The Sorcerer's DESTINY

BROCK E. DESKINS

The sorcerer stepped carefully into the ring of sigils painted onto the floor with the same paint used on his skin. Azerick focused his mind and drew in the Source before feeding it into the runes decorating the floor as well as those on his body. Flesh and stone began to glow with a silver, eldritch light, and the summoning chamber began to phase out of existence. His stomach leapt into his throat as he experienced the sensation of falling. What made it even more disconcerting was that it felt so much like his first trip to the abyss.

When the world came back into focus, Azerick found himself on a plateau of rough stone. Rivers of molten magma erupted from the ground and snaked across the rocky landscape before burrowing back into the rock and disappearing. Azerick could sense the titanic pressure and its desire to crush him like the insect he was as well as the intense heat threatening to immolate him. His staff thrummed in his hand as it too resisted the colossal forces acting upon it.

Azerick sent his thoughts into his staff, urging the arcanum sphere at its top to seek out its own kind. The staff pulsed in response, guiding its wielder along a path between molten geysers and pools of liquid stone. Azerick walked through the twisting labyrinth of the underground world, often backtracking and finding an alternate route in order to bypass an obstacle he could not gate past. He continually inspected his protective sigils despite their being far more indelible than any simple paint.

His staff pulsed more strongly, and Azerick soon spied a glow more silver than red. When he drew near, Azerick looked in wonder at the massive pool of liquid arcanum continually being fed by a geyser spewing the priceless metal more than fifty feet into the air. As he approached the arcanum lake, several globs began to form near the shore and rose out of its mirrorlike surface. The globs took on a featureless but humanoid form. Some were only slightly larger than he was, but others towered ten feet over his head. One of the silver creatures, one nearer his human size and vaguely feminine in form, approached closer than the rest.

To my sister Kellie,
As long as one person is reading this book, you will live forever.

CHAPTER I

Daebian rode the deep swells of the open ocean tucked in the bowsprit netting. Sea spray peppered his face with frigid droplets, salty like tears shed by the widows of sailors lost to the merciless dark depths. He lay at ease, comforted by the rolling and rocking of the waves, kissed by the briny beads while the wind whispered gentle promises in his ears.

He was an island of tranquility while chaos reigned all around him. The pirate ship had been running them down like dogs for the past half a day and was drawing nearer. The sailors of the merchant ship stretched as much cloth as they could in the rigging in the desperate hope of catching more wind and outrunning the pirates, but their efforts were destined to fail.

Captain Reid was brave and sought to make a name for himself just as Lord Giles had by bringing rare goods from far lands. It surprised Daebian to find a crew foolish enough to make the treacherous journey. Few sailed far from the shores of Valeria and Sumara, and none did so alone. Captain Bradley Reid thought by avoiding the established sailing routes he could outsmart the pirates lurking just outside the shipping lanes looking for stray merchant ships to pick off. He thought wrong.

As the pirate ship drew near, Daebian rolled out of his makeshift hammock and danced on the bow, ducking and dodging flung chain, shot, and crossbow quarrels. Any of the crew looking up from where they hunkered behind crates and whatever shelter they could find surely thought he was insane. Those near enough to hear him singing all the while were certain of it.

What are you doing? Annoyance tinged Klaraxis's thoughts as Daebian stood watching the pirates hurl lines attached to grapnels and begin boarding the ship.

"I am watching."

This is obvious. Why are you watching? You could slaughter this rabble with the power I give you. I hunger, and you wave my meal before me but do not let me eat.

"Firstly, I took your power; you did not give it. Secondly, you, like almost everyone else I have ever had the displeasure of meeting, lack vision. You know, for a demon prince who has existed for more than two millennia, your lack of foresight is pathetic."

What is pathetic is being subservient to not one, but two mortals.

"Yet that is your role. That should give you enough to think about to quell your incessant whining," Daebian replied.

The clashing of steel, shouts of anger, and cries of death filled his ears as the merchant crew fought with tenacity against the raiders, but their efforts were futile. A handful of pirates spotted Daebian leaning against the foremast and broke away from the main horde to engage him. Daebian shook his head and wagged a finger at the four men scrambling up the steps to the foredeck. Seeing only a well-dressed young man standing alone, greed and lust blinded the pirates, and they ignored Daebian's obvious warning.

The pirates rushed in, weapons held high to hack the boy down where he stood. Daebian kicked off the foremast and drew his sword in a single, fluid motion. He ducked low beneath the raised weapons of his attackers, brought his soul blade across in an arc, opening the guts of two of the pirates with a single swipe. With a flick of his free hand, he sent a gob of impenetrable shadow into the eyes of the man to his left, deflected the swing of the attacker to his right, spun behind the pirate, and stabbed him through the back. The blinded man howled in terror as he clawed at his face until Daebian silenced him with an easy, form-perfect thrust through his heart. The entire fight lasted less than the span of a deep breath.

He wiped his blade clean on the dirty jerkin of one of the pirates, leaned back against the foremast, and resumed observing the spectacle below him, grateful for Klaraxis's satisfied silence. The pirates had the majority of the merchant crew pressed back onto the stern and now had them outnumbered. Unable to reach their targets, several raiders broke off and began searching the ship for booty.

Spotting the lone figure on the foredeck, a few sought to relieve him of his wealth and life. Daebian once again wagged a digit at the approaching pirates while thrumming his fingers on the black jewel set in the pommel of his sword. The men looked at the bodies lying dead at the young man's feet, and after a brief pause to consider their options, wisely chose to go in search of valuables elsewhere.

Captain Reid, bleeding from numerous wounds and seeing he had less than half his crew still standing, called out for quarter. The raiders held back and waited for their captain to push through the throng of men. Daebian could not hear what they said, but Captain Reid and his men laid down arms, and the pirates corralled them at the farthest end of the stern.

The pirate captain and a host of his crew broke away while the rest guarded their prisoners and began plundering the merchant ship. He was a big man with a thick brown beard and wore a vast assortment of weapons hanging from loops affixed to belts buckled around his waist and crisscrossing his wide chest. He and two other men ascended the short flight of stairs to gain the bow.

"You killed four of my men easily enough. Why didn't you help your crew? Seems a man of your skill could'a made things a bit more difficult for me."

Daebian stood straight and addressed the captain. "Difficult? No, I would have changed the outcome of this fight."

The pirate smiled, revealing several gold teeth. "Then why didn't ya if you're so good?"

"I want to be a pirate." Daebian returned the smile.

"You look to be a boy of means. It seems it would be more profitable to ransom you."

"Seeing as how I stabbed my father with this very sword just before embarking on this fateful voyage, I would say it is unlikely you would see any profit from me in that regard."

The captain glanced at the dead men at Daebian's feet. The boy was too smart and too skilled with the blade. As captain, he needed to be the best amongst the crew, the undisputed leader. He had a bad feeling this man could upset that delicate balance. He wanted to kill the boy on the spot, but just one look into Daebian's black, soulless eyes made him reluctant to try. Perhaps the lad could be a strong tool if handled properly and with great care. He would have to ensure there was a quick blade at the ready should the boy prove the least bit threatening to his command.

"You certainly appear to have the skill for it."

"Captain, I have more skills than you can imagine."

"You can kill, that's for certain, but can you take orders?"

Daebian pursed his lips and looked up at the sky. "No."

Daebian's hand moved so fast, the captain was dead before he realized he had a foot of black steel through his heart. The crew moved at once. The two men flanking the now dead captain swung their cutlasses at the killer but met only empty air when Daebian fell back into the shadow of the foremast and vanished. He emerged hanging out above the deck in the netting below the crow's nest with one arm.

"Hey diddle diddle,
I pose you a riddle,
And you can tell me true.
Pirates are but seamen,
But when led by a demon,
What shall the fat merchants do?"

The assembled pirates looked up, slack-jawed and unsure what they faced or what to do. One of the men who had taken a swing at Daebian took a step forward.

"Give us their gold?" he answered in a nervous voice.

Daebian pulled himself back into the shadow of the crow's nest, reappeared just behind the man, and whispered in his ear. "Exactly."

The two men on the foredeck, as well as those crowding the steps, hastened away, desperate to put distance between themselves and what they all thought to be a demon sent to take them to the abyss for their wicked ways.

Daebian turned and addressed the pirates huddled below and hiding behind their drawn steel. "So what say you? Will you allow me to be your captain?"

"You killed Captain Dahl!" one of the men shouted.

"I did and made you richer for it."

"How's that?"

"I claim no stake in your haul this day. What was Captain Dahl's cut, twenty-five percent?"

"Thirty plus restocking and refitting," the man replied.

"The man was a pirate even to his own crew!" Daebian exclaimed. "I'll take twenty, including restocking and refitting, and guarantee you riches beyond your wildest imagination. Now, what say you?"

The men exchanged looks for several moments before the man with the courage to address Daebian spoke once more. "We say aye, aye, Captain."

"Fantastic!" Daebian beamed. "What is your name?"

"Tobias, sir."

"Tobias, I need a brave man I can trust to help me lead this crew. Can you be that man?"

"Aye, Captain, I can!"

"Outstanding."

"What would you like to do with the prisoners, sir?"

"Put them in longboats with food and water. I have need of their ship."

Tobias looked down at his fellow pirates. "You louts heard the captain! Rustle up those prisoners and put 'em in the water."

Captain Reid glared hatefully up at Daebian as his crew helped him into the longboat. "We're a week out to sea! You'll kill us setting us out in longboats!"

"Are you saying you wish to forego the use of the boat?" Daebian asked.

Captain Reid gritted his teeth and ordered his men to row for all they were worth, eager to put distance between him and the hateful young captain.

Daebian turned to his new crew. "Let's get to work on the rigging and sails. I want this ship repaired and the crew split between the two boats. No longer will wild jackals rule the seas. It's time for the wolf pack to take over."

CHAPTER 2

Azerick lay staring at the ceiling of Brother Thomas's infirmary. His patience for his convalescence at an end, he rolled off the bed and stood on shaky legs. He understood the severity of the trauma Daebian had inflicted upon him, but it still surprised him how long it was taking to recover. Klaraxis's demonic body could shake off and heal a horrific amount of damage in relatively short order, but having a soul torn from his body that was as much a part of him as his own was traumatic even for him.

The sorcerer found a robe and slippers in a closet, slipped them on, and made for the door. His movements were slow, and the stab wound in his chest throbbed with every movement. Whether the pain was real or the phantom echo of his son's betrayal, he could not discern. Brother Thomas appeared in the doorway, blocking his path.

"Azerick, you're up. How are you feeling?"

"Restless. I have spent the last week, a week of idleness none of us can afford, lying useless in bed."

The priest nodded. "You are the best one to gauge your wellness. How do you feel...spiritually?"

Azerick grinned. "Any remaining demons are all my own. It is like having a boulder lifted from my chest."

Brother Thomas clapped him on the shoulder and smiled. "It's good to have you back. I think everyone is probably in the main dining hall right now."

Azerick nodded, summoned his staff to his hand, and stepped out into the brisk morning air. The grounds were already bustling with activity. Classes had not yet begun, but many people were bustling about before having to perform their regular duties. Students and workers filed into and out of the big dining halls, and guards patrolled the walls and grounds in substantial numbers. Azerick returned dozens of greetings as he made his way across the compound and approached the new tower.

He paused just inside the parlor. Everything was as he remembered it. The crystal chandeliers hung from the ceiling emitting a warm light from the magical orbs set in the fixtures. The fine sofas and chairs were in the same place, and Lord Ebenezer Crowley lay curled up in front of the fireplace looking as though he had not moved since Azerick first brought him home with the exception of migrating from the old tower to the new. And yet he felt like a visitor, a stranger even. He had hoped the separation he had felt since his return would vanish along with the demon, but it was still there. Azerick steeled himself as he approached the dining room. He did not have time to dwell on self-pity.

All eyes turned to him when he entered the room, but Miranda was the first to react. She leapt to her feet and wrapped Azerick in a tight embrace.

"Azerick, you are up! How are you feeling?"

"I am well enough to get out of that infernal bed," he answered as Colleen made room for him to sit next to Miranda.

"You look rested," Allister said.

"I should. I have gotten more sleep in the past week than I have in the last eight or nine years."

Colleen asked, "Would you like something to eat?"

Azerick was pleasantly surprised to find that he did. Klaraxis's demonic appetite had left him bereft of the desire for normal food, but with him gone, the scents wafting from the dishes on the tables invoked a powerful craving.

"I would!"

Azerick let Miranda heap piles of food on a plate for him before they all started eating and talking about more mundane topics to cover simple breakfast conversation. He was able to learn much of how the students were progressing, the political climate, and supply acquisition and distribution just by listening to everyone around him.

"Ellyssa," Azerick finally interjected, "what do you think of our fighting strength?"

Ellyssa took a moment to compose her thoughts before answering. "Our troops are strong and disciplined. Against a normal enemy, they would far outmatch the best I can imagine. With the inclusion of the constructs, our fighters and mages are able to create an incredibly powerful bulwark against the ravagers. Whether it is strong enough is impossible to say, but we certainly have a chance. My fear is the dragons and the flying ships."

"We have successfully repelled the dragons in our training exercises," Rusty said defensively.

"We have repelled a few *illusionary* dragons with abilities we can only duplicate given our knowledge of the species. We have no idea how many they will bring or the power they can wield. I've seen Sandy decimate large tracts of land, and she is still considered a child amongst her kind. On top of that, we have no way of knowing what those ships will bring in the way of offensive capabilities. Even considering the additional wizards the Academy brings, if we scale up the number of dragons accordingly, I don't think we can withstand the inclusion of even a few more. The amount of power we must expend to withstand their attack drains us too quickly. Our mages will tire before we can defeat or drive away the dragons."

Azerick nodded as he stared at his empty plate. "I feared as much and have been thinking on this while laid up in bed. You have all done an extraordinary job, and none could do better, but I do not think it is enough."

"We can't train any harder, Azerick!" Rusty exclaimed. "We barely have enough time to recuperate between training exercises now, and we still suffer numerous injuries."

"Relax, Rusty, I am not suggesting such a thing. I know our people are at their physical and magical limits."

"Then what do you suggest?" Aggie asked.

"I suggest we raise our limits."

"How do you propose we do that?" Allister inquired.

"You say our mages fatigue too quickly due to the amount of power they must draw to withstand the dragons' assault. That being the case, we must make it easier for them to draw more power more efficiently from the Source," Azerick explained.

Aggie furrowed her brow and looked at Azerick dubiously. "You are talking about a Source pool."

"Every time I think you cannot surprise me with more impossible proclamations, you prove me wrong," Allister grumbled.

"What is a Source pool?" Rusty asked.

Aggie answered, "As most of you know, the power we tap into to fuel our magic is the residual energy seeping into nearly everything in our world from what we call the Source. The true Source exists on a plane of reality far removed from our own. When we harness it for our magic, it is sort of like filling a glass by sticking your arm out of the window when it rains. It works, but it's not efficient. A Source pool is much like it sounds. It is a direct well from where the Source springs directly into our world. It is the greatest dream of any practitioner of magic and nothing more than a theory wrapped in myth."

"It is more than a theory or myth. I have seen one. It is what Lissandra used to extract me from the abyss. Unfortunately, it died with her. I think she may have exhausted it in her final repair of the barrier in order to buy us more time. Whatever the case, we must create another one."

"You truly saw a Source pool?" Allister asked in awe.

"I traveled through it. It is—indescribable."

"Even so, no one knows how to go about creating one, not to mention the amount of power it would take to bring one forth is beyond imaginable," Aggie said.

"Raijaun and I, along with most of you, can do it…I think."

"Do you still have the power with the demon purged from you?" Allister asked hesitantly. "Are you still able to tap into the power of the abyss? From what I understand, that was a significant factor in the strength of your magic."

"I can still feel my connection with the abyss. I think because Klaraxis's body is a construct of the abyss, it still maintains a link to that dark power. In fact, without his constant vying for dominance, I can exert myself further without fear of losing control."

"Ah, yes, I always forget that little detail."

Rusty's jaw dropped. "Are you saying you are even more powerful than you were before?"

Azerick nodded. "In a sense. Technically, my power is the same, only now I can tap it to its full potential."

"The gods preserve us," Rusty mumbled under his breath.

"I assume you have an idea of how to accomplish this feat?" Aggie asked.

"I will have to consult the codex more, and since this involves a great deal of transdimensional magic, I will need your help, Aggie."

"Of course. I wouldn't want you to feel totally responsible for blowing us all up."

"Could it really blow us up?" Ellyssa asked.

"There is an enormous amount of power involved, and anytime you are trying to harness that much volatile energy you run the risk of losing control," Azerick admitted.

"How much energy are we talking about? How much damage?"

"Enough that the Scions and their minions might not have much to do when they get here."

"Oh, wonderful."

Aggie asked, "When are you wanting to make this attempt?"

"I need a few days to study the Codex Arcana and recover my strength. Just getting out of bed and eating proper food has made me feel better."

"All right then. We have a lot to do, and the Scions aren't going to give us any more time than they have to," Allister declared as he stood.

The others stood as well and filed out of the dining room to attend to their various duties. Azerick started to follow Raijaun to the lab until Miranda took him gently by the elbow.

"How are you feeling, you know, inside?" she asked.

Azerick smiled reassuringly and hugged her tightly. "Much better. I cannot promise I will be any less distracted, but my soul is more at ease. Hopefully, it will make everyone a little more comfortable. I'm sorry I cannot spend more time with you right now, but I need to talk with Raijaun about the barrier and creating the Source pool."

"I understand. It's going to happen soon, isn't it?"

"I think so. What will you be doing today?"

"I've been training with the martial students."

Azerick leaned away and arched his eyebrows. "Since when?"

"For more than a month. Maybe if you crawled out of your lab more than once a season you would have noticed," she teased.

"You're right, and I am sorry."

"It's mostly been one-on-one training with Alex, but recently I have been in the field with them so I can learn more of their troop formations and tactics. It's not as though anyone is going to let me stand on the front lines."

"We absolutely would not. When this is over, the people are going to need good, strong leaders. You must be there to fill that role."

"I know, but from what you have described, it is unlikely anyone will walk away with a clean blade, and I need to be as capable a fighter as anyone. Besides, it helps me take my mind away from Daebian." Azerick made a sour face and grunted in reply. "Azerick, please try not to hate him."

"I do not understand him enough to hate him or even be angry with him. I think I understand the Scions better than I do him."

"He's angry and jealous. So much happened so fast, I think it was just hard for him to adjust."

"No, acting out in jealousy or anger is capricious, and Daebian does nothing without knowing exactly what he is doing and why. I have a feeling Klaraxis has been influencing him for some time, but how much of his actions were due to the demon and how much was his own devious mind is anyone's guess. I just hope that whatever he has found to do with himself keeps him entertained."

"I just hope he's safe. Well, you have your things to do, and I have mine. See you tonight?"

"I will try."

Miranda put on a brave face despite the pain she felt from the rift still separating her from her husband. She understood what was at stake, and she accepted the fact the world needed her husband as much as she did, but such logic did little to ease her torment. Miranda kissed Azerick and sought out the drill grounds. Some vigorous swordplay would take her mind off her marriage and leave her too exhausted to dwell much on it later.

Azerick felt the divide between them and knew it would only grow wider despite the excision of his demonic passenger. There was just too much to do and too many things requiring his personal attention. He had lost valuable days of work recovering from the wound Daebian had inflicted. Azerick pushed his mortal concerns to the back of his mind as he descended the stairs to his laboratory, the only place he felt at home.

"Tell me of the barrier's condition," Azerick said as he entered the lab.

"It does not look good. There are numerous fractures and flaws throughout the expanse. It is all I can do to repair the most severe amongst them."

"How long before they are able to create a major breach do you think?"

Raijaun sighed and shook his head. "I don't know. They could create one now, for all I know. Given what I deduced from the remnants of their previous breaches, it would not surprise me if they could cause irreparable damage. I have no idea what they are waiting for."

Azerick looked pensive. "They are setting the board, placing their pieces before making their final gambit. Come; let us go see if we can buy some time."

Azerick focused his will on the huge gem in the center of the chamber. The light faded and the walls shimmered until there was nothing but the blackness of the transdimensional void. The darkness quickly lightened, and the shimmering screen of the world-enveloping barrier wavered into view.

"False Guardian, you have returned. You are different. You seem to have shed your demonic parasite, yet it was no doing of yours. Betrayal enshrouds you like a voluminous robe."

Azerick ignored the Scions' taunting and sent his consciousness throughout the vast expanse of the barrier. What he saw shocked him despite Raijaun's warning. Huge sections of the barrier looked like continent-sized stained-glass mosaics created by webs of fracture lines the size of rivers. The sorcerer had no doubt that the fallen gods could tear a hole through one large enough to send tens of thousands of ravagers pouring into the kingdom if they so desired.

"What are you playing at?" Azerick demanded. "Why do you hesitate to unleash your horde upon us?"

"You are not yet prepared. We desire you to experience the full terror and futility of resistance."

Azerick accepted the Scions' answer as a partial truth. He held to his theory that the Scions were not going to leave anything to chance and were preparing the board to their advantage. Azerick and Raijaun toiled for an immeasurable amount of time, sealing fractures and walling off lesser breaches until exhaustion forced them to leave the Scions' prison realm. Azerick was unsure of the hour when their consciousness finally returned to his laboratory, but he was certain it was late.

"Raijaun, why don't you go get something to eat and rest."

"Do you not need to rest as well, Father?"

"I do, but I cannot. I need to search the codex for information on creating a Source pool. Lissandra did it, so it must be in there somewhere. Raijaun, I am going to need your help with it. Your full help," Azerick emphasized.

Raijaun nodded grimly knowing the kind of pain he would endure by wielding all three forms of his magic in concert. "I will do what I must, Father."

Azerick smiled and squeezed his son's shoulder. "I know. You always do."

Raijaun left to get some much-needed rest and food while Azerick opened the Codex Arcana and spread its pages out before him. "I must create a Source pool. Show me."

The pages fanned and letters crawled across the sheets faster than the eye could read, but Azerick's mind absorbed every word and deciphered their complex and convoluted meaning almost without conscious thought. The codex held nearly all the answers to every conceivable question regarding magic, but it did not give up its truths easily for it did not think with a mortal mind. Its answers often appeared as riddles to the reader, and the more complex the question the more indecipherable the answer.

It took days for Azerick to compile a coherent method for creating the Source pool, days of not eating or sleeping; his only breaks were the times he spent with Raijaun to make repairs to the barrier in the desperate hope of staving off the inevitable invasion by just another day. It was with heavy footsteps that he finally emerged from his studies and joined his friends and family at the dining table.

"I presume your emergence means you have met with some success," Allister said in welcome as Azerick sat down.

"I have."

"From what Raijaun has been telling us of the barrier, I understand your grim demeanor, but I suppose there is more bad news at hand."

"A challenge to be certain. In order to create the Source pool, we need a lot of arcanum to act as a catalyst."

"How much arcanum?" Aggie asked.

"A thousand pounds."

"A thousand pounds!" Allister exclaimed. "There likely isn't a thousand pounds in the entire world!"

Allister's claim was not far from the truth. The amount of arcanum that went into the construction of Azerick's staff likely represented a year of mining and refining, assuming the dwarves had found a rich source. Arcanum was not found in thick veins like gold or silver, but scattered specks as if sprinkled by the gods in tiny pinches spread across the whole of the world.

"I discovered a source capable of providing what I require."

"Where in the world can you possibly find that much arcanum?" Rusty asked.

"The heart of our world is a molten mass of arcanum."

"No one has ever traveled to the center of the world. It is not possible," Allister insisted.

"A few have, but only Lissandra and her Guardians ever returned. I have discovered the method they used to travel there and can duplicate it."

"It cannot be as easy as you make it sound."

"It is not. Something lives at the heart of our world and jealously guards its hoard."

"What could possibly live down there?" Ellyssa asked.

"I do not know. Not even the codex was able to share that information."

Miranda wore a look of worry. "It sounds dangerous."

"There are elemental forces at work down there I will have to counter. I expect that to be my biggest challenge."

"Do you really?"

Azerick slinked a bit into himself. "No, not really."

"Father, you should let me come with you," Raijaun said.

"No, I need you to stay here and guard the barrier. You will have a great deal to do when I get back. Then it will be my turn to babysit the Scions while you recover."

"Azerick, are you sure this is a good idea?" Miranda asked.

"No, I'm certain it is a terrible idea, but like all my terrible ideas, it is the only one I see."

Miranda stood. "I can't do this anymore," she declared, then fled the room, struggling to hold back her tears.

"Miranda…"

Colleen stood and laid a hand on Azerick's arm. "Stay here. I'll go after her."

She found Miranda sitting on the sofa, weeping into her hands.

Miranda looked up when Colleen sat next to her. "It's never going to be okay, is it?"

"Azerick will be fine. He'll do this and come back."

"It doesn't matter. There will always be something else. Even if we survive this invasion, we will never be the way we were. Nothing will."

Colleen wanted to tell Miranda things would return to normal, that Azerick would settle down and be her husband again once it was all over, but her mouth refused to voice the lie.

CHAPTER 3

Azerick held perfectly still as Raijaun carefully painted the silver runes he described onto his body. The arcanum dust tinting the paint was worth a king's ransom, but it was crucial to allow him to withstand the elemental forces at play at the world's core. The sigils Raijaun marked him with were largely draconic in origin, and each one had to be perfect and painstakingly drawn. It took hours to complete them all, probably far longer than Azerick would be gone if everything went right.

Azerick had wanted to go to Miranda, but there was nothing he could say or do. He had to do this, just as he had to do so much more. He could promise things would be better afterward, but neither of them believed it. Chances were, there wouldn't even be an afterward. If he did not do everything he could, it was a certainty.

"I think that is the last of them, Father," Raijaun announced, then corked the small jar containing the last bit of arcanum paint.

Azerick carefully examined himself in the full-length mirror and declared Raijaun's work perfect.

"Are you certain I cannot accompany you?" Raijaun asked, not for the first time.

"You cannot. I need you here."

Azerick summoned his staff and walked as naked as the day he was born to the chamber he had prepared for the transport, careful not to mar any of the sigils on his body. Clothing would not last long in the hostile environment, and he saw no need in preparing any that could. It was much easier to protect his body which, thanks to Klaraxis's natural resilience, made the task even simpler.

The sorcerer stepped carefully into the ring of sigils painted onto the floor with the same paint used on his skin. Azerick focused his mind and drew in the Source before feeding it into the runes decorating the floor as well as those on his body. Flesh and stone began to glow with a silver, eldritch light, and the summoning chamber began to phase out of existence. His stomach leapt into his throat as he experienced the sensation of falling. What made it even more disconcerting was that it felt so much like his first trip to the abyss.

When the world came back into focus, Azerick found himself on a plateau of rough stone. Rivers of molten magma erupted from the ground and snaked across the rocky landscape before burrowing back into the rock and disappearing. Azerick could sense the titanic pressure and its desire to crush him like the insect he was as well as the intense heat threatening to immolate him. His staff thrummed in his hand as it too resisted the colossal forces acting upon it.

Azerick sent his thoughts into his staff, urging the arcanum sphere at its top to seek out its own kind. The staff pulsed in response, guiding its wielder along a path between molten geysers and pools of liquid stone. Azerick walked through the twisting labyrinth of the underground world, often backtracking and finding an alternate route in order to bypass an obstacle he could not gate past. He continually inspected his protective sigils despite their being far more indelible than any simple paint.

His staff pulsed more strongly, and Azerick soon spied a glow more silver than red. When he drew near, Azerick looked in wonder at the massive pool of liquid arcanum continually being fed by a geyser spewing the priceless metal more than fifty feet into the air. As he approached the arcanum lake, several globs began to form near the shore and rose out of its mirrorlike surface. The globs took on a featureless but humanoid form. Some were only slightly larger than he was, but others towered ten feet over his head. One of the silver creatures, one nearer his human size and vaguely feminine in form, approached closer than the rest.

"You trespass and seek to steal what is not yours," the creature said.

Azerick bowed slightly at the waist. "Forgive me. I was not aware this place and its materials belonged to another. My name is—"

"We know what you are called, and we know what you desire." The being pointed a finger at Azerick's staff. "Like speaks to like."

"You are made of arcanum?"

"We are arcanians. What you call arcanum is made of us. The bits you scavenge from the lifeless rock is the dust we leave behind when we ascend to our higher form and leave this shell of stone behind as we spread ourselves throughout the cosmos, seeding other worlds."

"Then I would ask you a boon. I am in desperate need of arcanum."

The arcanian's answer was blunt. "We know what you need and why, and it is not our concern."

"The Scions will destroy us! If they return unchecked, they could find you just as I did and come here."

"The Scions are gods and fully aware of our existence, but they concern us no more than your species. The arcanians are beyond such things."

"They will destroy my race! Do you not care?"

"We know thousands of worlds and tens of thousands of races. What is the value of one, or even a few, to us?"

"I cannot leave without what I seek."

"Then you shall stay an eternity."

"No!"

Azerick pulled at the Source, channeled it through his staff, and struck the arcanian with an intense ray capable of reducing the mightiest castle wall to little more than dust. If his attack had any effect on the creature, it did not show. The iridescent surface drank in the sorcerer's power without even a shudder.

The arcanian laughed with the sound of a thousand wind chimes. "Your magic cannot harm us. If we have no fear of gods, do you truly think you can concern us?"

Rage suffused Azerick's soul, and he grabbed at his abyssal power and twisted it into the Source with every ounce of his being. The subterranean landscape vanished from his sight as a wave of colossal force blotted out his vision and swept over the arcanians. The ground shook, crevices split open to spew more magma into the air, and stones the size of cottages rained down, exploding and splashing as they struck solid ground or liquid stone and arcanum.

Azerick tried to peer through the dusty haze and destruction. A glimmer of movement caught his eye just before a stream of arcanum burst through the miasma, hit him in the chest, and crushed his body against a cavern wall. The arcanian drew closer, the silvery tendril absorbing into its body as it approached, and stared into Azerick's face.

"Your species is young, and so I forgive your childish behavior this once. Leave our home and return to yours."

"I can't do that!"

Azerick grabbed at the Source and opened a gate directly behind him. The arcanian's "arm" pressing against his chest shoved him through the portal. The sorcerer closed the gate and cleanly severed the argent appendage. The shimmering substance splashed to the ground but instantly began drawing together and reforming like spilled mercury.

Azerick ran down the magma-lit tunnel unsure as to the course of his next action. He hoped the pools of pure arcanum were not the arcanians themselves, only the place in which they dwelled. If that were the case, perhaps he could find an unattended pool and take what he needed before they found him. Those hopes died within minutes.

He found a smaller pool tucked between two basins of molten lava and felt a glimmer of hope. Before he could finish etching the first runes onto the cavern floor, the arcanum pool expanded upward like an inflating bladder. A silver tendril snaked out of the swelling mass and wrapped itself around his body several times, forming a vaguely human shape behind it.

The arcanian stepped from the pool and approached. "Foolish human, you trespass in your desire to steal then pathetically attempt to assault us in our very homes. Should such a species deserve to exist?"

Azerick struggled futilely against the appendage holding him in place. "I have no choice! I do not act out of greed or desire to harm or take what is not mine, but out of desperation to save my and other races. Any people would do the same when no other options are available. Would you not do anything, violate any of your principles, to save your race?"

The arcanian tilted its head in thought. "You claim altruism. You claim to act on behalf of all who are threatened."

"I do."

"Then you will give us something in return."

"Yes! Anything!"

"Give us your son Raijaun."

Azerick felt as though the air had just been sucked from his lungs and the blood drawn out of his body. "My son?"

"What you desire is a part of us. In exchange for part of our essence, we require part of you. If you truly act on the behalf of all, the life of one surely is inconsequential in the grander scheme."

Azerick hated himself for even considering the creature's demand, but what it said was true. How could he place even his own son above that of nearly every race of his world? Still, his love and parental desire to protect his family warred with duty.

"What could you possibly want with my son?"

"We will demand a service of him, in a time of our choosing. He will be bound to that service by blood and the magic coursing through it."

"What can he possibly do for you that you cannot do yourselves? Your strength outstrips mine by orders of magnitude, and likely his as well."

"It is true that our power is beyond your kind, and even that of the gods in some ways, but we are like the mightiest of sailing ships in a world without water."

"What must he do? Will he survive your task?"

"Such a question we cannot answer. Does it truly matter when the fate of your world hangs in the balance?"

Azerick could not suppress the shudder coursing through his body when he answered. "No."

"Create your sigils upon the floor, and we shall provide you with what you require."

He felt the pressure ease from around his chest and fell to the ground when the arcanian withdrew its appendage. Azerick forced down the revulsion clogging his throat as he burned arcane runes into the ground with his magic. His task complete, the sorcerer created a second ring of sigils and stepped into its center. With a word and trickle of power, they flared brightly against the strange luminescence of the underground world, and whisked him up and away to his tower.

Raijaun waited within the summoning chamber and grabbed onto his father when he appeared and stumbled from the circle. "Father, are you all right?"

Azerick brushed Raijaun's hands away. "I'm fine."

"Were you successful? Were you able to get the arcanum?"

Azerick's voice caught in his throat, forcing him to cough to get the words out. "Yes. Go get Aggie and the others while I prepare the room."

Once Raijaun hustled away to do as he asked, Azerick sank to his knees and tried to hold back the shuddering sobs wracking his body. He had given up his son to creatures beyond his understanding with no idea of what they would do with him, and the knowledge that he would do it again if he had to sickened him beyond belief. Taking a deep breath to steel his resolve, Azerick made his way to the old tower.

Azerick had the summoning circle prepared by the time Raijaun and his core cadre arrived. Everyone understood what they were about to attempt, and their stony faces showed the seriousness of the endeavor and the effort it was going to take.

"Good to see you back, boy," Allister said. "Raijaun says you were successful in getting the arcanum?"

"We'll have it shortly."

"What do you need us to do?" Ellyssa asked.

"I will start a summoning. All you have to do is follow my lead and reinforce my weaves. Is everyone ready?"

The mages gathered around the circle and let their consciousness dip into the ether to touch the Source. Azerick fed arcane energy into the runes painted on the floor and sent tendrils of power deep into the ground, questing for the matching runes near the core of their world.

The ground shuddered as the two sides of the gate converged. The floor inside the teleport circle collapsed, creating a hole that vanished into blackness. Only Azerick knew it plummeted hundreds of miles to the core of the world. He sensed the presence of the arcanum just as the arcanians had promised.

Azerick pulled with his magic and felt the arcanum resist his magical commands to yield. The metal finally surrendered and began flowing upward when he felt Allister and the others add their strength to his. The ground trembled violently, and cracks began forming along the floor of the chamber. It felt as though they were in a tug of war with a team of recalcitrant horses.

A terrible noise like the side of a cliff face shearing away and crashing to the ground thundered up from the fathomless void in the floor. The entire tower quivered as if wracked by a chill. Dust wafted down from the ceiling and cast grit in their eyes as an eldritch glow shone up from the very bowels of the planet.

Silver light heralded the rushing body of arcanum, and for a moment, Azerick feared it would spew out of the well and drown them in molten metal. The flow began to ebb as it neared the surface, and the group of arcane masters received only a blast of hot air as if standing too near a blazing forge. A near-perfect disk of arcanum three feet across now adorned the center of the room.

"Is that it?" Ellyssa asked as she worked to catch her breath. "I was expecting it to be a lot harder than that."

Azerick smiled at his former apprentice. "That was just to summon the arcanum. The hard part is yet to come."

"Congratulations, Azerick, you are now the world's wealthiest man a thousand times over," Allister said with an amused grin.

"It is destined to be a rather short-lived accolade. Aggie, Raijaun, are you both ready?"

Raijaun nodded and Aggie answered, "Yeah, but I still think it's a damn fool thing to try, but I guess in these times even foolery looks good in the light of what we face."

Azerick used his magic like a chisel and began etching sigils upon the mirrorlike face of the solid mass of arcanum. Despite his perfect memory, he often referred back to the Codex Arcana to ensure everything was done to perfection just as the book described. Even with their complexity, Azerick finished carving the runes in less than an hour.

Aggie used her expansive store of knowledge to send her mind streaking across the cosmos to pierce the veil between dimensions. Once she had a firm grasp on the Source, she sent a tendril of power worming into the well of arcanum. She gasped as her magic flowed through the metal and hungrily clawed at the Source. What had been a mere trickle soon became a torrent of raging power and nearly broke free of her control, but Azerick, Raijaun, and the others came to her aid and helped stabilize the wild flow of magic.

"Raijaun, when Aggie opens the border between our reality and that of the Source, you will need to enshroud it in a net of all three elements of your magic in order to contain it," Azerick instructed. "Everyone else, follow my and Raijaun's lead and do the same."

Several heads bearing grim faces nodded as they exerted themselves to control the magical and elemental forces at work. Aggie nodded her readiness and opened the floodgate of pure, undiluted arcane power. The Source rushed at them as if from a ruptured dam of monumental size. The wizards looked on in terror with their sight beyond sight at the wall of energy hurtling at them and knew they were powerless to stop it. They poured their magic into a constraining weave despite knowing the futility of the attempt and braced themselves for oblivion.

Then their vision filled with the golden aura of Guardian magic as Raijaun seemingly wrapped up the colossal torrent in a weave of unimaginable strength and complexity, funneling it into a flow only just manageable. Azerick and the wizards added their power to Raijaun's, and together they were able to direct the Source but only with phenomenal effort. The tower shook as if assaulted by quarter-ton stones hurled by huge trebuchets. Sweat poured from the assembled mages and their muscles trembled as they fought to rein in a wild steed the size and strength of a titan.

Outside, pandemonium raged as the ground shook and buildings shuddered so violently they threatened to collapse. Students and faculty raced outdoors fearing such an eventuality. The arcane students found the Source frightfully chaotic when they reached out to it to shield themselves from falling slate shingles and feared that entire buildings might crumble upon them if the shaking did not cease. One young woman, not expecting the arcane surge, knocked down the wall of a nearby building and sent several people flying when the ward she conjured to protect herself materialized with the outward force of a small explosion.

Raijaun shouted as the agony of combining the three divergent types of magic warred within his body, but he fought through the pain and maintained his desperate control over the arcane battle taking place between worlds. Azerick saw his son now fighting a battle on two fronts but knew he could do nothing to help him except complete the spell as quickly as they could.

The mass of arcanum turned liquid once again and began roiling within the well. As the metal bubbled ever more violently, the mercurial sheen became even more brilliant and iridescent, taking on a reflective quality beyond imagination. Looking into the mirrorlike substance, one would swear they saw not just the reflection of the room or even the world, but all worlds and all things everywhere. It was like looking into the eyes of a god.

The world gave a final massive shrug before the wild flow of power surrendered and accepted its breaking. Exhausted and in enormous pain, Raijaun collapsed next to the shimmering pool of pure arcane magic. All of the assembled wizards sank to their hands and knees or propped themselves against the wall, fighting to catch their breath as muscles cramped painfully and their hearts felt ready to burst from their chests.

Azerick crawled over to his son and cradled his head. "Raijaun, are you all right?"

Raijaun opened his eyes and tried to smile but could not force it past the grimace of pain. "I will survive. I am very tired. I just want to rest now."

Azerick forced himself to his feet, draped Raijaun over his shoulder, and carried him to his room. He sat at the corner of his son's bed as Raijaun slept even as the pain wracked his body. Another pain threatened to tear Azerick apart as well.

"I betrayed you, Son, and I hope you will understand why even if you cannot forgive me. You deserve far better than this world will ever give you." Azerick kissed his son's forehead and sought his bed as the pain of the spellcraft warred with the agony of his breaking heart.

CHAPTER 4

Bron approached the fawn struggling against the snare cinched tightly around its rear leg and spoke softly so as not to startle the already frightened animal. Normally, being within a mile of an eight-foot-tall half-ogre would have sent the young deer into a panic so intense it may well have died on the spot from fright, but the druid's gentle words and presence brought comfort to the animal.

"Now club it so we can eat!" Trielle urged as Bron stroked the deer's silky coat.

"I am not going to kill a helpless animal, and you should be ashamed to even think such a thing," Bron admonished the wood sprite.

"But I'm hungry!"

"You're always hungry. You should learn a little empathy."

"Is that a song?"

"It is appreciating the feelings of others."

"Why would I want to do that?"

"Do you not remember how I saved you from a very similar situation all those years ago?"

"Yes! That disgusting spider was going to eat me!"

"You thought I was going to eat you too. How did that make you feel?"

Trielle thought about the day she met Bron. "I didn't like it."

"And this deer feels the same way. Understanding and appreciating that feeling in another is empathy. This animal has feelings just like you."

"It's a long-legged rat. A tasty long-legged rat. I'm pretty."

"The fawn is pretty as well. All animals have a unique beauty unto themselves."

"Well, I can talk!"

"Yes, often far too much."

The sprite's cheeks flushed with anger. "What's that supposed to mean! You better watch it, big stinky, or bedtime's gonna come early!" Trielle started jabbing her poison-laced spear at him as she buzzed around his head.

Bron ignored her tantrum as he always did and freed the young deer. Once free of the snare, the fawn bounded away into the brush. Bron smiled as he watched the fawn disappear into the forest.

"Look at that! Not even a thank you," Trielle complained. "Where's its empathy?"

Bron looked pointedly at the wood sprite. "I do not recall you ever thanking me for freeing you, and you can talk. How long ago was that, twenty years?"

"Your thanks is the knowledge of helping a superior being. Now, keep that feeling alive by getting me something to eat since you just let lunch run away."

"Do sprites even eat mammals? I am fairly certain you are largely vegetarian and insectivorous."

"We sprites are a very adaptive species. Now, hurry up. I know you are hiding some honey in that hole you call a home, and if that fat bear of yours has eaten it all, I'm gonna put him to sleep permanently."

Bron ignored the precocious sprite as he effortlessly carved a path through the thick forest without leaving a trace of his passing. His passage was as silent as it was invisible. His druidic knowledge and magic allowed him to penetrate the thickest brush and brambles as if he were on a well-traveled road.

As Bron neared the cave he called home, he listened to the wind and wildlife around him. The druid detected a change in the natural cacophony of the surrounding forest. To Bron's ears, the normally syncopated sonance of nature became more rhythmic and began a song as great as any created by the most talented composer. The druid followed the music in an irresistible desire to find its source.

"Hey, big stinky, lunch is that way!" Trielle shouted, then amped up the buzzing near his ear. When that failed, she jabbed the butt of her spear against the thick skin of his neck in an effort to herd him back from his deviation.

Bron stepped into the clearing where he preferred to commune with his goddess, Ellanee. Willow trees ringed the small glade and encircled the pond fed by a natural spring. A sense of overwhelming peace and oneness with nature infused his blood, as it would almost anyone blessed with the opportunity to visit this holy place—anyone except Trielle.

"Not her again!" the sprite complained.

Ellanee smiled at the sprite, fully accepting her nature and taking no offense in her behavior. "Hello, Trielle. Hello, Bron."

Trielle responded by sticking out her tongue, shaking her tiny backside at the goddess, and flitting into the draping bows of a willow tree. Bron knelt and bowed his head in reverence.

"Greetings, Goddess, and thank you for blessing my grove with your presence."

Ellanee knelt before her disciple and stroked his broad face. "Do not be thankful until you hear my reason for coming."

"Oh, the great cow goddess comes with bad news. What a surprise!" Trielle shouted from her hiding place in the trees.

"Your tidings are irrelevant," Bron rumbled. "Your presence is welcome no matter your reason. I am your faithful servant. Command me and I shall obey."

"I knew I chose my champion well. A great evil is coming. Ancient gods will soon break free of their prison and seek to destroy us, most the races, and enslave the few they allow to live."

Bron tightened his grip on his staff and fought back the rage building within him at the thought of anyone threatening his goddess. He forced calm into his heart and soul as his foster mother had taught him as a child.

"What can I do to aid you?"

"My fellow gods have each chosen their champions to spread word and make every preparation they can to combat these vile creatures. A human who helped turn back the tide of the undead that you also played a great role in destroying is uniting the humans, dwarves, and elves to oppose the usurpers, but it is not enough. The brutish races must stand with them just as they did two thousand years ago, or they will fail. You must be my emissary to the ogres, goblins, and orcs. I need you to do whatever it takes to convince them to fight next to their enemies."

Bron wagged his great head back and forth. "There is so much distrust between them and the *civilized* races, and they probably trust me even less. The ogres will look down upon me for my human heritage, and the orcs and goblins will distrust me for both my halves."

"Take heart, faithful Bron, for unlike the higher races, my beloved brutes have not forgotten the great war for their freedom, and they hate the Scions and their dragon overseers even more than the humans, dwarves, and elves. Convince them to accept you as my emissary, and they will accept their duty."

"I will do my best, Goddess."

"I know you will. It is why I chose you." Ellanee gestured at the ground between them, and a map of impossible accuracy and detail formed in the dirt, replete with towering mountains, lakes, and rivers. "The human gathering his allies has formulated a plan to meet the Scions and their horde in a small valley near where the Witchcrag Mountains and the Great Barrier Mountains meet. This is where they will need the might of the brutish races to defeat them."

"If it is within my ability, I will lead the brutes there," Bron vowed.

"Then go with my blessing, lovely Bron." Ellanee touched her druid on the head and vanished.

"Did you see that?" Trielle asked after fluttering down.

"See what?"

"She's getting fat. What's this about gathering the stinky races?"

"Ancient gods are returning and wish to destroy us all. Ellanee has asked me to gather the races to aid the world in defeating them."

Trielle's face fell slack. "We're going to fight gods?"

"And an unimaginable horde of evil creatures."

The sprite grinned. "Wahoo, the sprites are going to war!"

Her hungry belly forgotten in lieu of far more exciting things, Trielle flew skyward and raced home to announce the call to arms. While Bron returned home to gather a few supplies, a deep droning filled the air as hundreds of sprites beat their wings in a call that was heard for miles. Every sprite within hearing distance took up the message and relayed it throughout the vast forest.

Grumph, Bron's enormous dire bear companion, lay in front of the door to the druid's cave. Despite waiting for Bron to return and share his store of honey, Grumph protested loudly when he had to move to allow the druid to get inside.

"I don't know why you are complaining. The honey is not going to come outside. Perhaps if you stopped lying right in front of the door I would not have to disturb you."

Grumph responded by tearing a large furrow in the ground with a swipe of his massive paw and completely uprooting a tree that would have taken a woodsman several minutes to chop down. Bron ignored Grumph's tantrum just as he did Trielle's abrasive personality. When all of your friends were animals, such things did not register as the least bit out of place or inappropriate.

The druid selected a large pinecone, coated it with honey, and tossed it to Grumph who was filling the doorway with his massive head and chest. The dire bear gave Bron an appreciative grumble, carried his treat to a shady spot, and commenced licking it clean. Bron began rummaging around his tables, shelves, and cabinets for things to take on his journey. He selected pouches of herbs for their medicinal properties as well as a healing salve and a sack of dried tea leaves he was particularly fond of. He stuffed these, a tin teapot and cups, and a spare jerkin and trousers into a knapsack.

Taking up his staff, Bron stepped out of his cave and began his trek south and east. He knew the ogres lived in several remote valleys near some of the most treacherous terrain along the mountains, driven there by the continuous expansion of humanity. Most of the orc and goblin tribes also called the rugged valleys home as well, usually maintaining a tenuous peace, but sometimes not.

Bron had failed to notice the sprites' droning had ceased until it started up again and drew nearer. A great black cloud flew across the sky, undulating in a rhythmic dance that captivated the eye. The swarm swooped down in a coordinated dive until it hovered just tens of feet over the druid's head. Trielle broke away from the swarm and floated in front of Bron's face.

"Okay, big stinky, the sprites are assembled and ready to fight! Well, most of us. We couldn't wait around on the more distant hives. They'll catch up."

"The time to fight is not yet at hand."

"What?" Trielle exclaimed. "Do you have any idea how dangerous it is to get us sprites pumped up for battle then have nothing to fight? You're playing with fire, buddy!"

"I must travel to the ogre lands and enlist the aid of their kind as well as that of the goblins and orcs." Then we shall join the other races in the final battle for our freedom and survival. If you had listened, you would have understood."

"I don't have time to listen when it's time for action!" Trielle turned to the swarm hovering overhead. "False alarm, everybody. We gotta wait until big stinky talks to the king of big stinkies. We'll fight some gods later, I promise."

The sprite swarm gave Bron an angry buzz before zipping back to their hive to celebrate an overwhelming victory. Trielle lit upon Bron's shoulder and gripped the collar of his jerkin.

"Okay, so where are we going?"

"Several days walk to the southeast. You do not have to go. I am unsure how they will react to me, and it could be dangerous."

"All the more reason I need to go. Someone's gotta watch your big, stinky back."

"I have Grumph."

"Pfft, I can take care of that!" Trielle drew back her spear for a throw.

"It may be best to keep him with us."

Trielle sat back down on Bron's shoulder. "Yeah, you're right. You never know when we might run out of food and have to eat him."

CHAPTER 5

Tobias darted from patron to patron within the packed tavern. "Explain to me again what it is we're doing in Southport, Captain Daebian."

"Ever since Jarvin commissioned a proper navy, pirates have been relegated to little more than scavengers plucking at the carcass of a long-dead animal or snapping up tiny rodents to fill their bellies. We must adapt to this change or face starvation. We adapt by becoming predators instead of opportunists. A pack of pirates requires ships, and ships require a crew, which is what our fellows are out putting together now."

"Right, I understand all that. What I'm not getting is why, being pirates and all, we are sitting in a thrice-damned navy bar," the first mate hissed.

"What better ships to acquire than ones already outfitted for battle? It saves us a fortune in retrofitting. It's sound business sense, don't you think?"

"I think Captain Farique ain't much for change and will skin us all if these jellyfish don't beat him to it."

Daebian turned and fixed his second with a stare. "Who is Captain Farique?"

"You don't know who Captain Farique is?" Tobias asked incredulously. "Captain Farique owns the Black Sand Isles. He's the pirate king."

"Pirates have their own king?"

"It's an unofficial title. He likes to be called Captain, but it's all the same. It's his land and his safe harbor for most all who make a go at being a pirate. We even pay a tithe to him to enjoy his hospitality and not become targets of plunder ourselves. He keeps a pretty firm grip with five ships under his command and is the meanest sort of man I ever met."

"Really?" Daebian asked pointedly.

"Meanest don't mean scariest. Not anymore anyway."

Daebian stroked the tiny bit of stubble dotting his chin. "You know, Tobias, I have been at this pirating thing for a couple weeks now. I think I'm due a promotion, don't you?"

Tobias's face fell. "I think you're gonna get us all killed."

"Not all of us...probably."

"Captain, you're gonna go and cause a heap of trouble, aren't you?"

"Only for one of us. Which one of us is totally dependent upon the outcome."

"I'm just glad these jellyfish don't know who we are, or Captain Farique won't never get the chance to skin us and hang us from his yardarm."

"You are certainly right on that account. I do so deplore anonymity." Daebian stood and raised his glass above his head. "On behalf of my father Lord Azerick Giles, sorcerer extraordinaire, friend of the king, and the official bum wiper of the gods, I would like to show my appreciation to the men securing the seas by paying for every drink served in this bar until I depart for the evening. Be forewarned, I have no other pressing business for some time."

Daebian's declaration was met with a loud huzzah and a mass rush for the bar. Serving women struggled to fill orders until the barkeep brought in more help. The alcohol flowed and women began pouring in from the streets, finding the laps of many reveling sailors. Shots of rum and whiskey tore down the last vestiges of sobriety long before the night grew long.

"Tobias, I think it is time to start bringing in some of the boys."

"Aye, Captain. You know, if this works, you'll be known as the craziest, most brilliant pirate who ever sailed."

Daebian grinned into his glass and sipped. "You are stating an already established fact, but I appreciate your vote of confidence."

Tobias disappeared outside and reentered the bar a few minutes later with two of the crew. Every few minutes, two or three more of Daebian's men entered and joined in on the festivities, but they stared more at the partying sailors than the bottoms of their glasses. No one noticed when a few of the navy men stumbled out to get some air, relieve themselves, or decided to stagger back to their ship and were followed by a number of Daebian's pirates. Neither did anyone notice when the civilians returned a short time later, but none of the sailors ever did.

As the night wound down and the masses of drunk sailors dwindled to less than a score with nearly as many women sitting on their laps encouraging their revelry, Daebian stood on unsteady legs and addressed the crowd, slurring his words a bit as he spoke.

"Gentlemen, you have outlasted me and likely most of the swill in this place, so it is time for me to depart. Let us take one last glass to the streets and toast Southport."

Daebian led the crowd out into the night air, accompanying them in a raucous drinking song as they threaded their way down the cobbled avenues. The darkness of the early morning grew even blacker as the mob of revelers passed down a narrow street bereft of functional street lamps. Daebian turned to the mass of partiers when they stepped into an intersection.

"Fellows, this is where we must part ways." A loud groan of disappointment echoed from his new followers. "Do not despair, for the entertainment has not yet reached an end. Not for me and mine anyway. However, I am sad to say this is where your enjoyment meets its conclusion. Ladies."

The women hanging on the arms of several sailors smiled once at their escorts, nodded at Daebian, and disentwined their arms from the men before vanishing into the night. The navy men stopped singing and gave their benefactor puzzled looks. Confusion turned to fear when dozens of men appeared out of the shadows wielding truncheons and cutlasses.

Before the drunken men could utter more than a surprised exclamation, Daebian's men fell on them, bashing heads with truncheons and cutlass hilts. The pirates had the sailors beaten into submission in moments and donned their distinctive blue and white, broad-striped shirts.

"Tobias, how many men do we have at the ready?"

"Thirty-six new recruits plus our original crew. With the fellows we picked off through the night, we have forty-three wearing navy colors," Tobias dutifully reported.

"And the Watch?"

"Properly distracted in the upper commons."

"Fantastic. Let the festivities resume."

Daebian led his raucous partygoers down the docks to where the naval vessels were moored. The band of disguised sailors continued their shouting, singing, and cajoling all the way down the pier before stopping next to the moored ships.

"It's about time you lot finished embarrassing yourselves," a man called out from the deck of the ship. "Speak the password, and I'll lower the gangplank so you can sleep off your drink enough to pull your shift."

"The password is 'your mother's a trollop,'" Daebian slurred.

"Hilarious. Now give me the password, or you idiots can sleep on the dock!"

Daebian's demonic eyes peered through the darkness and found and memorized every shadow on the ship's deck. Walking into a shadow on the dock, Daebian stepped out onto the deck of the ship behind the guard on duty.

"The password is pirate," Daebian whispered in the man's ear.

Daebian plunged his sword into the man's back and casually tossed him overboard. He severed the ropes securing the gangplank in place before vanishing into another shadow and reappearing across the deck to cut down two more men before the first of his crew made it aboard. Despite there being only a nominal crew aboard the ship, Daebian needed to move quickly before they fully roused. Even a few men could pose a challenge if he did not get his crew on deck before they mobilized.

Piercing the darkness with his eyes, Daebian left the fighting behind him and leapt out onto the next ship. Sailors were already emerging from below decks and forming up, but they were too late to try to stop him. He quickly dispatched three men near the gunwale and dropped the gangplank for his men. The pirate captain stepped aside to let his men do their work as he sought out a third ship. The final object of his desire was moored two piers over, and even his enhanced vision was unable to discern a proper shadow for him to travel through.

"Gloom, come be my eyes."

A crow blacker than the night sky let out a caw, swooped down from an upper spar, and flew to the ship. Daebian used Klaraxis's power to see through Gloom's eyes. Able to identify the inky recesses on the far ship, Daebian leapt into the shadow ways and emerged amidst the alerted crew. Two men fell before the sailors were aware there was an enemy amongst them. Daebian blocked a strike from one man and ducked another before leaping through a shadow. He reappeared almost instantly several yards away and blanketed a large swath of the deck in unnatural darkness.

Men cried out in panic while Daebian sprinted across the deck and facilitated his men's boarding. By the time the pirates boarded the third ship, the first two were nearly under their control, the former crew, alive and dead, pitched overboard. Within minutes, the pirates secured the remaining vessel and cleared it of its original crew. Borrowing Gloom's eyes once more, Daebian stepped out onto the deck of the first ship.

"Tobias, what did you find in the stores?"

The first mate jumped when the voice spoke from behind him. "Fully loaded with oil flasks and all, Captain."

"Excellent. The wolves are now a pack, and it's time to go hunting."

Daebian sailed away from Southport with his three new ships. Behind him, the docks burned and cast the waterfront district in an orange glow. The flames licked into the sky as if to wave their farewell.

"Course, Captain?" Tobias inquired.

"South. I want to meet some old friends."

Thanks to the total surprise of the assault, the blackness of night, and the flaming distraction they left behind, pursuit was all but impossible. Even if the navy knew in what direction the absconded ships had travelled, the ocean was vast.

Daebian's armada of five ships sailed south for several days before creating a picket just below the land border between Valeria and Sumara. Stretching his watchers across more than fifty miles of open ocean, the pirates waited, vigilantly watching and lying in wait for their hapless prey to sail into their trap.

Although preferring to dine alone, Daebian chose this night to sup with his crew in the mess. He disliked the banal conversations of common men, fixated almost entirely on plunder, women, and drink, but he understood the importance of not setting himself apart from the crew. Daebian made the pretense of laughing at the punch lines of bawdy jokes or outlandish stories while he picked at his food, his mind focused on far more important things.

Tobias broke Daebian out of his pondering. "Captain, I know it's not our place to ask questions, but we been bobbing in the water for three days now, and the crew was wondering what it is we're waiting for."

"It is a good question, Tobias. The men are naturally anxious, and we do not want them to start questioning their purpose. You are ensuring they stay occupied?"

"Aye, sir. We been practicing what's written in them drill manuals we found in the officers' berths."

"Good. Knowing how your enemy fights is half the key to victory. As to your question, my father makes a major run to Sumara this time of year. We missed his ships heading south, but a more valuable cargo is returning north as we speak. We know they do not stray far from land for fear of pirates, so our picket has a good chance of spotting them. My father and his captains are no fools. It is unlikely they will be sailing alone, hence our wolf pack. A single pirate ship, or even a pair of them as I personally witnessed working in concert, has a poor probability of success. My father's men are well versed in shipboard combat, and his vessels are armed as well."

"Ah, so that's why we got these navy ships. We got them outgunned now."

"Partly, but a true genius can claim victory without firing a single shot. It is unlikely anyone outside of Southport knows about the theft of these navy vessels. Certainly no one south of the border does. We will use that temporary lack of knowledge to our advantage."

Daebian laid out the details of his plan to Tobias and ordered him to take it to all the crew in his command. Confused grumblings of misgiving met the instructions, but the crew accepted them, their fear of the enigmatic captain breaking through the resistance to generations of pirate tradition.

"Sails ho!" the lookout called from atop the crow's nest. "Two points port abeam."

Zeb pulled out a spyglass and scanned the horizon. He had three ships with him and a wizard, so he was not too concerned with pirates. As much as he disliked magic, he was glad Azerick had put a mage on each of his ships during these troubled times. Zeb saw the flare launch into the sky just as he made out the sails against the horizon from his position on the aft deck. Moments later, a second flare streaked skyward from far off the starboard rail.

"Eva," Zeb called to his wizard, "what do you make of that flare? Is it magic?"

The woman stared at the glowing light until it fell back into the ocean and vanished. "I do not think so. The trailing smoke would indicate it is alchemic, created by combining sulfur, charcoal, and saltpeter. Very few people are able to produce it outside the Academy."

"The military commissioned them wizards to make 'em for a while now. Is there any way you can get a better look at that ship and the one that shot off the second flare?"

Eva nodded and stood over a barrel of fresh water. She cast a spell and focused on the shimmering surface, willing it to produce the image she desired. Within moments, the clear image of a ship replaced the rippling reflection of her face.

"I have it, Captain. Would you like to see?"

Zeb stepped near the barrel and peered over the lip as if afraid a sea monster might be lying in wait for him. "That looks like a navy ship. It's flying their colors, and the armament is definitely military. Is that the ship to port?"

"It is."

"Can you show me the one off the starboard?" Eva waved her hand as if to brush away the image of the first ship and displayed the second one. "That's navy too, and they're both headed our way. I wonder what they want."

"What's your orders, Cap'n?" Balor asked.

Zeb thought hard for several seconds. "Order the other ships in close and subtly draw weapons from the armory. I don't know what's going on, so let's be prepared, but don't take any provocative actions." Zeb looked at the barrel of water. "And pour that water overboard and jettison the barrel."

Eva sent a magical yellow light soaring into the sky, the signal for the ships to converge and be wary of danger. An hour crept past and the navy ships drew ever closer. The lookout called out the sighting of a third set of sails appearing farther off the starboard beam.

"What do you think this is all about, Cap'n?" Balor asked nervously.

Zeb shook his head. "I don't have a clue. Everyone stay alert."

The merchant captain studied the crews aboard the approaching ships through his spyglass. The men wore the striped shirts and moved with the practiced efficiency of naval seamen. Everything he saw spoke of a legitimate naval operation, but Zeb could not shake the nagging feeling that a storm was brewing, and it was coming his way.

The lead navy ship raised signal flags, ordering the merchant ships to stand down and prepare for boarding. Zeb signaled the ships to drop anchor and comply, but he quietly passed word to remain on alert. The ships drew near, and a man in an officer's uniform stepped to the rail of the navy vessel and raised a megaphone to his mouth.

"I am Captain Tobias Munce of His Majesty's Royal Navy. Prepare to be boarded. Any interference in the performance of our duty will be met with force."

Zeb cupped his hands to his mouth. "I'm the captain of this vessel and senior member of this group. What is the meaning of this?"

"Due to the heightened state of war and the threat of political destabilization, the king has demanded an expansion in regular customs responsibilities," came the shouted response.

Zeb looked at the men gathered on the deck and the heavy weaponry trained on his ships. "Throw your lines then! Make fast for boarding!"

The crew of the navy ship threw lines across the short stretch of water between the vessels and lowered gangplanks once the merchant crew had tied them off. Sailors streamed across the gangplanks with Captain Tobias leading the way onto Zeb's ship.

"This is highly unusual, and I don't like it one bit," Zeb said to Tobias.

"It's not your job to like it, only to comply." Tobias began directing his crew to key locations on the deck.

Zeb gave Eva a sidelong glance. "The first instant this doesn't look legit, I want you to blast that ship to splinters."

"Let's not lose our heads," Daebian whispered into Zeb's ear. Eva let out a small squeak when Daebian poked her in the back with his sword. "I mean that quite literally."

"Damn your hide, boy! I took you aboard and made you a sailor! You have friends on this ship!"

"Which is why my people are not cutting yours down as we speak. Now, order your men to lay down arms and take a seat on the main deck."

"You just keep finding new ways to disappoint your father," Zeb hissed.

"He disappointed me first. Let this be the last time we mention him lest I become unpleasant. Now, order your people to stand down, and signal your other ships to do the same."

Zeb's face burned scarlet, and he gritted his teeth in barely suppressed fury. "Men, lay down arms and gather 'round the mainmast!" The crew's reaction was looks of confusion. "Do it, now! Balor, signal the other ships to do the same."

Balor looked about to argue but did as his captain ordered. He affixed several colored pennants to a line and hoisted them up. A minute later, both ships flew pennants of acknowledgment. Daebian's men quickly bound the hands and feet of the merchant crews. Daebian took the extra precaution of ordering gags in the wizards' mouths.

"Sorry about this, Eva, but we don't want anyone making this more unpleasant than it has to be."

Eva surprised Daebian by simply smiling coyly and biting down on the braided cloth he tied around her head. He then turned and addressed everyone aboard.

"For those of you who do not know me, I am Daebian Giles, outcast son of your precious Lord Giles. I understand this is likely a frightening situation for some of you, but rest assured I have no intention of harming you as long as you offer no resistance. Try to escape, fail to follow instructions, or offer my crew any form of violence or trouble, and you will be run through and tossed overboard. If you look off to starboard, you can see another of my ships approaching. That ship will carry a letter of ransom to my father, and when he pays it, I will release you all to go about your merry way."

It took a great deal of shuffling prisoners and crew to properly man all eight ships now in Daebian's command. He sent the smallest of his ships to convey his ransom demands while the rest of his pirate group sailed southwest into uncharted waters.

"What's next on our agenda, Captain," Tobias asked as he and Daebian shared a meal in the captain's quarters. "We made quite a haul with this run, not even counting whatever you get for ransoming the crew. The men are hoping we'll lay anchor so they can spend a good bit of their earnings."

"There really is little to do until our ship returns, and our crew is already stretched too thin between all our vessels. We are returning to the Black Sand Isles where we will hire more crew and wait for our ransom payment."

Tobias nodded. "Aye, and Captain Farique will be pleased with his share."

Daebian laid his fork down and looked at the overhead as he drummed his fingers on the tabletop. "I had forgotten about him."

Tobias was certain this was not a true statement. In the short time he had known the unusual young man, he was confident in thinking that Daebian had not forgotten a single event or word spoken to him since he was old enough to understand speech.

"We have one more audacious plan to enact, Tobias. I need you to visit with each of the crew and convince them to give me their full support. There will be a great deal of profit in it if we are successful."

"Do you think we'll be successful?"

Daebian grinned conspiratorially. "Tobias, I am *always* successful when I choose to be."

Good fortune continued to smile upon them as the seas remained calm and the winds gentle. It allowed Tobias to gather most of the crew together aboard a single ship, leaving a skeleton crew of men he trusted to maintain course on the others. It was cramped, and the smell of unwashed bodies was pervasive even in the open air of the main deck.

Tobias stood a few feet above the pressed mass of sailors atop the foredeck stairs.

"Men, we are heading home," the first mate announced, receiving a loud cheer from the crew. "But Captain Daebian has one more thing he needs before we take our shore leave and enjoy our spoils. As you probably know, Captain Daebian isn't one for taking orders from anyone, and he has set his sights on a higher position."

"There ain't no higher position!" a voice called out from the mob.

"There's one."

The crew began an uneasy murmuring as they began to understand what Tobias was saying. "He's a madman! Captain Farique commands nearly every pirate sailing the seas. He'll hang us all from his yardarms like wind chimes!"

"Captain Farique is just a man, and I think you all agree Captain Daebian is far more than that. He took our ship, four merchant ships, and three of His Majesty's naval vessels with barely a man lost. Do you think Captain Farique could do that? Captain Farique treats us like peasants, no more than serfs to toil in his oceanic fields for a pittance, for scraps he tosses down to us like dogs at his table. Captain Daebian will treat us right and give us our due. We will sit at his table and enjoy our spoils like knights and noblemen. Rarely does a man get the opportunity to raise himself above his allotted station. Do not pass up the one chance you have at achieving greatness!"

A cheer of assent rang out across the rolling seas. High atop the mainmast, a crow cawed out its approval as it spied upon the men below. Dropping a longboat and taking four oarsmen, Tobias returned to the navy vessel Daebian claimed as his flagship.

"Captain, the men have chosen to support you."

"Due in no small part to your wonderful speech." Tobias looked ill at ease, not knowing what kind of demonic sorcery Daebian had used to spy upon him. "You are much smarter than I had given you credit for. You would make a terrific ship's captain. Do you desire such a promotion?"

"There's few sailors who don't dream of commanding their own ship."

Daebian tapped his index finger against his nose. "It is unfortunate for you that I desire you to be by my side. You have earned my trust and confidence. I will cut you in for a full captain's share of the spoils, and you are second to no man save me. Does that suit you?"

"I serve at your pleasure, sir."

"Wonderful. Please bring me the wizard Eva and see to the ship."

"Aye, sir."

Tobias returned minutes later, gently pushing Eva through the door. Daebian motioned to the gag in her mouth and Tobias cut it free. If Eva was offended by her treatment, it did not show on her face. She took a seat in the chair Daebian indicated and smiled.

"Thank you, Tobias. I am sure Eva will behave herself," Daebian said in dismissal. "Nice to see you again, Eva. The former captain of this ship had some decent taste in wine. Would you like some?"

Eva glanced over her shoulder to her wrists bound behind her back. Daebian twiddled a finger and the rope became dry and brittle and fell apart.

"You have learned some new tricks," Eva said as she rubbed her wrists before reaching for the glass of wine.

"You have no idea the things I have learned."

"We all wondered what became of you after you left. You seem to have done rather well in such a short time."

"I do hate to remain idle."

"Is it true you stabbed your father before you ran off?"

"I did, and I took a bit of him with me when I left. How does he fare?"

"I'm not certain. I was put on ship duty and left with Captain Zeb shortly after you did. I cannot imagine anyone having the gall to attack Azerick. He is so powerful."

"He is also a bit stupid in some ways, and it is going to get him and a lot of people killed. How do you like ship duty? Is it preferable to being at the school?"

"I had never planned on setting foot on a boat in my life, but the constant training at the school was so stressful and exhausting I agreed to go when they asked."

Daebian quirked an eyebrow. "Father still actually asks people what they want? Well, that consideration certainly won't last much longer. Do you want to go back?"

Eva sighed. "They need me. Azerick says they need every wizard they can find to defeat the Scions."

"He is going to fail. What if I told you that you could be of greater use elsewhere?"

"Doing what?"

"Have you ever thought about being a pirate? It's a lot of fun."

Eva returned Daebian's smile and sipped from her glass.

CHAPTER 6

The forsaken gods of old hovered above their bleak prison world from within their crystal fortress. The Scions looked down at their countless minions clawing at the detestable barrier keeping them from their sole purpose for existing: the destruction and *enslavement of the mortal races.*

"The false Guardian's abominable progeny has been absent, and the barrier suffers from its absence," Zyn remarked.

"Our time draws near," Xar affirmed.

"I trust our weakening has gone undetected?"

"Indeed it has. We have successfully diverted the false Guardian and his mutant offspring's attention to other flaws."

"Let us take advantage of their neglect and awaken our pets."

"Agreed."

The Scions placed their hands upon the raised crystal sphere in the center of the room and focused their awesome power. A thin but incredibly powerful ray lanced out from the tower and struck the barrier. Unlike the previous breaches, this one was not intended to smash open a gaping wound to allow hordes of their violent killing machines through, but instead seared a surgically precise hole to allow their dominating consciousness to reach out into the mortal realm.

Sandy was luxuriating in her huge bed of deep, dry sand, heated with her magic to what humans would consider intolerable warmth. She had spent the last several weeks within the school grounds adding realism to the humans' training and improving her magic in the process. She enjoyed the one day off per week Azerick allowed them all to take so they could rest and reflect upon what they learned. Sandy hoped to reflect upon twenty hours or so of uninterrupted sleep.

"Hear us and obey!"

Sandy's head shot up and she searched for any sign of danger as fear gripped her heart and made her blood run cold. She had heard those voices once before when she was young, but she had dismissed them as a strange but frightful dream. She knew this was no dream, but a herald to a nightmare.

"Lord Giles, there are, ah, several men upstairs who, ah, wish an audience," Simon stammered.

Azerick looked up from the codex, turned on his stool, and fixed Simon with his gaze. "Who is it? I am rather busy to be entertaining guests."

Simon's fingers danced about nervously. "One is a messenger from King Jarvin. Another is a representative from Southport. The third is, ah, a sailor who claims to have a message from, ah, your son Daebian."

Azerick practically leapt from the high stool and crossed the floor. "What does he want? What did he say?"

"He, ah, did not share that information with, ah, me, My Lord."

Azerick's stomach fluttered anxiously with anticipation and trepidation. He desperately wanted to know what had become of his son, but he knew any message from Daebian was unlikely to be pleasant. In fact, it was almost assuredly bad news bringing all three men to his door. No one ever came bearing pleasantries these days.

"There is, ah, a matter I would like to discuss with you as well, My Lord."

"Of course, Simon. What is it?"

"Your treasury is down by seventy-three percent since we began funding the war effort. At our current rate of expenditure, I fear your liquid assets shall be exhausted within a year."

Azerick smiled and clapped Simon on the shoulder. "At least I can share some good news with you, Simon. We don't have anywhere close to a year before the Scions bust free and try to destroy us all."

"Oh, ah, I see," Simon responded quietly, then followed Azerick upstairs.

Azerick found all three men in the living room of the new tower, each standing with varied but equally nervous looks upon their faces. None looked eager to relay whatever message they were required to convey, so Azerick made it simple for them by addressing them in order of station.

"Which of you are from the king?"

"I am, My Lord."

"What is your message?"

"My Lord, King Jarvin requires your immediate presence to assist in resolving a dispute with several key nobles. All members are currently awaiting your arrival."

Azerick sighed, annoyed at having to delay his work to settle some petty squabbling. "Very well. Did you use the gate to arrive here?"

"I did, My Lord," the man replied, his discomfort at having done so evident in his voice and posture.

"One of my people will take you back. Please ask King Jarvin to assemble the council, and I will be there within the hour. Relay my appreciation to His Highness for indulging me. Haste is crucial at this point in the game."

"Yes, My Lord."

Azerick turned to the man from Southport as Simon led the king's messenger away. "What ill tidings do you bring?"

The man straightened and adjusted the collar of his shirt. "My Lord, Duke Beaumonte sent me with news of your son."

Azerick's lips compressed in a thin line. "What is it?"

"Just over a fortnight ago, a young man proclaiming to be Daebian Giles enacted a ruse and absconded with three of His Majesty's naval vessels, killing more than a score of men in the process. There have been reports of him using these vessels to dupe merchant ships into allowing him and his pirate crew to board and make off with their cargo, and in two known cases, their ships as well. He also left several fires in his wake."

"That is disturbing news. What is it you expect of me?"

"His Grace would like to know what form of recompense he can expect from you."

Azerick stared at the man until he practically wilted beneath his gaze. "Tell Duke Beaumonte my recompense comes in the form of advice. Inform every ship's captain that no official of the crown will conduct any kind of boarding party on open water. All ships will make for the nearest port to conduct any and all cargo or customs inspections. My son stabbed me through the chest. His actions are his own, and I accept no responsibility for them. Good day."

The representative looked about to argue, but a glare from the enigmatic sorcerer sent him scurrying for the door. Azerick turned his eyes to the last man in the room, who looked about to bolt for the door as well before relaying whatever message he held.

"Say your words and be gone," Azerick ordered, his tone soft and dangerous.

The man, a simple sailor given the look of his clothes and smell, held out a sealed letter with a shaking hand. "I weren't given no words, sir, just this letter, milord."

Azerick took the letter and examined the seal. Pressed into the black wax was a seal similar to his own, only the tower lay in a shattered ruin upon what he assumed were bodies. As he read the words neatly penned inside, his face flushed as his blood boiled. It was all he could do not to incinerate this man standing before him.

"Are you a member of Daebian's crew?"

"No, milord. I ain't never heard that name before. I mean, I heard it around the docks, but I ain't never met him. A man gived me a silver piece to bring that letter to you and a gold crown to deliver something you was supposed to give me."

Azerick read the letter three more times, but lashing his mind with Daebian's words only served to increase his ire. "Simon!" Azerick shouted, his demonic lungs issuing the words with enough force to set windows and bones vibrating.

The nervous steward raced through the door seconds later. "Yes, My Lord?"

Azerick handed the letter to Simon. "Fulfill my son's demand."

Simon read the letter, his eyes growing wider with each word. "Oh my. Oh dear. But..."

"Just do it, Simon," Azerick ordered softly.

Azerick's steward raced down to the treasury and reappeared moments later carrying a small, ornate box measuring just a hand span in width and a couple of inches tall. Azerick took the box and handed it to the courier.

"Tell your man to deliver this message to my son: there will be a reckoning."

The man ducked his head and made haste for the doors. Azerick rubbed his temples in an effort to massage away the pain building in his head. Looking skyward as if beseeching the gods for help, he sighed, summoned his staff to his hand, and made for the door with Simon following closely on his heels.

"Simon, check in on Raijaun for me. If he is feeling up to it, I need him to mind the barrier. I do not expect to be gone long, but now is not the time—"

A mighty roar thundered across the grounds. Clouds, angry and black, rolled in like the waves of a storm-tossed sea. Lightning streaked across the sky, splitting the clouds into the multiple panes of a giant, darkness-enshrouded stained-glass window. Azerick sprinted toward the commotion, his nerves on fire and his stomach churning with the realization that he had forgotten something terrible.

He came around the tower just in time to see Sandy smash her tail into the side of one of the school buildings, sending deep fractures all along its length. A second strike made the wall crumble and the roof cave in. Students began fleeing the wreckage through the doorframe still standing at the far end. Sandy swiveled her huge head toward the panicked children and reared back.

Azerick's body and magic acted before his mind fully comprehended what either he or Sandy was about to do. A near invisible ray of force struck Sandy in the side of her head, shifting her tooth-filled maw away from the scrambling students just as she unleashed a torrent of flame. Her fiery breath set the timbers of the collapsed building alight as if they were dried kindling.

Sandy directed her fearsome glare at the sorcerer and trumpeted another mighty roar along with a second jet of fire. Azerick raised a ward and felt the heat wash over him. His shield protected him from the intense flames, but the heat of it scorched the ground and cracked the stone all around him.

"Sandy, stop!" Azerick shouted.

The young dragon's only response was to leap at him, clearing the fifty feet separating them in a single bound. Sandy crashed down with surprising grace and swiped a big scaly paw at Azerick like a cat. The clawed hand caught him in his left side, sent him flying through the air, and tumbling across the ground. Had his body been as frail as the human form he took, the strike would easily have crippled or killed him.

Azerick rolled to his feet, his legs spread, and crouched in a defensive posture. "Sandy, block them out of your mind! You must fight them!"

Sandy appeared to claw at the sky and pulled down bolt after bolt of lightning. The powerful bolts stabbed at the ground, buildings, and humans scurrying for cover. The momentary shock of Sandy's attack passed, and the mages acted with expert proficiency, raising wards and shielding themselves and others from the elemental attack.

Sandy ignored the tumult around her and focused on Azerick. Azerick fed power into his ward as a dozen bolts converged into a single point aimed for the top of his head. Light flared all around him, blinding him in its intense luminescence. The sorcerer's ward fought against the lightning's awesome power, crackling and sparking in protest.

"Please, do not make me hurt you!" Azerick begged as the lightning strikes abated.

If Sandy was able to comprehend Azerick's words, she showed no sign of being able to comply with them. The dragon hissed out words in her draconic language and the ground beneath Azerick's feet turned to silt, enveloping him almost to his neck before solidifying and trapping him in a stony embrace.

The enraged dragon reared back, wreathed her mighty paws in eldritch power, and prepared to pounce. As she flexed her haunches in preparation for rending Azerick's head from his shoulders, a brilliant gold and silver ray struck Sandy in the side with enough force to throw her into a nearby building, collapsing its entire western wall and a large portion of the roof. Sandy burst from the rubble with a furious roar and breathed a colossal column of fire at Raijaun. Raijaun shielded himself from the flames and intense heat and braced himself as Sandy launched herself at him.

The ground exploded around Azerick as he thrust himself into the air with a beat of his demonic wings. The transformed sorcerer flew at Sandy, wrapped his arms and legs around her neck, and held on tightly. Sandy roared and flung her head around in an attempt to dislodge her attacker. Arcane energy crackled all over her body, wreathing her in a sparking aura of power.

Azerick gritted his teeth against the burning pain and hissed, "Forgive me," then slammed an open hand against Sandy's head and sent a powerful burst of magic straight into her brain.

Sandy slumped to the ground and lay motionless. Only the barely perceptible rise and fall of her thick midriff gave a sign of life. Azerick rolled to his feet and shifted back into his preferred form. Raijaun's shoulders sagged with fatigue as he dropped his ward and stepped toward Sandy and his father.

"What happened, Father?"

Azerick took several deep breaths to steady his voice as his emotions threatened to tear it and his heart apart. "The Scions have managed to breach the barrier and send part of their consciousness into our world to ready the dragons for their arrival."

"Does that mean the Scions are free? Has the invasion begun?"

"I do not think so. The dragons have all but vanished from our lands. I think most fled to faraway places after the Great Revolution. They will require time to organize and perhaps strengthen themselves before the battle begins. The Scions continue to strategically place their pieces upon the board before striking. Are you all right?"

Raijaun nodded. "I was not quite ready to expend so much energy so soon, but I am well. What of Sandy?"

Azerick looked at her and forced his eyes to staunch the tears welling up. "She is stunned and will remain so until I wake her. At least I hope so."

"Can you help her?"

Azerick thought for a full minute before answering. "I think so. Can you transport her to the laboratory?" Raijaun nodded. "I will need you to check the barrier while I am gone."

"Where are you going? Why now?"

"Jarvin needs a stick with which to beat his lords into submission."

"How long will you be?"

"Not nearly as long as I had first anticipated. This changes many things, my patience for stupidity paramount among them. Get Sandy to the lab and check the barrier. If the Scions have indeed broken through, you know what to do."

"Yes, Father."

Azerick sliced the air with his magic, opening a portal to bisect time and space. Stepping through, he appeared just before the east gates allowing admittance to the merchant district. Two wizards from his school stepped from inside a small guardhouse built to watch over the gates when their magical use was required. At least a dozen armored men stood watch and controlled the gates for their more mundane purposes.

"Prepare the gate," Azerick ordered as he strode toward them.

The two wizards exchanged glances over Azerick's unusually abrupt command but hastened to obey. The man and woman laid their hands upon the two pillars framing the wide gates and began channeling power into them. The guards ordered everyone approaching to stay clear while the wizards worked their magic. The guards needed little in the way of prodding as the runes inscribed upon the tall monoliths began to glow with eldritch light. Within moments, a shimmering screen stretched between the two columns before resolving into the landscape of Brelland's primary gate.

Three mages stood prepared on Brelland's side, alerted of the gate's activation by the obelisks at their end. Scores of ordinary citizens were hastening away from the gate while others stepped a short distance away and gawked. Azerick stepped through the portal without hesitation but paused on the distant end as vertigo washed over him. He sympathized with the ordinary humans for the effect traveling through the gate would have on them if even he felt such a strong sense of disorientation. He brushed aside his dizziness as well as his pity. He had no time for either of them.

Azerick appreciated the obvious militarization of the city. Barricades, racks of weapons, and cisterns of water were visible even this near the gates. Soldiers and conscripts marched through the streets, keeping them clear of anyone not gainfully employed. Tearing open another portal, Azerick stepped to the inner wall surrounding Castle Stonemount.

Despite having been warned of his impending arrival, the score of guards watching over the castle gate jumped and fumbled for weapons when he appeared. The men regained their composure and opened the walk-through gate so the sorcerer could pass without further challenge. The officer of the guard saluted when Azerick approached.

"I need you to send a runner to the castle and inform the seneschal or His Highness directly of my arrival. I hope the council has already gathered, but if they haven't, it is in their best interest to make haste. I have very little time to dally."

"Yes, milord!" the guard officer responded.

The man shouted for a courier, and a boy of no more than fourteen years, wearing a too-big set of light armor with a shortsword belted around his waist ran up and saluted. The gate officer relayed Azerick's order. The boy took off at a sprint and vanished. The soldier saluted once more as Azerick walked unhurriedly toward the castle. He could easily step there using another portal, but he wanted the council notified and assembled before he arrived.

The doors to the castle opened for him as he approached. Aaron Barker, Jarvin's steward, stood waiting for him wearing his robes of state. "Lord Giles, His Majesty and the council are assembled and waiting.

"What is it that requires my immediate attention?" Azerick asked without breaking stride.

"A conflict has arisen between His Majesty and Lord Atwater. Lord Atwater controls a large area between Brightridge and Argoth and has close ties with Duchess Paullina. Much of his land encompasses the agricultural regions of the Habberback Plains, which are vital to the kingdom's food production and distribution. Due to his vast wealth and plentiful food supply, he has assembled one of the largest individual armies outside of Brelland or Brightridge."

Azerick's face soured as he considered the implications. No single lord would have been allowed to assemble such a large force under normal circumstances for fear of usurpation. But with the mandated conscriptions and massive war effort, those restrictions were removed.

"What does he want? More land, titles, his own duchy?" Azerick asked. "Jarvin should offer him nothing more than five feet of rope and a six-foot drop."

"As well he would, only Lord Atwater's argument is held with measured support by others. You see, a vast army out of Sumara has appeared just across the border near Argoth. Duchess Paullina has moved the bulk of her forces to block the pass, but given the size of the Sumaran army, she could hold it for only a matter of weeks at best. Lord Atwater is even now marshaling his troops to march to Paullina's aid. Only Jarvin's insistence in holding this quorum has held them in place."

As ridiculous as the situation was, Azerick understood both positions. Valeria and Sumara were longtime bitter rivals and frequently in conflict. The southern provinces in particular would view any incursion into Valerian territory a hostile act no matter the assurances of Sumaran diplomats or even their king. Jarvin would have to mobilize a superior army to force Lord Atwater to obey, but he could not get them south before the renegade lord merged his troops with those of Duchess Paullina's, leaving the heart of Valeria nearly defenseless against the impending invasion.

Jarvin needed a stick to beat some sense into his wavering nobles, and that stick was Azerick. Azerick's anger only mounted as he strode down the corridors to the audience hall, and the chamberlain had to nearly jog to keep pace. Azerick was tired of the pettiness, tired of being the voice of reason, and tired of seeing his friends and family suffer. One of his sons was lost to him, possibly forever. His other son was exhausted and in agony from using his power to try to protect a people who would likely never fully accept him, and now Sandy lay in a state of unconsciousness from which she may never be allowed to awaken.

Aaron hurried into the audience chamber to announce Azerick's imminent arrival, knowing the sorcerer would not wait outside. The steward barely had time to speak his words before Azerick strode into the hall like a dark cloud moments from becoming a fierce storm. He surveyed those in attendance with a glance and recognized several of the attending lords as well as the Academy headmaster and a handful of senior wizards.

"Wonderful. Jarvin's dog is here to bark at us," a man declared vocally.

"Lord Atwater, allow us to conduct this meeting with civility," Jarvin admonished him from atop his throne.

"You speak of civility while Sumara marches on our borders, and then you bring in your thug to bully me into compliance like he has done so many times before. Not this time!"

"No one is here to bully anyone," Jarvin assured the agitated lord. "Lord Giles is here to apprise us of the current situation so we may make intelligent decisions based upon fact and not emotions brought about by old prejudices. Azerick, how stands our current situation?"

"Poor and getting worse," Azerick answered. "The Scions breached the barrier in a manner that allowed them to take command of the dragons."

"Have they escaped then? Are they on the march now?" Jarvin asked.

"I do not think so. This happened just before I departed North Haven, and I have not had a chance to inspect their prison because I am here dealing with this. Only recently is my son able to get out of bed due to the agony using his power causes him, and I just put down one of my dearest friends, but I cannot help any of them right now because I have to settle the squabbles of children! People are suffering and dying for all our welfare, including yours, but you still cannot see past your own insignificant existence."

Lord Atwater snorted. "Dragons, yet more of your nonsense. Several times my army, and others, have fought these creatures you claim belong to some ancient gods, and each time we defeated them handily. You once asked us what you would gain by having us build up our defenses. We only need look across Argoth's border for the answer to that. Oh, you were quite clever and very convincing, Lord Giles. Creating this fiasco so that we all build up armies so no one questions the power you are amassing was a stroke of brilliance. Your friends in Sumara attack us from the south while your army strikes from the north eliminating any further resistance to your plans of conquest. And do not think I don't know about this magic well of yours, all to increase your power so you can make yourself king. You have even managed to create a navy with your ships and your son's pirates."

"My son captured three of my ships and took the crew hostage, and the Source pool aids all who can channel magic."

"But none as much as you." Lord Atwater turned his eyes to Headmaster Florent. "Am I right, Headmaster?"

"From what little I know of such a thing, your argument appears correct."

"You may have the king and others fooled or cowed, but not me! I will not stand idly by while you march your foreign friends into my kingdom. Nor will I allow anyone to take what is mine. I bought my army with my gold, and I will use it as I see fit. They will march south and drive those desert dwellers back from whence they came. If the king wishes to hand over the crown to you then so be it, but do not expect me to toss in my gold or lands as well."

"This is your final word on the matter? Think well, Lord Atwater." Azerick's voice was as cold as a grave carved in the ice of the northern wastes.

"I have thought well and given my answer. Do not think to intimidate me, sorcerer. I am here under the king's protection and sworn word of safe passage."

"You, all of you, are fools if you think anyone can promise safety in these times."

Azerick thrust his staff at the nobleman. A black and silver ray lanced out of the arcanum sphere, struck the surprised man in the chest, hurled him from his seat, and pressed him against the wall fifteen feet above the assembled crowd. Several people cried out and made to race from the room. With his free hand, Azerick struck them all down with an invisible wall of force carrying the strength of an ocean wave.

Acrid smoke filled the room as Azerick's abyssal beam destroyed Lord Atwater's body and turned it into something unrecognizable. Azerick ignored several protests and even the ringing of armor and swords being drawn as guardsmen rushed into the room and formed a defensive wall around their king. When the arcane assault finally ended, nothing of the rebellious lord remained except for a black silhouette permanently scorched into the marble.

"Lord Giles, cease this at once! What have you done?" the king asked when Azerick finally acknowledged his protests.

Many of the nobles cowered on the floor where Azerick had casually tossed them, fearful they might well be the sorcerer's next target.

"I have carried out the execution of a traitor. Something you should have done the instant he opened his mouth in dissension."

"That was not an execution, it was murder!"

"If you did not ask me here to do what you did not have the stomach for, then why waste my time?"

"I asked you to come reason with them, convince them of the dire consequences of creating divisions within the kingdom!"

"You asked me here to be your stick to beat them into submission!" Azerick turned to the assembly. "The time for sticks is behind us! Now is the time of the sword, and I will put anyone to the sword who threatens the safety of the kingdom. Let us hope Lord Atwater's heir is of a more reasonable and tractable mind."

Jarvin quivered with fury. "You overstep the bounds of your authority. With a single act, you have undone what I have fought to create since I ascended the throne. I created this council so all have a voice. We have laws and courts to deal with matters such as this so no one man, not even the king, shall become a dictator. If I allow that to happen, then we are already lost. I charge you with murder, and you will stand trial!"

Azerick turned his baleful glare upon everyone in the room. "And who will arrest me?"

Jarvin's soldiers looked to their king but did not move. The fear in their eyes showed clearly. Jarvin looked to Headmaster Florent and her cadre.

"Is there nothing you can do?" he beseeched the powerful wizard.

"Our ability to contain or control Lord Giles has long passed. Even if I had the entire might of the Academy behind me, the destruction would be terrible, and the Scions would wash over us like a flood."

Jarvin looked back to Azerick standing impassively at the foot of the dais. "Historians will condemn you, Azerick Giles."

"I welcome their condemnation, for it takes a people to survive to have a history. Send your runners to Lord Atwater's heir and command him to order his soldiers to stand garrison in Brightridge. If he does not, inform him I will personally come and open a rift above his castle and send him and his entire family straight to the abyss."

"And if I refuse?" Jarvin asked through clenched teeth.

"Then you are a threat to the kingdom, and I hope *your* heir is of a more reasonable and tractable mind."

"I may not have the power to enforce my justice upon you, but I denounce you and strip you of all title and authority! When this threat has passed, know that I will use *every* resource at my disposal to see you tried and punished for your crimes if it takes my dying breath to see it done."

"If any of us survive, then I welcome your justice. Let the people decide if the man who saved them deserves your punishment."

"Will you submit to the judgment of the people and my sentence?"

"I will."

"On your word, on your sons, and on whatever may still exist of your soul?"

Azerick nodded before turning his eyes to Headmaster Florent. "I assume you have a method of communicating with the Hall of Inquisition. Please order them and Duchess Paullina's forces to allow Sumara to pass. They will then escort them north to the place of the final battle. If Senior Inquisitor Elias refuses, elevate Inquisitor Fennrick to his position. I feel he may be of a more reasonable mind."

Maureen looked to Jarvin who gave a single nod. "It will be done."

"The Scions are coming soon. I recommend you start moving the outlying towns and villages toward Brelland or Brightridge. Anyone outside the walls when they arrive will have little time to flee and will likely not escape the slaughter."

Azerick turned and left the stunned assembly behind him. Several minutes passed before anyone spoke or moved about. The gathered lords whispered nervously of what would become of them even if they survived the invasion. It was apparent that Lord Giles was beyond the power of anyone to control.

Jarvin motioned to Headmaster Florent to join him atop the dais. "We cannot allow this man to continue to exist unchecked."

"I would agree with you, Highness."

"Surely there is something you and your people can come up with to defeat him?"

"It depends on what exactly you mean."

"I mean that if by some miracle we prevail in this battle, Azerick Giles cannot live one minute to enjoy his victory."

"He swore to abide by your judgment."

"Promises easily made are even more easily broken," Jarvin countered. "We cannot take the chance. We need him if we are to have any hope of surviving this war, but he cannot be allowed to exist beyond its conclusion or all may well have been for naught. Can you create a weapon capable of killing him?"

The Academy headmaster thought for a moment. "I believe it is possible. Everything living can die."

"Good. Speak with Bishop Howarth. Given Azerick's particular physiology, the Church may be of invaluable help. Speak to no one of this unless their support is vital to its success. We cannot know where he may have ears."

"I understand. I just pray we are successful. If he learns we have turned against him, I honestly fear his retribution."

"He turned against me when he made his threats and murdered my subject while under my sworn protection. I must believe that even he has physical and magical limits, and those will be nearest at hand immediately following the battle."

"Who knows, maybe the Scions will kill him with their dying breaths," Maureen said with a wry smile.

"We can only pray it is so."

Upon returning to North Haven, Azerick immediately opened a portal to the tower entrance. He had not been gone long, and people were still hurrying about cleaning up the mess, clearing away the rubble from two collapsed buildings, and carefully searching for anyone who might be trapped beneath.

Miranda spotted him as soon as he stepped through the portal, broke away from the cleanup and rescue efforts, and rushed into his arms. "I was on the training field when it all happened. What's going on? What did Jarvin want?"

"He needed me to resolve a dilemma."

"Were you able to?"

Azerick inclined his head. "Yes, but not in a manner he liked. Miranda, I want you to know that no matter what happens, no matter the things I have to do, I do them for the sake of all humanity and beyond."

"I know, Azerick. What are you saying?"

"Do you know of Lord Atwater?" Miranda nodded. "I killed him just minutes ago. He threatened to block Sumara's soldiers from coming to our aid and secede if Jarvin tried to stop him. The king was extremely upset at my reaction. He denounced me, and I will stand trial if we survive this."

Miranda looked into her husband's eyes. "I know you did what you thought needed to be done. You are not an evil or selfish man, and Mother and I will stand behind you no matter what. All of North Haven will support you."

"No, you must not do that. I alone must face the consequences of my actions. If we prevail, Valeria will be shattered. She will need great people like you to gather up the pieces and make her whole again. You must stand with the king and keep our people united."

"You are asking me to abandon you!"

"I am asking you to do what must be done no matter how hard or painful it is, just as I have. There are times when necessity outweighs the moral right, as it did today for me, as it will for all of you one day. Let us pray those times do not come again in your lifetimes, but you must be prepared. Promise me."

Miranda swabbed away her tears on Azerick's chest. "I promise."

"Have you heard of what Daebian has done?"

Miranda nodded. "I do not understand him. My son a pirate! And now he has turned against people he called his friends. Why is he doing these things?"

"He wants to punish me for slights I have made against him, wrongs I cannot begin to fathom. He wants to show he is stronger than me, show that I am vulnerable."

"No wonder I have a hard time understanding this stupid war. I cannot even understand my own son. Is Sandy going to be okay?"

Azerick sighed deeply. "I don't know. I need to see what they have done to her, what kind of compulsion they have over her." Azerick looked off into the distance. "I wonder... Have you seen Allister?"

"He's out helping with the cleanup. What is it?" Miranda could only watch as he darted out the door.

CHAPTER 7

"When are we going to get there?" Trielle complained for the hundredth time that day. "We've been walking for days!"

"I have been walking for days. You have been mostly riding on my shoulders and complaining in my ear the entire way," Bron countered.

"You would complain too if you had to smell nothing but your stinky neck sweat the whole time!"

"You could get off me and fly."

"Why should I have to? It's your smelly neck that's the problem! When are we going to get to the valley of big stinkies?"

"We entered the valley two days ago."

"What?" Trielle shouted in Bron's ear. "We've been on this briar-entombed goat path for days, and I haven't seen a single stinky ogre."

"They are amazingly adept at traveling through this terrain and using their surroundings for camouflage. Three of them have been following us for nearly a day and half."

"Is that why that walking fur rug wandered off? What a coward! Where are they? I can't see anything." The wood sprite tried to penetrate the thick, nearly impassable thicket lining the narrow trail they were following but could not see into the brush and brambles more than a few feet. "I still should have smelled them." She looked at Bron's neck. "Well, probably not."

Only Bron's druidic mastery of wood lore enabled him to detect and track their watchers. Bron knew little of ogres other than they were hulking brutes with ferocious tempers and cruel hearts. The fact that the three monsters tracking him and Trielle showed significant patience and mastery of their environment surprised him.

Bron had chosen not to make a campfire when they had neared the Forsaken Valley, but seeing as their presence was now known and they were under close scrutiny, he decided to make a small fire that night. He set a pot of tea to boil over the low flames and laid several strips of salted meat on a hot rock to warm.

Trielle dropped down from the treetops shrouded in darkness and helped herself to the small jar of honey Bron had brought to sweeten his tea. The sprite dipped berries into the honey and ate them, often licking the fruit clean and going for a second coating.

"Most consider it ill-mannered to double dip," Bron chastised.

"Hey, my mouth is clean! The closest you have probably come to brushing your teeth was when I hit you in the mouth with a pinecone."

As usual, Bron ignored the insult they both knew was not true. "Did you find our friends?"

"Your friends maybe. Sprites do not befriend mean, smelly brutes, especially ones who spy on them."

"You befriended me."

"For which you continue to fail to show proper appreciation."

"I shall try harder. Were you able to see them?" Bron asked again.

"Yeah, I found them. Two are lurking a hundred feet to the north and one to the southwest."

"Hmm, if they meant us harm, I think they would have attacked already. Three ogres against one would not cause them to hesitate, I don't think."

"Obviously they know I'm here, too, and they are probably waiting for reinforcements."

"Obviously." Bron stood and peered into the darkened woods. "Would you all like to share some food and tea?"

Nothing moved for several moments, but as the minutes passed, three massive forms separated themselves from the darkness and approached. All three stood a full foot taller than Bron did and outweighed him by at least two hundred pounds. One ogre carried a human two-handed sword tucked into a wide leather belt, one a large axe, and the third a polished club of hardwood the length and thickness of Bron's arm. Despite their weaponry, none made any overtly hostile actions.

"You trespass, weak blood," the sword wielder said in a deep, gravelly voice. "We could kill you for that."

Bron watched Trielle dart to the treetops out of the corner of his eye. "Yet you have not, and for that I thank you. Would you like tea and meat?"

None of the three brutes answered, but they sat down around the small campfire. Bron interpreted this as acquiescence and handed each of them a strip of salted meat and a tin cup of honey-sweetened tea. He spied looks of appreciation upon the ogres' gruesome countenances as they tasted the venison and tea.

"Is it to your liking?"

"Salt is hard to get in our valley. Many days to the nearest mine."

Bron had expected these creatures to be far more brutish and barely capable of conversing. Their apparent civility and capacity for intelligent dialog continued to surprise him.

"My name is Bron."

"Golac," the sword wielder replied, then pointed to the one with the axe, and finally to the ogre gripping a club. "Krotko, Culk. Why do you come to our valley, weak blood?"

"Weak blood?"

"Your blood is weakened with that of a human. You are not one of us."

"I see."

Golac's words hurt him more than he had expected. Bron had grown accustomed to being distrusted and unaccepted by the humans, but he had not expected such rejection from the ogres. He had always reviled them, not just for the assault on his mother that had created him and ultimately killed her, but for the fear and hatred he received from so many humans. The fact that he felt pain at the rejection of those he detested came as a shock. He would have to meditate on this another time.

"I need to speak with your chief or king."

Golac shook his oversized head. "You are not one of us. Only those of the blood or Kin may speak with Sefket."

"Is Sefket your king or chief?"

"Sefket is chief and king for three more years."

"Who becomes king in three years?"

Golac shrugged. "One of the goblins."

"A goblin will be king of the ogres?" Bron asked, startled by such a revelation.

"It is the goblins' turn to be king of all the Kin. The Kin choose from those the goblins present at the gathering. He shall be king for five summers then we must choose a king from the orc tribes. He is king for five summers before the king is chosen from the ogres once again."

The existence of a somewhat democratic society amongst what the humans called the brute races fascinated Bron. The ogres were turning out to be nothing like he had imagined or heard about. He regretted not having more time in which to study their culture further.

"I must speak with Sefket, with all the tribes. There is a great danger coming that threatens all who dwell in this world including the Kin."

"Only Kin may speak with Sefket."

"Can you take my words to Sefket for me?"

Golac wagged his head to the negative. "Words are of no more worth than the one who speaks them. You are not Kin, you are not worthy, so your words are not worthy for Sefket's ears to hear."

"How can I prove my words are worthy?"

"You are weak blood. You must be judged worthy. You must become Kin."

"How do I become Kin?"

"Kramloc will decide," Golac answered.

"Who is Kramloc?"

"Kramloc is our shaman. He will decide if you are worthy."

"What if I am deemed unworthy?"

"Then we will kill you and eat your bug."

Trielle buzzed in the treetops. "Try it, you big, stinky ogre, and I'll put the whole lot of you to sleep!"

Golac glanced at the trees but otherwise ignored the sprite.

"How long will it take for me to meet Kramloc?" Bron asked.

"Two days."

"I hope I can prove my words are worthy. Perhaps I can convince you as we travel."

Golac smiled wryly and shook his head. "You may speak, but know your breath is wasted. None will listen until you are worthy. We will sleep now, but feel free to continue talking. You will have better luck convincing the trees than any of us."

Bron tried to engage his escorts in conversation the following morning and throughout the day, probing for information about ogre society and history, but the previously talkative Golac had gone as quiet as his compatriots, and his inquiries garnered little more than grunts and single-word answers to his many questions. Trielle remained silent and kept a considerable distance from the ogres, but Bron suspected most, if not all, of the pinecones falling from the few trees and striking them came from her and were not random droppings.

The druid did not try to elicit much conversation from the ogres on the second day. Bron satisfied himself by studying his surroundings, noticing a definitive increase in the number of paths and a decrease in the density of the otherwise impassable brush and briars filling the inhospitable valley. Near midday, the smoky scent of campfires and cooking meat reached his nostrils, and he knew they were getting close to their destination.

Several times Bron spotted or sensed movement in the thick foliage and felt the eyes of several watchers upon him as they neared the ogre village. He did not know what he would find upon entering their community, but what he saw surprised him. The paths converged onto what appeared to be a sort of town square. Yurts made of sticks, mud, and hide dotted wide dirt tracks through what appeared to be, with only a little imagination, a thriving, bustling town.

Ogres and even a few goblins and orcs wandered the lanes or sold trinkets, food, furs, and some metal items like pots, pans, tools, and a few weapons from tables and stalls set up to create a market square. Most deals were made based upon some established barter system, but Bron spotted a few coins exchanging hands as well.

Perhaps a mile to the north, a tall cliff face pockmarked with caves towered above the community. It was toward these cliff dwellings Golac guided Bron. Almost everyone they passed studied the stranger for a moment before returning to their business. The village was large and stretched all the way to the cliffs. Bron estimated there to be several thousand ogres living within and around it.

When they reached the base of the escarpment, Bron found steps cleverly carved into the face, creating zigzagging paths between entrances. When the surface proved ill-suited for stairs, stout ladders made of rough logs lashed together with rope provided a route to the more difficult to reach dwellings. Although they appeared well made and sturdy, Bron was glad he did not have to traverse them as Golac took him to a cave just a few dozen feet above the valley floor.

The instant Golac pushed aside the hide acting as a door, a plethora of odors, both familiar and strange, assaulted his senses. Herbs, barks, and crafted unguents wafted through the opening. The smell of distilled willow bark and other potions used to remedy a variety of ailments filled the cavern. Strange glyphs and crude images decorated the walls, scrawled there in paints made in much the same way Bron created his own pigments from bark, berries, and beetle shells.

An ogre stood over a table littered with dried herbs and bark, crushing some unknown ingredients with a stone mortar and pestle. He turned and faced the visitors when they entered without pausing in his amalgamations. Kramloc was a venerable specimen with long white tufts of hair sticking out from the sides of his head. Although stooped with age, he still topped Bron by several inches.

"Golac, why have you brought a weak blood to my cave instead of killing him the moment he trespassed in our valley? You know the laws."

Golac dipped his head. "Wise One, I found him unusual and chose to speak with him before executing him."

The shaman studied Bron for several seconds. "You always were a clever one. What does he want?"

"He claims to have important words for Sefket. He says we are in danger."

"Do you think his words are worthy of our king's ears?"

"I thought he might be tested and given a chance to prove his worth."

"So clever you are. I should train you to be my replacement for when I am gone."

Golac's face clouded and he took a deep breath before answering. "I am a warrior, Wise One."

"A good one as well," Kramloc agreed. "Perhaps you are destined for even greater things. Perhaps you shall be king one day."

"If the gods will it, it will be so."

The shaman turned his attention to Bron. "You say you have words for our king, words of warning?"

"Yes. There is a great—" Bron began.

"Silence, weak blood!" Kramloc barked. "You are not Kin, and you have not proven your worthiness. Until you have, you will hold your tongue and not insult us with your unworthy voice."

Bron suppressed his mounting anger and forced a sense of peace and calmness back into his heart. "Wise One, I understand this to be your way, your tradition, but what I have to say is a matter of life and death. Will you die for the sake of tradition?"

Kramloc stalked past Bron and held the hide flap open wide. "Look down there, weak blood. Our ways and traditions are all we have left. Everything else was taken from us by the people with the same blood polluting your body. If we give up that, then we are unworthy. Better to be dead than unworthy."

"There must be a way to prove I am worthy of sharing my words or Golac would not have brought me here."

"You will prove your blood is strong. You will fight, and you will win, or you will die. You will fight as an ogre, forbidden to use your goddess-given magic. Yes, weak blood, I know what you are."

"This is the only way?" Kramloc nodded. "Who must I fight?"

"You will fight our champion Bojan in the morning. I suggest you spend that time resting and reflecting upon what it means to be an ogre."

The shaman turned away, ending any further discussion. Golac opened the flap and ushered Bron out. The ogre escorted him back to the village and showed him to a small yurt near the center. The room had almost nothing in the way of furnishings with the exception of a pallet made of woven reeds to sleep upon and a small firepit in the center of the room.

"I will bring you water and food," Golac said. "Do not leave the yurt. It is forbidden for non-Kin to walk amongst the people unescorted."

Trielle zipped in through the smoke hole above the firepit the moment Golac departed. "Did you talk to the big, big stinky? What did he say? Can we go home now?"

"I cannot speak to their king yet. I must fight to prove myself worthy of gaining an audience. No one here will listen to me until then."

"All right, a fight! Finally, something interesting. So you club this guy, talk to the big, big stinky, and we go home and eat some proper food. See if you can wrap this up in the next hour or so, would you? I'm hungry, and the smell here is killing me."

"I do not think it is going to be that easy. I must fight their champion in the morning without using my magic, and if I do not win they will kill me."

"Like hell they will! I'll stab every one of them and put this entire smelly town into hibernation!" the sprite declared, then flew around the room stabbing at invisible ogres with her tiny spear.

"I appreciate your support, but I don't think that is a good idea. Kramloc says I must reflect on what it means to be an ogre."

"Well, you have the smell down pretty good, so it shouldn't take long to master the rest. Breathe more through your mouth, jam a finger into any opening up to the second knuckle, and poot like a buffalo."

"I do not think that is what he meant."

"Good luck then, because I can't see much else to them than that."

Trielle vanished through the smoke hole when Golac returned with a wicker basket containing food and a clay pitcher of water. He set the basket down on the floor and turned to leave.

"Golac, what can you tell me of Bojan?"

Golac turned, grinned broadly, and shook his head before leaving. Bron did not need any words to understand what he had just conveyed. Bojan would be a formidable opponent even amongst the ogres, and without his magic, Bron stood little chance of victory, but he refused to give in to despair. His goddess had set him a mission, and he would not fail. She would not let him fail. He spent much of the night meditating and praying to Ellanee and infusing a sense of peace into his troubled heart.

When Bron next opened his eyes, a pale, grey light seeped through the smoke hole, dimly illuminating the yurt's interior. He heard no uproar in the town, so he assumed Trielle had managed to stay out of trouble. When he saw her near the wall examining a small hoard of new beads, feathers, and stones, he had to amend that to at least she hadn't gotten caught.

The druid picked an assortment of fresh and dried fruits from the basket Golac had left and Trielle had failed to devour despite some obvious effort on her part. He had just washed his breakfast down with some water when Golac pushed through the flap.

"The hour is near. I hope you listened to Kramloc's words and took heed."

"I am as ready as I can be."

Golac grunted and motioned for Bron to follow. The druid picked up his staff and dutifully plodded after the ogre warrior. Golac led his charge farther to the east before turning north outside of the village. The path they followed showed recent signs of heavy use. Wherever they were going, they were not the first ones to arrive.

They were nearly at the base of the cliffs when Bron knew they had reached their destination. Golac led him down a narrow path descending between walls of stone and into a deep bowl. The surrounding boulders and high cliffs created a natural arena of sorts with hundreds of spectators gathered around the rim and along ledges cut into the walls. A resounding cheer arose when Bron stepped into the ring.

"Remember, you win or you die," Golac said before departing along the path they had used to enter.

Bron turned toward the center of the pit as a deafening roar from the crowd reverberated through his bones. He turned in a slow circle to locate the source of their adulations and watched in dejected disbelief when the biggest ogre he could imagine stepped into the arena. This was a true brute with little but malice in its heart and murder on its mind. He was what Bron had envisioned of the ogre race.

Bojan was a wall of muscle and barely restrained violence. He paced back and forth, swinging a club as long as Bron's staff and three times as thick with one hand. Even with Bron's magic, this creature would have been formidable. Without it, it seemed impossible. Movement atop the rocks drew Bron's eye. Kramloc stood upon the largest boulder surrounding the ring, looked down at the two gladiators impassively, and spoke a single word.

Bron did not understand the guttural word, but Bojan burst toward him at an astonishing speed with his club raised. Bron was barely able to leap and roll away as the huge bludgeon came crashing down in the spot he had occupied a split second before. The druid felt the earth shake with the weapon's impact as if it were crying out in pain from the powerful blow.

Bojan swept his club in a fierce backhand, and Bron was barely able to leap backward to avoid the swing. The ogre's attack took his weapon wide and left him open for reprisal. Bron darted in, struck Bojan hard in his midriff before spinning around and smashing the bronze-shrouded end of his staff into the ogre's back.

It was like hitting a tree covered in a thick layer of leather. The ogres might call him weak blood, but Bron made a formidable foe for most mortal creatures. Bojan grunted from the strike to his gut and took two involuntary steps forward from the one in the back. Such blows would have caused serious injury, or at least pain, to most creatures, but the ogre simply spun, slapped away a third strike with his bare hand, and smiled.

Bron backed away as Bojan strode confidently toward him, swinging his club from side to side as if scything down tall grass. The druid studied the way Bojan moved, gauging his speed and strength. He found them both to be terrifying. Bron focused his mind inward so he could calm his nerves and think. Unfortunately, Bojan was not of a mind to give him time to do either.

The enormous ogre rushed forward and swung his club in a lethal, horizontal arc. Bron ducked and rolled away, but despite his opinion that Bojan was unlikely to win any sort of spelling contest, the ogre was a skilled warrior and was prepared for the move. He kicked out just as Bron tried to roll away and caught him square in the ribs with a foot the size of a dwarf and just as solid. Bron felt himself lifted into the air and experienced the sensation of weightlessness for a full two seconds before crashing back to the ground and completing his tumble.

The crowd roared its approval and Bojan stomped forward, pressing his attack without needless showmanship. Bron rolled onto his hands and knees, the throbbing pain in his ribs eliciting a grunt of pain. The ogre swung his massive foot at his head like an enormous pendulum. Bron blocked the kick with his staff braced against his left forearm and slung a fistful of dirt and gravel into the champion's face.

Bojan dropped his club and his hands flew to his face, wiping frantically to clear his eyes. Bron stabbed out with his staff from a kneeling position and jabbed the end just below the ogre's sternum. Foul breath hit the druid in the face as the air was violently expelled from Bojan's lungs.

Bron raised himself to his feet and launched a flurry of strikes against the stunned ogre. The sound of wood and bronze striking thick, leathery flesh echoed over the crowd, competing to be heard over the roars of the spectators. Bojan staggered under the furious onslaught, trying to ward off the pummeling strikes with his hands and arms. Bron switched the target of his attacks from the head and body to the ogre's tree trunk-like legs, punishing the thighs and shins with strikes that would have cracked and shattered small timbers.

Bojan wavered and fell to a knee, his body quivering as he tried to support his body with his fists pressed against the ground. Bron held his attack for just a moment, unsure if this signaled defeat. Not hearing any sort of command from the stands and not wanting to give Bojan a chance to recover and resume the battle, Bron swung the end of his heavy staff at the back of the ogre's oversized head. A loud, meaty slap echoed across the pit then all was silent. Both the crowd and Bron looked on in stunned amazement at the staff gripped tightly in Bojan's huge fist.

"No," the ogre champion rumbled. "NO!" he shouted, drawing out the word until it became a roar of defiance.

Bron watched the jaundiced whites of the ogre's eyes turn red as his already bestial face twisted into rage-fueled hate. He stood, ripped the staff from Bron's hands, and flung it high into the air. It sailed behind him, creating a whumping sound as it twirled out of the pit and into the crowd of spectators, striking one unfortunate viewer between the eyes with enough force to stagger him.

The druid struck out with his fist, catching Bojan square in the jaw as he charged forward. The champion did not register the blow in the slightest. He grabbed Bron near the elbow with one hand and gripped him at his crotch with the other. Bojan lifted the half-ogre's stout body as easily as that of a child and ran across the arena with the druid held near head height before slamming him bodily against the unyielding stone cliff.

Stars and supernovas erupted behind Bron's eyes from the stunning impact. He once again felt the peculiar sense of weightlessness until his body struck the ground with a dull thud and a cloud of dust. His senses were so dazed, he barely registered the bone-crushing impact. Then Bojan was on him, pummeling him with fists like anvils until he sensed nothing but darkness until even that faded to oblivion.

CHAPTER 8

Daebian sat at a table within the seedy bar sipping at a mug of ale as he watched the comings and goings of the patrons and paid special attention to their conversations. The bar reminded him of similar establishments in North Haven and Southport but with an added underlying tension of barely restrained violence. In the hours he had been sitting here, he had witnessed five brawls and two knife fights. In none of the clashes did any sort of constabulary force arrive to end the squabbles or arrest those involved, and he enjoyed it immensely.

He was watching another small group of men who were moments from throwing blows when he felt a heavy hand land on his left shoulder. Daebian looked up without flinching at two large men standing behind him while three more took up positions to his sides and front.

"It's about time you all got here. I have been sipping this swill for the better part of the afternoon waiting for you to show up," Daebian said.

"You wouldn't be so impatient if you knew what Captain Farique is likely gonna do to you," the man with his hand on his shoulder replied.

"Trust me; I know exactly what is going to happen. You are going to drag me to your master, possibly rough me up a bit on the way, I'm going to propose terms to Farique, he's going to reject them and order me killed in some gruesome manner he thinks is inspiring, but I'll escape and kill you all before ending Farique's miserable life and assuming his vaunted position."

"They said you was different, and I said different was just another word for crazy. Seems I was right."

"Despite what is a common opinion of my mental state, it is not insanity driving my claims. It is the benefit of walking this world with my eyes open. I get to see everything. It's a shame so few others have learned to do the same."

"I knowed a few men who walked with their eyes open on account of Captain Farique slicing off their eyelids."

The five pirates shared a laugh and two of them jerked Daebian to his feet, relieved him of his sword, and searched him for more weapons. One of them then bound his hands behind his back with a length of cord and shoved him out of the bar and onto the street.

The dirt avenues were crowded with humanity's lowlifes and degenerates. Most of the buildings looked as dilapidated and neglected as the people themselves, having been built by timbers salvaged from ships no longer seaworthy. One of the few exceptions was the stone manor constructed atop the low hill overlooking the town and cove.

"You lookin' for your friends, boy?" Hamish asked. "They ain't gonna come save you. See, Captain Farique knowed all about your little plan, and his men done took them in just like we got you."

Daebian replied with an exasperated sigh. "Captain Farique *knew* my plan. You know, for someone who likes to do all the talking, you should learn to speak properly. Honestly, listening to you talk is like hearing an illiterate whore reciting the finest poems of our age. For that reason alone I might kill you first."

Hamish punched Daebian in the back of his head hard enough to make his knees buckle. Only the men holding onto his arms kept him from falling to the filth-littered street.

Daebian turned his head and smiled. "I will definitely kill you first."

The pirate thugs dragged their captive through the manor's gates and into the house. Daebian shook his head and rolled his eyes at the awful interior décor of what was otherwise a fine home. A pair of sentries stood watch at the end of the hall. One opened the doors and two of Daebian's captors pushed him into the room beyond while the others stayed outside.

The room was richly appointed with several bookcases stuffed with volumes of the written word and various curios. Two chandeliers provided rich, warm light for the eight men and one woman seated around a long table set in the center of the room. Daebian properly assumed these were the eight senior pirate captains and Captain Farique. Captain Farique was a swarthy man, likely of Sumaran descent given his name and appearance. He was of average build, but even seated Daebian could see he possessed exceptional height.

"Is this the source of all my troubles of late?" Captain Farique asked as Daebian was ushered in.

"Aye, sir. He's *Captain* Daebian for sure."

"Ridiculous, I have warts older than him. Did you have any problems apprehending him?"

Hamish shook his head and grinned. "No, sir. We picked him up in the bar just where Tobias said he'd be."

"Excellent. It appears these wild tales we heard of him were as fanciful as I had suspected. Have our men apprehended his crew as well?"

"Aye. Got 'em before they got off their boats. Didn't even put up a fight. Most of 'em even denied their captain." He gave Daebian a sharp jab in his short ribs. "Seems you don't inspire much loyalty in your crew."

Daebian rolled his eyes. "So it would appear."

"Sir, I took this off him as well." The man set Daebian's sword in front of Farique before returning to his captive's side.

The captain picked up the black-bladed sword and marveled at its dark beauty. "This is certainly an enchanting thing. I think we now know the source of this boy's mystique."

"Mystique? So my reputation has preceded me."

"Tobias told us everything about you."

"I hope it was flattering."

"He said you were a soulless devil who could strip a man's soul bare with a glance."

"So...yes."

"He also said you were supremely confident and always got what you wanted."

"The man has painted my portrait with the hand of a true artist."

Farique was obviously losing his sense of humor. "He failed to mention your arrogance, but I naturally assumed as much."

"That is because I do not possess such a thing. Arrogance is unwarranted confidence. Mine is perfectly placed, unlike the vast majority of your art and furniture."

Farique scowled at the boy's lack of proper fear. "Did you truly think you could throw together a few weak-willed sailors and take my helm? Did you think you were so clever that you could waltz into my home, in my kingdom, and take my throne? I have been a pirate longer than you have walked this world. Granted, you managed to accomplish a great deal in a surprisingly short amount of time. I particularly enjoyed hearing about how you and your men managed to abscond with three of His Majesty's naval ships. I should thank you even, for they will make a nice addition to my fleet."

"Did you want me to answer those questions, or were you just prattling rhetorically?" Daebian asked, for which he received another punch to his back.

"By all means, enlighten us as to your motives."

"Let me answer the first second and the second first." Daebian looked at Hamish. "I hope I did not confuse you. I was going to say latter and former, but then I would have had to explain what that was, and I just do not feel like getting into a lesson in vocabulary that would only bring us both a lot of stress. Back to the captain then. Yes, I do believe cleverness can accomplish a great deal more than simple brute force. Those ships are proof of that. How many ships have your pirates lost to the king's new navy? That brings us to your first question. Yes, I thought I could depose you with my ragtag band for the same reason I was able to do more with far less than any of your captains in recent history. Your tactics are a complete failure."

"It is tradition!"

"It is the same thing."

The room erupted in shouting with several of the pirate captains pulling blades and demanding the upstart's head served on a platter.

Captain Farique restored order. "I should let them cut you down like a dog, but you're a clever dog. If I can train you, perhaps you could be of use to me. Of course, you'd have to be on a short leash. We don't want you to bite your master. I'm going to give you one chance to save your miserable life. Stick close to my side, help me increase our profits, and one day you might even get a ship of your own if you prove loyal."

"Being something of a virtuoso, I cannot abide playing second fiddle to anyone," Daebian responded. "I would like to propose a counter offer."

"What would that be?" Farique asked with a grin.

"Retire. Take your flagship and whatever treasures you have amassed, pick any of the outer isles, and live out the rest of your days in peace and luxury." Daebian nudged his captor with his elbow and whispered, "This is the part where he orders my gruesome execution."

Captain Farique leapt to his feet and snatched the black-bladed sword from the table. "I should gut you with your own blade, you pompous little rat!" He jerked his head toward the door. "Flay him to the neck and hang him from my yardarm. Let everyone hear his screams and witness what happens to those who cross me."

Farique waited until his men shoved Daebian out of the room before addressing his senior captains. "Despite his arrogance, the boy is right. We need to do something about our declining profits. Thanks to his little stunt, the king's navy is swarming like a bunch of angry hornets."

"But do you think we can put aside our grudges and rivalries enough to work together? How do we split the spoils? What are the shares? Who decides the targets?" Marilyn, the one female captain asked.

A crow roosting on the outside window sill squawked loudly, cocked its ebony head, and peered through the lead-paned glass.

"It will take some time to sort out the particulars, but..."

Daebian was nothing more than a flash of movement as he launched himself from the shadows behind the pirate king's chair. A blade of ethereal shadow pierced the back of Farique's neck and erupted from his open mouth, silencing him forever. Every person in the room leapt from their chairs, drew cutlasses and daggers, and took several defensive steps away.

"Hold your steel or hold your guts!" Daebian ordered.

"We could cut you down right now!" one of them shouted.

"You could try, but you would fail and die."

Seeing that no one was about to put his threat to the test, Daebian shoved Farique's body out of the chair, retrieved his sword from the table, and sat down. Channeling a tendril of abyssal power from the jewel gripped in his hand, Daebian set the stone back into the pommel of the soul blade.

"It's true, you do possess dark magics!" one of the pirates barked.

"I do, and you had best listen to me and think well on my offer."

"We swore oaths to Farique!"

"Oaths only live as long as the one to whom they are made."

The pirate leaders looked to each other, wondering if anything this creature said could be believed. "Farique's man said they had your men. Your man Tobias gave them up. We don't have to make no deals with a demon!"

"Ordinarily I would rather stab you than argue, but I do like to talk about my cleverness. Tobias did precisely as I told him and carried out his job excellently as I have come to expect. Farique never captured my men, you great bunch of idiots. Those buffoons of Farique captured my prisoners who were kind enough to pose as my crew in exchange for promises of release. Well, most of them were my prisoners. My men have been in place for days and are right now securing each of your flagships."

"Impossible!" another spat. "You'd need half the men on the island to take those ships!"

"No, I would need nearly seven full crews and three wizards. The fact your ships were nearly stripped of men in order to take mine made it that much easier."

"Farique has wizards too!"

"He had some hedge wizards who seriously lacked the formal military training of mine. I killed those glorified street corner charlatans last night and replaced them with my people. A few illusions and a couple transmogrifications and I had the perfect people aboard hours before the first blade cleared a sheath." Daebian leaned onto the desk and stared at the pirates intently. "Let me make one thing very clear. If you go against me you will lose. It is not a guess, or a gambit, or boasting, but a reality as solid as this desk and the dead man lying behind it. Are you all getting it now? Yes? Then let us stop this needless display of bravado and get down to business."

"What do you want?"

"I already have what I want. What I have to offer is for your benefit. Pledge your loyalty to me, and convince everyone else to do the same. I believe Farique's tithe was twenty percent? I will take only fifteen. You retain your ships and crew, but you answer to me and follow my orders. Your way of conducting business no longer works. Pirates can no longer strike out as individuals because the merchants and navy now travel in packs. How many ships have failed to return to the isles these past two years? We can no longer operate as individuals. We must form a powerful pack like wolves. Will you be part of my pack?"

"What if we refuse?"

"Then you die. I have many good men who would love to take over your ships. I would wager there are men amongst your own crew who would leap at the promise of a captaincy. The choice is an easy one. Pledge to me and profit, or hold on to oaths made to a dead man and join him."

"You're nothing but a petty tyrant!"

"No, I am a beneficent tyrant, at least to those who show proper fealty."

The end was a forgone conclusion. Despite the seriousness with which they had all made their oaths, everyone there held one ideal above all others—profit. Each of the captains swore oaths to Daebian and sealed it by making a shallow cut above their left breast.

"There we are, one big happy family," Daebian crowed as he leaned back in his chair. The door opened and Tobias stepped warily into the room. "Perfect timing, Tobias! How did it go?"

"Just as you predicted, sir. Farique's men took in the prisoners and our watchers while the rest of us set upon the flagships."

"You were successful?"

"Aye. There were a few bloody skirmishes and we lost some men, but we captured the lot of them, mostly thanks to your wizards."

"Fantastic! The captains have pledged their loyalty, and I have promised them their ships back." Daebian addressed his officers. "Return to your ships and spread word of my new regency."

"Just like that, sir?" Tobias asked.

"Yes, just like that. Do not look so worried, Tobias. My captains know that if they break their oaths, I will hunt them down and send them straight to the abyss where their souls will languish in tortured agony for all eternity. We will reconvene this meeting in three days."

The senior captains filed from the room, urged by the pointy blade of real fear. Not one of them doubted Daebian's willingness or ability to do just as he promised.

"Tobias," Daebian called out as the pirates left the room.

"Yes, sir?"

"Find me a decorator. This place is just awful. If you happen to find the one responsible for this travesty, have him or her beaten. This is inexcusable."

His first mate saluted. "Aye, sir."

CHAPTER 9

Azerick found the old archmage near the center of the destruction using his magic to shift stones and timbers. Dozens of workers and soldiers loaded debris into carts and wagons to be hauled away or stacked elsewhere to be used for rebuilding. Brother Thomas stood nearby with another of his Chosen to provide aid to any injured they found.

Azerick stepped next to the cleric. "How bad was it?"

"Fourteen injured, three seriously, but no fatalities, praise Solarian," Thomas replied.

"Praise him indeed."

"What happened?"

"The Scions pierced the barrier and dominated the minds of the dragons just as they did before." Azerick's face twisted in a mix of anger and self-loathing. "I should have prepared for this! I knew about the dragons, and I should have devised some way of preventing it from happening."

"Don't beat yourself up, boy," Allister said reassuringly. "You've had a goodly number of things occupying your mind. We'll figure out a way to fix this."

"That's what I have come to see you about, Allister. I was thinking that maybe the compulsion the Scions put on the dragons is not much different than the one used on Hati," Azerick explained, referring to the woman a hobgoblin shaman had mutilated by attaching the wings and talons of a blood hawk to her and mentally dominating her as part of a grotesque army. "Perhaps we can free Sandy as we did her."

Allister stroked his beard. "Yes, it's certainly possible, but I imagine these gods have a far more formidable form of domination. Then again, the dragons have vastly stronger wills, so perhaps there exists the possibility."

"I would like to try as soon as possible."

"Go ahead, Allister," Brother Thomas said. "We haven't found any injured in the last half hour. My Chosen are doing a fine job of tending our wounded. If I can be of any assistance with Sandy, please come get me."

Azerick clasped the cleric's shoulder. "Thank you, Thomas. I will."

The two powerful spellcasters descended the stairs of the new tower and made their way to the large laboratory located beneath. Raijaun was there stroking Sandy's scales. Azerick's heart broke upon seeing the thick chains securing her to the floor and the iron muzzle keeping her jaws clamped shut.

"Father, you are back. How did it go?"

"About as badly as it possibly could, but I was in too much of a hurry to return to take the time to devise a solution acceptable to all. How is she?"

"Still asleep. I thought it prudent to restrain her in case she woke up before you returned."

"It was a wise decision. How fares the barrier?"

Raijaun's face dropped. "The barrier is in a shambles. I hardly know where to begin to make repairs. I reinforced a couple of the worst breaches, but at this point I fear our efforts will not make much difference. There are dozens of weakened areas the Scions could exploit if they had a mind to. I am surprised they are not already through."

"They do not want to expend the energy to create a full breach. Best to bide their time to allow the barrier to fail so their power is at its full potential when they arrive. Despite their boasting, I am certain they are wary of facing us and our gods with less than their full strength. Let us just be thankful for their patience."

Raijaun nodded. "I have been studying the compulsion they have placed upon Sandy. It is unlike anything I can imagine. It is vastly complex and supremely powerful. I dared not do anything but observe it."

Allister grumbled, "If only both your sons showed such wise restraint. All right, let us see what we are dealing with here."

The three of them used their magic to delve into Sandy's mind and studied the complex magic surrounding it. Azerick could see Allister's arcane hands gently probing the weave in an attempt to unravel its secrets. Azerick too plucked at the ethereal strands holding the powerful magic together. The power, convolution, and sheer scope of the magic the Scions employed was incredible, but Azerick expected nothing less. There was another aspect to it, far more insidious than the spell used on Hati. The weave of magic did not just surround her; it appeared as though it was part of her. The strands burrowed into the very essence of her spirit. After more than an hour, Azerick and the others were forced to give up their current approach.

Allister wiped the sweat from his wrinkled brow. "I'm not going to lie to you, son; that is some formidable work. It was like pushing water uphill. As soon as you stop pushing, it flows right back into place."

"Then I will have to devise some sort of dam," Azerick responded. "Did you notice how the magic was attached to her aura? It reminds me of how my and Klaraxis's souls were intertwined. I will have to find a way to separate them."

"Can you do that, Father? Can you block them from controlling her mind?"

"I think so, but she is unlikely to thank me for it."

Daebian stood looking through the big picture window of his hastily refurnished office. He turned when the door opened and Tobias entered with Captain Zeb. He smiled at his former captain and took a seat behind the enormous desk.

"Captain Zeb, I am glad to see you well. How are your men?" Daebian inquired.

Zeb did not return Daebian's pleasantries. "What do you want now, *Captain* Daebian? Or should I say King Daebian?"

"Actually, I am going by Commodore Daebian, but King Daebian certainly has a nice ring to it. Perhaps at a later time. As to what I want, I want many things, but I assume you refer to this particular moment in time. I wanted to thank you and your men for helping me pull off my little ruse. It avoided a great deal of bloodshed."

"You didn't give us a whole lot of options."

"But options you had and were free to exercise them anytime. But as I told you and your people, few of them would bring a ransom and were therefore worthless to the pirates. Worthless things tend to get tossed into the sea."

"You put my people in that situation! You play with people's lives like they are your toys!"

"It was for the greater good," Daebian countered.

"It was for your own good!" Zeb raged.

"What good could possibly be greater than that?" Daebian looked curiously to his first mate. "Why do people always give me that look when I make such statements?"

"I'm guessing they don't understand the concept."

"That is why I keep you around, Tobias, to help me understand the minds of lesser men." Daebian narrowed his eyes and pointed a finger at his second. "There it is again, right on your face!"

"No, sir. Probably just got something in my eye, sir. Lot of sand getting in everything around here."

"Hmm, curious."

"You promised to set my men free," Zeb said.

"I did and I will. Tobias, get the door."

Tobias opened his mouth, but before he could form the question, someone knocked. The second mate snapped his mouth shut and opened the door. A sailor stepped into the room bearing a small box clasped between his hands.

"And the object of your salvation has arrived!" Daebian announced dramatically as he stood and took the box.

"What is that, sir?"

Daebian sat back down, opened the small chest, and withdrew the precious coin from inside it. "It is our ransom, Tobias."

"It seems a bit small to me, sir. Is it magical?"

"It is better than that. It is recognition."

"I'm sure its importance is lost on my simple mind, but the men will find spending recognition a bit difficult."

Daebian waved a dismissive hand. "They have earned far too much to complain. There are greater things in this life than gold, but I understand the baser desires of lesser men. Take a share for each of the men from my treasury to keep them appeased."

Using his abyssal power, he bored a small hole through the gold disc and threaded it onto the leather cord to join the nearly identical one already in place. He then retied the necklace around his neck.

"That is what all this chicanery was for?" Zeb demanded.

"That and your ships, but mostly this."

Zeb shook his head. "I don't understand you, boy."

"Nor does anyone else, and they never will. Tobias, get Zeb and his men on a ship and send them home."

"Aye, sir. What next?"

Daebian stood and gazed out the window and across the sea to the northwest. "We wait."

"Wait for what, sir?"

"The end of the world."

"How is it coming along?" Azerick asked Raijaun as he painted his final rune upon Sandy's scaly hide.

"I am nearly complete with the last one, Father," Raijaun called from Sandy's other side.

Azerick and Raijaun had spent the past several days painstakingly drawing glyphs upon Sandy's body in hopes of blocking out the Scions' mental domination. No spell Azerick could conceive of was capable of stopping the compulsion from taking hold the moment the blocking spell wore off, so he was forced to create a more permanent solution. Perhaps he could have devised something better given more time, but time was something none of them had to spare. He just prayed Sandy would forgive him.

"I am finished. What do we do now?" Raijaun asked.

"We must etch them into her scales and bind them to her spirit to create a permanency to them. Because much of what we have done is draconic in origin, we will need your Guardian magic to make them indelible and imbue them with power. It will be fatiguing, but it should not be painful for you."

"I would do it regardless to protect her. I just hope she does not hate me for it."

Azerick laid a hand on his son's shoulder. "The blame will be all mine. I will bear the burden of her anger like I have so many others. Sometimes, I think perhaps that is my primary purpose in all this, to be the shelf upon which all others may place their anger, pain, and hatred so they might work with those they once considered enemies."

"Whatever few may dislike you today will revere you tomorrow when their eyes gaze upon the rising sun that would have been denied them had you not done what you must. They are children, fickle and self-serving, and they do not know what is good for them until they become adults and can look back on the sacrifices you made for them."

Azerick felt like weeping under his son's praise. Kind words were so rare these days, and he cradled them in his heart so they might warm him against the freezing touch of duty. It was the candle he prayed would be sufficient to light his way even as darkness continued to press in.

Azerick hugged Raijaun tightly. "My wise son. Are you ready?"

"I am."

"What you must do is very simple despite the power involved. You must feel out every sigil upon Sandy's body and gently feed your Guardian magic into their forms. The runes will drink it in, and in great quantity, but not too quickly. Sandy's magic will recognize your Guardian power as a kindred spirit and bond with it. This will keep the runes empowered much like I do with my staff when I must draw power from it."

Raijaun nodded and reached for his Guardian magic. It was strong but comforting, like a stern but loving parent there to guide and protect him, but it demanded respect. He walked the magic over Sandy's body and traced the runes painted on her scales with a thousand invisible fingers. He felt every sigil beneath his magical touch as if they were burned into his own flesh and gently began coaxing the golden tendrils of magic into their forms.

The runes began to glow then hissed as they burned, filling the room with an acrid stench like that of burning hair. Raijaun flinched inwardly but maintained his focus as he continued to pour power into what seemed a bottomless vessel. The runes drank in his magic and Raijaun began to fatigue, but he sensed the power growing within them.

Sandy's form was nearly lost within the brilliant aura of light the runes emitted as they absorbed Raijaun's power like parched soil drinking in a summer shower. Raijaun felt himself nearing his limits, but he also knew the runes were reaching theirs. When the arcane glyphs finally reached their full capacity, Raijaun drove his magic deeper into Sandy's body, found the core of her draconic power, and wove the threads of magic together to create a permanent bond between her and them.

Azerick grabbed his son as he took a couple of stumbling steps back, and guided him into a nearby chair. "Are you all right?"

Raijaun took several deep breaths before nodding. "I am very tired, is all, but there is no pain."

"You did very well. Go to your room and rest now. I am afraid I will need you again very soon."

Raijaun was too tired to ask why and plodded up the steps to his room. Azerick knelt beside Sandy's big, wedge-shaped head and stroked her brow. He dreaded waking her, and not just because he feared his preparations could prove inadequate, but because of her reaction when she saw what he had done to her. What he had done was far more than mar her brilliant scales. Sandy's dragon name, given to her by her mother, translated as 'Beautiful One Whose Scales Shine with the Glory of the Morning Sun.' Azerick's solution had destroyed not just her scales, but her very identity as a dragon and the only real connection she had with her mother.

With a deep sigh of remorse, Azerick removed the iron muzzle and laid his hand upon Sandy's brow. "Awaken."

Sandy's eyes fluttered for just a moment before she leapt away and cast her head back and forth, her eyes wide with panic. The chains holding her in place clattered loudly and groaned in protest. Azerick took several hasty steps back and raised his hands.

"Sandy, it's okay. You're safe now."

"The Scions, they called to me! They commanded me! I tried to block them from my mind, but they were so loud and their voices had so much power."

"Can you still hear them?"

"Barely, like the echo of a whisper."

"I have blocked them from your mind as best I can."

"How? What…?" Sandy craned her neck around and looked at the runes covering her body. "What have you done to me?" she whispered.

"I had to create a permanent magic to protect you."

"So many?"

Azerick swallowed and took a deep breath. "No, but I wanted to make you stronger so you would be better able to protect yourself."

"To make me a better weapon for you to use, you mean!"

Azerick dipped his head in shame. "Both statements have merit."

"You had no right!"

"No, but I had great need. Sandy, I'm sorry. I should have expected this, but I thought of you like family, more like a daughter than a dragon."

"If I was truly your daughter then you should have protected me!"

"I am sorry, Sandy. I failed you."

Sandy's jaw worked to form words, but her fury was too great to give voice to them. She wanted to demand that he fix her scales. She wanted to ask if she had hurt anyone, but her pain crushed reason. She glared at the chains and summoned her magic. The steel glowed hot and she snapped them with ease. With a furious roar, she slashed at the empty air and tore a great hole in space. To Azerick's eyes, it looked as though she were leaping straight for him, bent on tearing him apart, but she vanished through the gate halfway to him. Even from beneath the new tower, Azerick was able to hear her pain-filled bellow as she flew away.

It was with a heavy heart Azerick made his way up the stairs. Although he was as strong as a team of horses, Azerick felt as though his feet weighed a thousand pounds each as he struggled to lift them to the next step. He found Miranda, Aggie, Allister, and Rusty waiting for him in the parlor when he emerged from the winding staircase.

"Azerick, are you all right?" Miranda asked.

Azerick halfheartedly returned her soft embrace. "I am well enough."

"We heard Sandy make such a racket before she flew off. We weren't sure if she had attacked you again."

"No, Raijaun and I were able to block the Scions' influence."

"She seemed mighty upset when she lit out of here," Allister said.

"The methods we employed were unpleasant. She needs time to adjust. On that matter, I feel it urgent to make an adjustment as well."

"What kind of adjustment?" Rusty asked.

"Sandy's domination makes it clear that the Scions are very close to escaping. There is no longer anything Raijaun and I can do to stop or even slow them. One of our greatest weapons is the Source pool beneath the old tower. North Haven will be the first city to fall when the Scions and their minions attack, and we cannot lose the well when it does."

"How do you propose we prevent it?"

"We must move it."

"You want to move an entire tower and the single most concentrated source of magic in the known world?" Rusty asked.

"In a sense, yes. What I want to do is shift its existence so it is hidden but we can still tap into its power."

Aggie's face went ashen. "Boy, you better not be proposing what I think you are."

"We cannot afford to lose the well. Without it, our mages will fatigue too soon, and we will be defenseless against the dragons."

"The elves failed in their attempt to do this very thing and nearly made themselves extinct in the process!"

"I witnessed what they did, and I understand the mistakes they made. The elves tried to move too much too far. We will only be shifting the tower a short ways outside of our reality. It will present far less of a challenge than what the elves tried. The elves also did not have a Guardian or a Source pool to aid them."

"It's still damn insane!" Aggie protested.

"But I will make the attempt all the same. My chances are far better with you to help guide me through the passages between worlds."

The old mage looked ready to slap him, but her shoulders slumped and she shook her head. "Damn us all for fools then. If you're so set on destroying us before the Scions get here, then so be it. But mark my words, boy; you had best start listening to your elders. I don't care how much power you can channel, it's no substitute for experience!"

Azerick nodded. "I know, Aggie. It is why I ask for your help, and I would not try such a thing if I was not confident in our chances of achieving it. It will take several days to prepare. Raijaun should be recovered by then. I just hope the Scions give us that much time."

CHAPTER 10

Reality returned to Bron with the sound of rushing water. A mixture of odd scents filled the air, and he found himself staring at the grey stone of a cavern ceiling when he finally managed to open his eyes. He turned his head left and recognized the crude paintings on the wall as the ones belonging to Kramloc. Turning his head to the right, he saw the shaman bustling about near his table of herbalist equipment.

"Do you know why you lost?" Kramloc asked without turning.

Bron worked his tongue around in his mouth and managed to answer. "He was bigger, stronger, and a better fighter than me."

The shaman turned toward him holding a hollowed-out and dried gourd. "No, you lost because you have yet to acknowledge your other half. You still cling to your goddess and humanity, and it weakens you. If you do not understand what it means to be ogre, you will always be weak."

"Then why am I still alive? Why did Bojan not kill me, or are you going to execute me in some horrible public spectacle?"

Kramloc shook his head. "That is what you expect of us. Nothing but cruel monsters who revel in causing pain and death, and you are partially correct. When in the bloodlust, we can be quite savage, but we revere death even more than life. I allowed you to live because you needed to see what it means to be ogre before I can expect you to become one. I also believe your words are worthy and wish to offer you another chance."

"If you think my words important, why do you not just hear them?"

"Because it is not our way. Your words may be worthy, but you are not. You must understand what it means to be Kin."

"How do I learn that?"

"You cannot. To understand what we are, what you are, is a matter of heart and blood, not one of mind. It is not logic to be studied, it is raw and elemental. It is passion, anger, and courage. No creature can learn those things."

"If I cannot learn it, how am I supposed to understand it? How can I prove myself worthy?"

"You simply must be. Accept your other half and be ogre."

"You still answer me with riddles."

"Your confusion and ignorance do not make my words a riddle."

"What happens now?"

"I will share with you some of our history, and perhaps you will begin to understand and even accept your heritage. Then you will fight Bojan once more on the morrow."

Bron winced in pain. "I do not think I can get out of this bed much less fight."

The shaman smiled. "You will be able to fight, and you will win, or you will die. Drink this."

Bron took the gourd and brought it to his mouth. The smell made his eyes burn and he balked. Looking at the shaman, he held his breath and poured the concoction down his throat. It felt like Bojan had just hit him again. His stomach twisted into a knot, and his blood burned as if on fire. His vision wavered, and the room began to spin. Bron tried to steady his sight by focusing on one of the images painted on the wall. It seemed to help for a moment until the drawing began to move. He closed his eyes, but the images still danced in his mind as drums beat a deep rhythm. His heart took up the cadence as it thrummed in his chest.

Bron was unsure when he had fallen asleep, if indeed he had, but when he next opened his eyes, dim sunlight was creeping through the flap covering the opening. As the light slowly began to intensify, Bron knew it was already dawn.

"Let us hope the light of a new dawn illuminates the dark corners to which you have banished your better half."

Bron followed the voice and found Kramloc sitting in a roughly constructed chair and wondered if the shaman had slept at all. If he had not, then he obviously did not need it because he looked far more refreshed and prepared to face the day than Bron felt.

"Stand," the shaman ordered. "You have no time to lie about."

Bron wanted to do nothing except lie there, but he mustered his strength and forced his stiff and aching legs over the side of the bed. The dull pain from numerous abused muscles elicited a hiss of discomfort, and he fought to stand. Bron paused, sitting on the edge of the bed before pushing himself to his feet.

"I cannot fight Bojan in my condition," Bron insisted.

"Your human blood declares you once again by speaking falsehoods. You can and will fight. You simply cannot win."

"Then this will be an execution."

"If you make it so, yes. Those who are not Kin cannot leave this valley. It is our last refuge, and it must remain secret. If you wish to live you must become Kin."

"What now?" Bron asked, deciding it was pointless to wage any further protests.

"You will go to the Passage of Lore. Perhaps if you see our history, you will accept and even embrace your heritage. Then you will face Bojan once again so we may see if you have learned anything."

"Embrace a people who violated my mother and created me so that I could live as an outcast? Embrace a people who only value violence to prove their worth and who murder a messenger without hearing the words that might prevent their doom? Show me your cave and carry out your execution, but I will not accept the savagery of your kind. If I am to die, it will be with the peace and love of Ellanee in my heart."

"Such a human conviction." Kramloc said, then walked out of his cave.

Bron followed the shaman down the narrow cliffside path, his bones and muscles aching the entire way. They followed the face of the escarpment for more than a mile without coming across another ogre. Had he not been so focused on his discomfort, Bron might have pondered the lack of activity in the previously bustling community.

Kramloc stopped before a narrow fissure in the mountainside. It looked as though a giant axe had split the cliff face in twain. The sky was a narrow strip of blue several hundred feet above the passage.

Bron could not see the end, but he had the feeling it opened into another region of the valley.

Kramloc handed the gourd to Bron. "Drink this. It will help prepare you for what you face."

Bron looked at the vessel with its noxious contents, and his stomach twisted in anticipation of its vileness. "I would rather not die with that foulness in my body."

"It is not a request. If you hope to have the slightest chance of victory, you will drink it."

The druid took the flask and stared at it for a moment before he pulled the stopper, steeled himself against the awful taste and unpleasant effects, and downed it in a single gulp. Despite holding his breath in an effort to keep from tasting it, the vile liquid still traced a bitter, revolting path down his gullet and into his stomach. He shuddered, fought back the cramping nausea the concoction induced, and steadied himself against the vertigo washing over his mind.

"Follow the path through the Passage of Lore. Pay special attention to images painted upon the walls, and perhaps you will finally understand your heritage. At the end, you will find Bojan. If you have learned what the passage shows you and accepted your other half, you may have a chance of victory. If you do not, then your journey through this life is over, and I hope you find a greater path to follow in the next one. You will fight as an ogre, without magic, or you will forfeit your life with dishonor."

The shaman's words came to him as if from the bottom of a well, but he understood them and took several wavering steps into the fissure. Only a few yards in, Bron saw innumerable images painted upon the walls, covering the rocky surface for as far as he could see. He braced himself against the wall with an outstretched hand to catch his balance. The painted image of an ogre writhed beneath his palm. Bron snatched back his hand and saw that all the pictures were moving and dancing around like marionettes on strings. The druid shook his head in an attempt to break the hallucinations created by Kramloc's foul brew, but still the paintings moved. Deciding there was little else he could do, Bron took several cautious steps down the path. The animated pictures continued to draw his eyes, and he began to study them in more detail.

Starting at the images nearest the entrance, Bron began to piece together their meaning. They were not random drawings, but a history in art form. A dragon watched over a cluster of humans, dwarves, elves, ogres, goblins, and orcs as well as other races. High above the dragon, faceless heads towered over them all. He could see and feel their disdain despite their lack of features.

One of the ogres stood up from his labors and hurled a stone at the dragon. Other ogres, followed by the rest of the figures, took up stones and cast them at their overlord. The dragon reacted with terrible ferociousness, and many of the figures perished, but they succeeded in bringing the dragon down. Man, elf, dwarf, and brutes danced and reveled in their victory until the faceless ones descended and hurled flaming mountains against them, extinguishing their lives in the blink of an eye.

In another painted montage, dwarves beat upon metal blacker than the heart of the abyss. Elves stole the secret of the faceless ones' power and shared it with the humans. The human wizards and dwarves used this power to enchant six magnificent sets of armor, one for each champion of the major races. The elves created creatures born of elf and dragon, and together the mortal races battled for their freedom and lives.

The world trembled beneath the terrible power of the faceless ones. The Scions shattered entire mountains and raised greater ones in their place. Dragons and gods struck back at their revolting slaves, blood flowed like rivers, and death raged across the world like a fierce wind. Still the mortals fought and died, but none so greatly as the brute races. The powerful ogres often led the vanguard of the attacks, fearlessly throwing themselves into the maws of the dragons and against the blades and claws of the monsters summoned by the faceless gods. Even the goblins, thought weak and cowardly by most, swarmed their enemies with their vast numbers. Leading every battle were the six heroes of the races, their black armor shedding the blows of their enemies as surely as the blood refusing to mar its gleaming surface.

Still the people died and their cause seemed bleak, so they prayed for help, sending their pleas out into the cosmos for anyone who would listen. When all seemed lost, their prayers were answered. Four beings proclaiming to be gods gathered the elves, their champion, and their strange Guardians and took the fight to the faceless ones' celestial home. Without the faceless ones' divine power, the dragons and their minions began to fall, and the war turned in favor of the mortal races. The elves lost their hero and many of their Guardians, but they managed to banish the faceless ones with the aid of the new gods.

Many races, fearful of this new freedom and desiring safety and peace above all else, hid themselves away deep beneath the earth. Those who chose the light of the sun lived in peace — for a time. Never content, the humans began expanding. The elves retreated in the face of the growing human populations. The other races tried to coexist with the humans, but their cultures and need for land to live upon collided. Humans refused to abide by borders, and clashes with the brute races ensued. The Kin tried to fight back, but their numbers suffered decimation in the Great Revolution like no others. Blood flowed once more until they threatened to finish the job the faceless ones left incomplete. The brute races chose to retreat farther into the mountains and valleys considered too inhospitable to be desired by the humans.

The paintings grew still once more as Bron tried to decipher their meaning. His blood still burned, but now his head swam with the images and their significance. Everything he had held true regarding the ogre and their Kin was in question. Deep in his heart, he had held hatred for what they had done to his mother and for the pain of his own existence. For the first time, he wondered which was the nobler race.

By the time Bron reached the end of the passage, his head had cleared and his balance was back to normal. Most of the aches and pains had dulled to shadows of their former selves. The crevice opened into a small glade measuring a few hundred feet across and was surrounded by high walls created by the network of bare, stone ridges. Tracking his eyes along the peaks of the ridges, it appeared as though the tiny valley continued farther on. Movement ahead of him snapped his attention to the center of the small clearing. Bojan stepped out of a cluster of cottonwood trees and stood smiling at Bron, greatly anticipating their rematch.

Bron scanned the walls of the glade once more, but he and the ogre champion were alone. This was not a match to be viewed by spectators for their enjoyment. This was a fight to the death, held to defend each warrior's ideals and sense of duty and purpose. Bron summoned his courage and faith, trusting in Ellanee to help him complete his mission.

A shrill cry brought his attention to a small cage hanging from one of the cottonwood trees. "B.S., get me outta here!"

His heart sank seeing Trielle in a cage, her tiny hands tugging futilely at the bars. "Let her go! This is about me, not her."

Bojan said nothing and just stood smiling. The druid hefted his staff, slowly approached Bojan, and desperately ran tactics through his mind. He could not even consider trying to break through the massive ogre's defenses. Trading blows was out of the question. Due to his size, Bojan had a slight reach advantage as well. Bron's only option was to strike quickly and slowly grind the ogre down, much like trying to chop down a large tree with a hatchet. Only this tree was intent on falling upon him and crushing his body to a pulp.

Bojan stood nonchalantly, confident in his strength and previous victory, as Bron approached. He did not even lift the end of his club from the ground. Bron thrust at the ogre's face with the bronze-capped end of his staff, which Bojan simply batted away as if shooing a pesky fly. Bron retracted his staff and leapt back. It was a needless gesture as Bojan only stopped leaning on his club and plopped it onto his shoulder. The ogre extended his hand with a smile and made a beckoning motion.

The druid was not about to let his pride and anger at Bojan's casual dismissal of his fighting prowess goad him into acting rashly. Bron circled the ogre, searching for an opening. He lunged in, starting his swing high but dropping it low in mid-stroke. The crack of wood and metal striking flesh resounded across the glade. Once again, Bron leapt away instead of pressing his successful attack.

Bojan swept his club off his shoulder and flexed his offended leg without letting the grin slip from his brutish face. He did finally adopt something of a fighting stance, obviously deciding the battle had begun in earnest. Bojan made a few noncommittal swipes at his opponent, which Bron easily avoided. Bron answered the moves by thrusting and slashing at Bojan whenever the club whisked past, but Bojan was able to deflect them with his weapon or slap them away with his hand.

Bron dug the end of his staff into the soil near his feet and flung it at Bojan's face. The warrior was not about to be caught by the same trick twice and turned his head and shielded his eyes with his hand. Bron took advantage of the opening, striking Bojan's upraised arm, spinning around behind him, and clouting him in the back of the head. Bojan spun around with a roar of real anger and pain, but a hard jab to his stomach dropped him to his hands and knees. His fierce shout became a choking struggle to regain his breath. The druid pressed his attack, landing kick after kick into Bojan's shoulder and side.

"Yeah, get him! Aim for the groin!" Trielle shouted.

Bron felt a brief glimmer of hope until Bojan exploded from the ground with a fury-filled shout of rage. The ogre champion burst up beneath him and hurled the druid twenty feet through the air. Bron had barely come to a tumbling halt in the dirt when he saw Bojan take a few powerful strides and leap. The huge ogre came down like a meteor, crushing his huge fist into Bron's face. Still bellowing his incoherent battle cry, Bojan lifted his foe and repeatedly slammed him against the ground.

Bron felt the air blasted from his lungs, and his world swam in a wash of vertigo as his brain crashed against the inside of his skull as if trying to escape. He felt himself airborne once more before striking a small tree hard enough to snap it partway up its trunk. He tried to stand, took several stumbling steps, and fell heavily back to the ground.

He looked through bleary eyes at Bojan as the big ogre casually retrieved his club to finish the job. Bron steeled himself to accept his fate and failure. Bojan looked at the stunned druid a moment and began walking toward Trielle's cage.

"I think I eat noisy little bug before I kill you," Bojan said with a cruel smile.

Until now, Bron was unsure if Bojan was capable of speech. "Leave her alone! I failed. It is me you are supposed to kill!"

"Her not Kin. Only Kin leave the valley."

"Give me my spear and we'll see who gets eaten!" Trielle shouted.

Brave Trielle, defiant and fearless to the last. Hearing her shouts filled him with sorrow. Seeing such a spirited life about to be extinguished for his failure brought on the intense anger he worked so hard to suppress. The casualness with which Bojan and his kind would kill another being who meant them no harm made him furious. He would not sacrifice his honor to save his life, but he would not let Trielle die for the sake of his morals.

Bron's furious roar filled the tiny canyon as he grabbed at the power of nature. He called to the tree holding Trielle's cage and poured his energy into it to make it grow, lifting Trielle out of Bojan's reach. Another cottonwood snaked down with unnatural suppleness, wrapped several willowy limbs around Bojan, and flung him halfway across the clearing.

"You fight me!" Bron raged.

Bojan stood with his characteristic smile and dusted himself off. "Finally, you fight like an ogre."

Bojan's words were lost to the blood rage pounding in Bron's ears. As Bojan stalked toward him, Bron punched both his fists into the ground, burying them to the wrists. Earth and stone grew up his arms and sheathed his body in an elemental carapace. The druid rushed at his foe and swung a fist that now looked more like a small boulder. The blow landed against Bojan's chest and threw him back several yards.

The ogre rolled to his feet with a shout of rage and barreled into Bron, hoping to use his awesome mass to bear the druid to the ground and crack him open like a nut. Bojan may as well have been trying to push over a mountain as Bron fused his shell with the ground at his feet. Bojan rebounded from the immovable object and took two staggering steps away.

Bron reeled back and crushed the ogre's face with another powerful blow. Bojan flew parallel to the ground for a score of feet before landing in a groaning, pain-filled heap. The enraged druid was not finished yet. Bron uprooted a leg and stamped his foot. The ground beneath the prone warrior buckled and became a wave, carrying his huge body back to his relentless foe. Bron raised a powerful leg and kicked at the oncoming ogre. Ribs cracked and Bojan went rolling again. The druid began stalking toward the now silent and immobile figure, intent on crushing the last vestiges of life from his body.

"Now you know what it means to be Kin."

Kramloc's words penetrated Bron's mind, and he turned to find the shaman standing just a few yards away. Bron's fury demanded he crush the shaman as well, but he forced a measure of calm into his heart and listened.

"What do I know of being an ogre?" Bron gasped as he struggled to regain control of himself. "Being a creature of uncontrolled rage and violence? Is that what it means to be Kin? Is that what you wanted me to learn?"

Kramloc shook his head and nodded toward the cage holding Trielle. "It means doing whatever you must, to be willing to sacrifice everything to win and protect your Kin. We survive because we refuse to submit, no matter the cost to any individual. Kin comes before self. You abandoned your ideals and your honor to save your friend. That is what it means to be Kin. You have seen our history. You see how the sacrifices, the honor, and bravery of our people have been forgotten or discarded by all but the Kin. It was not us who drew first blood and encroached upon the human lands, yet we are called the brute races. Come, our king is eager to meet you."

Bron looked to the fallen Bojan. "What of him?"

"He will recover. Come, let us retrieve your friend so we can hear your words."

"What of Trielle?" Bron asked as he used his magic to bend the tree low enough to reach the cage.

"Sprites are fickle creatures. Her kind's poor attention span makes it unlikely she could remember the way here if she wanted to."

Trielle buzzed out of her cage when Bron pried open the door. "Who's got a poor attention span? I'll show you some attention, you big, smelly lump of troll poo!"

Trielle began pounding on the shaman with her tiny fists, kicking him in the head, and yanking on his long, white tufts of hair. Kramloc ignored her as he led them through a narrow fissure at the rear of the grotto. The passage ran a nearly straight path until it opened into another, larger canyon.

"You planned for this all along?" Bron asked as they walked in single file through the cleft.

"I created a circumstance. How you reacted to that circumstance I could not foretell."

"What if I had continued to refuse to use my magic as you dictated and Bojan beat me again?"

"Then he would have killed you, and your words would have gone unspoken. There would be no third chance."

"Have there ever been other half-ogres who have found their way here?"

"Very few."

"I imagine it is rare for anyone to stumble upon this valley."

"It is rarer a weak blood lives to draw more than a few breaths before the humans destroy it."

It was a sobering reminder of human intolerance. As a druid of Ellanee, Bron was taught to revere all life, even the life of creatures like these ogres he had hated for so long. It saddened him to know that had his foster mother not protected him, even the people of their tiny community, every one of them professing to revere nature and worship Ellanee, likely would have left him to the elements to die, assuaging their conscience by claiming it a *natural* death for an unnatural creature.

"Still, I cannot imagine many of them could beat your champion. Were any able to achieve victory?"

Kramloc twitched his head. "Victory was never measured as an external achievement. All true victories reside within. Look at us here. We live in the midst of this rugged valley, forced from our rich ancestral lands by the humans, but not one of us feels defeated. The humans would be pleased if we all simply died, but we still live on. We thrive even here, and nothing they can do will ever take that away. It is what makes us worthy."

"You continue to astound me, Kramloc. All my life I believed the ogres to be nothing more than animals, worse, monsters, yet you continue to show me so much wisdom and pride."

"Sometimes we are monsters when we feel the need. Our nature is not always what most races would view as pleasant or civilized, but it is who we are. It is our way, and we make no apologies to anyone for it. Do humans apologize to the deer or the fish they kill and consume? Do they apologize for killing the Kin and stealing their lands? No, and we expect no apologies from them either. It is their way."

"But as an intelligent species, can we not choose a better way? The brutality of my own creation shows there is great room for improvement if only someone made the choice to change."

"Who chooses what is the better way? By whose standards should all society be based upon? Should humans dictate to ogres how to behave? Should dwarves dictate to elves? Your conception was surely an unpleasant event, but would this world be better had you not been born? Think on the lives you have touched and the things you have accomplished. You are a favored son of the All Mother, and I would surmise your worth has been weighed countless times and found acceptable. You are worthy, Bron. The All Mother found you worthy, and now your Kin have declared you worthy as well. Only you continue to question it."

"Others have questioned it for most my life."

"Why do you value their opinion above your own? Like victory, your true value must be measured internally. All else is ultimately meaningless."

Bron looked at Trielle, now clinging to a tuft of Kramloc's hair and sleeping on his shoulder having thoroughly exhausted herself trying to beat the ogre into submission. She was small, rude, and obnoxious, but she was intensely independent and free-spirited. She would never allow anyone to define her and would certainly never accept anyone's judgment of her character or worth. She was who and what she was, and she loved every bit of herself. She would never change to try to appease another. Bron envied her in that regard.

He had little time to mull over the wise shaman's words as the slot canyon widened into another small gorge creating a natural stadium. The stadium seats were carved into the rock in a series of ascending benches and filled to capacity. The bulk of the races present were ogres, but hundreds of goblins and orcs also occupied the stadium in a few small groups.

Bron and Kramloc approached the end of the stadium and stood before a raised section upon which were gathered three parties of the brute races. A score each of orcs and goblins flanked three ogres, one of which sat upon a simple throne of carved stone.

Bron stepped closer to the shaman and whispered, "I assume the one upon the throne is King Sefket, but who are the others?"

"They are the high chiefs and chiefs of the goblin and orc tribes."

"Are they here for me? I did not think you had that much confidence in my victory."

"The tribal chiefs have been here for several weeks. Many of the tribes have settled within or near our valley because of the increase in human activity. Most feared it was a prelude to war against the Kin and sought counsel to decide what to do."

"I wish my words were going to prove those fears false, but I am afraid they will not."

The arrivals reached the foot of the large dais, and Kramloc began speaking without waiting for recognition or obeisant ceremony. "Sefket, chieftains, I am pleased to introduce our newest Kin. This is Bron, favored son of the All Mother. He has proven himself worthy and has words he wishes to share with the Kin."

Sefket was an impressive specimen of his people. He stood strong and proud, although he was nowhere near as massive as Bojan was. Despite his slightly lesser stature, there was cunning in his eyes the champion lacked, and it spoke a great deal as to what the Kin found worthy in a leader.

"The Kin welcome you and your words, Bron, favored son of the All Mother."

"Thank you, King Sefket. I only wish my words were pleasing ones. Wise Kramloc told me of your worries concerning the human activity, and I am afraid they do herald the coming of war."

A great murmuring arose around the stadium in chorus with hundreds of bestial roars and the shaking of weapons. Sefket raised a single hand and the gorge fell silent.

"Are the humans resuming their former battles, or have they decided to turn their swords against the Kin once again?"

"Neither. The focus of their preparations is a far more terrible enemy, one who threatens all the races, including the Kin. I walked through the Passage of Lore, and I know your people—our people—remember the Scions, those you call the faceless ones. The All Mother, Ellanee, asked me to come to you, to warn you, and to ask you to lend your might to the other races in this battle. I know the humans have been unfair and even cruel, but I must ask, will you fight with them so that all may share in the victory once again? The higher races may not admit it, but we all know that without the might of the Kin, they will fall, and so shall we all."

Sefket turned and addressed his people in his powerful, commanding voice. "We all hear our Kin's words, and I find them worthy. Shall we hide in our valley and wait for the enslavers to come destroy us, or do we remind the so-called higher races of our worth?"

The combined shouts of the Kin were deafening. The stone trembled as thousands of feet stamped against stone. Bron could not discern a single intelligible word, but anyone could interpret their meaning.

Sefket turned to each of the high chiefs. "Ranko, Hagas, I declare it time to unseal the Tomb of Legends." Both chiefs nodded and Sefket looked to his shaman. "Kramloc, we have decided it is time to open the tomb. Do you agree?"

"I do, Sefket." Kramloc motioned to Bron. "Come, Bron, you should witness this. The Tomb of Legends has not been opened since we first sealed it more than a thousand years ago."

"What is the Tomb of Legends?" Bron asked as he followed the shaman shuffling up the steps to the pinnacle of the dais.

"It is where we entombed the original heroes of the Kin. We brought them all here when the humans forced us from our lands and entombed them within, along with their fabled armor."

"What armor is that?"

"You will see." Kramloc's smile spoke of eager anticipation.

Sefket and the two high chiefs stood at the wall backing the high platform upon which they stood. Detailed images of ogres, orcs, and goblins doing battle with dragons and other strange creatures stood out in deeply carved relief. The king and the chiefs each pulled a gold medallion suspended by a thick chain from beneath their leather jerkins. Separating the discs from the chains, the three leaders set them into shallow depressions carved into the cliff face and stepped aside.

Kramloc and one of the goblins and orcs took a few steps forward and began chanting. Bron could not understand the language, but he sensed it was ancient and felt the power building behind the guttural words. The medallions began to glow with a faint nimbus of light, and the stone began to vibrate. The dull grinding of rock against rock resounded through the gorge as a large slab of stone sank into the floor of the raised platform to reveal a spacious, smoothly carved interior.

The walls bore engravings similar to those covering the outside face. Bron thought the figures were all Kin until he spotted a single dwarf occupying a place of prominence in the center of the far wall. But no matter how intricate the engravings, all were eclipsed by what lay in the center of the tomb.

Three marble plinths acted as the resting place for the bodies laid reverentially upon them. The remains of an ogre, orc, and goblin lay head to head like the spokes of a wheel, each bedecked in armor of impossible blackness and trimmed in gold. Although the dust lay thick throughout the tomb, not a single speck marred the depthless ebony metal.

"What is that armor? Where did it come from?" Bron whispered.

"These are the suits bestowed upon each of the races' heroes in the time of the Great Rebellion. Although they are the masterworks of the dwarf Dundalor Ironforge, only the ogres possessed the strength to beat the metal into sheets for forging."

"What kind of metal is it?"

"No one knows. The metal was a gift from the gods. What it is, where it came from, or how it was forged is a secret lost to time. Perhaps the dwarves still know, but we do not."

"You said this tomb has been sealed since you fled your old lands. If the armor was powerful enough to help defeat dragons, did you not think to use it to defend yourselves against the humans?"

"No. The armor was created to help us defeat an immortal foe, and the humans also possessed the armor. To have hero battling hero was unthinkable. It would be an insult to the gods and the price we paid for our freedom. The Kin also knew that if we were to use it against the humans, then it would only be a matter of time before we used it against each other, so we sealed the armor within this tomb with our most worthy only to be opened in the time of our greatest need and with the unanimous consent of the three great tribes."

Bron looked on as the three shamans spoke words of reverent prayer before gently removing the armor from the mummified corpses and strapping them onto their chiefs. Several descriptors ran through Bron's mind as he gazed upon the fully armored warriors, but the word regal stood to the fore. The druid never thought he would use such a word for any of the brutish Kin, but the profound look of courage, strength, and purpose in their eyes could not be expressed in any other way.

The three leaders marched from the tomb and faced their people with their arms held high. The mountains shook as the Kin roared their approval. The sound was as inspiring as it was terrifying, and Bron felt a surge of pride to be called one of them.

Sefket turned to Bron. "The Kin stand ready, favored son of the All Mother. Lead us to our field of glory."

CHAPTER II

The men heard the wagon rumbling down the rutted road before they could make it out through the lightless evening. The carriage left narrow wheel tracks where the last of the snows sought refuge within the shadows draped across the roadway. The sections not covered in the frigid white stuff were a muddy slop that spattered the pair of mules' legs and bellies as they dutifully pulled their burden down the treacherous path, a sucking, slurping sound punctuating each rising hoof as dirty water rushed in to fill the depressions they made with each step.

As the wagon drew near, three highwaymen emerged from the trees and stepped just inside the ring of flickering light cast by the lanterns hanging off each side of the driver's buckboard. Two of the men pointed cocked and loaded crossbows at the wagon driver's heart, leaving no question as to their intent. The driver reined in his mules with a sharp tug of their leads and calls of "whoa."

"It's a foolish man who travels these roads alone," the brigand without a crossbow called up to the driver.

"I won't argue that, but it's a big assumption on your part to think I'm alone."

"I think you're bluffing. We been waiting in this spot for hours and ain't seen another soul."

"Are you willing to bet your life on that?"

The speaker turned to his two accomplices. "Watch the woods." He then turned back to the man on the wagon. "You seem like a clever fellow if a mite foolish. What's your name?"

"Most folks just call me Fetch."

"Well, you just go and fetch me whatever gold you pulled out of these streams and mountains."

His cohorts chuckled at their leader's pun. "Hey, boss, these mules ain't got no brands."

"That makes our job a lot easier. I guess we'll be taking them too."

"Look at him. He ain't hardly got no legs. Is he a dwarf?"

"Naw, ain't no dwarves gonna be driving mules on these roads. He's a half-man, ain't ya?"

Fetch glowered down at the robbers. "What I am is under the employ of someone you don't want to cross. Are you certain you wish to sell your lives so cheaply?"

"I don't know who your boss is, but he ain't here, is he?"

"On the contrary, I have been here the entire time." A shadow detached itself from the base of a stout tree and approached them.

Both crossbows swiveled to point at the speaker's heart. The man was tall, lean, and impeccably dressed in dark clothing. The fact he was able to blend so easily into the shadows and get the jump on the brigands may have been the source of the men's sudden fear. It could also have been the fact that not a single speck of mud dared touch his shoes or clothing as he stepped nonchalantly toward them, seemingly oblivious to the lethal weapons aimed at him. Whatever the reason, the highwaymen felt a sudden shift in the balance of power, and it made them very nervous.

The leader of the band tried to put on a brave front and spoke. "Who are you?"

"I am Landrin Bailey, lord governor of End's Run. You men are guilty of crimes against its citizens."

The brigand leader searched the trees for any signs of movement or sounds that might betray the presence of soldiers. "You look to have come unprepared, Lord Governor."

"It is you who are unprepared for me. I sense the evil intent within your hearts and know you meant to murder my man after robbing him of all his possessions."

"Well, we can't have folks running off and telling the local constabulary."

"For your crimes of robbery with intentions of murder, the punishment is death."

"Only ones dying here tonight are you two. Kill them."

The first man turned his crossbow back to Fetch to carry out his orders. The half-man squeezed the lever of the crossbow he had picked up from beneath his seat while the thugs were distracted by Landrin's arrival and buried a quarrel in the man's heart, killing him instantly.

The second robber loosed his bolt and stared in mute shock when the lord snatched it from the air like a fly. The brigand dropped his weapon and reached for his sword. Landrin drew his slender rapier, sprinted across the fifty feet of open ground, and kicked the man in the chest before the blade cleared its sheath.

Landrin darted to the leader of the gang and slapped his sword from his hand hard enough to send it flying deep into the forest before his partner's body struck the ground with a wet thud and soft mewling of pain. He pressed the tip of his sword against the man's throat.

"You have two choices. You can spend the next five years in my dungeon serving a purpose, or I can execute you here and now."

The thief's voice trembled. "W-what sort of purpose?"

Landrin smiled and revealed a long pair of fangs. "My purpose."

"No, I won't!" he cried, trying to back away.

"So be it."

The vampire silenced his cries with a swift thrust through his heart and walked over to the man huddled on the ground holding his bruised and broken ribs. Landrin did not even have to speak before the man gave his answer.

"Please, don't kill me! I want to live, please!" He held his quavering hand up beseechingly.

The ride to End's Run was long, bumpy, and unpleasant, particularly for the highwayman trussed up and lying in the bed of the wagon. It was the darkest, loneliest hours of the morning by the time they reached the earth-filled double walls of the kingdom's northernmost town. The men guarding the gates opened them wide without challenge.

No one knew what the governor and his man did on these occasional late night forays, but none were curious enough to ask. Landrin was as respected as he was feared, and none pried into his affairs; not that anyone likely would regardless of his status. End's Run was a wild frontier, although much less rough now that King Jarvin had appointed Landrin governor, and people tended to leave others to their affairs as long as they were left to theirs. Even now, the sounds of raucous laughter and merriment drifted across the settlement from a few of the taverns and inns that never closed their doors except to keep out the cold.

Fetch guided the mules to the small northern gate leading to the cobbled lane winding its way to Landrin's mansion. The road was steep, snaking up the hillside to the mysterious home created overnight using magic from a scroll given to him by Solarian, god of light. Between that and the governor's enigmatic nature, he rarely had visitors, something for which he was very thankful, and this night more than others.

"Take our guest to his cell," Landrin instructed his valet. "I will be in the chapel."

"It still bothers you, don't it?"

"The necessities of my existence will always trouble me."

"Don't see why." Fetch nudged the wheel of the wagon with his boot. "This fellow gets to cool his heels in a reasonably pleasant little cell for a time then go on his merry way. Anywhere else in the kingdom and he'd be swinging by a rope next to his friends."

"Sometimes the measure of one's death is more important than the measure of one's life, something of which I am keenly aware."

Fetch knew there was no point in arguing when Landrin was in this sort of mood. He had tried on several occasions to convince his friend and boss that taking blood from men or women who would otherwise have been executed was no different than milking a cow, but Landrin remained morose for days after taking in a new prisoner, and nothing would cheer him up. Only his devotion to Solarian brought him any measure of peace.

Landrin entered the chapel room of his home and knelt before the huge golden disc suspended from the ceiling set to capture and reflect the rays of sunlight that would stream through the stained-glass window behind him come morning. Devotions were normally performed at sunrise and sunset, but Landrin's heart was heavy, and only Solarian's cleansing light could ease his suffering.

"Solarian, lord of morning, god of light, forgive me for my actions this night and continue to bless me with your radiance. Though I cannot walk within your luminescence, I thank you for your love and guidance and will forever be your servant. Anything I have and everything I am is yours to command."

Golden light filled the room, and Landrin could feel the awesome power only a god could radiate wash over him. He felt the breath he had not drawn in the past couple of decades catch in his throat. Landrin slowly turned on his knees and saw the silhouette of his god in the center of a dazzling aura.

"Solarian, you grace me with your presence once again," Landrin intoned.

"Not even close," a sultry feminine voice replied.

Sharrellan dropped the brilliant glow surrounding her and laughed softly. "Forgive me, Landrin. My humor can sometimes be a bit cruel."

"Why do you come and defile this holy place with your presence?"

"I have a service I require you to perform."

"I do not serve you. I serve only Solarian, so be gone from my home."

The goddess touched an alabaster hand to her exposed cleavage in mock offense. "Such rudeness. Most of my subjects would be overjoyed by a visit from their beloved goddess."

"I am not your subject! I belong heart and soul to Solarian."

"It is a shame your beloved Solarian does not hold you in such high regard. Do you think the god of life and light has anything other than pity for you? You are an undead monstrosity, and he finds you repulsive beyond few other things in this world. I, on the other hand, think you are fabulous. Your soul belongs to me whether you like it or not."

"I have given myself to Solarian, and you cannot take that away!"

"You are correct; I cannot take a soul from another god. Fortunately, he was perfectly happy to give it to me."

Landrin's eyes dropped to the floor and he whispered, "He would not do such a thing."

"Could and did. Who do you think helped you become what you are?"

"You are the cause of my existence?"

"With Solarian's blessing. Now stop being so pouty. This is important."

Landrin's world shattered. He felt betrayed as everything he had done to prove himself worthy of his god's love crumbled to dust. He had tortured himself, denied the needs of his existence only to find rejection.

"What do you want from me?"

"I want you to do the job for which you were created."

Sharrellan produced a scroll from nowhere and held it out to Landrin. The vampire reluctantly took it and read its contents. He leapt to his feet, fury mingling with disgust as he hurled the parchment back at the goddess of death.

"I will never be a part of your vile schemes! Good people died to thwart this perversion of magic, and I will not mock their deaths by trying to complete it!"

Sharrellan sighed and rolled her eyes. "Honestly, Landrin, I thought you were clever. Like you, that entire debacle was created for a purpose."

"You gods use us like toys. What purpose is worth the lives of thousands?"

"The lives of millions. Evil is coming, and it seeks the annihilation of nearly all the mortal races. Certain people needed to be guided along a path so they could rise above the rabble and provide the leadership the people need in order to have a hope of defeating these foes."

"Did you fail? Are the gods not as infallible as you like us mortals to believe?"

"You no longer get to count yourself among the mortals," the goddess countered. "We are capable of making mistakes, most of which involve the inability to foresee every potentiality revolving around free will. But this was not one of those times. Our efforts to prepare for the coming invasion have been almost flawless."

"Then you raised the wrong one. You should have kept one of your willing devotees on hand for this, because I will have no part in such desecration," Landrin insisted.

"You are the perfect choice. Anyone who desires to use such power is ill-suited to wield it. Your ability, undead nature, and apprehension make you the only one we trust with the responsibility."

Landrin shuddered. His skin felt alive as it crawled in revulsion. "You said you were successful in your preparations. Why do this then?"

"Because it is not enough. We have studied our position, placed all the pieces upon the board, and in none of our gambits are we successful."

Landrin studied Sharrellan's terrifyingly beautiful face and saw the fear beneath her haughty façade. "You are afraid."

The goddess let her true emotions surface for a brief instant. "We are all afraid. We fear for our subjects and for our own existence."

"You ask me to desecrate brave men and women who have given their lives to protect their homes and families."

"Their souls will have departed this world. The magic you employ will only affect the shells once housing them. Landrin, if you refuse to do as I ask, then evil will swarm over the races and destroy them."

"Why do you bother to ask me? Can you not just command me as your pawn? Why do you not do it yourself?"

"The answer to both is free will. We are forbidden by a power higher than even the gods understand. You must make the choice for yourselves. Will you sacrifice your morals for the continued existence of this world's people?"

Landrin stared at the rolled vellum on the floor but did not move to pick it up. He abhorred his existence and could never visit anything resembling it on another. If this was the only way to save the people, perhaps it was time for them to die. No, he could not decide for all of humanity and beyond whether they deserved to live or die. They must be given the choice, and to do that, they must survive.

"I want something in return."

The goddess smiled coyly at the creature who was once a man. "Most people would consider their lives a proper reward."

"I told you the last time you sought to manipulate me that I place no value on this false life."

"All right, what do you desire?"

"You will give my soul back to Solarian. When I finally meet my end, I will return to bask in the shining god's light."

"Even after he cast you aside? Landrin, I would give you everything you desire within my realm. You would have power and luxury beyond your imagination."

"Yet I would still be your pawn. Better to be an insect under the sun than a god drowning in darkness."

Sharrellan's laughter ended with a resigned sigh. "Sometimes, you humans are just like dogs. No matter how hard you kick them they always come scurrying back to their master's feet. Very well, I will offer your soul back to Solarian, but I cannot guarantee he will accept it."

"We all live and die by the choices we are given. Even gods are given choice, and I choose to wager my soul on his."

"Then he shall have it, and I truly hope he rejects it. There are few people I am genuinely fond of, and your obstinacy has made you one of them."

Landrin ignored the goddess's compliment and picked up the scroll. "How much time do I have to prepare?"

"None whatsoever. You must leave immediately and begin your preparations the moment you arrive. Ancient gods and their innumerable minions are outside the walls and are moments from breaching them. Make haste, Landrin. The world depends upon it."

Sharrellan vanished before his eyes without a sign of her departure or having ever been there. Landrin studied the scroll in his hand and wanted nothing more than to cast it into a fire, but he could not. He had a duty to perform, and no matter how distasteful, he would do it.

"I thought we were friends."

Landrin turned and found Fetch standing in the doorway. "Of course we are friends. Why do you say that?"

"You talk to gods and don't think to ask them to make me taller?"

He smiled at the half-man, grateful for his ability to ease his troubled soul in even the darkest of moments. "I like you just the way you are."

"Says the man who don't have to use a step stool to mount the privy. It sounds like we got some work to do. Do you want horses or mules?"

"Speed is of the essence. I will summon a mount. It is the only way to get where I must go quickly enough."

"I've eaten a dead horse, but I never thought I'd ever ride one," Fetch responded with a grunt.

"Fetch, you do not need to be a part of this."

"It sounded to me like everyone is going to be a part of this. These legs may not be able to reach the privy, but I'll stand and fight like any man."

Landrin clapped the half-man on the shoulder as he passed through the doorway. "Fetch, I think you are a giant among men."

"You can carve that on my headstone. 'Here lies Fetch, the world's shortest giant.'"

Landrin enjoyed one of his rare laughs as he walked out of his home and into the dark night. Revulsion swept over him as he delved into the forbidden art of necromancy and sent black magic out across End's Run and into the surrounding land. It took only a few minutes to find what he sought lying buried beneath a couple of feet of earth.

The undead steed pawed its way through the soil and galloped through the trees and up the hill to the manor, staying outside the walls of the town and away from the eyes of the townsfolk. The animal was in decent shape, having died just yesterday after it had gotten into a toxic mass of highland ragwort. Fetch arrived with a pack stuffed full of supplies and his crossbow slung across his chest just as Landrin cinched the saddle on tight.

"Well, at least it doesn't smell...that bad."

"You do not need to go with me, Fetch."

"If you think I'm going to miss out on a gods-given quest, think again. I ain't seen much beyond the tops of people's legs in my life, and I ain't about to miss this."

"Do you need help mounting?"

"Either that or you conjure up something my size. I saw a dead raccoon on the road when we came in."

Landrin laughed again, truly grateful for Fetch's company, and lifted him onto the back of the undead steed. Fetch was his only real friend since his transformation and a vital link to his humanity. He leapt straight into the air and came down to take an easy seat on the saddle.

"Show-off," Fetch muttered behind him.

"Hold on tight. This is going to be a rather intense ride."

Landrin spurred the horse with a thought, and the undead mount exploded into motion. Fetch cursed loudly as the trees flew past as slightly darker blurs against the backdrop of the night-time sky. That single exclamation became a near unending torrent of vulgarities when they left the road and continued the breakneck pace through the forest. Mile after mile the nightmarish creature ran, long after any other living mount would have collapsed from exhaustion.

The horse sprinted through the trees and leapt obstacles without breaking stride, reacting instantly to its creator's mental commands. In the few hours before dawn, Landrin's mount carried them a distance that would have taken days using a living horse. The primary reason for his haste showed itself as the sun began to lift over the horizon. The forest was slowly changing from black to grey when they spotted the ancient citadel carved into the cliff. Unlike the last time Landrin had seen the structure, it looked truly abandoned and lifeless now. He reined in his mount just before the entrance of the fortress and lowered Fetch to the ground where he promptly fell over.

"They need to make horses with narrow rumps for folks like me who lack a notable inseam," the half-man complained as he lay on the ground.

"Fetch, I need to get inside. Are you all right?"

Fetch waved a hand. "Go, I'll manage. I just need a minute to pop my legs back in their sockets."

He sent his steed away to return to the earth, left Fetch to recover, and hastened inside. Landrin shuddered as he entered the fortress and navigated his way down the dark halls to the central chamber. Even after so much time had passed, he could still feel the presence of the lich he had fought.

The shattered remains of the massive black crystal still lay scattered about the room. He paused and whispered a prayer to those who had died to prevent exactly what he was about to enact. Shoving aside his deep reservations, Landrin gathered in the Source and sent hundreds of magical tendrils creeping along the floor. The wisps of magic began pulling every crystal shard into the center of the chamber. As the fragments conglomerated, they began to fuse back into a single mass. Within minutes, the crystal was whole and resting back within its cradle.

"Well, that was something to see," Fetch remarked as he walked into the room.

"I suppose you are wondering what this is all about."

"That and why I bother to do so much sweeping. It seems you have a more efficient way to get the job done."

"Something is coming that has even the gods scared," Landrin explained. "You recall the night the dead rose?"

"Kinda hard to forget rampaging zombies."

"It is going to happen again, only this time I am in control. Sharrellan, and I assume the other gods as well, do not think the living can defend against whatever is coming, so she asked me to aid them by raising the dead."

"So the zombies are going to be on our side this time?" Landrin nodded. "It still sounds damn unpleasant."

"It is, but it is vital, or so she tells me."

"Do you trust her?"

"No, but I believe her. She is afraid, and if the gods are afraid, we should all be terrified."

"All right then. If it's all the same to you, I think I'll go see if I can hunt down some fresh food while you do your horribly unspeakable magic."

"Thank you for your understanding and words of comfort."

"I call 'em like I see 'em."

Fetch dropped his pack in the room, checked his crossbow and quarrels, and left to hunt some game. Landrin stared at the black crystal for several minutes before unrolling the scroll and reading the magic contained within the words burned into the vellum. He used his magic to guide the rapidly building power, drawing it toward the tower. Outside, an unnatural fog began to form, surely ruining Fetch's plans for a good hunt. It would take days for the power to accumulate, so Landrin forced himself to relax and settle into the rhythm of the magic.

CHAPTER 12

A zerick slowly circled the old tower, studying the runes painted on its sides and carved into the ground around it. It was the fifth and final inspection of their work. The school was silent for the first time since its founding. Azerick had ordered everyone not needed for what he was about to enact to stay well clear of the grounds. Thousands of anxious eyes focused on the old tower stabbing above the wall from the training fields.

"Azerick, are you certain you must do this?" Miranda asked. "Aggie said it is very dangerous."

"There is an element of danger, but I must hide the tower and the Source pool so the Scions do not destroy it. We cannot lose this valuable a tool. I will be fine."

"You always say that."

"And I always return."

"Barely!"

"I have to try," Azerick insisted.

"What if we lose you? Are you not as vital as this pool?"

"No, I'm not. Raijaun and the others will stand in my stead. This was never about me, but about all of us. It is about standing together, never surrendering, and doing whatever must be done to ensure our survival. We all must play our part, and this is mine. Now, please go stay with the others."

"I want to stay here. What if something goes wrong?" Miranda asked.

"What will you do if it does? If I could do this alone I would not risk my best people in this effort, so there is no reason to risk your life as well."

"I don't want to lose you again."

"You won't."

Azerick could not bring himself to tell her he was already lost. He had inhabited the body of a demon lord and had made enemies of the king and the Academy. There was almost no one of power who would not like to see him banished or dead. He was uncertain how this war would conclude, but he knew there would be no happy ending for him.

"Just go now, please."

Miranda kissed her husband deeply before climbing astride her horse and galloping through the gates. Azerick waited until she was out of sight before turning to those gathered. Twelve of the strongest mages residing at the school stood in a loose group with mixed expressions. All were aware of the challenge ahead of them and the potential for disaster.

"It's time," Azerick announced. "Everyone, go take your places."

There was no arguing. Every argument that could be made had already been voiced, and Azerick was not going to be deterred. The tower must not fall, no matter the cost. Despite his reassurances, he knew this was a risky endeavor. The elves had failed in their attempt to do this, but they had overreached themselves. At least, Azerick hoped that was the source of their failure.

His people encircled the tower, each one of them standing at a precise location like points on a compass. Once Azerick started the spell, no one could move an inch from their spot. They were not just casting a spell, they were each part of the spell's form, and any deviation would destroy it and possibly themselves.

Azerick entered the tower and descended into the old laboratory; the heart of the tower where the Source pool now resided. Stepping into the chamber was like walking into a sauna, only it was a wave of arcane power washing over him instead of moist heat. In another room, the crystal allowing him and Raijaun to travel to the Scions' prison beckoned. Azerick ignored its calls, knowing there was no longer anything they could do to delay the fallen gods' return.

Stabbing his staff into the tower floor, Azerick began weaving the spell of translocation. Outside, the runes flared and he felt the others add their power to his. He used his staff as a focal point and to anchor him to the tower as the veil between worlds began to part. The ground beneath his feet trembled as the world resisted the attempt to steal part of it away.

Buildings shook, shedding roof tiles like a dog shaking water from its fur until they cracked. A section of the outer wall collapsed beneath the violent quaking. Aggie wanted to stop the spell now, but they were committed, and disrupting it at this point could be more disastrous than continuing. She was certain the tower would collapse and bury Azerick beneath it at any moment, but a closer look showed the tower was not shaking at all. It was the world around it reacting violently while it stood in an eye of relative calm. It gave her hope, and she shouted her observation to the others to reassure them. She could feel the anxiety in their shared magic, and it was crucial they not let fear distract them, or they could yet lose control just as the elves had.

Some of the weaker structures on the school grounds began to collapse, and deep fissures radiated out from the base of the old tower. Several of the mages looked at the expanding web of cracks as they crawled outward. Ellyssa glared at one running between her feet but refused to allow it to distract her. The ground collapsed around the tower as if it were being swallowed by a massive sinkhole, but it did not fall.

It hovered over the pit, displaying the outside walls of the subsurface rooms. Then it began to fade. At first, it looked as though it were being cast into darkness by the setting sun despite the illumination of everything around it. Then it began to lose solidity, and for a brief moment, everyone could see Azerick in the central chamber with a look of total focus etched upon his face. A moment later, there was nothing but a massive hole in the ground and the destruction it left behind.

Azerick's world turned grey then stark white. Color slowly began filtering in, and he could define shapes around him. For a few seconds, he could see through the walls and floors above him and gazed upon the light and the tops of trees of the outside world. Azerick was exhausted and took several minutes to steady the muscles now trembling like an old man afflicted with palsy.

Finding his balance once more, he reached into the silver liquid of the Source pool. The pool radiated with power, but not like the burning heat of a fire. It was warmth, love, strength, and the sweetest promises ever whispered into one's ear.

He had to use his intense focus and will to keep himself from allowing it to pull him into its comforting embrace and consume him. Azerick pushed back and used his mind and power to shape the living Source into the tool he needed. He withdrew his hand from the pool and admired the shining metal lying in his open palm. To anyone else, it appeared to be nothing more than an impossibly brilliant door handle, and that was what it was, except it was far from ordinary.

Slipping the handle into his pocket, Azerick made for the stairs leading up. For a few frightful moments as he stood in the doorway of the foyer, he thought the spell had failed, but Azerick quickly realized he was somewhere else. The air was completely free of the smells of humanity. No tangy odors of forge fires or sweet smells of food cooking in the kitchens tinged the air. No voices or the sounds of mock battles played across the grounds. It was silent, and the air was almost sterile. Azerick's tower stood as the only building for as far as he could see, and he suspected it was the only one in this world.

The sorcerer stepped from his tower and gazed across the open field and up at the mountains looming behind him. It was identical to the place he just departed, except no man had ever set foot here before. Every tree that had ever grown and not fallen to age and the elements still stood tall, safe from the axes and saws used to create the training grounds, farms, and pastures.

It was beyond peaceful; it was tranquil. Silence lay over this world like a blanket shielding it from the horror his world was about to face. Azerick was almost able to fully relax for the first time in years until the silence of the place went from serene to disturbing. It was not just quiet, it was devoid of sound and life. Then someone threw a mountain on him.

Azerick erected a ward just as the sky vanished and something colossal came crashing down. His ward flared violently as it fought against the crushing weight of the world-eclipsing form trying to grind him to dust. Azerick poured power into his shield and was launched forward like a cherry pit being squeezed between an enormous thumb and forefinger. He rolled and tumbled inside his magic sphere for over a hundred yards until the trees brought him to an abrupt halt.

He leapt to his feet and stared in disbelief at the creature that had nearly crushed him into paste. The dragon, if that was what it truly was, was both awesome and terrifying. Its serpentine body was a river of rippling, multihued scales with eight legs and four wings. How something that size could fly was beyond him. It was easily five hundred feet long, and Azerick figured he was probably underestimating it as his mind refused to fully acknowledge its greatness.

"You trespass in my world, sorcerer. You plant your unnatural home and defile the purity of this place, and for that, you shall die."

The dragon's voice struck Azerick like a wave and nearly knocked him back off his feet. Before he could respond, fire engulfed the world. Azerick raised another ward and was barely able to shield himself from the hellish flames. The trees around him exploded under the intensity and were reduced to ash in the span of a breath. The ground turned black and cracked as every particle of water evaporated. Azerick struck back with a massive fist of invisible force, snapping the flame-spewing jaws closed and rocking the dragon's head back.

"Stop!" Azerick shouted. "There is no need for us to fight. I do not wish you any harm."

"You, harm me?" The dragon's laughter shook pinecones from the trees not destroyed by his fiery breath. "I am Ancalon, Father of Dragons. I am as old as this world. You are a child who has picked up his father's sword and now thinks he is a great warrior. You have no idea of the meaning of power. I smell the blood of one of my children upon you, so I will show you real power."

Azerick thought back and understood Ancalon must mean the dragon who had stolen the Codex Arcana from him. "I had no desire to harm him, but he gave me no choice. Do not make the same mistake."

Ancalon gave another rumbling chuckle. "Insect."

The Father of Dragons slammed a mighty paw against the ground, causing it to heave and buckle. A huge section of earth and rock rose out of the soil like a geyser and blasted Azerick hundreds of feet into the air. The sorcerer ripped open a gate near the apex of his rapid ascent and transported himself back to the ground behind the great wyrm.

Azerick gathered in the Source as fast as he could. Ancalon sensed the power building behind him and spun to face the intruder. He was swift for such a colossal creature, but Azerick was faster. The sorcerer released a powerful blast of arcane energy directly into the dragon's face, knocking the gargantuan creature back a hundred yards. Ancalon's clawed feet dug furrows in the ground deep enough to bury a wagon as he scrabbled for purchase.

The dragon responded with a roar of fury that hit Azerick with as much force as a strong wizard's spell. Azerick raised a boulder the size of a cottage from the ground and launched it with the speed of a loosed arrow. The boulder struck Ancalon between his enormous eyes and shattered into a spray of gravel. The beast shook his head, raised a mass of earth the size of a large house, and dropped it on the infuriating sorcerer.

Azerick tore open another gate and leapt through just before the million-ton rock smashed into the ground and caused a small, localized earthquake. The cloud of dust kicked up from the assault made it nearly impossible for Azerick to see, but Ancalon was so large he did not have to. His amalgamated ray of arcane and demonic magic pierced the dust cloud and struck the dragon low in its side between its two sets of wings.

Ancalon roared in pain and fury. No mortal creature had ever caused him harm before. This sensation was new and unacceptable. The dragon sent his magic into the sky, and enormous thunderheads rolled in to answer his call. The wind began blowing furiously, and lightning arced across the black clouds. Ancalon grabbed those bolts with his magic and hurled them at the human creature.

Azerick felt one and then a multitude of powerful lightning bolts strike his ward. Arcs of tremendously powerful electricity struck his shield and the ground around him by the hundreds. His hair stood on end, and tiny motes of electrical energy crackled across his flesh and clothing even inside his protective bubble. He sent magic deep into the ground and forced a lake to rise beneath them. Ancalon's lightning electrified the water and sent its power coursing through the great dragon's body. Azerick jabbed the arcanum point of his staff into the ground and added his power to the assault.

The dragon screeched once more, beat his powerful wings, and flew into the dark sky. Azerick chased him with flaming orbs and brilliant beams of arcane energy, scorching scales and eliciting more bellows of outrage. Ancalon streaked skyward until his gigantic form was nearly lost from view. The dragon grew bigger in Azerick's vision as it plummeted from the clouds. He was sure Ancalon meant to crush him with his bulk and rend him apart with the talons of all eight feet stretched toward him. The Father of Dragons suddenly altered his course and raced horizontally across the sky. Azerick could hear the leathery flaps of his wings cracking like whips under the titanic forces battering against them.

"I tire of this game. You are not welcome here, and I cast you out of my world!"

Ancalon's talons tore a gash in the sky itself. Azerick realized what the dragon had done just a split second before the rift tore him from the ground and sucked him into its interdimensional maw. The sorcerer twisted in midair, pointed his staff toward the tower, and called upon the silver substance of the Source pool. Pure Source material poured out of the windows and doors and expanded into a shimmering silver bubble. Azerick was unsure if his hasty shield would prevent the dragon from destroying his tower and the well, but he had no time to try anything else. It was an instinctual measure of desperation.

The rift swallowed Azerick whole, and his stomach lurched as he spun and tumbled through dimensions. Down through the gullet between worlds he fell, stars and suns streaking by like fireflies. Millions of miles, meaningless in this place between places, flashed by in seconds, minutes, possibly hours. Time had as little meaning here as distance. A white scar appeared in the distance, a rent in space opening to his destination.

Azerick was spewed out of the non-space and into a world of life and color. Wind rushed past Azerick's body as he plummeted toward a sea of green just a couple of hundred feet below. Hastily shifting into his demonic form, he snapped open his great, bat-like wings to arrest his fall. The jungle canopy seemed to explode as hundreds of thousands of birds or some kind of flying animals took to the sky with a hellish shriek. Knowing he had no time to stop his plunge, Azerick directed his descent toward a strip of water barely visible between the expansive spread of foliage.

The sorcerer struck the water with a great splash, and he once again found himself tossed about, tumbling through the rushing torrent of water as the river swept him downstream. His wings less than useless, Azerick once more adopted his human body and struggled to keep his head above water. The speed of the river made Azerick feel as though he were trapped on the back of a runaway horse desperately trying to throw him. He kicked and paddled furiously to reach the shore and to avoid the occasional boulder peeking out of the water. The former was a complete failure, and the latter achieved only marginal success.

Azerick grunted and cursed in pain whenever he failed to avoid one of the immobile obstacles. The river bashed, bruised, and abused his body for mile after punishing mile. He did not know if his demonic body was capable of drowning, but if it was, it could not be much longer in coming. Only his fight with the demon lord Drak'kar could match the punishing brutality of the river.

Azerick detected a change in the tone and tempo of the torrent's rage, and he knew the river was about to unleash an entirely new hellish experience upon him. He thrust his head above the water and saw open sky a few dozen yards ahead. The sorcerer kicked and pulled furiously at the water, but it refused to loosen its grip on him. The river flung the human flotsam over the cliff and bore him downward under the force of the powerful cascade.

Azerick struck the water below with great force, but the resulting splash was lost amidst the awesome amount of water crashing down in an unending deluge. He prayed the plunge was a prelude to some sort of respite, but if his gods could hear him in this world, they chose to ignore his pleas. He had just enough time to take in another lungful of air before he was swept away once more. Another brutal mile raced by, then another and another. His world had become little more than flashes of green and the spray of white water as the river, sped along by gravity, tried to flush him like a toxin from its system.

Undercurrents continually pulled him down and bounced his body along the riverbed before hurling him upward once again, usually just in time to bash him against another rock cutting through the raging water. Azerick felt himself lifted into the air once again only to come back down hard a second later. Several times the river dropped away and deposited him onto a smooth stone shelf just a few inches below the surface. It was akin to being forcefully thrown down a giant flight of stairs.

His final drop ended in a splash and notably calm water. For the first time in what felt like an eternity but probably spanned only twenty or thirty minutes, Azerick was not rushing downstream and bashing into rocks. He kicked his feet until his head broke the surface and he found himself in something of a large pool below a multi-step waterfall. There was still a substantial current, and it was quickly pushing him toward another nightmarish stretch of water. Azerick paddled desperately for the shore and dragged himself onto the muddy bank.

Lacking the strength to pull his head out of the muck, Azerick simply lay there, fighting to catch his breath and taking inventory of his numerous wounds. Realizing there were more areas of his body in pain than not, he quickly gave up on the endeavor and simply luxuriated in being stationary. He slowly began moving parts of his body to work out the rapid onset of kinks and to reassure himself that he still could.

He crawled to his feet and surveyed his surroundings. High mountains loomed over a dense jungle. The river cut the only clear path he could see, but the thick vegetation grew right to the banks and stretched out over the water in most places making it impossible to follow it in either direction. A steamy, heavy mist blanketed the treetops in wispy vapors, filling in the few breaks in the otherwise impenetrable canopy.

As his exhaustion wore off, it gave his rage the energy to surface. Ancalon had delayed him and could even now be destroying his tower and the Source pool. His people needed him and the pool to defend against the Scions, and the dragon had proven to be a detriment to them both. Azerick reached out to the Source in order to scour away a swath of this damnable jungle and bleed away some of his rising anger only to find he couldn't. Where the vast river of arcane power once flowed, there was nothing but a barren landscape.

Real fear did the job of vanquishing his anger as he realized he was trapped in this world with no magic with which to flee it. Azerick quickly took control of his mounting anxiety and refused to let panic inhibit his ability to think his way out of this predicament. If what he understood of the Source was accurate, it was nearly impossible for this world to be completely bereft of magic. The Source flowed throughout the universe, shaping worlds and creating life. Even if this world was ancient and the Source had somehow dried up, there must still be a remnant of it somewhere. Azerick sent out his focus once again, this time searching for small pools or rivulets of power instead of the enormous sea present in his world.

As he expected, it was there in the trees and the ground all around him like the mists floating high overhead. It was as weak and insubstantial as the fog as well, but a person can trap enough mist to provide water to drink, and so he could trap enough of this power to open a rift back to his world. He could gather and hold the arcane energy in some runes, but it would take time to build them up to the level he needed to enact such a spell. If only his studies in rune carving had come to him as naturally as his sorcery had.

He nearly laughed aloud when his staff thrummed gently in his hand as if to remind him that he had a concentrated source of power at the ready. He would still need the runes for a spell of that complexity, but at least it was now possible to do it without waiting weeks or months for them to trap enough energy to be useful. Azerick scanned the sky through the slash in the jungle created by the river and saw the scar left by the rift hovering near the top of a barren mountain poking above the green canopy like a giant grey wart. The scar represented a weakness in the barrier between worlds, and it was his best chance at reopening a passage back home.

"All right, what else do you have?" Azerick shouted in challenge to the jungle.

A creature that would look perfectly at home in the abyss stepped out of the dense foliage as if in answer. It stood more than a head taller than Azerick did but sported far more mass than even his demonic form. The skin all over its body was dark green, mottled with black bony plates, and spikes grew all around its head. It was bipedal with arms slightly longer than its legs. A pair of eyes rested close together above a pronounced set of jaws overflowing with long, sharp teeth too large to be concealed by its nearly nonexistent lips.

"Remind me never to ask this horrible place that question again."

"Where is he?" Miranda shouted, her anxiety increasing with every hour Azerick failed to return.

It was now the second day since Azerick and the tower disappeared. Everyone had remained hopeful the first day, assuming Azerick was simply creating defenses to further conceal and protect the tower, but as dawn of the second day crept over the horizon, many began to fear something terrible had happened.

"We aren't sure," Allister answered calmly. "The passage of time gets a little strange when you start slipping between worlds and realities. It could be only a couple hours has passed where he's at. Do you remember how it was when he was in the abyss? Far more time passed for us than it did him."

"But what happened? Where did he go? Do we know anything at all?" she demanded. Her voice quavered with fear, and she stood on the verge of tears.

Aggie said, "I have tried to scry him, but my skill cannot pierce the veil between worlds. I'm sorry, Miranda."

"We do know the spell was successful and that the tower and Father reached the location he sought. I cannot glean any more information than that," Raijaun added.

"I knew this was going to happen! I knew one of these insane ideas of his was going to fail and he would never return! Does he even think about the people he is leaving behind and how much they depend on him? Does he care?"

Aggie stood and embraced Miranda. "Of course he cares. He cares so much that he is willing to risk his life to protect us all."

"For once I wish he would just protect me, and yes, I know exactly how selfish that sounds, but he's my husband. Isn't a wife allowed to be selfish once in a while?"

"Of course you are, dear." Aggie drew Miranda in close and let her weep into her shoulder. "We both know that if your roles were reversed, there is nothing you would not do to defend your people, even if it meant sacrificing your own desires. Your heart is aching and cries out, but your mind knows Azerick is doing what he must."

"I am so afraid, Aggie," Miranda sobbed. "My son is gone, and if I lose Azerick, I will have no one left."

Several sets of eyes sought out Raijaun, but no one commented. Raijaun glanced at the floor but showed no other outward sign of having been hurt by her statement. Miranda was frightened and grieving, so they let her vent her frustrations.

Aggie turned her toward the kitchen. "Come, let us sit and have tea in silence while the others figure out a way to find that fool husband of yours."

"Does anyone have any ideas on how to bring Azerick back or at least find out where he is?" Rusty asked after Miranda was out of the room.

"We know where he is, or at least where he was," Raijaun answered.

"Azerick said something about the elves having their spell go awry. Could that have happened to him? Could he and the tower have gone somewhere else?"

"No, I maintained a connection with my father for several seconds after he and the tower made the shift, and both arrived precisely where they were supposed to. I did not detect any secondary temporal disruption that might have changed that."

Allister said, "We must assume he ran into a problem returning here. Can we open a rift to go find him?"

Raijaun nodded his head. "Creating a portal is possible, but it will be difficult and dangerous since none of us has a significant connection to that world. If he does not return, I may make the attempt anyway, but I do not think it is the wisest course of action. I will need time to study the codex in order to create a spell to reach the same geographic location within the same timeline if we run out of other options."

"All right, see what you can do to rescue him if it comes to it. What about the Scions? How is their prison holding?"

"The stone Father and I use to send our consciousness to their plane is in the old tower, so I can no longer provide a current assessment."

"That's just great!" Rusty railed. "Why did he take the only way we have to watch the Scions with him?"

"Their prison has degraded to the point where our repairs would amount to little improvement, and Father needed to keep the crystal safe for the final battle. Given what I last saw, I strongly suggest we begin moving everyone to the city. It is likely only a matter of days until they break free and launch an all-out assault."

"We're just going to abandon the school?"

"Defending the school was never an option. North Haven will fall and the school with it. Once we know the Scions and their horde are near the city, we will start evacuating the citizens. Our job is to get as many people through the gates as possible and to destroy as many of our enemy as we can before retreating."

"I really hate this plan," Rusty complained bitterly.

CHAPTER 13

Heartrending rage inundated Sandy's soul with an intensity she had never felt before. She beat her wings furiously, desperate to put as much distance between herself and the source of her misery as she could and as quickly as possible. But even as she left the school and Azerick far behind, she keenly felt every rune etched upon her body, and there was no way to run from such a desecration.

Sand dragons were not built to be swift or agile flyers, and despite her strenuous efforts, she was not fleeing nearly fast enough. The young dragon focused her anger and willed her muscles to work harder, but they were already pushed to their limits. The more she demanded, the angrier she got as her body refused to obey. The harder she tried, the more the runes itched and demanded attention.

Reaching the limits of her irritation, Sandy turned her thoughts to the hated sigils. She could clearly see the shape of every rune on her body and trace each line within her mind. Ancient dragon memories handed down from her parents and grandparents and every ancestor from the beginning of time floated to the forefront of her mind. Most of the runes tapped into the vast power of the elements, much like her innate dragon magic. She picked out a rune tied to the element of air and called to it. The rune answered, flaring brightly, and a fierce wind struck her from behind. Sandy fought to maintain control, canting her wings and forcing her flight to straighten by using her tail like a ship's rudder to correct her course.

Gaining control, she caught the powerful blow with her wings and streaked across the sky. The feeling was exhilarating, and she marveled at the speed with which the ground retreated far beneath her. She was certain no sand dragon had ever flown so swiftly. Even the great cloud dragons, who rarely set a scaly foot upon the ground, would be hard-pressed to match her speed.

Sandy called out to the wind once more, another rune flared, and a gust came at her from the side. Banking her enormous wings, she dipped sharply to her left and raced for the ground with breathtaking speed. Despite her initial thrill, the cost of this new power quickly reasserted itself, and her rage renewed. Sandy desperately needed a release before the anger consumed her.

Runes flared all over her body, wreathing her form in a light so bright she looked like a meteor streaking across the sky. Sandy unleashed the pent-up energy with a furious roar. A massive sphere of crackling energy, fire, and electricity as big as her body raced ahead of her and struck the ground. The titanic assault incinerated trees, melted stone, and caused the earth to buckle and heave for hundreds of feet in every direction.

Sandy pulled up from her dive so close to the ground she could feel the heat of the scorched earth wash over her belly scales, the only scales on her body not ruined by Azerick. She released a massive jet of flame as she sped just a few feet above the ground, creating a line of fire nearly a quarter-mile long before arcing back into the sky. The young dragon raced upward on a magically conjured wind until the raging inferno beneath her appeared no bigger than a small campfire. At the apex of her ascent, she flipped over backward, tucked her wings close to her body, and plummeted once again.

Once more, she commanded the runes to summon a colossal amount of elemental power and unleashed it at the hapless ground, creating a gigantic crater of scorched earth beneath her. A powerful wave of fatigue washed over her, and fear replaced her anger as the ground rose up to meet her. She desperately sought out the power of her glyphs and received only a feeble reply.

Adding her innate magic to that of the rune, she summoned an anemic wind. Spreading her wings wide to catch the updraft, her body began to level out, and the approaching ground slowed. Her muscles ached, and the bones in her wings felt ready to snap as they fought against the wind pressure. Her bones held, and she managed to regain some altitude, but she was exhausted now and her stomach demanded sustenance. It was apparent her new power was far from limitless.

Far in the distance, she spied a herd of elk sprinting across an open glade, likely spooked from her assault on the valley. Even as tired as she was, it did not take her long to reach the bounding animals. It was a big herd, and Sandy killed and partially cooked half a dozen of the creatures with her fiery breath in a single pass.

She set down lightly amongst the charred remains and began eating voraciously. There was well over a thousand pounds of meat lying smoldering in the clearing, but she did not doubt for an instant her ability to consume every bit of it.

With her belly full, sleep became the dominant voice demanding her attention, so Sandy curled up in the open glade with two elk unconsumed and fell asleep. They would make a fine breakfast in the morning.

Unwanted faces and voices filled her dreams that night. She awoke to find her body twisted and deformed. Azerick stood over her with a face bereft of emotion.

"What have you done to me?"

"It is for the best, Sandy. I needed to make you stronger so you were more useful to me."

"You ruined me!"

"I made you better."

"You have no right!"

"Right is whatever I deem necessary for the survival of my people."

"What about my people?"

"Your people are the enemy."

"They are an unwilling enemy!" Sandy insisted.

"It does not matter. Had I not been able to block the Scions' control, I would have destroyed you too."

"You did," she whispered.

Sandy leapt into the sky and flew as fast as her wings could carry her. She raced south toward her desert home, the Scions' horrible voices commanding her to kill all the while. She ignored their whispered demands and pushed them to the back of her mind. A new voice, soft and loving, ascended to the forefront of her consciousness.

"Mama?"

"Come home, child"

Sandy commanded more speed, and the forests of northern Valeria flew past and became the massive fields of the Habberback Plains before turning into the red stone and sand of the Great Sand Desert. Her homing instincts took her straight to the cave she and her mother called home burrowed within the Bloodstone Mountains.

"Mama?" Sandy called out as she hesitantly stepped into the cavern.

"Come inside so I may see you. It has been so very long."

Sandy followed the sound of her mother's voice to the large cavern at the rear of the cave. Her mother had spent years carving out the sandstone to create a good home for her beloved daughter. She looked upon the deep claw marks in the stone and gently ran her muzzle over them.

"Who are you?" Sandy's mother demanded when she entered the cavern.

Sandy's voice quavered and caught in her throat. "It's me, Mama."

"No, my daughter is beautiful! You mock the name I gave her. You are not my child!"

"Mama, it *is* me!" Sandy cried.

"Be gone. The sight of you injures my heart and wounds my eyes!"

"Mama!"

"Go!"

"Mama!" Sandy shouted, then started awake.

She peered across the meadow wavering through her tears. The sun was just an arcing sliver peeking over the horizon. Sandy glanced at the two elk carcasses, but she had no appetite. She lay her head back down and prayed for the ground to swallow her up and make her just another mound of earth and grass. She thought her dreams had returned to haunt her when another voice intruded on her mind, but this one was deep and soft and held no malice.

Come to me.

Fear ran through her body. The voice felt so much like that of the Scions, only this one was not commanding her to kill.

"Who are you?"

Come to me.

"Where?"

Follow my thoughts, and I will show you the way. You know how. It is in your blood, child.

Sandy did not know to whom the voice belonged and wanted to ignore it and push it from her mind, but it continued to coax her with its deep and sonorous timbre. It felt like the reassuring words of a beloved grandparent, and she desperately needed reassurance now. Gripping the two remaining elk in her powerful hind claws, Sandy pushed into the air, summoning a helpful lift of air with her runic power. Carrying two adult elk would have been a challenging task, but the aid of her new magic made it almost easy to manage. She liked this new power, and it infuriated her to acknowledge it. It was an abomination. It made her an abomination, but it came so easily, and she hated herself for it.

Her artificial winds kept her aloft and speeding toward the Great Barrier Mountains far to the east. Sandy could feel the power stored within the runes had not fully recovered from her colossal outburst yesterday, so she took a more conservative approach to their use. Summoning the guiding winds proved to be a simple task and did not tax her strength. As long as she did not throw a giant, fiery tantrum, she could keep the winds blowing for some time.

The voice drew her like the needle of a compass. Sandy flew onward, never deviating and never losing her way. Soon, the towering peaks of the god-forged mountains loomed over her. She had never felt so small and insignificant in her life. Hundreds of peaks stabbed into the sky so far that if a person could stand upon their crests they would be cast in perpetual twilight.

Sandy heard the voice coming from above her, so she pumped her wings and soared upward where the air thinned and it became a challenge to breathe. Her wings found less and less resistance, and she surely would have faltered without her summoned wind to lift her like an invisible helping hand. She blinked hard when an enormous section of the cliff face wavered in her vision. For a moment, she feared the lack of air was affecting her senses, but then the stone vanished and revealed a gigantic cave dug into the side of the mountain. Sandy knew this was from where the voice came.

Gliding into the cavern was easy. It was so wide even her fully outstretched wings did not come close to brushing the sides. Sandy hesitated and examined the cave's surface. Most of the stone showed clear but greatly aged claw marks, and the floor was worn smooth except for some deep gouges left by taloned feet. The thick layer of dust indicated that even the most recent of those marks were made ages ago.

"Come inside. No harm shall come to you, child."

The voice came to her from farther inside the cave and not from within her mind. Sandy shuddered as the awesome power of the voice made her scales—her mutilated scales—vibrate. Dangling the two elk from her mouth, she slowly walked deeper into the cavern. The shaft remained straight and uniform, giving evidence to its constructed nature.

Only when Sandy had walked hundreds of yards into the mountain did the tunnel begin to widen into a great cavern. As she approached the chamber, a deep inhalation came from farther inside. She could feel the breeze it created caress her scales as some titanic creature drew in a great breath.

"You are younger than I had suspected, decades from a respectable mating age. I suddenly find you slightly less interesting." A soft chuckle echoed through the chamber.

"Who are you," Sandy asked.

"You are a guest in my home. Proper protocol dictates you give your name first."

"I'm sorry. I did not know."

"It is all right. The stench of humanity is heavy upon you. I suspect you have had more social experience with those crude creatures than with your own kind. What is your name?"

Sandy growled out her dragon name and felt the lie it now was catch in her throat. "My friends call me Sandy."

"Beautiful One Whose Scales Shine with the Glory of the Morning Sun. I should like to see such beauty. Sand dragons always were lovely to look upon."

Soft light illuminated the colossal cavern, and Sandy gasped at the sight of her host. Near the back of the chamber reclined a summit dragon older than the mountain in which it dwelled. Its mass was awe-inspiring, dwarfing Sandy the way her mother did when she was just a hatchling. His body was stark white and mottled with grey splotches, like stones jutting out of a snow-capped peak. A wave of ancient power and wisdom washed over her and made her knees buckle. The sudden anger she felt radiating from him made her flatten herself to the floor.

"Who has defiled you?" the venerable dragon demanded in indignation when he beheld the child's magically etched scales. "I sense the hand of a human involved, but something else as well. You have been touched by one of the elves' Guardians. What human and Guardian desecrated you?"

Sandy's mind was awash in confusion and uncertainty. Was Azerick her friend, her surrogate father? A few days ago, the answer would have come readily to her lips, but everything had changed so fast.

"Forgive me, child. My momentary anger has caused me to break protocol. I am One Whose Power Makes the Mountains Tremble. Now that formalities have been properly established, you may refer to me by my familiar name of Mordigar." Mordigar smiled at Sandy stretching submissively on the floor. "Relax, Sandy, I am not angry with you. You do not need to fear me. I imagine there is a long tale leading to your condition. Humor an old dragon and tell me about it."

Sandy stood back up and forced herself to meet Mordigar's eyes. "I brought something to eat. Would you like it?"

"Ah, how very appropriate of you. There is a bit of dragon in you after all. It has been centuries since I ate, and I admit it has been difficult for me not to be rude and snatch those lovely creatures from you."

"Take them both," Sandy offered. "I gorged yesterday, and I am still full."

"Guests must share in meals for protocol's sake." Her host severed the haunch from one of the elk with a deft slice of one claw. "Tell me of how this human and Guardian came to violate you so horribly."

"I was young, only two years old when my mother died. Azerick found me when he came into my cave for shelter. He shared his food and water with me. He was kind to me, and I followed him."

"If he was kind, why would he disrespect you and your mother in such a way?"

"The Scions took hold of my mind. I tried to resist them, but I could not. Azerick and his son Raijaun, he's the one with the Guardian magic, made the runes to protect me from them."

Mordigar studied the glyphs for a moment. "Now I see, but there is far more there than needed to protect you."

Sandy nodded. "He wanted to make me stronger so I could protect myself. That's what he said."

"You think he sacrificed your beautiful scales to make you a better weapon to use against the Scions?"

"I—I don't know. Partly, I guess."

"It would certainly fit their nature, but you say he has been kind to you for years. Had he used you for his own sake in the past?"

"No. He even died to rescue me and his human foster daughter from other humans who wanted to use us as weapons."

"He died?"

"It's another long story. He is a very powerful sorcerer. Death was mostly an inconvenience for him."

Mordigar chuckled. "As much as I distrust and dislike their kind, only humans are defiant enough to oppose even death and somehow triumph. Do you think he was remorseful about what he had done to you?"

"I think so. Does it matter?"

"That is something you must decide. Only you can decide what is more important to you. Is it your departed mother and the name she gave you, or the man who raised you, loved you, and even sacrificed his life to keep you safe?"

"It just hurts so much," Sandy said.

"Only true love does. Give it time. Answers often elude us until we stop trying to seek them out."

Sandy listened to her elder's wisdom and tried to absorb his words, but her pain ran deep and hot. She needed time to let it cool before she could search through the ashes of her emotions for answers.

"I told you about me. What about you? You must have seen so much in your lifetime. Why are you not under the Scions' control?"

Mordigar stared past his young guest and back up the river of time to an age long ago. "I have indeed seen and done much. I was there when the races rebelled, and I saw enough slaughter to dread the Scions' return. Like many of our kind, I isolated myself from the world, partly in fear and partly in shame at my actions. I entered the long sleep only a few centuries after we were freed from the gods' control. We knew our kind was marked for extinction, so we hid and slept. It was the Scions' call that woke me just days ago. Then I sensed your power and pain being unleashed and called to you."

"But the Scions cannot control you now?"

"My pride says it is because I am too powerful, but I think I am simply too stubborn. Their voices are muted, and the Scions are only able to command the young from behind their prison walls, but that will change once they break free and come fully into our world. Then, not even my cantankerous nature will provide a defense against them."

"What will happen then?"

"I will seek the destruction of the small races. If you choose to align yourself with them, then you and I shall be enemies. You will have to kill me to protect those you love."

"I could not kill you!"

"You can and you must if you and your family wish to survive. Do not look so forlorn. I am old, and I have no desire to be anyone's slave. Most every dragon you slay will thank you for their freedom. It is the way of our pride. Better to be dead than relegated to the duties of a cur."

"Morality and sentimentality aside, I do not have the power to kill someone like you."

"You have more power than you know. Sand dragons are far from the biggest of our kind, but your natural tenacity is unmatched. Your runes contain an awesome power if you learn to use them to their full potential. I can help you in that endeavor, though I fear our time together will be brief."

"You would help me kill our kind?"

"I would help you free us all. Tell me, do the Guardians still stand their vigil?"

"Azerick says they are all gone. Only his son Raijaun stands as a true Guardian."

"Then things are truly bleak. What of the small races? Do they stand united and strong?"

"I do not know. Azerick has been fighting to unite them and creating plans to defeat the Scions, but he struggles just to get the humans to work together. I don't know about the rest of them."

"It sounds as though your friend is working very hard to save everyone," Mordigar said.

Sandy dipped her head in acknowledgment. "Many people say he has become obsessed with it. People who once revered him now fear or even hate him. His own family is broken and suffering because he cannot take the time to tend to them properly."

"Despite what the stories tell us, few heroes are revered or even recognized in their time. It is not until the dust settles and people see the sacrifices a person made by putting others' needs before their own that they are appreciated."

Although Mordigar spoke of Azerick, Sandy knew his sage words were meant for her. She felt selfish for being so angry with Azerick. He had given up so much for so many people, and she had cursed and forsaken him for a name and pretty scales just like so many others.

"You said you can help me be stronger?" Sandy asked.

"Indeed. You have felt and used some of the runes' power, but that was only in their most basic of forms. The real power lies in combining them and devising ways to control the elemental forces of nature, often in very subtle ways, to achieve the greatest results. I fear we have little time, but I will show you what I can. But first, I could really use a proper meal."

Sandy made room for Mordigar to pass and followed the venerable dragon down the passage. Mordigar's colossal size made it impossible for him to stretch his wings out inside the tunnel. Instead, he threw his enormous bulk over the edge of the cliff and began a heart-dropping plummet to the ground several thousand feet below. He extended his massive wings and soared over the valley long before he came near the rocky ground. Able to unfurl her wings inside the tunnel, Sandy had no need to make the free fall but chose to anyway just for the thrill of it.

Just a few hundred feet from the ground, she summoned a powerful updraft to launch her skyward. Sandy quickly caught up with her elder as he glided along the high air currents. She streaked past Mordigar with a loud roar and a short burst of flame before circling back and making several tight loops around him as small flares of runic power punctuated each daring maneuver.

Mordigar chuckled at the youngling's antics with his deep basso rumbling as Sandy took up a steady position on his left. Sandy felt like a sparrow chasing after a hawk next to him. She could not contain the grin spread across her face at the joy of flying with her own kind. She had never realized how much she missed being with another dragon until now. It felt as though she were truly home for the first time since her mother died. Her smile faltered as guilt washed over her for feeling this way after everything Azerick had done to make her welcome in his life. Sandy felt outright horrified when she looked at Mordigar and thought about the possibility of being enemies one day soon. She pushed the idea from her mind and chose to live for the moment and accept the joy it brought her.

"We will stay close to the mountains to avoid attention," Mordigar said as they glided high above the base of the towering range. "There, perhaps three hundred feet above the foothills."

It took Sandy only a moment to locate what Mordigar had spotted. A large herd of mountain goats perched along the narrow ledges and outcroppings picked at shoots of grass growing between the rocks. A lone male called out a bleated warning when he sensed the predators gazing down upon them from on high. Sandy made to dip her wings and dive upon the tensely wary animals, but Mordigar stopped her.

"Wait. There are numerous avenues through which they can scatter and flee. I have an enormous appetite, and chasing dozens of goats all across the face of the mountain is needlessly exhausting. Study the terrain, look for areas where you can herd them together, and use your magic to corral them."

Sandy scanned the rocky terrain and spotted a deep gulley. "The washout there would channel them together. Once inside it, they would naturally follow its course downward along the easiest path."

"Very good. Use your magic to get them into the gulch."

Sandy took just a moment to formulate a plan and plunged toward the nervous prey. The goats bolted in the opposite direction just as she had expected. Earth runes flared along her body as she conjured pillars of stone ahead and above the fleeing animals, forcing them to turn toward the washout. The goats, seeing only a single route of escape, leapt into the wide cleft and bounded down the mountainside.

Mordigar flew to her side. "Excellent, now think on how you can blend the elements to capture as many of them at once as you can."

The young dragon thought less about magic and more about the forces of nature and how they acted alone and in concert. It would be a fairly simple task to swoop down and strafe the goats with her fiery breath, but she knew that was not what Mordigar was trying to teach her. Earth and water runes lit up her form for a brief moment.

Heedless of the impending danger, the goats continued their headlong dash toward the base of the mountain. Seconds before reaching the bottom where they could scatter, the ground beneath their narrow hooves gave way, and the hapless animals tumbled into the large sinkhole Sandy had created just beneath the surface. A few of the rearmost goats leapt to the side and scrambled past the pit.

"Let them go," the elder dragon said when Sandy made to go after them. "We have enough and do not want to decimate the herd in its entirety. Some must be left to repopulate."

Sandy nodded her understanding and followed her new mentor as he dived toward the terrified goats trying to leap and scramble out of the hole. A short burst of Mordigar's intense flame breath ended their frantic attempts at escape. The two dragons set down near the edge of the hole. Sigils flashed and the ground beneath the goats rose up to create a smoking platter of roasted meat.

"Very nicely done. One should not eat off the ground like an animal when it can be avoided. You are as clever as you are lovely."

Sandy was glad dragons could not blush. "My scales are hideous, but at least I am better suited to catching lunch."

"Do not let your outward appearance define you. You are far more than your scales or your birth name. Your mother chose your name out of love and what she felt best suited you. Now, as you reach maturity, you must decide on a new name, one that befits your character and actions. Do you think I came out of my egg and made the mountains tremble beneath my awesome power?"

"I suppose not. What was your birth name?"

"It was so long ago I have forgotten. What else have you learned other than how to catch a meal?"

Sandy doubted the old dragon had forgotten a thing, but she let him change the subject without further prodding. She had thought there was far more to this hunt than simply capturing food. Mordigar was the type to make every action one of learning.

"I could manipulate my enemy on the battlefield in much the same way," Sandy answered.

"Excellent. Killing your foe is not the most challenging aspect of warfare. Getting them into a position in which you can kill them with the least risk and greatest effect is the true key to battle. A courageous warrior will face an oncoming horde and sell his life dearly. A smart warrior will kill his foes before they even know they have been engaged. He is then free to seek more enemies to slay."

"I understand."

"I have no doubt that you do. Eat up. We will both need our strength."

Despite her earlier assertions of not being hungry, the use of her rune magic had quickly eaten up her reserves, and Sandy eagerly tore into their meal. She gave Mordigar several sidelong glances as she dined, wondering if his comment about them both needing their strength meant more than just her training. Sandy wished she had the power to make this time with him continue so they would never face each other as enemies. She knew she could not, and Sandy finally understood all of the sacrifices Azerick had made for the sake of the mortal races.

CHAPTER 14

Headmaster Florent strode the streets of Southport wearing a simple set of robes with the hood pulled up in place of her official robes of office. It was best if as few people as possible knew of her comings and goings this day. There were numerous questions that were best not asked, and if even a hint of their answers were discovered, it would mean instant execution. She deeply disliked these cloak and dagger schemes, but the safety of the realm was at stake, and the king himself had ordered her actions.

She approached one of the gates made magical with the help of Azerick's son and beckoned to the Academy officer on duty. The man walked cautiously toward her then made to clasp his hands in front of his chest in salute when he saw her face beneath the hood. A sharp hiss from the headmaster stopped him before he could make the deferential motion.

"Headmaster, what brings you to the gate?" Magus Welch's confusion was evident on his face and in his tone.

"Absolutely nothing, because I was never here," Headmaster Florent responded.

The magus gave a short nod. "I understand."

"You cannot possibly understand what never happened. I was never here, and I never asked your people to open the gate to Brightridge. If anyone asks why you activated the gate, you will tell them it was to test your crew."

"I understand...I think."

"Don't think, just open the gate."

"Yes, Headmaster."

"Who?"

"Nobody, I was just going to run my people through a quick drill."

"Good work."

Magus Welch hastened back to the gate and began barking orders. A bell started ringing, its cadence signaling a live drill. Guardsmen stopped traffic and ushered travelers away from the gate. Two more wizards appeared and began channeling power into the pillars framing Southport's northeastern trade gate. The runes carved into the stones lit up, and a shimmering screen stretched across the divide. Although she could not possibly see it, Maureen knew a nearly identical scene was playing out in Brightridge.

The headmaster kept her head down as she bustled through the gateway. She fought the wave of vertigo and nausea associated with gate travel as she stumbled through to the other side. She tried to imagine the chaos of tens of thousands of people using the gates with the threat of slaughter stampeding them through. Maureen shuddered at the thought of the death rapidly approaching the kingdom. A second tremble shook her body knowing she was planning the execution of the man seemingly doing his damnedest to save them.

Brightridge showed every level of militarization as Southport did. Patrols roamed the streets in numbers nearly equal to civilians, and not a man or woman walked unarmed. Massive ballistae were mounted and manned on nearly every roof capable of supporting them. Borrowing a tactic from North Haven's ships, the defenders strung thick chains and ropes between roofs to impede dragons from landing and rampaging through the streets.

Only the stoutest buildings could hope to stop one of the powerful creatures, but anything that could slow or hinder them was worth the effort. Wells, buckets, and huge cisterns of water sat at almost every intersection, ready to extinguish the inevitable flames. Like Southport, every building not occupied had been razed, its timbers carted off to limit combustibles or used in the construction of barriers or weaponry.

The people traveled with the cautious and furtive movements of a city already under siege. When they moved, they stuck close to the buildings and watched others traversing the streets with looks of support as well as suspicion. Almost no one stood idle. Teams of men and women looked over fortifications and continually sought ways to improve them. Anyone not gainfully employed stayed indoors unless they had urgent business elsewhere.

Headmaster Florent likewise stuck to the shadows cast by the buildings as she made her way toward the Temple of the Sun, avoiding eye contact with the few other pedestrians. She had only visited the great religious center twice before, but finding it was a simple affair despite Brightridge's vastness. Only Castle Brightridge exceeded it in size within the city, and no structure or complex in all of Valeria came close to matching it in splendor. The polished gold dome of the central structure shone like a second sun setting in the heart of the city. On a clear day, it was impossible to gaze directly at it without fear of being struck blind by its brilliance.

"Headmaster," a voice called out, breaking her out of her rather singular focus.

Maureen gasped and instinctively drew in the Source when a man stepped away from a darkened alcove. She started to chastise herself for her carelessness, but she quickly deduced that this man was far more adept at this sort of game than she was. He was not large, perhaps a couple of inches shorter than she was, and sported a lean build. Although he wore the unadorned robes of a priest, Maureen knew his skills and duties did not involve preaching or tending to the less fortunate.

"Forgive me for startling you, Headmaster. My name is Brother Sweet, Anthony Sweet. Bishop Howarth informed me of your impending arrival and requested I escort you to him."

The headmaster stiffened her composure as if his unexpected presence had not bothered her in the least. "Proceed, Brother Sweet."

The priest took a position to her right nearest the street. Although he led, the man was never more than a half step ahead of the formidable wizard. Maureen doubted it was out of any distrust of her but from years of habit never to put his back to anyone. The man moved with the graceful economy of a skilled fighter, but his lean stature suggested he was not a typical holy warrior.

"Brother Sweet, how familiar are you with the nature of my meeting with Bishop Howarth?"

"Intimately, Headmaster, but do not be concerned. Only the bishop and I know of the existence of this meeting or its details. I have the bishop's full confidence, and I hope to have yours as well. Not even Jarvin, who approached the bishop with his problem, is aware of my role."

"And that role is…?"

"The swift and preferably subtle execution of the fell spawn Azerick Giles."

Brother Sweet's calm assuredness in carrying out his task convinced the headmaster he had done this sort of thing before, although she was certain never against such a powerful foe. Bishop Howarth must have had more success in discovering a way to kill the sorcerer than she had, hence his request for the meeting and Brother Sweet's involvement.

Maureen had little else to ask the man, and Brother Sweet volunteered no further information or conversation whatsoever. They soon came to the outer boundaries of the Temple of the Sun. The walls surrounding the mini city were thick bars of wrought iron twelve feet tall, supported by pillars of white marble every twenty feet.

The entire complex was designed so that nothing could cast a substantial shadow anywhere on the grounds. The polished main dome and numerous smaller domed minarets reflected the sun onto the surrounding buildings in such a way as to destroy most forms of daytime darkness. To combat the summer heat, fountains dotted the courtyards, gardens, and larger gathering places inside and around the temple complex.

Brother Sweet led his charge around the outside of the central temple and entered a small garden area near the southeast corner. He directed the headmaster to follow him down a very narrow opening between the wings of two buildings. The passage made an abrupt right and ended at a solid iron door. It was the only place on the grounds she had seen where anything less than total daylight was allowed to exist.

The priest produced a large cruciform key with the symbol of the sun stamped in its handle. The door opened with remarkable ease and silence despite its stout construction. Brother Sweet made a sweeping gesture to usher the wizard in ahead of him. Headmaster Florent was not surprised when the man would not negotiate the narrow stairs leading beneath the heart of the temple with her at his back.

She stepped past the unusual priest and descended the stairs. The air was noticeably cool and stale. Headmaster Florent spied the flickering light of a lamp or torch at the base of the stairs some twenty feet down. Given the angle of the construction, she could not see into the chamber below until she reached the bottom. Maureen found herself in the outer foyer of what was almost certainly a vast crypt. A stone table surrounded by oak chairs occupied the center of the room. Upon the table lay a folded cloth obviously concealing something beneath. The only figure in the room was Bishop Howarth.

"Welcome, Headmaster Florent. I trust Brother Sweet has made a favorable impression?"

"He seems very capable, Bishop. Congratulations on your appointment. I apologize for my late tidings. It has been a rather hectic time."

"It certainly has, and I appreciate you coming so quickly."

The headmaster crossed to the large table and ran a finger through the dust accumulated on the back of one of the chairs. "You certainly chose an apt location for this meeting."

"I believe this is where Bishop Caalendor held many of his meetings during the usurpation. It seems to do well in holding onto the secrets discussed within."

"You *believe* he made his plans here?" Maureen asked, arching an eyebrow at the head priest.

The bishop smiled at her veiled accusation. "I was never a part of his schemes. The former bishop knew me for a staunch moderate and never included me in his plans."

"I shall take your word on it," Maureen replied. "Jarvin trusts you. If that trust is misplaced then let it be on his head. I am hoping you called me here because you have had more luck finding a solution to our mutual dilemma than I have."

"Are you saying nothing in the great stores of artifacts hoarded by the Academy is capable of killing this creature Lord Giles has become?"

"I am not saying that, but let us be clear. This is an assassination, not a battle to the death, which neither of us could be assured of winning. His death must be instantaneous. To try and fail to kill him is to court disaster. The Academy has the power to scour a city clean off the face of the world, but so does he. That sort of battle is the last thing we need or might be capable of winning after we fight these false gods."

"If you expect him to act in such a cataclysmic way if he learns of our intent, perhaps we should reconsider this plan in its entirety. I like to think well enough of you that you find this sort of action undesirable."

"The only thing I am certain of is his total unpredictability. He might just shake his finger at us and paddle us like errant children, or he may send a mountain crashing down upon our Academy and temple. No, personal feelings aside, Azerick is too great a threat to the kingdom to be allowed to roam free. Gods, he murdered a notable lord in the king's hall with no more feeling than squashing a fly."

Bishop Howarth nodded. "I understand Lord Atwater's actions were treasonous and warranted execution."

"Not without at least a semblance of a trial. Even if Jarvin secretly applauded Azerick's solution, publicly he cannot support such ruthless, dictatorial actions. So this is where we stand. Do you have what we need to accomplish it within that bundle on the table?"

"I believe so." The priest pulled back the cloth to reveal three swords lying beneath.

"Swords?"

"Not just any swords: the Swords of the Saints. Do you know of the elves' disastrous attempt to leave this world and take their entire physical nation with them?"

"Vaguely. They tore open some kind of rift and nearly destroyed themselves."

"The rift they opened allowed numerous demons to escape the abyss. This was before the creation of Solarian's Light. The Church had no holy warriors with which to battle undead or demonic scourges at the time, so we prayed to Solarian to aid us when dozens of them crossed the frozen north and terrorized our kingdom. His answer came in the form of four swords, blessed by him for the specific purpose of destroying demons."

"I only see three."

"Brother Sweet carries one."

"Assassins within the Church? You surprise me, Bishop."

"Sometimes in order to bring the light, one must strike from the shadows. I am sure you have a few people of such skills within the Hall of Inquisition?"

Maureen nodded. "We do."

"You know Lord Giles better than I. Do you think this will be effective against him?"

"From what I understand, he was originally possessed by a demon but later died. His soul then travelled to the body of the demon that possessed him, thus becoming the possessor. My sources tell me his son, Daebian, stabbed him with a very special sword that pulled the demon's spirit from his body. So we have a human soul in a demonic body. Whether that is sufficient to make him especially vulnerable to these blades I cannot say. Such a thing is more within your expertise."

"Quite right. A demon's soul is much like a bloodstain. Once it defiles your clothing, it will always leave a trace no matter how much you scrub. So there is an element of the demon's essence still within Lord Giles who possesses its physical form despite what he likes to show the rest of us. I am certain the Swords of the Saints are capable of killing him swiftly. There exists but one other conundrum we must recognize."

"What is that?"

"His son."

"Which one, the pirate or the monstrosity? It is a toss-up as to which is the more dangerous."

"If Daebian tried to kill his father, I doubt he will have any objection to anyone who might finish the job. What can you tell me of his other son? How might he react if we execute his father?"

The headmaster pulled out a chair and sat down heavily. What had been a distasteful but necessary action was quickly spilling over into talks of massacring a family line.

"I know how horrible this sounds," Bishop Howarth said, "but we must consider all the possible consequences of our actions."

"Raijaun is very powerful, possibly a match even for his father if he ever truly embraces his gift. But he is also kind and steady. He came to the Academy to help us create the gates. I am certain he overheard many unkind words regarding his existence, but he never showed any anger or aggression. He rather reminded me of his father when he first came to the Academy, only much more mature and less volatile. I cannot say how he will react. No one can be more fearsome than a peaceful man pushed to fight."

"But could we destroy him with the swords as well if it became necessary?"

"He was created with the physical and spiritual essences of Azerick, so he too should be as vulnerable as his father. If we are considering killing him because of a potentiality, where do we draw the line? Do you think Lady Miranda, Duchess Mellina, or the people of North Haven will simply turn a blind eye to his execution? Azerick Giles is practically worshipped in that city."

"Insurrection is a problem for the king. Mine is dealing with unholy abominations threatening our world and way of life. First and foremost are these Scions and their horde. A very close second is Azerick Giles. If his son remains peaceful, I have no problem leaving him be. But if he decides to threaten our people like his father has done, then I will spend my last breath putting him down as well. Are you willing to stand and do the same?"

The headmaster ran her hand lightly over the hilt of one of the swords and stared blankly for several moments. "I am."

"I thought as much. I suggest you take the swords to His Majesty as quickly as you can. I suspect you shall keep a blade for one of your special officers?"

"It is my intent."

"Good. Jarvin will then have the other two to dole out as he sees fit. This will allow us to strike from multiple angles. If one of our agents cannot reach him, our odds are greatly increased that someone else can. When would you like to depart?"

Maureen rolled the swords into a bundle and tied them with a length of cord. "The sooner we set this in motion the better. My sources tell me we have very little time."

"What transpires in North Haven?"

"The idiot created a Source pool then tried to shift it to another plane just as the elves attempted to do with their entire nation."

The holy man's face paled. "Dear god of light, what happened?"

"The fool apparently succeeded, only no one has seen him in two days."

"What about the barrier?"

"I'm not sure, but it is bad. The son says he can no longer do anything to maintain it. Whatever is going to happen is going to unfold very soon."

"Weeks, months?"

"I am betting more likely it is days. Did you know dragons have been spotted flying in the skies?"

"I had heard some gossiping but have seen nothing myself."

"The ones we have seen appear to be mostly younger dragons and are staying away from the large cities. The garrison still in Argoth managed to bring one down a few days ago when it got too overzealous. I must assume it was not prepared to face the wizards left behind."

"Why do you think only the younger drakes are mucking about?"

"I can only theorize, but my guess is whatever power the Scions have over them is not strong enough to dominate the elder dragons—yet."

Bishop Howarth looked hopeful. "Perhaps they never will."

"Unlikely. The Scions had complete dominion over the dragons during the Great Revolution. I imagine that will return when they are free of their prison."

"It sounds like you should probably hurry. Brother Sweet will see you back to the gate."

The Academy's headmaster clutched the bundle of swords beneath her robes and climbed the stairs with Brother Sweet trailing just behind her. The man was so unobtrusive that Maureen had forgotten he was even in the room until it was time for her to leave. The priest led her back toward the gates by a different route from which they came with the same quiet professionalism he had displayed throughout the entire meeting.

"Brother Sweet, how many men have you killed during the course of your duties?"

"Five, Headmaster."

"Five? Forgive me, but that does not seem like many given what I assume is your primary mission."

"One should not keep score to give testament to their abilities. It cheapens the lives of those we must take. I was brought to the seminary when I was four years old. By the time I was seven, the brothers recognized a natural affinity for many of the skills I now employ. I have been training for a moment like this nearly all my life. When the moment comes, you can almost be certain it will be I who thrust the first blade."

"Just know this, Brother Sweet; Azerick Giles is not a man. He has not been one for many years. Underestimate him and you will likely doom us all."

"I would never commit such a sin, Headmaster."

"Good luck to you, Brother Sweet."

"May Solarian's light shield you from the darkness."

CHAPTER 15

Azerick stared into the too-small eyes of the creature and saw nothing but rage and malign intent. He took two steps back but stopped when his feet touched the water. The deep pool, high-sided cliff, and rushing river afforded no escape in that direction.

The sorcerer raised his hand and spoke softly. "Look, I don't want to be here any more than you want me here. So how about you just go back into your jungle and I leave your territory?" The creature responded with a growling hiss and lunged with its clawed hands outstretched to rend him to pieces. "Of course not."

Azerick leapt to the side and brought his staff around to strike the beast hard in the side of its bony head. The creature stumbled and fell headlong into the pool but quickly regained its feet. It splashed out of the water but took a moment to study Azerick. Its foe was stronger and faster than it had anticipated, and it knew it faced a powerful adversary.

Azerick held his staff out before him as he slowly backed away from the creature. Broad green leaves brushed his arms and the back of his neck as he penetrated the dense jungle. Refusing to surrender its foe to the jungle, the vicious monster rushed forward, slashing at Azerick with its lethal claws. Azerick backpedaled, ducked, and parried the swift attacks with his staff, but the creature struck with the speed of a cat and the power of a draft horse.

Azerick felt every jarring blow in his bones with each successful parry. He blocked another stroke but failed to avoid a swift left paw immediately following his successful blocking of its right. The sharp claws shredded his shirt and tore deep, bloody furrows in his right shoulder. Azerick's anger mounted and he struck back, no longer willing to stick to the defensive. Now it was the creature's turn to withdraw and fend off the intruder's assault. Wood and arcanum struck flesh and bony plates with a series of resounding clacks. His frustration at not being able to call upon his magic to end this fight grew, and his blows began raining down even faster and harder.

The monster's knees buckled, and he thought the battle was drawing near its conclusion until something leapt onto his back. Azerick felt half a dozen claws sink into the flesh between his neck and shoulders. Fetid breath assaulted his senses as the creature brought its fang-filled maw down toward his throat. He reached over his shoulder with his free hand, grabbed his newest attacker by the wrist, and flung it into the trunk of a nearby tree.

It was the same sort of creature only much smaller, probably a full head shorter than Azerick's human form. Azerick had no time to contemplate the greater meaning of this new arrival as the larger of the brutes let out a roar and charged. Its assault was wild and frantic as it tried to sink its claws into Azerick's flesh. A swift kick sent Azerick stumbling backward into the rough trunk of a tree. He ducked and felt chunks of bark rain down atop his head as the brute's slashing claws tore it to splinters.

Azerick sought out a small amount of power stored within his staff and sent it into the arcanum ball affixed to the end. He hated to use even that limited bit, but he needed to end this fight and get back to the site of the rift. He rolled past the creature and struck it hard in the gut when it turned to face him. The monster doubled over as the air was blasted from its lungs. Azerick then brought the arcanum end of his staff down onto the back of the beast's head with a bright flash of expended arcane power. The brute's eyes rolled back in its head and its skull split under the impact.

A cry and a hiss brought Azerick around just as the smaller creature lunged for him. He struck the creature in the midriff with his staff, flipped it over his head, and shaping the arcanum ball into a spear, pinned it to the ground. The creature let out a high-pitched shriek that made Azerick's ears ring until it fell silent. The larger brute groaned and reached out a hand toward the smaller one before closing its eyes and exhaling its last breath.

Studying the larger creature, he determined it to be the father of the smaller one. The younger one had obviously come in defense of its parent who may have acted only to defend its young from Azerick's unexpected intrusion. Given the look of the creatures, a fight may have been unavoidable as they appeared to be powerful predators. The last thing he wanted to do was stand around and wait for the mother to show up. Propping himself on his hands and knees, Azerick retrieved the door handle from his pocket, stuck the shaft into the dirt, turned, and pulled. The handle pulled out of the ground with no effect.

"Of course. I really hate this place," Azerick mumbled.

Scanning the trees overhead, he picked an opening in the dense canopy created by the river, shifted into his demonic form, and launched himself skyward. Azerick pumped his leathery wings and rose above the light-dampening hood that cast this world in perpetual gloom. The moment he reached the unfiltered light of the sun, thousands of winged creatures with bodies the size of cats, bat-like wings, and large hooked beaks burst up from the jungle canopy like a second skin being shed and blown away.

The mass converged into a huge swarm and enveloped Azerick, biting and slashing at him with beaks and talons. Azerick fought back, striking them with his staff and snapping their necks with his bare hands, but they showed no fear and their numbers were legion. Within moments, Azerick's body sported numerous bleeding gashes, and his wings were in shreds. Diving for what he hoped was the relative safety of the jungle floor, he struck the treetops and let gravity drag him down. The foliage was so dense he had to practically swim through it as he pulled himself down, all the while being harried, scratched, and bitten by the flying creatures.

Azerick burst through the lower canopy and plummeted forty feet to the jungle floor. He managed to slow his fall only slightly with his ruined wings. He lay on the ground looking up at the canopy overhead, listened to the angry screeches of the flying creatures, and counted the numerous injuries inflicted upon his body. He eventually gave up inventorying his aches and just tried to catch his breath and let his wounds heal.

"I really hate this place," Azerick growled again.

The borghast beast sniffed at her dead mate and child. The blood was hours old, almost half a day. Borghasts were the undisputed rulers of this world, and their hunting territory was vast. It had to be when so few animals would willingly come within ten miles of the top-tier predators. Sticking her bony snout in the air, the matron picked up the strange scent of her mate and child's killer. She did not recognize it, but that came as no surprise. Few creatures would attack even a young borghast much less one guarded by its father, and any creature capable of that feat was powerful.

It did not matter to her. This creature killed her mate and it would die. Borghasts mated for life, and it was unlikely she would choose another. She had waited until she was at the height of maturity before choosing her young, virile male in hopes of producing a strong offspring. There was not another of her species for hundreds of miles. She put her nose to the ground and found the scent of blood. She flicked out her tongue, committed its taste to memory, and began loping through the jungle with preternatural silence. The killer would die, and she would make a nest of its bones to seek solace in her future of lonely isolation.

Azerick shoved the huge green leaf away from his face as he pressed through the inhospitable jungle, which elicited another shower of warm water soaking him even further. Not that he could get any wetter if he jumped into a lake. The jungle was hot and steamy, and droplets of water covered everything. Every piece of foliage he pushed aside or brushed against brought on a brief but soaking rain shower. He hated the jungle to the point he actually longed for the dry, weatherless world of the abyss.

Fighting through the vegetation and the constant deluge made it difficult for him to focus enough to grab at the few wisps of the Source to recharge his staff. It was a painstaking endeavor as the Source was a grain of salt amidst a pile of sand, and it was up to Azerick to pluck it out. Not only was the Source almost nonexistent, so were the signs of any life larger than whatever tiny lizard or mammal scurried about the jungle floor or climbed through the leaves. He never caught sight of the creatures and was aware of their presence only through the sound and tiny rainstorms made by their furtive scampering.

He was grateful he at least had his staff, and not just because it would provide the only real source of power required to reopen the rift. The arcanum blade, shaped at the end, sliced through the tough vines and thick stalks trying their best to prevent him from reaching his destination. If it were not for the fact he could feel the energy seeping through the rift's scar, he would likely have walked in circles for an eternity, unable to even find the mountain above which it lay.

Azerick stopped and listened as the hairs on the back of his neck stood on end and a chill ran down his spine. Nothing moved within the jungle around him. The chirping of tiny wildlife and the buzzing of insects were gone. Even the dew covering the broad leaves of the plants seemed afraid to fall. Something was close by. Something dangerous. Azerick tried to see past the foliage, but his vision barely stretched beyond the length of his staff.

The sorcerer stood as still as a statue and listened, but he heard nothing other than the sound of his breathing and the rhythmic thumping of his heart. The moisture dotting his brow was no longer solely from the pervasive mist fogging the air. He was in the midst of something dangerous, and he had no idea where it was. But it was very close.

The wall of vegetation to his left exploded in a mass of shredded leaves, stems, and stalks as something huge and powerful burst from hiding. Azerick tried to turn and leap away and felt the sharp burn of the creature's claws carve furrows down his shoulder blade. The force of the blow sent him crashing into the brush and would have shattered the bones of a mortal man.

Azerick rolled to his feet and held his staff out defensively. The creature paused and growled as if to study him or was just surprised that he survived and was still able to fight. It looked much like the other two he had fought with its too-big teeth, ridiculously large claws, and bony plates and horns covering its leathery body, only this one was significantly larger and angrier than the others had been.

"You must be seeking vengeance," Azerick said despite assuming the creature could not possibly understand his words. "I did not mean to encroach upon your territory, and I am sorry if I killed those you cared about. They gave me no choice except to defend myself."

The borghast matron studied the creature crouching before her, unable to comprehend how it was not dead or crippled. It was a small, weak-looking animal. How could it have killed her mate and child? It made soft, almost mewling sounds. Was it whining in pain, or were they sounds of communication? She was unsure but did not care either way. It had killed her family and destroyed her legacy. It would die.

The borghast beast lunged and Azerick tried to dive away again, but he was too slow. The creature was amazingly swift for being so large and powerful. It wrapped the clawed fingers of both hands around his chest and waist, lifted him from the ground, and went careening through the jungle. Leaves and branches whipped him as if he were running a gauntlet of punishing schoolmarms wielding switches. The forest was a blur of green; the only clear, fixed point his vision could find were the baleful eyes of the borghast beast and its wicked, slavering jaws.

Azerick's body twisted and contorted as he shifted into Klaraxis's form. His transformation was swift, and the borghast matron was not able to adjust to the sudden change in equilibrium. Azerick and the creature went tumbling still locked in an embrace. He brought his staff in front of him just in time to prevent the beast's jaws from clamping onto his head. The borghast beast bit down on the staff, shook its head, and tore it from Azerick's grasp. Azerick got his legs between him and the monster and heaved, sending the creature crashing back along the trail of crushed and shattered foliage.

The matron spat the stick from her mouth and tried to understand the sudden change that had come over the creature. She did not know how it could transform into something completely different and obviously more powerful, but that did explain how it was able to kill her family. She would have to be more cautious in her attack, but she would never relent.

Azerick got to his feet at nearly the same time as the creature. The two foes squared off perhaps thirty feet apart, studied each other's movements, and formulated plans of attack and defense. The borghast moved first, launching itself across the short span separating them in a second. Azerick leapt to the side and used his freshly healed wings to lift him up and away from the beast's path. He summoned his staff to his hand in mid-leap and swung it in a powerful arc, clobbering the creature in the side of the head.

The borghast matron tumbled from the force of the blow but quickly shook it off and gained her feet. She was bigger than this creature and likely stronger, but it was swift, smart, and far from weak. It fought well, but she was cunning too. She would need to figure out a way to use her territory to her advantage. The intruder had wings, but it did not try to fly off. It must know about the wallix roosting above and the death they represented for anything encroaching upon their treetop homes.

Azerick and the creature stood staring at one another once more. He thought perhaps his strike had stunned the creature, but its eyes were focused and caught every movement and twitch of his muscles. His ears picked up the sound of the river raging a short distance off to his right. A plan leapt to mind and he ran as fast as his legs would carry him and the resistance of the jungle allowed. He had gotten the jump on the beast, but it was more adept at navigating the thick vegetation than he was.

Before she was able to devise her next attack, the shape-shifter bolted for the dense jungle. If it thought to lose her in the undergrowth, it was a foolish attempt. Nothing could escape a borghast on the ground.

Azerick jumped into the air and used his wings to lift him over the thickest obstacles but kept well below the towering treetops. Despite the numerous vines crisscrossing the jungle like a ship's rigging, he was able to glide through the openings between trees enough to put some distance between himself and the creature desperate to kill him.

The matron raced furiously after the cowardly killer and roared her anger when it flew above the undergrowth and began gliding through the trees. It began outpacing her, but her sense of smell allowed her to follow the creature even after it fled from sight. Let it run. Borghasts were tireless hunters. She could and would track it around the world if need be. It would eventually tire, but she never would. She knew the river was nearby and wondered if the creature was going to try to lose her by flying over it. It was a risky attempt and almost as dangerous as flying above the trees. The wallix rarely flew into the jungle itself, but they would dive toward the river and attack anything wandering away from the protection of the shadowy interior.

She flicked out her tongue, tasting the air and "seeing" beyond the concealing foliage. She picked up the creature's heat pattern and the electrical impulses its body generated. She slowed her pace and stalked forward, licking at the air and processing the vast amount of information it relayed to her brain. The killer had stopped near the edge of the river, perhaps aware that to try to fly across held significant risk. She quickened her pace without concern as the roar of the rushing water easily masked any sound she might make. The matron peered between the large fronds and spotted her foe standing in a slight clearing, looking across the small gorge cutting a twisting path through the jungle.

She tensed her muscles, dug her toe claws into the soil, and burst through the undergrowth, holding her furious bellow until it was too late for the creature to avoid her attack. The black-skinned killer spun just in time for her to rake her claws through his throat and down to his abdomen. The borghast matron faltered in mid-flight when her talons failed to find purchase, and her body met no more resistance than if her foe were made of fog.

She tumbled as she hit the ground and dug her claws into the dirt to arrest her slide toward the chasm's edge. Somehow, the creature had managed to deceive her eyes and had not been where she thought he was. She did not understand what kind of chameleon power allowed it to do such a thing, but she would not fall for it twice. It may be able to trick her eyes, many creatures in the jungle had such abilities, but it could not fool her tongue. She had been overconfident of the kill, but she would not miss again.

Azerick felt the wind generated by the monstrous creature's passage through his illusion gently caress his skin. He needed to hide very close by in case the creature was able to discern the nature of his ruse through scent. His attacker clawed at the ground to prevent going over the edge, but Azerick was not going to let that happen. He charged the borghast beast and struck her in the chest with his staff as she stood. The strike sent her arcing over the cliff and plummeting toward the raging water. The fearsome flyers exploded from the treetops in cacophonous fluttering of wings and squawks and swooped down after the falling, howling creature. The borghast struck the water with an imperceptible splash, and the wallix arced back into the sky and returned to their arboreal aerie.

Azerick watched the river wash the creature away as it did him. He hoped the water carried it just as far and that the creature would give up its pursuit of him. The sorcerer knew the desire to be fruitlessly optimistic. He sensed the vengeance raging within the creature's heart and recognized it as a mirror of his own. They would fight again unless he could escape this world.

He glanced up at the treetops and was glad he had not tried to cross the expanse. He figured out a swifter form of travel and put it to use, gripping the tree trunks with his claws like a squirrel and leaping and gliding across the open spaces. If the river carried the borghast as far as it did him, and with this swifter form of locomotion, he should be able to put at least two days between him and the creature. Hopefully, he would have enough time to tear the rift back open and escape before it found him again.

Despite his best efforts, Azerick could not help but think about his home and what they were facing, wondering if they too were fighting for their lives at this very moment. The Scions had been close to escaping when he shifted his tower. If they broke free while he was trapped in this world, the consequences could be disastrous. He needed to get back, and there was little to nothing he could do to hasten his return. It would take more than an hour to replace the power it had taken just to create his minor illusion. Azerick pushed his fears to the back of his mind. They would only serve to distract him, and distractions would get people killed.

Azerick swung from vines, flew through clearings, and leapt from tree to tree when the jungle became too dense. He was grateful for Klaraxis's strength and ability to fly. Were he required to make his way through this inhospitable place as a human, the fate of his world would likely be decided before he ever had the chance to escape it. Movement became trickier as the ground began sloping upward and the distance between trees became greater. Patches of open sky managed to break through the green ceiling in places, some large enough to tease small swarms of wallix into chasing him a short distance until he was able to reach a denser section of forest.

After hours of climbing and gliding, he finally reached the plateau atop the mountain. Had he been forced to walk, the trip would have taken days, days he did not have. He did not even have the hours he was spending, but his control over the situation was limited. Although the trees blocked his view, he could feel the remnants of the rift cutting a jagged scar across the sky. Azerick sent his otherworldly senses out to probe the tear between worlds, and as he had suspected, he found the veil thin and frayed. It would heal over time and disappear, but it was still raw enough that he should be able to tear it back open even with the paltry power at his disposal.

Azerick began to formulate what he would need to do in order to achieve his goals and blessed Duncan for his education in rune magic. Despite this world being nearly bereft of the Source, there was still power within the elements, power he could harness with runes. He stared down the mountain slope and faced a quandary. He could begin carving the runes he needed to open the rift, but if the creature appeared and attacked him it could disrupt his work. He had an idea to lay a trap and hopefully conclude their battle, but it would take time, time he did not have to squander. How long would it take the creature to track him down again, assuming it did not drown? If he focused on opening the rift, he might be able to leave this place before it caught back up with him. That scenario was unlikely. It was simply going to take too much time to gather enough energy to open the rift.

He studied his surroundings, most notably the clustered trees and draping vines. Azerick searched his memory and brought his engineering texts to the forefront of his mind. His plan was a simple one, but the execution was very complex. He started by climbing the green trunks of the trees and gathering long strands of vines. He wove them together using line splicing techniques Balor had taught him and created a single braided rope hundreds of feet long.

Azerick set the rope aside and formed the arcanum ball on his staff into an axe head, making it look much like a halberd. The mystical metal cut into the tree with ease and carved out a large wedge in the trunk with only a few minutes of chopping. Studying the lay of the ground and the formation of the treetops, he chose another tree and began hacking at it until it too had a large chunk cut out of its base. The wallix squawked and took to the air, but they returned once Azerick moved on to another tree.

Azerick took up the huge, coiled length of vine and threaded it as close as he could get through the treetops without attracting those flying nightmares. He wedged his staff between two moss-covered boulders and tied the end of the vine to its middle. Azerick grabbed another vine, secured it near the top of the last tree, and pulled with all his might. Angry wallix took to the skies as the tree swayed, groaned, and cracked as it tilted sharply.

The vine snapped taut and pulled the other trees down with it. This moment would determine if his plan had a chance of working or if he had just wasted half the day. The row of trees leaned and cracked in succession but did not fall as the vine supported their weight and kept them upright but leaning several degrees. Satisfied his trap was not going to collapse under its own weight, Azerick set to work painstakingly carving runes onto the ground, rocks, and trees with the claw of his index finger.

CHAPTER 16

Daebian stood with the four incensed ships' captains aboard his flagship as they watched the pirate crew liberating the holds of the merchant vessels of their precious contents. Daebian's men swarmed over the captured ships lashed together to make their plundering as efficient as possible. His ten pirate ships had little trouble driving off the three naval vessels escorting the merchants, sinking one of them, and capturing their prey.

Tobias approached and knuckled a salute. "Commodore, we're near finished transferring the cargo."

"Excellent work, Tobias. Spread my regards to the crew for their flawless execution."

"What are you gonna do with us and our crew?" one of the merchant captains demanded.

"Normally, I would confiscate your ships and either set you adrift in longboats or hold you for ransom, but I am in a bit of a hurry and do not have the time to spare to make them seaworthy. Therefore, you are free to go."

"And how do you expect us to go when you took all our spare sailcloth?"

Daebian shrugged. "Row, swim behind it and push, sew your shirts and knickers together and make a sail for all I care. Just be thankful I leave you with those options. Most are not afforded such luxury."

"You're a cold-hearted bastard!"

"Such rudeness when I have been nothing but hospitable. I tried to play the good host and even offered you drinks."

"I'd sooner drink with Sharrellan while demons strip the flesh from my bones than with gutter filth like you."

"Be very careful, Captain, and do not mistake my current pleasantries as a disinclination to kill you. Say the wrong word, and I will run you through and have no trouble enjoying my lunch."

The irate man pressed on heedless of Daebian's warning. "I know your father. I cannot imagine the disappointment he must feel for siring the likes of you."

"And you found the magic word, congratulations."

The merchant captain still wore the sneer on his face, ignorant of the black sword running through his heart until he collapsed upon the deck in a rapidly expanding pool of his own fluids.

Daebian pulled his sword free, wiped it on the man's trouser leg, and slammed it home in its sheath. "I don't care if you carry him off or dump his carcass into the sea, but get off my boat." The three remaining captains each grabbed a limb and carried the body away without a word. "Tobias, order the ships cut loose, and get someone to throw some sand on this mess. Once our sails are repaired, plot a northwesterly course with all haste."

"Aye, sir!"

"Eva," Daebian called out.

The young mage answered Daebian's beckoning and climbed the steps to the stern. "Did you need me, darling?"

Daebian smiled, wrapped her up in his arms, and kissed her. "You performed wonderfully once again."

"I do aim to please, Commodore," she responded with a giggle.

"I need you by my side, but I cannot promise to keep you safe where we are going. It may be beyond my power to do so. If you like, I will order a ship to carry you to North Haven, or wherever you wish to go."

"Do you want me to go?"

"I do not, and I need you to better the odds of what will be the riskiest gambit of my life, but you may well die doing so."

"I have made my choice, and that choice is to be by your side. I have lived more in these past weeks than most experience in their dullish lives."

Daebian hugged her tightly. "I will do everything I can to protect you."

"I have the utmost faith in you."

"Let us both pray our mutual confidence in me is well placed."

"Very good, now ask the stone to release its grip," Mordigar instructed. "One does not command the elements to do anything, or you risk having them turn on you."

Sandy did as she was told and coaxed the rock clinging to the mountainside to let go of its hold. She first sent out her innate magic to urge the stone to fall and activated the power of her runes to enhance and empower the effect. A great slab of rock separated from the escarpment and began sliding down the steep slope before tumbling and breaking apart in an avalanche of destruction. The veritable river of boulders crashed into the trees below, snapping them off at the trunks, and sending a great plume of dust into the air.

"Excellent, you have a natural affinity for stone and earth. These will be your most powerful weapons. Use your imagination to shape them to be as formidable as you can make them. You will need it to face what will be overwhelming odds. Let us take to the sky and work on your flying."

Sandy dutifully followed Mordigar into the air without question or comment. Most of her training was done without her speaking, although her mentor did encourage her to ask questions. She played the role of an attentive student and did not waste time with unnecessary conversation while her training was in progress.

She chased after Mordigar and took a position off his left wing. Despite his enormous size, the elder dragon was a swift flyer, and only by summoning gusts of wind to assist her could she keep up. She was able to outmaneuver him to some degree by using her magic thanks to her smaller size, but her lack of experience in aerial combat showed, and she had yet to achieve any sort of victory.

Mordigar executed a series of rolls and loops and weaved through canyons as Sandy worked to keep up and imitate his maneuvers. He watched his protégé as she mimicked his flight and noted every missed turn or poorly executed roll or bank.

"You are fighting the air currents and needlessly exhausting yourself," Mordigar told her. "Although the air is impossible to see, it is as real and substantial as any of the elements. You must work with them, not against them. Feel, smell, and taste the currents and pockets of greater or lesser density. Use those to assist your maneuvers and plan your moves accordingly. Do not force the air to do what you wish, but do what the air allows. Do you understand?"

"I do."

"Good, now fly off and attack me. Show me what you have learned."

Sandy banked to the left and Mordigar to the right. She flew a long circuit around the mountain for several minutes before climbing to a higher altitude. It did not take long for her to spot Mordigar drifting along a warm air current, pretending to be oblivious to everything around him. Sandy adjusted her angle, matched his heading, and called on a tailwind to silently catch up to him. She brought her wings in close and angled them to prevent the wind from rustling the leathery membranes and betraying her approach.

She kept herself centered on the bright disc of the sun just in case Mordigar happened to glance in her direction. A smile spread across Sandy's face as she neared striking distance. She curled her toes inward so her sharp talons would not rake Mordigar's back as she homed in on the spot just ahead of his wings. A moment before she could deliver a thump between his shoulder blades, Mordigar dropped ten feet, rolled onto his back, and delivered a stunning blow to Sandy's side and belly with his tail.

Sandy suddenly knew what a fly must feel when it gets swatted as she began an uncontrolled tumble to the ground. She writhed in midair, twisted her wings, and slung her tail around in an effort to right herself and regain control. She was still falling too fast to regain altitude. Runes flared across her body, and a great geyser of water sprang from the lake below and struck her in the belly. She rode the column of water into the lake where she struck with an enormous splash and a brief shout of profanity that got cut off as she began coughing out large quantities of water.

Mordigar landed next to the lake with a dull thump and a powerful wind kicked up by his wings. "You failed."

Sandy shook her head and looked up at her mentor. "You think? What did I do wrong? I had the sun at my back just like you told me to."

"Having the sun at your back is not always optimal, particularly when it is also at your foe's back. I was able to see your shadow on the ground, and when yours and mine converged I knew you were within striking distance. Also, you must use your magic to part the wind in front of you. I was able to feel the air pushing ahead of you upon my back."

"Oh. You didn't have to hit me so hard."

"I have confidence in your abilities and cleverness. I felt you were ready for more vigorous training."

"Well, you nearly killed me! How would that have made you feel?"

"If my assessments were misplaced then I would have felt annoyed with having wasted my time on you."

"Oh."

"Do not dwell on what could have been. Focus on what is happening now. I have seen people of all races waste a lifetime on what might have been. Ruminating on things you can no longer change is to squander the preciousness of life. Learn from what has happened and move forward. Are you ready to continue?"

"I am."

"Good, now listen well. You will certainly be outnumbered, particularly in the sky. This means you will find yourself on the defensive far more often than not. However, a good defense can prove to be even more effective than a desperate offense. Take to the sky, and I shall show you."

Sandy heaved herself into the air and Mordigar followed, rising into the sky in lazy, concentric circles as the warm updraft aided their wingbeats. The ground fell away then sped past as the two dragons took up a game of chase. Sandy dropped lower, and Mordigar dived to follow. She spied his shadow rippling along the contours of the ground and watched it catching up to hers. She waited until the two silhouettes nearly converged, rolled onto her back, and lashed out with her tail just as Mordigar had done to her. The giant wyrm grabbed her tail and yanked it with enough force to make her yelp in pain and throw her roll into a tumble.

"You will not surprise me with my own tricks. You are neither stupid nor unimaginative. Use your cleverness to devise countermoves of your own. If you try to fight your foes with tooth and claw, then you are on a short path to defeat."

Sandy accepted the rebuke and studied her surroundings as Mordigar had taught. She called upon the power invested in her runes and summoned a powerful wind to increase her speed. She understood now why Azerick had done what he did and knew it was a painful choice for him to make knowing it would hurt her deeply. Without the runes, Mordigar and most other dragons would make short work of her in the air, but with them, she was a match for almost any of dragonkind and better than most. She sensed the use of dragon magic and knew Mordigar was calling upon his own innate abilities to speed his flight in order to keep up.

The younger dragon dived for the ground and glanced behind her to ensure her mentor was close behind. Azerick's rune magic was not her only source of power, however. Using her sand dragon heritage, she called up a fierce dust storm and flew into the heart of it. Despite the drop in visibility, Sandy was far from blind. Racing through the gritty cloud, she barked out short, sharp roars, and her ears created a sort of map in her mind as it processed the returning echoes. One of the advantages of spending a great deal of time beneath the surface was the ability to see without one's eyes.

"Very good, young one!" Mordigar called out behind her.

Sandy darted for a series of ravines and deep fissures cutting through the mountainous region like knife wounds on the skin of the world and pulled her dust storm along behind her. She weaved around jutting rocks as she raced through a twisting labyrinth of cuts and draws. Despite Sandy's obscuring cloud and evasive moves, Mordigar stayed close on her tail, and she could hear him chortling his pleasure at her seeming inability to shake him.

"I may not be able to see well, youngling, but my memory is impeccable despite my great age."

Sandy knew Mordigar was following her by sound as well as memory and led him toward her trap. She remembered a low waterfall spanning the gap between the walls of one of the canyons along which tracked a narrow but deep river. Sandy called to the stones lining the canyon, pulled them free with her magic, and bombarded the elder dragon.

Mordigar swooped right and left, avoiding most of the stones and letting his powerful wards deflect the others. Sandy knew the old dragon would not be fazed by such a simple assault, but that was not her intent. Her earth runes flared and the waterfall's riverbed rose several feet. Sandy skimmed just over the crest with Mordigar practically shadowing her every move. With any luck, he would not differentiate between the magic used to raise the ground and that which caused the continual dust storm and falling stones.

Sandy heard a great splash and vociferous cursing when Mordigar struck the lip of the falls. He began laughing when he realized what his student had done, but Sandy was intent upon cutting that laughter short. He was off balance, and it was now her best chance to make a decisive strike. As Mordigar floundered and struggled to right himself, Sandy reversed her course and summoned a powerful spout of water from the river.

The column struck the massive dragon under his left wing, throwing him further off balance. Mordigar cursed again but did not have time to get inventive with his expletives as Sandy struck him in the back and conjured a gust of air to add power to her attack. Her mentor was unable to counter the triple onslaught and crashed into the river.

Sandy landed on a sandbar and beamed as Mordigar dragged himself from the river and coughed the water from his lungs. She could tell he was trying his best to look fiercely dignified but gave up the pretense and laughed heartily.

"Well done, little one! I am wet and hungry. Let us leave this place and get something to eat."

Student and master lay curled into two scaled mounds, one large, one beyond enormous, digesting their heavy meals. Sandy was just on the edge of consciousness when Mordigar tensed and anxiously raised his head.

"I fear our time together is at an end," he said in a strained voice.

"No, there is too much for me to learn still!"

"It would take me a century just to begin to teach you all I know, but that was never my intent. I showed you how to mix the colors. It is up to you to paint your masterpieces. You are tenacious and brilliant, and it will carry you far. The Scions are breaching the walls of their prison. You must leave now. Once they come through, we will be enemies."

Sandy's stomach twisted into a knot and she denied his words with every fiber of her being. "No! You can fight them. We will fight them together!"

Mordigar bent his head down and nuzzled her cheek. "It is not possible. Believe me when I say I have tried and with the most powerful of motivations."

"I cannot fight you. I won't."

"You will!" the ancient dragon roared. "You will fight me and you will kill me, because if you do not, I shall certainly kill you, and I cannot live with that. I am old and I am tired. I have suffered at the hands of these so-called gods, and I do not wish to do so again."

"What did they do to you?" Sandy asked softly.

Mordigar's eyes became haunted as the ghosts of the past peered out of them like windows to his soul. "I once had two daughters. You remind me of them both so much. My eldest was kind and wise beyond her years. My younger was fierce and full of fire. She had so much she thought she had to prove."

"What happened to them?"

"The war happened. My little one died in the fighting, unwilling to back down no matter how terrible the odds. My older daughter survived the insurrection, and when the Scions were banished and the dragons were no longer under their spell, she tried to be a bridge between us and our former enemies. She thought she could be an ambassador to help the freed people rebuild their lives and repay what we had done to them. The humans pretended to be willing to talk, but it was a ruse. They did not believe we too were victims and only saw us as the tyrants who oppressed them.

"They killed her before she could speak a word of peace. I know we have only spent a few days together, but for those few days I had a daughter once again. I will not lose another! So when I tell you to fight me with every ounce of strength and every bit of cleverness you possess, you will do it if you give one fraction of a damn about me!"

Mordigar softened his tone and Sandy felt the mountain cease its trembling. "It is a mercy for me and a chance for you to live the life my daughters never got. Do this for me, *One Whose Brilliance Outshines The Sun*. Survive this and tell the races we too lived as slaves with less free will than they."

"I will save you, Mordigar, I swear."

"Survive and you will. Now go, the barrier is falling."

Sandy ran down the short passage, hurled herself into the air, and flew desperately westward. She was buoyed with new wisdom and a new name, but she dragged an anchor of despair behind her. She had known no other dragon in her life but her mother, and this one was about to be taken from her too, and long before it was time. Her mind flashed to the Scions. The rage and hate filling her was greater than any she had felt in her entire life. Even her breaking at the hands of the Sumaran lord paled in comparison, and she swore to unleash every bit of them upon the Scions and their horde. She was more brilliant than the sun, and she would explode in a supernova to scorch them from the face of her world.

CHAPTER 17

The river swept the borghast matron all the way back to her nest site near the pool below the falls before she was able to extract herself from the water. She was exhausted. Borghasts were not strong swimmers, but her desire to seek retribution on the crafty creature kept her struggling to stay afloat until the river calmed enough, she could drag herself to safety. She rested for an hour before resuming her hunt, following the killer's stench through the jungle despite its traveling through the trees and rarely touching the ground.

The borghast matron raced through the jungle, tearing at the foliage with wild abandon as if she were swimming through a lake of impenetrable green water and leaving a wake of shredded vegetation. Small animals fled from her path as she tore a wide swath through the jungle and clambered up the slope toward the mountaintop.

It took her nearly a day to reach the mountain, and it would take several more hours to scale it. Her instincts told her the creature was drawn to the strange tear in the sky. Perhaps it had fallen out of it and was trying to get home. She could not allow that to happen. Her mounting fatigue did nothing to ease the fury raging inside her. Every burning muscle and labored breath acted as a bellows pump, stoking her anger to even greater intensity until it burned so hot, she was certain it would consume her.

Darkness fell and still she pressed on. Her eyes had no trouble seeing in the pure blackness of a jungle too dense to ever witness the light of the twin moons or the star-dotted sky even on the rare occasion that the clouds allowed them to gaze down upon their world. A light drizzle began to fall as she neared the high plateau, and she slowed to a predator's hunting pace. Unlike her earlier reckless, destructive sprint through the jungle, there was no tearing of leaves or snapping of branches to betray her presence.

Heavier droplets of water cascaded down her face as she pushed her head through a thick wall of leaves and spotted her quarry scratching in the dirt and on rocks and trees. It seemed a peculiar thing to do, and she wondered if it was looking for food. The creature finished what it was doing, moved away, and began scratching on a tree trunk once again. When it moved to another spot farther away, she slinked from her concealment to see what it was doing.

The gouges were made with deliberate care with straight lines and uniform arcs and circles. Were they territorial markers? She flicked her tongue at them and recoiled. There was something grossly unnatural to them. It tasted bitter and made her tongue tingle like a nearby lightning strike. Her first instinct was to destroy them. No creature dared to claim territory belonging to her, but that might alert it to her presence. Better to leave them for now.

The matron slipped back into the thicker brush and crept closer to her family's killer. It was near the edge of the plateau and only a few yards from where she was hiding. The creature was strong, but not quite as strong as she was. Nothing in this world was as strong as a mature borghast. It might be cleverer, but it lacked her ferocity. She could defeat it, but she had to be careful and respect its capabilities.

She waited until the killer was bent over a large stone jutting from the dirt and fully engaged in its marking before charging from her hiding spot. She aimed for the creature's neck in hopes of inflicting a fatal wound, but it must have sensed her attack and rolled away at the last second. Her claws cut deep wounds into its shoulder and upper arm. She chose not to press her attack and instead raced into the jungle and disappeared into the darkness.

Azerick felt a soft tremor in the ground beneath his feet and instinctively rolled to his right just before the beast's claws ripped new gashes down his left arm. In the fraction of a second it took to get to his feet, the creature was gone. The only evidence of its existence was the blood running down his arm. He was amazed at how swiftly and silently a creature that size could move. There was not the slightest rustle of branches to betray its presence despite Azerick knowing that it was stalking him just beyond the range of his sight.

He turned in a slow circle, gripping a stout branch in his hands and holding it defensively before him. Azerick was as prepared as he could be for this confrontation, but his nerves tingled with real fear in anticipation of the next assault. He spun toward a noise in the brush to his right and set himself for the charge. Once again, he had not detected the creature's presence until it was nearly upon him. Azerick had to dive forward and felt the creature's claws tear into his side before he even saw it. He twisted and swung his club, but the borghast was already gone, vanishing into the night like a vengeful jungle spirit.

Azerick realized he was not dealing with a mere animal, but a creature of cunning and intelligence. Perhaps not on a human level, but enough to know how to ambush, use distractions, and thrust and retreat to bleed him out without risking the danger of a head-on fight. He could not afford to stand here and let the creature pick him apart. Azerick sprinted toward the site of his trap. It was more open, and there were fewer places for the monster to launch its ambushes.

The sorcerer raced for the stand of trees he had prepared. A flash of movement cut across the path ahead of him. He stopped and listened, searching the darkness for any sign of the borghast. Of course, there was none. Even the wind seemed afraid to blow for fear of drawing the creature's attention. The only sound was the heavy drumming of his heart. Azerick hefted his club and felt foolish for taking a small amount of comfort in its feeble defense.

He took a few more cautious steps toward his trap and barely registered the dark shape detach itself from the trunk of a nearby tree twenty feet above him. Azerick swung his weapon with all his strength just before a massive weight bore him to the ground. The dull thud of the tree limb striking the monster's bony armor broke the silence permeating the jungle.

Azerick dropped the feeble weapon and used his hands to push the snapping jaws with their dagger-sized teeth from his throat. His arms trembled beneath the strain as drool rained down on him and fangs clashed inches from his face. Azerick gasped as the creature raked the claws of one foot down the length of his thigh. He could feel his blood pouring freely from the horrible gashes as the borghast tried to raise its foot high enough to disembowel him.

The lethal movement sacrificed the matron's position and allowed Azerick to get his leg beneath her. Heaving with all his might, he flung the borghast beast off him and sent her crashing into the brush. Wasting no time to worry about his injuries, Azerick rolled to his feet and ran. His left leg felt mushy and slow to respond to his dictates to run. Gritting his teeth through the pain, he leapt into the air and used his wings to glide across the tangling undergrowth. No longer concerned with stealth, the borghast crashed through the brush after him. His leg buckled when he came down, but he quickly righted himself and began a loping hobble toward his staff.

Seeing her prey wounded and trying to reach its weapon, the borghast matron barreled headlong through the thick jungle in pursuit. A vine stretched taut and low across her path tripped up the matron and sent her crashing to the ground. With a frustrated roar, she dug her claws into the earth and charged forward. The killer's leg had finally given out and it was fetched up against a large boulder, desperately trying to stem the bleeding. She needed to finish this fight before it could reach its weapon.

A slender tree sprang upward with a whoosh of air and the sharp crack of a whip. A strong tug on her ankle sent her falling once more. She was far too heavy for the trap to lift her from the ground, but it did slow and infuriate her. The matron slashed at the vine cinched around her ankle. The intruder had not moved and lay just a couple of hundred feet away, its face contorted in pain, weak from blood loss. She tore at the vine keeping her from her vengeance with her claws and charged ahead only to find a web of crisscrossing vines set to trip and entangle her. Refusing to allow anything to keep her from her prey, she began hacking and clawing her way forward.

Azerick watched the creature slash its way toward him, snarling and alternating hateful glares at him and the vines impeding its progress. His nerves were raw, and it took all his discipline to wait and not act too soon. Forcing himself to remain calm, he waited until the creature was in the center of his trap before he sprang it.

He summoned his staff to his hand, effectively pulling the linchpin holding everything in place. Everything started to go as planned until the tree nearest him snagged in the branches of the one next to it. Dropping his crippled ruse, he leapt up, sprinted to the tree, and cleaved its trunk with a mighty swing. The tree fell, pulled the cords tied to the others, and began the cascade effect he had hoped for.

The borghast matron tore another vine free from around her leg and looked up to see her prey appear to shake off its injury and begin running. She roared, thinking it was trying to escape, but it stopped and hewed into a tree with its strange weapon. The tree toppled, and others within the area cracked and fell as well. The strange marks the creature had scratched into the trunks exploded and trees began raining down around her.

Real fear set in as she desperately tried to avoid being crushed by the falling timbers, a feat made especially challenging due to the numerous vines strung across the area. The matron leapt high into the air and hurled herself at the killer, leaping and bounding over the woven strands. She was only a few yards away from achieving her revenge when a massive weight fell across her back and pinned her to the ground.

The matron heard her ribs snap and felt the air blasted from her lungs. She struggled to work her way free but found her efforts futile. She tasted blood in her mouth and tried to draw a breath to shout a final curse and found the attempt equally useless. She hated this creature more than anything in the world, but it was a good death.

She died battling a superior predator instead of growing old and feeble until the day her instincts demanded she walk into the jungle and surrender her life and territory to a more worthy borghast. She looked up at the rare opening in the trees and basked in the glow of the twin moons peering through a break in the clouds. The matron sensed the creature's approach and opened her eyes as its shadow fell over her.

"I am the Hand of Sharrellan. Death finds all those who fall beneath my shadow." Azerick raised his staff, the arcanum spear tip gleaming in the moonlight, and thrust. "But not today."

Azerick used his spear as a lever and heaved, lifting the tree just a scant couple of inches, then pushed a stout branch beneath it. His efforts provided just enough relief to allow the borghast matron to breathe. He sat on the fallen tree near the matron and examined his wounded leg, which was already on its way to mending.

"I know you don't understand me, but I am going to talk anyway. Not that there is much else for either of us to do but talk and listen. I am sorry about killing your family. They were your family, weren't they? I could see it in the hatred you had for me. I know that hatred very well. It too set me on a path of violence, and it killed me, only I came back. I came back so I could kill some more. It seems like my only purpose for existing has been to end some person or another. I always told myself it was necessary, that it was for the greater good, and that I didn't have a choice. But I did. I always had a choice no matter how unpleasant it might have been. I chose to put myself in situations that could only be resolved through killing another. So many times, I could have chosen to distance myself, to let the cards fall where they may. When did it become my responsibility to save everyone? When did I gain the right to impose my sense of morality on the world?"

Azerick looked down at the trapped creature which appeared to be hanging on his every word. "I'll tell you when: the day I was born a human. It all started when I was a boy in Southport…"

CHAPTER 18

Ghost raised his black muzzle to the night sky and released a long, wailing howl. Wolf finished tying off another lethal trap and looked up into the trees to check the placement of one of his many ropes strung through the branches. He had spent more than a year making roadways of ropes and bridges through the trees and creating thousands of traps to show the invaders they were not welcome in his woods. Borrowing from the vast cache of arms Azerick's people created, he had dozens of bows and hundreds of arrow quivers hidden in the treetops of the thousands of acres of forest he claimed as his.

"For crying out loud, would you give it a rest?" Wolf groused. "You've been shouting at the sky for the past week. It's a new moon, and all your whining won't make it come out."

Ghost turned his golden eyes on Wolf, huffed loudly, and resumed his howling. A glimmer of light caught the corner of Wolf's eye and drew his attention to the west. There was a glow far out on the horizon as if the sun were rising, but it was a white light not orange, and it came from the wrong direction. Brilliant bolts streaked out from its epicenter and cracked the sky like a massive burst of lightning, only it continued to split the sky like cracks across glass.

"Way to go, stupid! Your shrill caterwauling broke the sky!" Ghost looked at Wolf and glared. "Yeah, I know it wasn't you. This can't be good, and you know I'm going to get blamed for it."

Raijaun bolted upright and nearly fell to the floor as he rolled out of his bed seconds before realizing he was awake. His heart raced, and a cold sweat traced lines down his grey skin. It was an odd sensation. He could not ever remember sweating before. He ran to his window and discovered the source of his fear. Raijaun sent half a dozen intense orbs of light streaking out of the window to hang in the air and illuminate the entire school grounds.

A bell clanged in alarm at nearly the same instant he lit up the grounds. Raijaun threw on a robe, grabbed a ready travel pack, and raced down the stairs. He called into Miranda's room on his way down, but she was already standing in the stairwell by her door, sword held ready in a white-knuckled grip.

"Raijaun, what is it? Is Azerick back?" she asked.

"No, the Scions have breached the walls of their prison and torn their way into our world. We need to get everyone to the city."

"Go, I'll be down in a minute."

Raijaun nodded and ran down the remaining stairs to the ground floor. He met Alex and the mage leaders just outside the tower. The school was in a controlled uproar as people hustled to pack gear, load wagons, and ready themselves for war. Only minutes had passed since the alarm sounded, but Alex and most of his warriors were already fully armed and armored and leading the efforts to mobilize. Such was the state of their constant readiness training.

"Is this it?" Alex asked.

"It is," Raijaun answered. "Has anyone seen Peck yet?"

"Here, sir!" Peck's voice called out from behind the group before pushing his way to the fore.

"Peck, are your riders ready to move?"

"Already saddled and mounted."

"Get them out as quickly as you can, warn the towns, and get to Brelland."

Peck saluted sharply. "Yes, sir!"

"Has there been any news of Azerick?" Allister asked.

"None whatsoever."

"How are we supposed to fight these things without him?" Rusty asked.

"We will fight exactly as we have been trained to," Raijaun answered. "We are not going to win this war today, so it is not an immediate issue."

Allister gave Raijaun a grave look. "What if he does not come when we meet them in the valley?"

Raijaun's stoic façade slipped just a bit. "Let us pray we do not find out."

Miranda burst through the front door of the tower fully armored with her helm in her hand. "What are we doing?"

"Everyone is preparing to move to the city," Raijaun answered.

"What can I do?"

"Nothing here. You should take a platoon of our people, ride ahead, and inform the duchess so she can prepare the city."

Wagons, horses, and ranks of people on foot massed in an orderly column stretching out of the gates and pointing toward North Haven. In less than an hour, every man, woman, child, and farm animal went from dead asleep to ready to march with a few of their worldly possession strapped to their backs. A plaintive wailing echoed over the caravan from the distant woods.

"Did we send someone to get Wolf?" Miranda asked as she took the lead of her guard contingent.

Ellyssa shook her head. "The idiot refuses to abandon his woods. I have tried talking him into leaving with us a hundred times over the past year, but he refuses to budge."

Miranda pressed her lips into a thin line of dismay, but she understood the young man's conviction. Were it not for Azerick's insistence, she would stand and defend North Haven until the last drop of blood drained from her body. Only her husband's belief that her greatest value lay in fighting the battle and restoring civilization after the war convinced her it was more important to survive than die needlessly.

"All right, but inform everyone guarding the gates to keep an eye out for him in case he changes his mind. It looks like you are all ready to move out. I will ride ahead and apprise Mother of the situation. I am sure she and General Brague have already roused the army, but she will need to know exactly what is happening even if I have little to share at this moment."

"Be careful, Mother," Raijaun said. "Father said they would likely come from the sea, but it is not unreasonable to think the Scions might be able to gate smaller units onto the mainland as they have done in the past."

Miranda smiled, a hint of tears gleaming in her eyes. She leaned over in her saddle and hugged her stepson. He was so tall now she could wrap her arms around Raijaun's neck while seated upon her horse. Azerick rarely showed his demonic form, but the image of it was burned into her mind for all eternity. Raijaun looked so much like him now, and being reminded of his absence tore at her heart.

"Raijaun, I know I have been a terrible mother, but know that I love you. You are a good boy, and I am so proud of you."

"It's all right, Mother. We all do the best we can. I think you tried harder and did far better than most women would have done if faced with such an unusual situation."

"I was blind. You were always the good son."

"All good mothers are blind when it comes to their children. It is the side effect of unconditional love. Do not give up on Daebian yet. I do not think any of us can understand the enigma he represents, but I know he will be a vital role in this tragic play that is unfolding."

"But for which side?"

Raijaun shook his head. "I cannot begin to guess."

A knocking at the door roused Daebian from his sleep. He disentwined himself from Eva's arms, pulled on his trousers and boots, and stomped to the door. He yanked open the portal and glared at his first mate in mock agitation.

"Are we sinking?"

"No, sir. We're near the coordinates you set."

"Ah, excellent." Daebian turned to Eva. "Best rouse yourself, dear. I'll be needing your other fantastic skills soon."

"You are awful!" Eva laughed.

"And you sound just like my father." Daebian grabbed a shirt and followed Tobias onto the deck. "I am rather awful if you consider the fact that I am technically only ten years old."

"Put that way, Eva is the deviant."

"She is, isn't she? I will have to punish her for her wickedness later. Have we spotted anything yet?"

"No, sir, but that ain't surprising. What is it you expect to find out here? Begging your pardon, Commodore, but the men are getting a mite uneasy. We're in the middle of a barren sea, and now the sky's cracked open like the shell of a boiled egg."

"When war comes and battle is met,
Blood will spill and rivers run red,
Men will die, their hearts filled with regret,
While the victors stand in a field of the dead.
The coward will run away and hide,
The fool will fight for honor and pride,
But the wise man will…"

Daebian looked to Tobias to finish his rhyme.

"Do his damnedest not to die?"

"Will choose the winning side. War is upon us, and it is time to choose our allegiance."

"If it's the same to you, I'll still do my damnedest not to die."

Daebian clapped him on the shoulder. "Please do. You are a good man, Tobias, and it would be a great inconvenience for me to replace you."

"Aye, sir, I wouldn't want my death to inconvenience you."

"I appreciate your consideration."

"So, war is coming and we need to pick a side, but who's coming? There ain't nobody out here but maybe a crazy Northman or minotaur ship."

"I assure you, they are coming, and they are far more frightening than Northmen or minotaurs."

A shout from the crow's nest rang out. "Sails two points off starboard!"

"And there they are. Let us see what we have."

Daebian pressed his spyglass to his eye and scanned the horizon. Just peeking over the edge of the world were the sails of several ships. As Daebian watched them draw near, it became apparent these were not ordinary ships.

"Captain!" the lookout shouted.

"I see it, and it's Commodore!" he shouted back. "It looks like my father was telling the truth. They do have flying ships."

Tobias took the spyglass Daebian offered. "Dear gods above. What are we going to do about those?"

"We are going to go apply for a position."

Tobias's face fell slack. "Something tells me this ain't the parlaying sort of applying."

"Not a chance."

"What is it you have in mind?"

"We're pirates, what do you think?"

Tobias sighed and studied the flying armada. There were two dozen ships of similar size with a massive dreadnought flying in the center. The hulls were an off-white and smooth without the visible seams of timber-constructed ships. It was as if they were carved from a single enormous bone. Their sails were a shimmering screen like a soap bubble flattened into sheets and hung from masts and yardarms.

"I suppose we might be able to pick one of the smaller vessels off from the rear if they ignore us and fly past."

Daebian narrowed his eyes.

"But you want the big one."

"Damn right I want the big one."

"You have a plan for snatching it?"

"Two stupid statements in a row. You're slipping, Tobias."

"Sorry, sir, I guess I'm a bit put off from seeing flying ships."

"I suppose I can understand that. After all, you're only human. Bring as many men onto this ship as we can cram aboard and have the others hold their positions here." Daebian turned toward his cabin. "Eva!"

Eva appeared from his stateroom and bounded up the steps to the aft deck. "Yes, darling?"

"I will need you soon."

"Are those ships flying?" she asked as she looked at the vessels sailing above the horizon.

"They are, and that is what I need you for. I need to get our men onto the flagship. Can you open a gate onto their deck?"

"I should be able to, but using the gate is disorienting. They will be vulnerable for a few seconds until they get their feet back under them."

Daebian smiled. "Not a problem. The enemy will be sufficiently distracted."

Non-essential crewmen began shuttling over from the other ships in Daebian's fleet and soon filled the hull and decks of his flagship. Once aboard and prepared for combat, his ship set an intercept course for the flying armada. The fear aboard the human vessel was palpable, and the smell of sweat permeated the decks. Men gripped swords and knives in trembling fists and said prayers to Serron.

The flying ship drew closer and matched his course to intercept. Apparently, the invaders were as interested in him as he was in them. Creatures swarmed the gunwales and scurried through the thick, web-like rigging, looking eagerly down at the seemingly helpless human ship.

"Gloom, find me an open window so I might slip inside and introduce myself."

The crow squawked an acknowledgement and flew toward the Scion ship. Daebian watched the vessel grow larger through Gloom's eyes and was soon circling above it. Scores of four-armed insect-like creatures swung from rigging and scampered up masts and across yardarms with gravity-defying sureness. He picked out his point of insertion, stepped into the shadowy doorway on his vessel, and emerged on the deck of the enemy ship.

Daebian leapt from the darkness with blinding speed, slashing at the creatures, rigging, and lines in an effort to create as much chaos as he could. Despite their heightened alert status, nearly a dozen creatures fell to his black blade before the hue and cry of a general alarm began sounding across the ship. Daebian ran from shadow to shadow, leaping out of the darkness to cut down an enemy before darting away and reappearing almost instantly somewhere else on the deck.

From high upon the rigging, Daebian saw the glimmer of Eva's gate rippling in the air near the center of the main deck and it begin disgorging his crew. He used his abyssal power to conjure a fog as black as night and shrouded the deck around the portal in darkness. Accustomed to fighting on the rolling and pitching decks of a ship, his people were quick to regain their balance and took up defensive positions, shot crossbows into the inky fog, and waited for the monsters to leap out of the darkness.

"Tobias!" Daebian called down from his perch.

The first mate looked up from the eye of the black fog and spotted Daebian in the rigging. "Yes, sir?"

"Fight your way to the wheel and keep us away from the other ships!"

"Aye, sir!"

Daebian began to clear away the black miasma so his people could take command of the wheel and hopefully the ship. Leathery-skinned, multi-limbed crew leapt through the vanishing haze, stabbing and slashing at the human invaders. His crew fought back valiantly despite the freakish nature of their foes. The humans gained the momentum, largely thanks to Daebian's surprise assault and their sudden arrival via Eva's gate, and began cutting a path toward the stern.

A slight tremor in the line alerted Daebian to the presence of an enemy who must have had extraordinary stealth to be able to nearly catch him unaware. He ducked just in time to avoid the sword aimed to take off his head. The blade struck the mainmast with a dull thud and buried itself nearly an inch into the glossy substance. Daebian looked into the furious, multi-faceted eyes of one of the spider creatures as it wrenched its blade free. Its leathery carapace was a deep burgundy instead of the dull grey of its crew.

"You will pay for your brazenness, pathetic human!" the creature hissed.

Daebian narrowly avoided the creature's thrust and concluded that he was at a significant disadvantage when it came to fighting and maneuvering in the rigging. His escape options were limited, and a swift kick eliminated them. Daebian twisted as he fell, desperately searching the rapidly rising deck for a shadow. He spotted the long sliver of darkness created by the mast, but he was on the wrong side of it. Sending his demonic power outward, he grabbed the shadow, pulled it beneath him, and opened it wide.

He fell into the shadow and vanished into the deck. Failing to identify an exit before diving in, he flew through the shadow ways and risked a blind jump using his intuition. Daebian tumbled out of the shadow ways into a room steeped in darkness and stained with a faint red light. His body came to a stop when it struck a wall of fleshy solidity, and he leapt to his feet. He clamped his mouth shut to stifle the gasp struggling to get out and held his breath.

Thousands of ravagers packed the hold from wall to wall, seemingly stacked on top of each other as they gazed at the glowing red orb floating several feet over their heads. A few of them rumbled at Daebian's intrusion but did not move. Daebian let out his breath as he saw that the ravagers were in some kind of torpor, likely the only way to transport the vicious creatures without them tearing each other apart.

"That's all right, don't get up. I was just leaving," Daebian said as he stepped back into a darker patch near the hull and leapt onto the deck.

The deck was awash in yellowish ichor and streaked with red blood. Bodies of both humans and monsters lay scattered about like unsecured cargo crates tossed around in a storm. Tobias and his boarding crew were near to gaining the wheel, but they struggled against fierce resistance from both their front and rear. Daebian hacked at the backs of the mob trying to get to his men and forced a large number of them to turn their attention to him. He leapt from shadow to shadow and cast sections of the deck in darkness that only his eyes could pierce, striking out like a phantom to thrust his blade into the backs of his enemies.

A large portion of the main host broke away to deal with him and relieved the pressure on Tobias's forces enough for them to resume making headway toward the ship's controls. Daebian's superior reflexes and ability to use the shadow ways kept him from harm's reach until the ship's captain nearly dropped on top of him. He rolled to the side just as the captain plunged from the rigging and carved a long divot into the deck with his sword.

"Stand and fight me, cowardly trickster!" the creature snarled as it charged in, swinging a pair of crescent blades.

Daebian leapt away and to the side, narrowly avoiding the dual strikes. The red creature was fast, and it took all of Daebian's demonic enhancements to match him in speed and strength. He looked for a point to access the shadow ways, but the creatures had him surrounded, and the captain's assault was relentless.

Sensing his opponent's intention, the captain shouted, "Keep him from the shadows!"

Daebian charged a knot of creatures and cut two down in rapid succession, but three more took their place to deny him the shadows he sought. The attempt cost him as he felt the searing pain of a blade cut across his back. He leapt into the air and tried to flip over his foe's head, a move that would have worked had it been human. The spiderish captain sprang upward and intercepted the human's trajectory. Using one of his free hands, he grabbed the invader and slammed him down onto the deck. Daebian twisted away from the plunging blade and kicked the creature in the abdomen with enough force to knock it away.

He leapt to his feet, but the furious captain was already charging back into the fray. Discarding finesse to the wind, he ignored the human's thrust and felt the black blade carve a deep gouge in his leathery body plate. He grabbed the human's sword arm with one hand, his belt with the other, lifted him from the ground, and charged through his own crew to slam Daebian against the mainmast.

The captain leaned in as he drew his blade back. "Time to die, vile human," he hissed.

Daebian smiled as he glanced at the shadow the creature cast over him. "Not today."

Daebian focused his energy on the shadow and fell into it, pulling the spider-like captain into the shadow ways. Daebian emerged near the far rail and promptly closed the dark portal, leaving the two halves of his foe occupying opposite sides of the ship. Seeing Tobias and his forces having a hard time securing the wheel, Daebian called out to his companion.

"Gloom, go find Eva."

Gloom dived from a lower yardarm straight for the ship sailing below. The ship and sea rushed toward him as Gloom swooped onto the deck and lit upon the rail near the wheel. Eva gasped when Daebian appeared from nowhere and grabbed her wrist.

"I wanted to keep you away from the ship, but I need you."

"It's too far away for me to open a gate now."

"Don't worry, I'll get you there."

"Okay, what do you need me to do?"

"Follow me, brace yourself as we step into the shadow ways, and then start kicking some serious butt."

Eva put on a brave smile. "All right, I'll come save you."

Daebian returned her impish grin and pulled her into the shadow ways. She gasped when the world went black around her and an icy chill caressed her warm flesh like the cold hand of death. She breathed deeply and luxuriated in the touch of the relatively warm sea air when she and Daebian emerged onto the deck of the flying ship. Not even the sight of the carnage and furious battle between humans and monsters prevented her from relishing being out of that hellish passageway.

"Be a dear and clear my ship of these creatures," Daebian said with a smile.

Eva did not return the look but did as she was bid. Focusing her mind beyond the physical world, she called out to the Source, shaped it to her will, and unleashed fire and destruction into the rear of the Scions' minions. Daebian defended their rear from the few stragglers or those scampering through the rigging while Tobias and his men finally got the break they needed to push through to the ship's controls.

A large host of defenders stopped their assault on the humans to their front, turned, and charged headlong toward the hated wizard. Eva raised an invisible wall and smiled as scores of monsters slammed into the barrier like a flock of birds flying into a giant window. She then split the wall down the middle, rotated it outward from the center, and used it to shove the creatures toward the railing. The invisible walls forced dozens of the monsters over the edge while others clung desperately to the rail or fellow shipmates.

Tobias and a handful of men reached the wheel, dispatched the operator, and formed a bulwark atop the aft deck stairs. The wheel looked much like any ship's wheel, but several levers also stuck out of the deck like corn stalks, their purpose incomprehensible to him. The first mate grabbed the wheel with both hands and kicked one of the levers with his foot. The ship lurched hard to port and plummeted, shaking dozens of the enemy and a few humans off the deck. Tobias grabbed the lever he had kicked with one hand, pulled it back into place, and straightened the wheel.

"Ray, Leon, Kardal, grab those levers!" Tobias ordered. "That one is sway, that one surge, and that one heave. Let's not do heave again."

Daebian appeared behind Tobias and asked, "Do we have it?"

The first mate visibly jumped. "I really hate it when you do that! Aye, sir, I think I got the gist of it. I saw Eva. Is she okay by herself?"

Daebian looked out across the deck and saw Eva leap through one of her gates, appear on the bow, and strike down half a dozen more of the spiderlike crew. "Yeah, she's fine. My father's people have trained well for this. Now get us away from those ships."

Several of the smaller vessels swooped in and were close enough for the crew to try to leap across from their higher decks and yardarms. Tobias spun the wheel and tapped Ray on the shoulder.

"Hard to starboard, Ray. Everyone hold on!" Tobias shouted.

The ship rolled right and slid away from the nearest enemy vessel. The sudden separation caused most of those trying to leap across to find nothing but empty air beneath them and plunge hundreds of feet before striking the open ocean.

"Commodore, they're catching up! I don't think we can outrun them in this tub unless I'm not doing something right."

Daebian thought a moment. "We need to lighten the load. Any volunteers to hop over the side? No? Okay, wait here, I have an idea."

Daebian stepped into the shadow ways and found the shadow leading to the ship's hold. Once again, the packed ranks of ravagers barely acknowledged his presence as he squeezed past them and made his way to the port bulkhead. He found the ropes attached to what appeared to be large doors or ramps set in the sides of the ship to facilitate loading and unloading. Daebian hacked several of the ropes free and stepped back onto the deck near Tobias.

"Everyone get a good grip! Tobias, roll us hard to starboard."

"Aye, sir! Ray, hard to starboard on my mark...mark!"

The pirate shoved the lever all the way to the right and held on for dear life as the ship rolled its deck nearly vertical. Ravagers began pouring out of the hold by the hundreds and plunged into the ocean. Fireballs streaked past and lightning raked the exposed hull as the chasing ships began firing their weapons in an attempt to slow them, or failing that, destroy them altogether.

"Tobias, straighten us up. You men get on those deck weapons!"

The ship regained an even keel, and Daebian's remaining pirates ran to the rail and manned the strange weapons attached to them. The weapons vaguely resembled heavy crossbows or scorpions except they were rune-inscribed and the arms did not have a string with which to launch a projectile. Unsure of what else to do, the men loaded rods made of a strange metal and also inscribed with runes into the groove, aimed them at the pursuing ships, and squeezed the trigger.

The rod shot from the weapon as if it were an ordinary bolt, but shortly after leaving the weapon, the runes flared and it became a bolt of lightning or a fireball. Accuracy was hampered by both sides performing evasive maneuvers, and most of the shots went arcing across the sky without causing damage, but enough were hitting them to cause Daebian and his crew some concern.

Time seemed to stop, the wind from their forward motion ceased, and no one on the deck moved. A dreadful aura of menace and supreme power fell over the ship like a dense fog. This was the moment Daebian had been expecting and dreading. This was the moment where his brazen gambit would pay off or he and his crew would die.

"*Enough. I will not have you destroy my ships no matter how amusing your little display.*"

Daebian focused his thoughts into the soul stone. "*Klaraxis, can you draw part of my essence into the gem and keep safe my secrets?*"

"*It is feasible, but only if the creature does not look for them here. You are toying with gods, not some mortal wizards you can easily fool.*"

"*You had best try your hardest, particularly in regards to your existence. And, demon, if you try to do me any harm, I will toss your gem into the ocean where the most exciting thing you will see is the underside of the occasional fish for all eternity.*"

"*I know my place, my son. More importantly, I know what is best for me.*"

It took all of Daebian's substantial will to draw his thumb over the razor edge of the blade exposed above the lip of its sheath. A rivulet of blood welled up and disappeared as the soul blade pulled it in along with part of his soul and the memories it contained. Not even the powerful influence of the Scion could prevent the shudder racking his body as part of his very existence was stripped away and forced into the black gem.

The Scion's voice filled his head. *"Tell me why I should not kill you immediately. You may speak now."*

Daebian felt the invisible constriction around his body slacken. He turned around and found the Scion towering over him. The creature was impossibly thin, like a voluminous robe hanging on a broom. Its flesh was a pallid grey and it had no mouth, nose, or ears. Its eyes were overly large and looked as though they were carved out of the clear night sky with stars gleaming and far away galaxies swirling in an endless black universe.

"For the very reason you have not done so. I am interesting," Daebian answered.

"You destroyed a great many of my minions. Do you think so highly of yourself that I will not exact retribution? Your actions are an affront to my power. For this alone you deserve death along with the rest of your kind."

"Your minions, of which you have plenty, are meaningless tools whose only value is in achieving your goals. Good leaders are far more valuable and much harder to find. It takes a great act to warrant the attention of someone so powerful. Anything less than what I did would not be paying proper tribute to your greatness."

The Scion paused as it considered the strange human's words. *"I am Zyn, but you will call me master."*

Daebian knelt and delivered his line with the smoothness and mastery of the world's greatest actor and with the conviction to fool even a god. "I am yours to command, master. I am Daebian—"

"I know everything there is to know about you, slave." Zyn held his long-fingered hand a few inches over Daebian's head. The Scion's psychic probing felt like nails being driven into his brain. *"You are the son of the false Guardian, but there is no love lost between you. How incredibly interesting. You struck him down but did not kill him."*

"It was the only mistake I will admit to ever making in my life. I thought I could cause him greater pain by letting him live for a time."

"Indeed. You have an unusual power, but you are not a wizard or sorcerer. That blessing has saved you from immediate execution. However, there is a wizard amongst your crew. She will of course have to die."

"Master, I beg a boon in addition to you graciously sparing my life."

"*You wish me to spare the woman. This cannot be done. She and her entire tainted bloodline will be exterminated.*"

"She is a valuable tool. Without her, I could not have accomplished taking this ship and attaining my position, and you would have been denied your greatest general."

"*You think very highly of yourself.*"

"My greatness is second only to my masters' no matter how distant that divide may be. Please, let me use her until you achieve your goals of eradicating the wizards and enslaving the wretches of humanity."

"*You please me, slave. I will grant you your wish. She will live until I order you to kill her. If you hesitate, I will destroy you both.*"

"Your will be done, master. May I ask for one more favor?"

"*Never has a creature asked for more when I have already given it its life, but I know your request and once again I am amused. My answer is yes, when the time comes, you shall be the one to kill your father.*"

"Your greatness is matched only by the generosity you bestow upon your worthy servants."

"*You had best prove your worth, or I shall quickly revoke my favor, and you will suffer greatly.*"

"I will please my masters."

Daebian looked up but Zyn was gone. The air once again blew across his face, crewmen moved about on the deck, and the ship continued to cut a swath through the air.

"*Klaraxis, that was the most unpleasant experience of my life. Let us avoid doing it again. Keep those memories safe. I will need them later.*"

"*Of course, master, I am your humble servant.*"

"*Your sarcasm is not appreciated.*" Daebian shouted, "Stop shooting, the ship is ours!"

The other Scion ships had already ceased their attack and returned to formation around the flagship. The human crew members were unsure what to do and stood around while the few remaining Scion minions resumed their duties as if nothing had happened.

"What now, Commodore?" Tobias asked.

"First, I think I deserve a promotion to admiral."

"Congratulations, Admiral. You want me to commission a new hat for you?"

"First, I want you to commission a muffle for that sarcastic tone of yours."

Tobias grinned. "Aye, aye, Admiral."

"Then I want you to put the crew to work. How many did we lose?"

Tobias looked out across the deck and took a quick count. "I'm guessing near a hundred. Might be less depending on how many recover from their wounds."

"We'll need to join our floating ships and replace them. I also want to get some human crew on a few of the other flying ships as well. You seem to have a handle on steering the thing, so you can instruct our other captains."

"Aye, sir. So this is the side we're choosing?"

"It is."

"All right, so what happens next?"

"We go and conquer a kingdom."

CHAPTER 19

Miranda looked at the generous amount of food spread across the long table within the castle's elegant dining room. "I feel guilty eating in the palace dining hall when tens of thousands of our people are eating such simple fare in the streets or atop the walls."

"Rank has its privileges, my dear," General Brague stated flatly, "particularly when in the garrison where resources are more readily available. Be thankful for it. We will all be sharing camp rations soon enough. Soldiers need to see their leaders standing strong and above the hardships of the common man. It gives them courage and something to focus on when we do step into the fray, risk our lives, and bloody our blades on our enemy. Wars are won within the hearts of men, not on the backs of mounts or the bodies dead upon the ground. Would you revere the gods if they toiled in the fields, filthy from simple labor and suffering the hardships of mortals?"

"Are we likening ourselves to gods now, General?"

"To inspire people to throw themselves at almost certain death, we must be a close second in reverence and more substantial than the gods."

"Well said, dear," Duchess Mellina commended him with a smile. "Miranda, you saw how the people rallied when we threw ourselves at those detestable mercenaries. Were our presence and actions common, a simple matter of course, the effect would have been lost, and more would have died. Be thankful we are able to feed and shelter them at all. If we are all forced into the valley as Azerick speculates, I expect to see much deprivation should the war last beyond a week."

Allister asked, "What of the food stores we have been collecting these last few years?"

The Duchess frowned. "Most have gone to feeding the populace. We have concentrated our populations mostly within the cities to supply the war effort. We had to feed thousands of people who normally would have been largely self-sufficient. The summer's crops are also not ready to be harvested. Had we just a few more weeks to bring in the harvest, our ability to survive a siege would have been extended by weeks. As it is, immediate rationing will have to take place once we reach the valley just to stay fed for more than a week."

General Brague added, "Don't forget about our allies. The Sumarans are bringing tens of thousands of soldiers. They are traveling fast and will have a limited amount of food within their baggage train. As their hosts, we will have to feed them as well. The elves are coming, hopefully, from the far north. They will not be able to carry a great deal of food either and will likely forage for most of their provisions en route. Who knows what the dwarves will bring if they even come to our aid and have not chosen to stay hidden beneath their mountains?"

"Father has assured me the dwarves are coming, but he has heard nothing from the elves. Given what I have seen of the invaders and our own preparations, it is unlikely the war will last long enough to cause more than moderate hardship where hunger is concerned," Raijaun said. "Victory or defeat is likely to be decided long before we begin suffering from famine."

"You're as joyful to be around as your father," the general rumbled.

"Optimism without realistic expectations is rarely productive." A bell began tolling across the city and was quickly joined by others. "I believe my case has just been made."

Everyone cleared the room and ran for the battlements, grabbing weapons and donning armor that were never more than an arm's length away. The entire city was abuzz as soldiers and citizens scurried like ants in a disturbed nest. Miranda took a spyglass from one of the soldiers manning the castle battlements and scanned the horizon. The ships stood out clearly against the fractured sky as they drew inexorably closer.

"Could they be our ships or refugees perhaps?" Miranda asked as she peered through the spyglass.

Raijaun shook his head. "No, look at the hulls. There is a sliver of skyline beneath them and it grows larger. Those ships are not sailing on the sea but above it. They will be ferrying the invasion force."

"There aren't that many," Miranda observed. "They cannot conquer us with so few, can they?"

"The ships are larger than anything we can build, and the creatures likely need little room. The Scions would not attack unless they were supremely confident that their numbers were sufficient for the task. Do not think of them like ordinary pirates or invaders. Whatever their stratagem, it will be unlike anything we have seen or are likely prepared to face."

"Can we begin the evacuation now?" the duchess asked.

"Yes. It should be too late for them to alter their plans now. Order the gate activated and move the civilians through with all haste. I will contact the Academy and inform them of the attack. I must assume this is only half the invading force. The Scions will not leave Southport alone to strike at them in the rear. They will want to destroy the largest concentration of wizards above all other considerations except exacting my and Father's death."

Allister hustled for the gates to give the order to begin evacuations. General Brague took a contingent of castle guards to spread the word and to let the soldiers see that their leaders were there and ready to fight alongside them. Raijaun plucked the speaking stone from a pocket in his cloak and focused his will upon it.

"Headmaster."

It took only a moment for the reply. "Raijaun?"

"Yes, Headmaster. The invasion has begun. Have you seen any sign of the enemy yet?"

"No, nothing yet. We have had a few reports of small attacks outside the city, but nothing more substantial than we have seen over the past year."

"I expect you will see their flying ships within a day or possibly even the next few hours. It appears they are unconcerned with waiting to coordinate a simultaneous assault."

"Should I order the evacuation of the city now?"

Raijaun thought a moment before admitting to himself he did not have the answer. "I do not know, Headmaster. I waited until we saw the enemy approach to evacuate North Haven to limit their ability to react. I am certain the Scions will know precisely where we are going the moment the gates activate and align. Whether it is in your best interest to act now or wait, I cannot say, and will leave it to your wisdom. I will tell you this: the Scion ships will be here before we have time to evacuate everyone. That is going to cost us lives. Part of me wishes I had acted sooner, but logically I know that doing so could have had even worse results."

"I understand." The headmaster's voice lowered. "Has there been any word of your father?"

"I am afraid not, and I would be lying if I said I was not deeply troubled by his absence."

"We are all praying for his quick return. Thank you for the information. I will put my people on heightened alert."

"Fare you well, Headmaster."

"And you."

Maureen broke the connection and breathed a sigh of relief and worry. She knew their chances were very poor without Azerick's help, but part of her hoped he had met his end so she and the king would not have to bloody their hands. She looked down at her wrinkled and aged hands and rubbed them together vigorously. There was already too much blood staining them to ever be clean again. With another heavy sigh that did nothing to relieve the burden she carried, the headmaster grabbed her staff and went to alert her people.

"Is Southport also under attack?" Aggie asked as Raijaun slipped the stone back into his pocket.

"Not yet, but it won't be long."

Aggie watched the ships approach, now close enough to be seen with the naked eye. "Raijaun, are all the invaders on those ships?"

"Those ships carry the initial invasion force. They will create a beachhead where I must assume they have another method of bringing in reinforcements. It would be highly impractical to transport their entire army by such mundane means."

"The ships appear vulnerable. If our mages attack them directly, we could prevent them from landing their forces and do a great deal of damage."

"I would be very surprised if the ships are as vulnerable as they appear, but the strategy is certainly sound."

"I'll take more of our mages to the seawall and see if we can't swat at least a few of those things out of the sky."

"I know I do not need to say it to someone as learned as yourself, Aggie, but please be careful. We cannot afford to lose our wizards in the opening gambit."

Miranda said, "I should go down there and lead the repelling forces."

"My Lady, I think it is better if you stay near me. You are but one more sword amongst many right now. The people will need you later, and Father would never forgive me if anything happened to you."

"I just feel like I should be doing something."

"You are, Mother. You are a symbol of hope, and in these times the people need that far more than another fighter or martyr."

"I suppose you are right."

Miranda knew from the smoke and the sounds of battle that her people were being pushed farther into the city as they lost ground with every passing minute. The noncombatants were nearly through the gates, and it was almost time for the rest of them to begin withdrawing as well. For the most part, it appeared as though things were going as planned. That all changed when a dragon came crashing down atop a nearby building and flattened it beneath its great bulk. Miranda sprinted behind a defensive fortification as the air around her became a fiery conflagration.

The dragon pulled itself from the wreckage and swatted away the humans attacking it like insects. Miranda looked up and stared into the dragon's eyes, eyes fixated on the stone columns of the gate. The Scions knew what it was and now set out to destroy it before any more of the humans escaped to safety, no matter how temporary that refuge might be.

Soldiers and mages sought to stop the beast as it tore at the stout ropes and chains strung across rooftops to prevent just such an attack.

Spells and arrows sliced through the air and hammered against the dragon's defenses. The dragon tore down entire buildings as it bulled its way toward the gate, hurling fire and huge chunks of wreckage at the tiny defenders.

A second massive crash shook the battlement and knocked Miranda from her feet. When she stood back up, the Daughter of North Haven faced another dragon bent on destroying the gate and anyone in its path. Some of the few soldiers still guarding the gate charged the creature in a show of futile bravery. Others fled through the portal along with the mass of refugees, their courage having met its limit.

Miranda ducked behind the low wall once again as fire filled the plaza. The scent of charred flesh and the screams of those unfortunate enough not to die immediately made her vomit into her throat. With no sign of reinforcements in sight, Miranda choked down her bile, hefted her shield and sword, and charged the colossal creature.

The dragon craned its neck back to unleash another blast of incinerating fire, and Miranda knew her part in this war was over. She raised her shield to cover her face and aimed her blade at the creature's softer underbelly in hopes of inflicting at least a minor wound before she met her end.

Miranda closed her eyes as she heard the deep inhalation heralding her death. Had she kept her eyes open, she would have seen the third dragon drop from the sky and sink its talons and fangs into the back and neck of the creature about to kill her. Although smaller than the dragon she attacked, Sandy was equipped with some of the most powerful jaws and sharpest claws in the dragon kingdom, and they had no trouble piercing the armor-like scales and sinking deeply into the flesh beneath.

Miranda dived away as the two titans thrashed, destroying buildings and crushing everything in their path. Stout beams snapped like twigs as the two dragons fought and clawed, but the outcome was never in question. Sandy clung to the dragon's back with a grip it had no chance of shaking loose. Runes flared with a brilliant blue light along Sandy's forelegs as she sent a powerful surge of electricity into her foe's body, stopping its heart and struggles in an instant.

"Sandy, praise the gods it's you!" Miranda cried as she climbed to her feet.

Arrows and crossbow bolts arced over her head and bounced off Sandy's scales as Miranda ran toward her friend. Sandy growled. Miranda skidded to a stop and spun to face the soldiers and mages rushing to what they thought was her defense.

"Stop! She's a friend!" Miranda splayed her arms wide trying to wrap them around Sandy's neck. "I'm so glad you're okay."

"I am better now," Sandy acknowledged. "The coastal side of the town is pushed back to the second wall and quickly retreating to this position. The east and south walls are being overrun and falling back to the second wall now. They will lose it soon as well. I will go and try to pull some of the dragons away and steer clear of the city as best I can. Humans seem to have a problem distinguishing one dragon from another."

"Thank you, Sandy; just be careful." Miranda turned to the mages and soldiers. "Spread the word to the others not to target the glowing dragon, and be prepared to get our people through the gate."

Miranda watched the orange flames and black smoke stab at the sky as her beloved city, her home, burned and inhuman invaders ravaged it. Her eyes traveled to the strange ships flying above the city hurling fire and lightning, and she imagined the people dying with each flash and concussive blast. Her tears rained onto the bloodstained cobblestones as if to extinguish the flames of her crumbling city.

Raijaun saw Sandy take to the air after defeating one of the dragons trying to destroy the gate. Her runes flared as she conjured powerful winds to aid her flight and launched harassing attacks at the dragons wheeling about over the city. He smiled at her cleverness and skill when several dragons chased after her and gave the mages defending the city a much-needed respite.

It was difficult to see the farthest lines of battle as more than half the city was burning, but it was clear the humans were in a fighting retreat to the magical gate. With more than half the remaining dragons distracted by Sandy, the greatest problem in getting their people safely through the gates were those flying ships raining down destruction from beyond the range of most of the wizards' spells.

Looking at the sky, Raijaun began gathering power. Anyone with the ability to see into the ether would have found themselves blinded by the gold and silver amalgamation of Guardian and sorcerous energy limning his form, spewing arcs of arcane energy like the spray of a cascading waterfall. Gale-force winds whipped around his body, and ominous clouds rolled in like an avalanche across the sky.

Daebian felt the wind pick up and saw the wall of clouds forming as he directed his crew to destroy the city he once called home without the slightest bit of remorse. He reveled in the destruction, finding a sort of dark poetry in the chaos he had helped unleash. He turned his eyes from the death and flames back to the clouds. The rolling vapors had massed, taken on a sort of solidity, and began racing toward him and his ships.

"Tobias! Those clouds have the stink of my brother all over them. Put our arse to the wind and make for the sea!"

"Aye, sir!"

Tobias spun the ship's wheel as others pulled levers and signaled the other vessels using flags and flares. The crew grabbed ahold of whatever fixed object they could find as the cloudbank struck with the force of a wave, lifting them and propelling the ships along its face. The stern of Daebian's flagship lifted higher than the bow, putting the vessel at a steep decline and forcing crewmen to cling on for dear life. Tobias and his two operators fought to control the pitch and avoid flipping end over end. One ship failed to do that, and the stern continued to rise until it could no longer maintain the precarious balance and tumbled, spilling crew into open air as it fell and shattered against the sea's surface.

A second ship managed to regain control before suffering a similar fate when a dragon, caught in the same unnatural storm, lost control of its flight and smashed into the aft deck, killing the operator and destroying the controls. The dragon flailed in the tangling lines as the ship plummeted, sharing the same fate as it and its crew.

Daebian peered through squinted eyes and saw Eva, a rope wrapped three times around her waist securing her to the mainmast, fighting to maintain the concentration required to work her magic. He was unsure what she was doing, but from the way the ship eased its wild bucking and rolling, he surmised she was enacting some sort of ward at the ship's stern.

The cloud pushed them farther out to sea like a piece of flotsam until North Haven was a speck on a distant shoreline. The roiling wall cloud slowed and became more vaporous, and Daebian and his fleet found themselves lost in the midst of a dense fog. The strange mists dispersed, and Daebian made a quick count of his ships. His tally came up five vessels short from his original number until he spotted a black dot in the distance coming to rejoin the armada. He had lost three ships today thanks to his brother and one to the wizards during the first hour of battle.

"Well played, little brother."

"What was that, sir?" Tobias asked as he shook the cramps out of his hands caused by the death grip he held on the wheel.

"Point us back to shore, Tobias." Daebian turned when Tobias failed to carry out his command. "Tobias!"

Daebian felt the stifling weight of dread drop over him like a frigid, wet blanket. Nothing moved on the deck, not even the breeze. It took only a moment for him to find Zyn looming as dark, powerful, and malevolent as Raijaun's cloud.

"*Your father was not in the city. Where is he?*"

"I do not know, master. I cannot imagine what would have kept him from this battle. It would not surprise me if he managed to get himself killed. The man has a significant lack of foresight."

"*No, he is not dead, but his absence is disconcerting. We do not like surprises like these gates the humans used to flee our righteous justice. Why did you not inform us of their existence?*"

"Why did you not pluck it out of my head with the rest of my thoughts?"

Daebian cried out as a sharp pain lanced through his brain. "*Do not be impertinent, slave!*"

"Master, I meant no such thing! I meant only that I could not tell you for the same reason your all-knowingness did not discover it in my mind. I did not know about them. I know I cannot keep secrets from you, great master, and would not if it were possible." Daebian felt the pain lessen as he braced himself on his hands and knees near the Scion's feet. "We are returning to the battle to slay our enemies."

"The battle is over, for now. Most of the humans escaped through their gates to the city called Brelland. You promised me a leader of unparalleled ability yet your wretched brother defeated you and destroyed some of my ships. I allowed you to keep your pet wizard as a reward for your cleverness. Perhaps I should revoke it for your failure."

A thin line appeared across Eva's forehead and blood trickled down her face.

"Master, she is the only reason this ship survived my brother's magic! If you kill her now, she will be but one of many dead this day. Surely the lives of your servants and this vessel are worth keeping her until the races are properly crushed and subservient?"

"Perhaps you are correct." Five of Daebian's crew collapsed lifelessly to the deck. *"But examples must be made. Do not fail again, slave."*

Zyn vanished, the oppressive pall lifted, and things moved once more. Eva wiped her brow and stared at the blood covering her hand. Daebian strode briskly to the main deck and helped Eva untie herself from the mast.

"Are you all right?"

Eva wiped the blood from her fingers onto her sleeve. "I think so. What happened?"

"Just a visit from one of our lords and masters."

"I take it he was displeased."

"I think it is the duty and desire of gods to be displeased. It is the only time they are happy."

"Daebian, what is going to happen to me after this war? Your father said the Scions will kill everyone who can wield magic."

Daebian laid a hand on her shoulder. "I won't let that happen."

"Can you prevent it? They are gods, Daebian."

Daebian snorted and waved a dismissive hand. "The gods suffer from the same weakness as my father. They are blinded by their own power and feelings of invulnerability. It is what has probably gotten my father into whatever bind he now finds himself and how I have been able to hide some of my thoughts and memories from our masters. I have no doubt they could find and tear out whatever they wished from inside my head, but they think so little of people like us and so highly of themselves they do not bother to probe that deeply. They have blinded themselves to all but the most obvious things."

Eva smiled and pressed against Daebian. "You think more of yourself than any man or god I ever met."

"Yes, but my faith is far better earned." Daebian turned and shouted. "Tobias, turn us around and lead our ships back to North Haven!"

"Aye Aye, Admiral!"

CHAPTER 20

So I shifted my tower between dimensions and disturbed the sleep of some giant dragon," Azerick said. "We fought and he tossed me into your world. That's my life story and how I got here. It's quite a lot when I sit down and actually think about it. I think the worst part of all this is that it has become normal, almost rote. What kind of life is that?"

The borghast matron sighed deeply. The killer had been making noises for two days almost nonstop. She wished it would simply kill her and be done with it. Instead, the creature sat on the tree pinning her helplessly on the ground barking noises at her. It even brought her food and water. If this was its method of torture, it was a bizarre one.

Azerick's hand hovered over one of the runes etched into the face of a large boulder. "Well, I think it is time for me to go."

The sorcerer gripped his staff and used it to feed power into the runes and enhance the latent energy trapped within them. It was an agonizing effort, like trying to breathe through a very small tube. His mind and magic demanded more, but there was no more to give. The runes began to glow, faintly at first, but they steadily grew brighter as they shaped the meager magic leached from the rock, trees, and air. When the power reached its crescendo, Azerick released it.

Four searing rays shot upward, creating the luminous outline of a massive pyramid stabbing into the sky, and struck the weakened scar in the veil between worlds at a single point. Thousands of wallix took to the air with loud squawks and began circling the strange lights with uneasy, territorial aggression. The sky tore open like a sail in a storm. Azerick could feel the magic pouring in from the other side. He inhaled the ethereal power with his mind and body like a drowning man gasping in a lungful of air.

He leapt and pushed himself skyward, shoving against the air with his wings. With a backward glance, he motioned to the tree trapping his foe. Abyssal magic happily answered his call, causing the wood to rot, crumble, and release its prisoner. The wallix swarmed after him the moment he breached the treetops. Azerick used his magic to coax more speed as the swarm closed in behind him and created a cloud so massive it blotted out most of the land.

"Come on, you rabid vultures!" Azerick shouted as he raced for the pupil in the rift's eye. "I've got a big meal waiting for you if you're so damn hungry."

Azerick pushed through the rift, urging the ravenous, angry wallix to give chase. The alien world vanished as the sky swirled into the strange, twisting ether of the space between worlds. He emerged hundreds of feet above his tower and spotted Ancalon's colossal form curled around it, basking in the radiating energy of the Source pool. Azerick pulled in his wings and went into a steep dive. Rolling onto his back, he opened a massive portal directly behind him and in the path of the pursuing Wallix.

"Hey, Ancalon, I thought you might be bored, so I brought you some friends to play with!"

The Father of Dragons looked up just as the flock of wallix entered the portal. The gate's exit point opened just over his head, and the swarm of ravenous creatures burst through like the snowflakes of a furious blizzard. Ancalon roared in outrage and indignation as thousands of beaks and talons dug under scales and sought out vulnerable areas to claw and bite. The creatures were little more than the irritating nuisance of bedbugs to the great dragon, but they stoked his rage and he lashed out. Fire rippled over his body like a windblown robe, incinerating the pests in their entirety.

The Father of Dragons searched the sky for his tormentor. "Sorcerer, I will take great pleasure in devouring you, body and soul!"

Azerick pulled in the power of the Source pool until he was certain taking in any more would consume him and leave not even dust to be carried away on the winds of this shadow world that looked so much like his home. He fed the energy into his staff until it thrummed with power demanding to be unleashed. He fell from the sky just as Ancalon looked up, shouted, and brought the arcanum ball down upon the dragon's head with a mighty overhead chop.

Azerick's comparatively diminutive size made the attack look almost comical, but there was nothing amusing about the power with which it struck. Ancalon's world blacked out for a brief second, and his head swam as the blow shook him to his core and staggered him. A massive shock wave rolled through the air in a perfect ring, stripping and brutalizing every nearby tree that had managed to withstand their first battle. Azerick used his wings to arrest his fall, reeled back, and delivered a second, identical blow that drove the colossus to the ground. A cloud of dust substantial enough to make a small city vanish within its choking haze billowed up around the dragon's body.

Azerick rode the dragon's fall to the ground, stood on the back of his neck, and jabbed the now spear-tipped staff beneath Ancalon's scales and into the base of his gigantic skull. Arcane energy crackled over the staff, waiting to deliver a jolt directly into the dragon's brain.

"Enough!" Azerick shouted. "I am not your enemy, but I will be your executioner if you do not cease this childish tantrum!"

Azerick felt Ancalon's body tense beneath him before going limp with a hurricane-like sigh of surrender. "How pathetic a father am I that I have twice failed to protect my children?"

"I am not a threat to the dragons, Ancalon. The Scions use them, and I must protect my family and my people. It is the Scions who are the enemies of us both, so stop fighting me and help destroy them."

"I cannot fight them. I tried the first time they invaded my realm and lost."

"Why did they come here and leave you be if they were victorious?"

"Father of Dragons is far more literal than a mere title. My blood runs through the veins of every dragon in existence. Thousands of years ago, those creatures came and took some of my blood like leeches. Through it, they are able to bind my children to their will and use them to act as your overlords."

"If you help me, we have a chance to break that link and free them," Azerick urged.

"We cannot. Although I am the master of the spaces between worlds, I cannot go to any of them. You are obviously powerful, but you are not enough to be more than a nuisance to them."

"I know that challenging gods sounds ridiculous, but we have done it before and triumphed."

Ancalon snorted derisively. "Gods…"

"You do not believe them to be gods?"

"What is a god but a being with the power to control another?"

"Then help us. There is far more than just me to fight these creatures and their unholy minions. My son has the blood of dragons running through him. Does that not make him a child of yours as well, a child fighting your most hated enemy?"

"He is a Guardian?"

"He is, and he is brave and kind and wise beyond his years. He is fighting for what is right and is willing to die to save the peoples of our world. Will you be a coward and hide here, or will you fight for your children like a true father would no matter the cost?"

The Father of Dragons rumbled deep in his chest. "I am no coward. I would fight those false gods with the last drop of my blood, but I cannot leave this place, and they are not likely to willingly come here."

"Then I will force them to come here with your help. I cannot easily open a gateway between worlds, but you can. Share your runic knowledge with me so I can lay a trap for them. Our gods' presence in my world is limited by their nature and a higher power, but I suspect the same does not hold true here."

Ancalon's eyes narrowed in thought. "You are correct. Their power and presence would have no limitations here. I do not know if your gods' strength is up to the task of posing a real challenge to the Scions. In your Great Revolution, it took them, the power of a dozen Guardians, and the host of the elven nation to bring them down. I felt the death of every Guardian and know there are no more with the exception of your son."

"Fortunately, my son is exceptional," Azerick responded. "There is also me and you. I do not know if we have the power to slay these creatures, but I know this is our best and only chance."

"Very well, sorcerer. I can show you how to open a rift to this world with my help, but it will be up to you to force the Scions through it.

Once through, we face another challenge in keeping them here. Their ability to cross dimensions is as great as mine."

"Hopefully, their desire to kill me and our gods is great enough to make them stay. This will present them with the best opportunity to kill us all and be done with us. I have spent these past years positioning our pieces on this board as best I can, but I cannot guarantee the actions of the other players."

"Indeed you cannot." Ancalon drew a complex sigil in the ground with a single massive claw. The furrow created by the etching was deep enough to provide a proper grave and so large Azerick had to hover above it to get a proper view. "The Scions will not willingly leave their citadel until it is time for them to personally engage in battle with your gods. It is the seat of their power much like the Source pool within your tower. Place these markers in a position to surround their fortress and activate them when they are at their weakest. I will sense their power and add my own strength to it. Even so, the Scions will resist, and I do not know if even our combined magic will be sufficient to bring them over without first having weakened them in some way."

"How can we weaken them?"

"I do not know. It will be up to you to find a way."

"Ancalon, I do not know what has happened since I have been gone. Do you know where my son is? Have the Scions started their invasion yet?"

The Father of Dragons closed his eyes and peered through the veils between worlds with his senses. "A number of my children gather near the cities you call Brelland and Brightridge. They are angry, and there is much magic being unleashed there."

"Then we have already lost our coastal cities," Azerick muttered to himself. "Can you send me to Brelland?"

"Easily."

Ancalon pointed a talon at the sky and ripped open a hole in space. Azerick flew upward and dived into the swirling, multi-hued mists and auras. His heart raced with the fear of what tragedies might have befallen while he was away. Were Raijaun and Miranda all right? Were they able to evacuate the cities as planned? Did Sandy still hate him and abandon them? He feared for Ellyssa, knowing she would put herself in the face of danger and never yield despite what wisdom might demand. He could not lose another family. Just the thought of it threatened to drive him into madness.

CHAPTER 21

Wolf watched the flying ships return through his small brass spyglass. They were barely visible against the smoke-shrouded horizon as North Haven burned just a few miles away. The largest of the vessels broke away from the others and appeared to be coming toward him, but it cut a path toward the school. The half-elf blinked back tears as the ship began raining fire and lightning down onto the now empty tower and buildings, setting another blaze to obscure the view of his sky. The school was his second home, but Wolf was still surprised at the strength of his emotions on seeing it razed to the ground.

"They should have stayed and fought," Wolf said bitterly to Ghost. "They should have fought for their home like us. They won't take my home without a fight."

Wolf turned his spyglass back to the city and saw large groups of the creatures called ravagers gathering outside the eastern wall. One of the ships was lowering a pair of obelisks by means of ropes and pulleys, while a few, slightly more human-looking creatures, helped guide them into place.

Within minutes, the obelisks stood as a matched pair perhaps two hundred feet apart. A minion at each obelisk inserted a rune-inscribed disc into a matching recess in the stones' surface. The disc flared brightly, and a shimmering gate sprang up between the two pillars. Hordes of ravagers and other creatures streamed through the gate, and Wolf soon gave up trying to count them.

"New plan, Ghost. We will let them pass through our woods, but we will take a toll from the stragglers at their rear. Hey, don't give me that look! I might be idealistic, but I'm not suicidal. You know, for

someone who bathes using his tongue, you are very judgmental."
Ghost cocked his head. "I bathe plenty! If you are through disparaging
my character and hygiene, I would like to focus on the plague of
monsters bent on killing us and everything else in this world."

The ravagers did not move with the ordered discipline of soldiers
but in massive herds tens of thousands strong. Most of these herds
headed in a south-easterly direction, likely on their way to Brelland and
stopped only long enough to decimate any homes and towns in their
path. A smaller group of perhaps three to four hundred broke away
and headed due east just a few miles south of the Northern Range.

There were only a handful of small settlements to the east, and
Azerick had made sure they were all warned to leave. Wolf had seen a
group of Peck's riders going in that direction a few days ago. Still, it
was unlikely they had reached all of the homes dotting the forest, and
there were always those who would refuse to go and would fight for
their homes no matter how ridiculous such an action was. Wolf found
he was able to relate to those foolish people. If these creatures thought
they could just traipse through his woods unmolested, they were
wrong.

Wolf and Ghost padded through the forest as quickly and silently
as a soft breeze after the ravagers. The pair ran at an oblique angle to
head off the much faster-moving invaders. Wolf and Ghost caught up
with the tail end of the marauding band just as the forest resumed to
the east of what was left of the school. Wolf considered the stupidity of
his actions once again as he sighted down the shaft of his arrow before
releasing it into the back of one of the creatures' necks. Two more
arrows were in the air even as the ravager plowed face-first into the
ground and tumbled to a halt.

The mass of ravagers skidded to a stop and searched for the
ambusher. One of the creatures took a deep breath through its nose and
locked eyes with the half-elf. Wolf put out one of those beady black
orbs with another arrow and the chase began. The ravagers let loose
with shrieks and howls as Wolf slung his bow, grabbed a rope tied
higher in the tree, and swung through the air. Ghost raced along below
him while ravagers clawed at the ground in pursuit.

Ghost sprinted away into the shadows. The only sign of his
presence was the brief but furious sound of battle when a solitary

ravager got too close. Wolf swung from ropes and darted across shaky rope and plank suspension bridges he had spent the last couple of years erecting throughout hundreds of acres of his forest. He also had a dozen bows and scores of quivers packed with arrows tucked away in the branches and on platforms, wrapped in oilcloths to protect them from the elements.

Wolf used the platforms and bridges to pepper the ravagers with arrows until he ran out or they began climbing the trees to get to him. A ravager stepped onto the shaky bridge spanning the gap to the tree he was perched in, but Wolf knocked it off with an arrow to its chest. Ravagers began climbing trees all around him, and he knew it was time to move on. Grabbing another rope, Wolf swung out across the span between trees and raced across his primitive bridges with ease. The ravagers were not adept climbers and had a far more difficult time following him. Most leapt from the trees back to the ground where they possessed a significant speed advantage.

The half-elf led the creatures through areas rife with all manner of traps designed to cripple, maim, and kill his attackers. Whip traps and spike boards impaled bodies, and snap traps pierced the ankles and legs of dozens of ravagers. Wolf swung out over a wide expanse, released his grip, and leapt to a mace trap hidden high in the trees. He grabbed the rope and heaved with his legs, riding the thousand-pound spiked log like a sled racing down a steep hill. Wolf used his weight to guide the log into the tightest knot of ravagers and smiled as he plowed through dozens of the monsters, pinning several on the log and crushing a host of them before arcing back up and leaping into another tree at the apex of its swing. A sharp cry brought his attention to the north.

"Ghost!"

Wolf leapt from tree to tree using their branches like a squirrel when he lacked ropes or bridges to make the crossing. He found Ghost surrounded by ravagers, looking like a piece of flotsam in a sea of murderous creatures. The big wolf kept his backside to a massive tree as the ravagers closed in around him. His black coat glistened with fresh blood, not all of it belonging to his enemies.

"Ghost!"

Wolf began showering the ravagers with arrows in hopes of creating an opening for his best friend to escape through, but there were simply too many of them. Wolf swung to the massive fir tree towering over Ghost as ravagers began clawing their way into the branches below him. He looked at Ghost helplessly and continued loosing arrows into the mass of snarling bodies. He could hear more of the creatures crashing through the forest not far away. He and Ghost were less than seconds from being overwhelmed.

Wolf grabbed some shredded, pitch-covered tinder from a pouch on his hip and stuffed it into the recesses of a dry pinecone. He fought to control the shaking in his hands as he struck steel against flint, sending cascades of sparks onto the highly flammable fibers. The pitch-laden tinder snapped and popped as it burst into flames. Wolf touched the burning cone to a branch over his head, setting the dry needles aflame before pitching the fiery pinecone into the brushy ring surrounding the tree.

A small fire erupted almost immediately as the parched needles and twigs combusted. Wolf grabbed at the cones and drier branches in reach, touched them to the expanding flames just over his head, and hurled them into the forest, driving some of the ravagers away from Ghost and erecting walls of fire between him and the packs of ravagers racing toward them.

He had gained Ghost some time, but now they were both surrounded by ravagers and fire. More of the killers arrived, lunging at the expanding flames and darting away. A few braved the fire and leapt over or simply charged through, ignoring the searing of their flesh to reach Ghost. Wolf launched shaft after shaft into those that disregarded the fire.

Ghost was capable of handling any single ravager who got past Wolf's sniping, but they were both tiring, and the tree they used as a key to their defense was being consumed by flames. In the next few seconds, the ravagers would cease their hesitation and rush Ghost, and all Wolf could do was look on helplessly, exacting revenge until he ran out of arrows or burned up.

Ghost looked up at Wolf and saw him grip the hilt of his sword as he prepared to throw himself into the throng of vicious monsters before deserting his friend. Ghost's body contorted, his black fur vanished, and he stood on the naked legs of a human.

"Throw me a rope!"

Wolf's eyes went wide, but he dropped a rope without hesitation. Ghost used his human arms to scamper up the line as the ravagers leapt through the ring of fire and slashed at the air where he had been standing. Ghost climbed hand over hand up the rope until he took a perch next to a glaring Wolf.

"You and I are going to have a very long talk if we survive this," Wolf said. "How long have you been able to do that?"

"Since I was about five."

"You don't think that was something worth mentioning in all these years? Oh my god, you were there when I was with Becky and Louise! Oh, you were right there watching when I was with Rachel, you furry little pervert!"

"It's not that big a deal."

"Hey, it's plenty big enough!"

Ghost rolled his eyes. "Not that, the…do you really think this is the best time to have this discussion?"

Ghost looked at the ravagers sinking their claws into the thick tree bark and slowly making their way up its surface even while the branches above his head combusted and sent a wave of searing heat against his unprotected skin. "I suppose not, but you can bet we're going to talk about it later. Can you swing?"

"I'll learn."

Wolf grabbed a rope and pulled it to him. "Hold it just below my feet. We'll have to swing together since you didn't bother telling your best friend you could turn into a person."

"Let it go already! I'm sure you have secrets too."

"Not as many as I thought I did just a few minutes ago."

"Are you referring to Rachel?"

"I am referring to Rachel."

"It wasn't a secret. She told everyone."

"How do you know?"

"People talk around me."

"What did she say?"

"It was flattering."

Wolf smiled. "I guess it's okay then. Still, women are blabbermouths. You keep your big yap shut."

"I kept this from you for the last fifteen years. Do you think I'm going to share it with someone else? Now, those things are right below us and our rope is on fire. If your rope is still strong enough to support us and your massive ego, I would really like to leave now."

"Right."

Wolf and Ghost swung out over the leaping, snarling ravagers like monkeys on a vine. Wolf released his grip and threw himself at the tree ahead of them with a master's practiced ease. Ghost tried to emulate his friend's move, brushed the branch with his fingertips, and fell. The branches whipped and scratched his body before he landed on a stout limb. A ravager leapt up, grabbed a lower branch, and took a swipe at Ghost with its blade.

Ghost gripped the limb above him and threw his legs up and over it just as the knife sliced through the air below his back. Wolf buried an arrow in the creature's face and sent shafts streaking into the ones trying to climb up. Ghost heaved, kicked, and managed to pull himself onto the limb and gain Wolf's higher position.

Wolf glanced at the scratches now covering Ghost's human skin. "I bet you wish you were wearing trousers about now."

"Not nearly as much as I wish I had friends who did not put me in situations that have me fighting for my life."

"Then your life would be boring."

"Yes, but at least it would extend beyond the next hour."

"True, it appears I underestimated how challenging this was going to be."

"The cave Ellyssa was living in when she went crazy isn't too far from here. Its opening is narrow, and I think we can defend it."

"Great, then we can starve to death."

"Do you have a better plan?" Ghost asked, "Because, so far, yours are not quite panning out."

"I have a brilliant, two-part plan. Part one, shut up. Part two, we use the zip line running across the creek and hopefully gain a little ground on them. There's not much in the way of trees near the mountains, so even if the wind shifts, we should be okay as far as the fire goes."

The pair fled through the trees as quickly as they could, using the terrain to slow their pursuers. When they reached an area where Wolf had not strung ropes, zip lines, or bridges, it was a mad dash across the ground, often just yards ahead of certain death until they found safety in the treetops once again. The trees began to thin, and it was a long run to the tree near the banks of the river where Wolf had a zip line to get across. They found a game trail cutting a tunnel through the dense brush and used it to navigate their way through the natural obstacle while the ravagers tried to tear their way through, behind, and around them.

Wolf and Ghost climbed the stout oak and scampered to the upper arms of the majestic tree. The river was less than a hundred feet across, but the zip line ran almost five times that length before ending at the nearest suitable tree. From there, the trees shrank and dwindled near the base of the mountains where erosion and rocky terrain limited their growth.

"There's only one pulley," Ghost noted.

"Jump onto my back and hang on."

Ghost wrapped his arms around Wolf's neck and locked his legs around his waist. "Can you hold me?"

"Yeah, but now I'm really wishing you had trousers."

Wolf gripped the pulley bar tightly and threw himself off the small platform. The two flew over the river as ravagers howled their anger. The bulk of the creatures raced up- or downstream in search of a way across, a few leapt onto the rope and tried to shinny across it, and several jumped into the river and were swept away. The pair reached the far side, and Wolf drew his shortsword the moment Ghost dropped off his back and severed the rope with a quick swipe, sending the ravagers trying to cross into the river.

Ghost shifted back into his wolf form the instant they touched the ground and loped beside Wolf as they raced for the cave. It was almost two miles to the southern base of the mountains, and they were at least a mile west of the cave entrance. Wolf ran at a pace between a jog and sprint, but when he heard the howls and calls of the ravagers behind him, he urged his body to greater speeds. As the ravagers rapidly gained on them, Wolf knew he would not be able to reach the cave before the ravagers ran him down.

Wolf felt a tingling at his side like static. He gripped the wolf-headed hilt of his sword and felt it grow warm to the touch. The half-elf focused on the strange blade and felt energy pouring into his body and fueling his muscles. He urged his legs to move faster and they obeyed. The feeling of speed was exhilarating as the ground sped past, and Ghost had to increase his pace to keep up. Wolf knew he still lacked the speed of the ravagers, but he might just be fast enough to make it to the cave.

From the corner of his eye, Wolf spotted three of the creatures racing at them from the south, sure to intercept them before they reached safety. Ghost peeled off and struck the lead ravager in the chest. The two foes went down in a rolling, slashing, snarling mass. The other two were intent on killing the half-elf and ignored the two creatures locked in combat. One ravager leapt at Wolf, its bone blade held back for a powerful strike. Wolf ducked low and whipped his black steel blade in a swift arc, lopping off the creature's right leg at the knee.

The second monster came in low, slashing at Wolf's thigh. Wolf leapt, twisted in midair, and cut a deep gash across the ravager's shoulder blades. He took a few stumbling steps as he landed but continued to race on. The ravager fell and came charging out of the cloud of dust it raised in its tumble. Wolf continued to sprint, knowing that if he stopped to fight the beast, the others would be on him in an instant.

He tensed as the ravager bore down on him, ready to lash out the moment it came within reach. A black blur struck the killer as it jumped at Wolf's back and took it to the ground. He cast a quick glance back, saw that Ghost had the creature by the throat, and knew the outcome was already decided.

The ravager lay still, and Ghost raced just ahead of the onrushing horde. Wolf glimpsed Ghost off to the side and heard the ravagers closing in behind them. He saw the dark cleft in the rock just ahead and leaned forward, demanding even more speed from his exhausted body. His legs felt numb, and his lungs burned with every labored breath. He let out a bestial snarl as he jumped through the narrow fissure just behind Ghost.

Ravagers piled against the opening, slashing and clawing in their attempt to force their bodies through the gap. Wolf hacked at the arms thrusting into the cave and littered the ground with dismembered limbs until the creatures finally chose to give up their siege and gathered just outside, snarling, pacing, and occasionally taking out their frustrations on each other.

Wolf bent double trying to catch his breath then began shouting out and limping around the cavern. "Ow, hamstring cramps! My legs aren't designed to go that fast!" He looked out at the ravagers pacing outside and at the spring near the back of the cave. "It doesn't look like they're going anywhere anytime soon. At least we have water. Not sure if we can eat those arms I chopped off. You want to take a taste?"

Ghost's expression clearly indicated he did not. Instead, he sat on his haunches and began howling, his shrill cry echoing off the stone walls.

"Yeah, it's going to take about ten minutes of that before I throw one of us outside to those things."

Ghost cast him a sidelong glance but continued his vociferous calling. After twenty minutes of Ghost's caterwauling, Wolf was about to chastise him once again, but responding howls from outside the cave cut off his complaint. Moments later, yips and cries filled the air, and Wolf heard the padding of innumerable feet strumming against the ground. The ravagers ceased their growling and quarreling as hundreds of wolves plowed into their ranks in a fury of snapping jaws and flashing teeth. The two sides fought with wild viciousness, heedless of their injuries until they could fight no more. Blood soon painted the ground and rocks, most of it that of the ravagers.

The battle was over in minutes leaving dead ravagers littering the ground. The wolves did not escape without losses of their own, but not as many as Wolf first thought. Several fallen members of the massive pack began to stir and soon stood once again. Only the blood matting their coats gave any indication they had been seriously injured just minutes before. A big, silver female broke from the pack and approached Wolf and Ghost. She sniffed Ghost and began nuzzling his neck. Her body contorted, and she wrapped her now human arms around Ghost's neck and hugged him tightly.

"Oh, my boy, I thought I had lost you all those years ago."

Ghost shifted and returned his mother's embrace. "Thanks to my friend, I was never lost."

Luna turned to Wolf who stood with a look of incomprehension on his face. "Thank you for being a friend to my son. Your kind and mine have long treated each other well, and I am grateful."

"*My kind* never did much for me, but I'm glad we're friends."

"Do you know of the lupins?"

"Not until today."

Luna smiled. "We are very reclusive and secretive by nature. Do not think ill of my son for keeping that secret even from you. You must have many questions."

"Just one at the moment. Would it kill any of you to carry a pair of trousers?"

CHAPTER 22

Jerry stared out at the darkness beyond the walls. "Was it as bad as our training?"

"It was so much worse," Kari answered. "They were so fast and vicious. They climbed up the walls and just kept coming no matter how many we killed. The worst part was the smell. Ellyssa and the others never prepared us for the smell of death."

"I'm just glad they brought some of us back to the wall. If it's half as bad as you say, we'll need everyone we have hurling wizard fire to hold them back." Jerry leaned forward against the parapet. "Did you see that? It looked like something moved near the farthest fire."

Kari looked out at the large bonfires casting orange light over sections of the surrounding area outside the walls. Shapes flitted around the glow of the fires; their silhouettes darker than the softly illuminated ground around them.

"Hopefully just some animals. Let's light 'em up."

The two young wizards grasped a tiny tendril of the Source, shaped it into a simple spell, and sent it arcing over the wall. When the white balls of light reached the desired location, they burst into miniature suns, destroying the darkness for hundreds of yards in all directions. Within seconds, dozens more streaked across the sky and brought an unnatural daylight over most of Brelland.

"Dear gods, we're all going to die!" Jerry shouted.

Ravagers packed the field for as far they could see. Hundreds of thousands of remorseless killers charged the castle walls, their bloodcurdling howls loud enough to shake the stones beneath the defenders' feet. Massive trebuchets began launching colossal stones and flaming cisterns of oil followed by the smaller catapults and ballistae.

"Hold yourself together and follow your training!" Kari shouted, then began weaving her spells.

Snapped out of his shock, Jerry followed her example. He fought through his terror and began hurling magic at the approaching horde. All along the wall, destruction rained down as magic, arrows, stones, and fire slew the invaders by the hundreds. Despite the incredible onslaught, it was like throwing stones at a lake. Ravagers filled every void created by the brutal attacks and piled against the walls in mounds of bodies clawing their way to the precipice despite the defenders' unyielding brutality.

"Fire up the gates and watch the skies!" Ellyssa shouted as alarm bells rang throughout the city.

Brelland boasted three magical gates to facilitate the evacuation of nearly a quarter of a million people packed within its walls. Paired obelisks stood midway down three wide avenues leading to a large, circular plaza. It was deemed the best area to facilitate the evacuation of so many people, but it left them vulnerable to attacks from above. Cables and chains stretched between rooftops and iron tower frameworks to hamper dragons trying to land in the plaza and destroy the gates, but they did nothing against their magic or terrible breath weapons.

Thousands of citizens already crowded the streets, and they began pushing toward the gates before the mages charged with their operation could even activate them. A massive camp lit by torches and magical light replaced the cityscape behind the gates as the portals sprang to life. Wizards sent lights streaking into the sky as dragons swooped down and began spewing fire and hurling magic at the scurrying forms below. Wards flared throughout the plaza as the mages erected magical barriers like huge umbrellas against the rain of destruction.

The dragons' assault was intense as the enormous creatures swooped low, struck at the humans, and raced away into the night in a series of unending sorties. Wizards not tasked with defense lashed out with their magic, forcing the dragons to evade their spells and making it difficult for them to unleash their fury with any accuracy. Huge ballistae launched spears with enough force to punch through even dragon hide, and catapults flung lengths of chain or cables capped with iron balls to foul their wings.

Ellyssa watched a large green dragon dive low and draw in a massive breath. She drew in the Source, wove a twisting braid of magic, and struck at the creature. The ray lanced from her outstretched hands and hit the dragon in its scaly side. The powerful mage continued to pour energy into the spell, training it on the dragon like a stream of water trying to extinguish a fire.

Maintaining an attack of this sort required intense concentration and was mentally and physically exhausting, but her anger helped fuel it. She smiled when her magic tore through the dragon's wards and scales to inflict a grievous injury. The oil keeping the leathery membrane of its wings supple began to burn and left a trail of smoke across the sky before the dragon plummeted and crashed through several buildings. Soldiers and mages raced to the site to ensure it did not rise again.

Ellyssa turned just in time to catch a glimmer of movement out of the corner of her eye. She dived to her left as a dark, child-sized shape hurled itself at her from the darkness of a nearby building. She felt pain flare across her back just above her kidney and the warm rush of blood. Ignoring her injury, she rolled to the side and prepared to blast the creature to pieces. A stream of arcane orbs smashed into the knife-wielding, blue-skinned creature before she could attack it. The luminous orbs drove the creature to the ground and left its body a smoking ruin.

"Are you okay?" Roger shouted as he ran to Ellyssa's side and pressed a dressing against her wound.

Ellyssa nodded as she used a bandage from her satchel to tie Roger's wadded piece of cloth in place. "Yeah, it only cut me. How did that thing ignore my wards?"

"I don't know, but we better keep an eye out for them. I would also like to know how they got into the city and this close to the gates."

The two wizards felt the ground tremble beneath their feet and noticed discordance with the normal rumbles of war. A section of the road sagged before crumbling into a large hole. The fissure widened and stretched until it reached one of the gates' pillars.

Ellyssa and Roger looked on helplessly as the obelisk fell like a sawn tree into the gaping wound. To add a nightmare atop the horror, ravagers began pouring out of the crevice like roaches into the street. The creatures hacked at the nearly defenseless people trying to flee, causing pandemonium as women grabbed children and tried to run only to find there was nowhere safe to go.

"They're in the sewers," Roger said hoarsely.

"Just like the vermin they are," Ellyssa snarled, then began drawing in the Source without reserve. "Time to squish some rats."

Several mages sent red balls of light streaking into the sky to indicate their dire emergency. Thousands of soldiers left their defensive positions and converged on the plaza with all haste. Hundreds of cavalry arrived and laid into the ravagers with sword, spear, and arrow as people fought for their lives or just tried to break free from the chaos and escape.

Ravagers continued to spew from the hole in the street, and others could be heard above the din opening up elsewhere and expelling more enemy into the heart of the city. A massive column of fire fell from the sky, striking the gaping fissure at the gate and incinerating scores of ravagers as they tried to climb out. The ground shuddered and the walls of the crevice collapsed leaving a smoking trench in its place and sealing off the ravagers' point of egress.

Ellyssa and Roger ran to Raijaun as he touched down with a beating of his wings near the fallen gate. He struck out with his awesome power, cleaving through masses of ravagers but also humans. The battle was so chaotic, the combatants locked in such fierce struggles, it was not always possible to fight the enemy and avoid collateral damage. It tore at his soul knowing that some of his magic brought down friend as well as foe, but he knew he had to force the invaders back to protect the gates, and he continued the barrage.

"Raijaun, they're coming through the sewer!" Ellyssa shouted.

"And the aqueducts, I imagine."

"Can you fix the gate?" Roger asked.

Raijaun shook his head. "No, the obelisk is gone. This is very bad. Continue to hold the plaza. I must see to clearing the aqueducts of these invaders before they get too entrenched within the city and prevent our people from reaching the gates. With only two functional gates, we will have to defend the city far longer than anticipated."

"Can we hold long enough?"

"I do not know. Clear the surrounding buildings of civilians and do whatever it takes to hold the remaining two gates. If you think you are going to lose this position, destroy the gates so the ravagers cannot use them."

"But if we destroy the gates…"

"If we lose the gates, we are already lost. At least those in the valley will have a chance to flee."

Raijaun leapt and thrust his body into the air with the powerful beating of his wings. From his aerial vantage point, he saw the situation was possibly even direr than he first thought. Fires were burning in several locations within the upper district as ravagers clambered out of the tunnels beneath the city and onto the streets. Furious battles raged across several blocks as wizards, warriors, and citizens fought with the tenacity of cornered animals. Raijaun reached into his cloak pocket and focused on the speaking stone.

"Headmaster, there is dreadful news."

The Academy headmaster's stressed voice came to him a moment later. "It is grim here as well, Raijaun. The ravagers are charging the walls, and I'm about to order the gates opened."

"Wait! Do not activate the gates yet!"

"Raijaun, there must be half a million of those things blanketing the countryside, and I have a city packed with more than two hundred thousand people to evacuate. I don't have time to wait."

"The ravagers came through our sewers and aqueducts. The moment you activate the gates, they will know precisely where they are and will come streaming out in the middle of the city. They undermined one of our gates and destroyed it already."

"Dear gods above," Maureen gasped. "Can you still flee?"

"I...don't know. You need to flood the tunnels beneath the city or fill them with fire. Do whatever it takes no matter the damage."

"Understood. Thank you. We may owe you our lives again, Raijaun."

"Duty accrues no debt. Protect the gates and get everyone out."

A powerful blow blasted the air from his lungs as taloned paws wrapped around his body and drove him toward the ground. Raijaun and the dragon struck hard enough to bounce once before settling in a cloud of dust and churned-up earth. The dragon's grip loosened enough from the impact to allow him to twist around just as the creature's massive jaws snaked down and tried to snap his head off.

Raijaun's muscles burned and his arms trembled as he held the huge head at bay. Hot, sticky drool poured from the dragon's maw onto his chest and face. The Guardian sought his spiritual center, found tranquility, and shaped the Source with a thought. The dragon roared as electricity coursed through it. Raijaun felt the dragon fight back with its magic, dampening the spell's power and forcing it to arc harmlessly into the air.

The dragon squeezed harder and called upon its magic to return the powerful jolt. Raijaun cried out and his body convulsed from the arcane attack. The dragon's head came down as his arms failed. A gust of wind blew over him, he felt the thud of something heavy striking the ground nearby, and the pressure on his arms eased then vanished. Raijaun opened his eyes and saw that Sandy had her jaws clamped behind the dragon's head. The dragon tried to fight and roll away, but Sandy was cutting off its airway and its struggles quickly ceased.

"Thank you," Raijaun said as he stood. "It is a good thing you were here."

"I've been flying around the edges and picking strays off from the herd. I'm getting pretty good at it. When I saw you fly out of the city, I figured you'd catch someone's attention and might need help. What are you doing outside?"

"Ravagers are in the tunnels beneath the city. My guess is they are coming in through the aqueducts to the north or the sewers' exits to the south."

"That's not good."

"No, it's not."

"Let's get up there then. I'll help."

When Raijaun and Sandy neared the channel directing a man-made river beneath the city, they discovered Raijaun's hunch had been right. Hundreds, possibly thousands, of ravagers crowded around the opening to the aqueduct. A canal led to the aqueducts just under a mile from the city's curtain wall. The canal disappeared into a tunnel running below the ground and into the labyrinth of waterways. A dam and floodgate controlled the amount of water flowing into the city, and this was Raijaun's destination.

"There are so many of them!" Sandy exclaimed. "And those are only the ones we can see. Who knows how many there are already inside?"

"It's not going to matter. Have you ever seen a pond get struck by lightning?"

Raijaun landed atop the dam's control house and turned a large iron wheel. The floodgates opened and water poured into the canal. The wall of water slammed into the masses of ravagers wading in the channel and swept them into the cavernous pipes below the city.

"Now we just need the lightning," Raijaun said to Sandy.

Sandy grinned. "I can do lightning."

Sandy and Raijaun called upon their magical powers and sent bolt after bolt of electricity into the canal. The electrical current coursed through the water and electrocuted scores upon scores of invaders. They pressed forward and aimed their bolts into the mouth of the aqueduct, sending the killing jolts as far as they could beneath the city. They then sent rays of freezing cold into the water. Ice instantly formed where they struck. The air filled with the popping and cracking of ice expanding all along the flow of water.

The entrance to the aqueduct became completely clogged with ice but still they directed the intense cold into the channel. As the water froze beneath the city, it expanded, crushing everything inside the tunnels and buckling several streets. The pair stopped when the air around them became so cold it burned like fire. They stepped away from the intense cold and admired their handiwork.

"I don't think they're getting in or out of there again," Sandy commented.

"I just hope it was soon enough to avert disaster. I must return to the gates. We stopped them here, but there were already hundreds if not thousands within the walls." Raijaun looked up into a sky lit almost as brightly as daylight from the constant barrage of magic and dragon fire streaking into the air and crashing down onto the city. "The dragons have increased their assault as well, so we are far from safe."

"I'll try to harass them as best I can, but I'm staying away from the city."

"I understand. I am almost anticipating someone lashing out at me thinking I am one of these creatures. Humans are a rather shortsighted people. Be careful. That was a lot of power we used just now."

Sandy glanced at her inscribed scales and smiled ruefully. "I have a lot of reserves."

"Have you forgiven us?"

"I have come to understand, and I suppose understanding is a large part of forgiving. Better a hideous body than a beautiful corpse."

Raijaun stroked Sandy's chest. "You could never be hideous."

"Thank you, the flattery of a five-year-old means so much to me."

Raijaun laughed and opened a portal above the city. He stepped through into smoke-tinged air and made a quick survey of the damage. Fire teams worked furiously to control the burning buildings while soldiers and wizards battled the ravagers still wreaking havoc inside the city and repelled those climbing the outer walls. The walls held and the enemy inside appeared to be contained to pockets of resistance away from the gates.

Raijaun glided down to the plaza and saw that the battle here had been brutal. Bodies littered the ground, and most of the nearby buildings lay in ruin. Those still standing appeared ready to fall at the slightest urging. Noncombatants packed the plaza, but they were not moving as swiftly as they should. Raijaun's stomach felt like it was about to implode when he saw the reason why. Only one of the gates still stood. The other lay in a mass of rubble near the end of the street.

"Raijaun!" Ellyssa called out as she shoved through the mass of people.

"What happened?"

Ellyssa had to swallow to get the words out. "We lost another gate. The dragons started dropping those little blue creatures from the sky like stones. We had our best wards around the gates, but they just went through them like they weren't there. One of them struck right next to the eastern gate and exploded."

Raijaun raised his hand and focused on the ruined gate. "Runic magic of a destructive nature. The Scions will not allow any of their minions to wield magic, but they are not beyond using them as vessels for it when needed."

"We've managed to keep the dragons from dropping any more of those things now that we know the danger, and they have mostly given up doing so. Can we get everyone out with just one gate?"

"I don't know," he lied. "Just keep everyone moving as fast as we can. I need to speak with the king. There are some hard decisions we have to make."

Raijaun opened another portal and stepped into the hall Jarvin had declared as the war room. As he expected, the king was there with his generals and strategists. Leaves of paper lay on the table in front of him, reports in chronological order and separated by key locations. All eyes looked up and hands went reflexively to sword hilts.

"My apologies again, gentlemen."

Jarvin waved a hand. "We are all agitated. I am very glad to see you. My reports from the gates are sketchy and third-hand at best."

"The mages and soldiers there have been extremely hard-pressed. I expect their reports to begin reaching you soon."

"I hope you can fill us in on what you know until they do."

"The situation is beyond dire, Your Majesty. Ravagers entered the sewers and aqueducts through the northern waterway. Sandy and I managed to flood the tunnels and freeze them solid."

"Sandy is one of the wizards?" Jarvin asked.

General Haskins answered, "That's Lord Giles's pet dragon, isn't it? I heard he had one of those. What kind of mad sorcerer would he be without a pet dragon?" The general laughed loudly.

"Sandy is a dear friend and considered family. She is no one's pet and has been risking her life fighting for our cause. It would be ill-advised to show her disrespect again," Raijaun warned, his voice as frigid as the northern wastes.

The laughter abruptly ceased and General Haskins looked chagrined. "My apologies. My attempt at levity was poorly applied, and I meant no disrespect."

"How bad was the damage to the gates?" Jarvin asked, getting back to the task at hand.

"Nearly total. We have lost two of the three gates to the surprise assault and some unexpected tactics."

"What of Brightridge? Have you been in contact with Headmaster Florent?"

"I warned her of the assault from the sewers. They had not yet come under attack, so they had a small chance to counter it. I lost the speaking stone while in combat with a dragon and have not spoken with her since."

Jarvin nodded, his face ashen. "Is our plan still viable? Can we evacuate the city through just one gate?"

"From what I saw of the multiple battlefronts, it is unlikely we can evacuate the city in its entirety. That is why I came here now, because only you can choose our course of action."

"What are our choices?"

"Stand and fight to the last man and send word to the valley for everyone to flee. Some will survive in the world to come, although most might prefer not to. Our other choice is to give our fighting forces priority of the gates, particularly the wizards. If all our allies have answered the call, we will have a substantial force waiting at the valley, but they will require all of our mages if they are to make a stand. It is possible that we might still win this war there, assuming Brightridge is able to reach the valley mostly intact."

"You would abandon nearly half the city and leave those people to the hands of those monsters?"

"No, sire, you would. I would stay and defend the gates. The amount of power I can wield is substantial if I hold nothing back and allow it to consume me. I should be able to oppose the Scions and their horde long enough for most of the fighters to get away."

Jarvin stood and smashed his fist against the table, upsetting several brass figures placed on a map like chess pieces. "You give us a devil's choice! We're damned no matter what we choose."

"It is not I who force the choices but our situation. I merely point them out."

"No, I will not abandon my people. Not one person. Not even to save ourselves. If we do that, then we are no better than these false gods. It is best not to exist at all than to give up the one thing that defines us."

"Hear, hear," his officers declared.

"Then there is but one last thing we can do."

"What is that?"

"Pray for a miracle."

CHAPTER 23

Azerick grabbed hold of his fury and clutched it to his heart like a mother cradling her babe. He reached behind him with his magic and pulled up a chunk of granite the size of North Haven's castle. The miniature mountain streaked after him and followed its master into the rift like a well-trained dog. Azerick and his mountain appeared several thousand feet over the city. Below, dozens of dragons wheeled about, spitting fire and hurling magic at the people within. Beyond the walls, ravagers covered the land like writhing crimson snow, their bodies stacked against the walls in several places like deep drifts with the humans fighting furiously to shovel them away.

The rift spit his colossal boulder out like a cherry pit, and it fell inexorably to the ground. Azerick fueled its descent with his magic, shattered it into hundreds of pieces, and energized them with arcane power. The ravagers and at least half a dozen dragons found themselves pummeled by a meteor shower the likes of which had not been seen since the near world-shattering battles of the Great Revolution. Hundreds of fiery stones struck with enough force to shake the city and knock people from their feet. The meteors shattered the ravagers' drive to the city and the ground upon which they stood.

"What new kind of hell is this?" Jarvin shouted as his war room shook, paintings fell from walls, and his recently uprighted battle figurines fell across the table once again.

The terrifying impacts continued, and all within were certain the entire castle would soon crumble around them. Candelabras and braziers toppled, and men raced about on unsteady legs to ensure they did not set fire to the room. Raijaun lit the room with his magic and saw the pale, fearful looks of everyone turned in his direction.

"Raijaun, what is happening?" Jarvin asked.

Raijaun raised a hand as if feeling for a draft. His concern vanished and a smile spread across his face. "Father has returned."

"Thank the gods," Jarvin murmured along with the others in the room.

After only a few minutes of tense silence, a bright, thin line split the air near where Raijaun had gated into the room earlier. The portal widened and Azerick stepped into the room wearing his more comfortable human guise. Jarvin's hand unconsciously fell to the hilt of the sword resting at his hip.

"Father, it is good to see you well. We have been very worried since you did not return as expected. I suspect something went amiss?"

"You could certainly say that."

"Let me guess," General Brague interrupted, "you ran out of people to aggravate in this world so you found another to pick fights in."

"Actually, it was two worlds."

"Forgive me. Perhaps one day I will learn to stop underestimating you."

"I pray we all live so long."

"Azerick, I am heartened to see you back," the king said.

"Are you?" Azerick turned back to his son. "How are Miranda and Ellyssa?"

"Miranda is seeing to the moving of refugees. Ellyssa has been battling at the gates but fares well. Sandy has also returned and is providing a great deal of help distracting the dragons and pulling them away from the battle over the city."

"I am relieved. I feared that I had driven her away irrevocably. Has she forgiven me?"

"She has come to understand why you did it and accepted its necessity. Father, there is an urgent matter we must attend to. We have lost two of the three gates. The ravagers managed to get beneath the city and struck where we least expected it despite having reinforced our guards there."

"I must take much of the blame," Jarvin said dejectedly. "Your son advised me to place a larger force to guard them, but I took some of them away and put them back on the walls. It seemed that was the more immediate threat at the time. If we die here, it is my fault."

"Possibly, but I have no intention of us dying here. It goes against my plans, and that I cannot allow. Accompany me to the gates, Raijaun."

Azerick opened another portal and stepped through. Raijaun followed and they both entered the plaza through a narrow alley. Masses of people packed the plaza beyond the alley trying to get through the single gate while soldiers and mages tried to keep them orderly. It was a battle they were losing, and Azerick's cataclysmic return had panicked them even further as they feared the Scions had finally appeared to destroy them once and for all. Ellyssa and Roger saw Azerick and Raijaun emerge from the narrow cleft between buildings and broke away from the crowd.

"Azerick, you made it back!" Ellyssa shouted, wrapping him in a tight embrace. "I'm sorry. I tried to protect the gates but I failed."

"You did not fail. You did your best, and I'm sure you are the reason we have any left at all."

"Raijaun and Sandy are the ones who stopped them from coming into the city."

"You all did your part, and I am proud of you. Show me the ruined gates."

It took some shouting, shoving, and even some magic to push through the mass of people, but most moved out of their way when they saw Raijaun towering over them.

"So, it was you making all that racket," Roger noted as he shuffled beside them.

"It was. I do like a grand entrance."

"Where did you go? What happened?"

Azerick stopped and looked at the shattered remains of the toppled pillar. "We don't have time for that now."

"Can you fix it?" Ellyssa asked. "The other one is even worse. An exploding goblin blew it up."

"Goblin?"

"Whatever they're called. They are dark blue and kind of look like Grick."

"They can also ignore our wards and walk right through them," Roger added.

"Is there any way to make another one?" Ellyssa asked.

"I can't, but I know someone who may. Fortunately, I have not been idle while I was away and made a friend."

"How big a fight was it before you became friends?"

Azerick grinned. "Pretty damn big."

He reached into his pocket and retrieved the door handle made of arcanum. Jabbing the end of it between the stones of a nearby wall still standing despite the rest of the building lying in ruins, Azerick turned the handle and pulled. A section of the wall opened up as if it were a door on well-made hinges. The interior was dark except for the glowing silver pool in the middle of the chamber.

"What is that?" Raijaun asked, indicating the handle.

"It is a piece of the Source pool made solid. It allows me to return to the tower."

"Could you not have used it to return home?"

"I had no connection to the pool from where I was, so could not open a doorway. It also only works one way, so do not let this door close behind me."

Azerick walked into the chamber containing the Source pool and up the stairs to the living room. Exiting the outer doors of the foyer, he stepped back into Ancalon's world and found himself staring into the dragon's massive eyeball.

"You have returned."

"I need your help."

"So soon? I hope this is not indicative of the level of give and take for our alliance."

Azerick ignored the dragon's barbed words. "I created a series of gates to allow my people to flee ahead of the Scions and their minions. Two of the three have been destroyed. With their loss, we cannot evacuate Brelland before they overrun us. Can you create a rift in my world to replace them?"

"I felt your gates when you activated them, though I did not know their true purpose. Primitive but effective devices. Yes, I can open the channel you require. Since I now know what they are, I can use your gates as markers to know where to create the entrance and exit points of an acceptable rift."

"Thank you, Ancalon; we are all in your debt."

"Only if you survive and we are triumphant. Remember our bargain. There must be no retaliation against my children when this is done."

"I will do everything I can to ensure it."

"Then there will be no debt between us."

Azerick returned to his tower and the doorway that would send him to his world. Something impacted his face the moment he stepped through, leaving a stinging heat on his left cheek. He braced himself as Miranda began punching him in his chest and calmly waited until her fury subsided.

"I'm told you have arrived only to catch your back as you vanish once again with no idea whether or not you are coming back!" his wife railed, then punched him again. "I thought you were dead! You cannot keep putting me through this. It's not fair."

Azerick held her close as she collapsed against his chest and wept. "I'm sorry. I do not mean to be so selfish, but I am back now, and I am not going anywhere."

"Promise me."

"I promise, not until I must face the Scions. If I do not return from there, then it will not matter anymore."

Miranda pushed off Azerick's chest, forcing aside her wifely concerns and resumed her duties as the daughter of North Haven. "We need to get the people out of here."

"I have addressed the issue. Get everyone clear of the area, particularly from around the gates. Tell the crowd that we are going to open another portal to get them all through, but they need to step back."

"Can you do that?" Ellyssa asked.

"No, but I have spoken to someone who can."

The soldiers and mages urged the pressing crowd to back away, issuing promises to any who resisted and clouts to their shoulders and bodies when words failed. They had barely cleared the area when the air tore open in a line bisecting the two destroyed gates. The rift opened wide like the mouth of a giant, invisible creature to reveal the valley hundreds of miles away. The valley defenders scurried about and formed ranks, unsure what the rift portended.

"That should facilitate our evacuation. Continue to defend the walls as best you can until the noncombatants are safely through. If we begin to get overrun, retreat to the secondary defensive line. This is not the place to stand and die. We will punish them as best we can, but reaching the valley is our priority. I have greatly expended myself of late and need to rest."

"We can manage, Father. Where shall I find you?" Raijaun asked.

"I will take a room in the castle. Jarvin will know which one."

Azerick opened a portal and stepped into the small room he had stayed in during one of his previous visits. He lay upon the small bed and allowed his exhaustion to pull him into a rare period of sleep. The Scions mocked him in his dreams as fire, flood, and ravagers scoured his home from the face of the planet. He fought the fallen gods in a fierce battle until only he and they remained, fighting atop a mountain made of the dead. The world below was in flames, creating a place more hellish than anything found in the abyss.

A soft rapping at his door pulled Azerick from his nightmares and back into the godforsaken world of reality. He did not startle nor wake in the cold sweat such dreams would normally induce in a person. His life had long been a thing of nightmares, and they no longer affected him. Not even the awareness of his apathetic reaction bothered him anymore.

"Come in, Raijaun."

Raijaun opened the door, ducked low to clear the frame, and entered. "Father, the bulk of the evacuation is complete."

"What is the hour?"

"Mid-morning."

"How do we fare at the walls?"

"Thanks largely to the destruction you inflicted upon your return, we were able to hold the outer walls for nearly ten more hours. We have retreated to the inner curtain wall and are facilitating the evacuation of our fighting forces."

"All right. Let's make sure we get everyone through. Our job is done here, and there is no reason to stay and fight."

"Some would believe dying to protect their homes is reason enough."

"That is because some people are idiots who do not see that dying wins nothing but death. Only by surviving and fighting will they earn something worth dying for."

"You sound like Daebian."

"There are times I feel he has the right of it." Azerick sighed at the thought of his son. "Come, everyone will need our help to retreat through the rift. Are you rested enough to take on an entire army with me?"

"I have been resting in place and using my power sparingly for this purpose. Despite knowing the pain it will cause me, I am looking forward to giving it back to these vile creatures."

Father and son walked through the abandoned halls of Castle Stonemount, likely one of the last few to do so. A palace once teeming with court attendees, residents, and an army of servants, only the hollow sound of their feet striking stone and marble, the cacophonic war raging outside, and the pervasive smell and thin haze of smoke now took residence inside.

The fouled air grew thicker the moment they exited. Black smoke rose in hundreds of curling columns toward the sky where dragons wheeled and dived, spewing fire and hurling magic at the retreating defenders. Azerick looked into the distance and saw several black specks in an aerial duel only visible to his and Raijaun's keen eyesight unless one had a spyglass at hand. Through the bright flares of light and the exchange of fiery breath, Azerick knew Sandy had not left them and still fought to bring even a slight respite to the humans by pulling some of the dragons away from the city.

Azerick and Raijaun did not have to travel far to reach the forward lines of battle. They held the inner curtain wall, but their defense was tenuous. The wizards knew they were soon to retreat and so fought with little reservation, keeping the ravagers at bay and preventing the dragons from tearing through the wards and wreaking uncontrollable havoc.

"Azerick!" Alex called out as he jogged toward the sorcerer.

Alex's armor showed the ravages of war, what was visible of it beneath the layer of black, viscous blood. His eyes were a mirror of his armor: weary, battered, and fatigued but still resilient and refusing to yield.

"We cannot hold here much longer."

"You do not have to. Pull everyone away from the wall and move with all speed to the rift and the remaining gate," Azerick instructed. "Raijaun and I should be able to slow them enough to give you all time to flee. Is the inner-city still ours?"

"Mostly. A few bands of ravagers and an occasional dragon manage to break through or sneak their way inside, but so far we have been able to strike them down or push them back. We should have little trouble with any that might be terrorizing the city between us and the gates."

"Good. The moment we create a break, order everyone to the rift." Azerick turned to his son. "I know this is going to cause you a lot of pain. Are you ready?"

"I will manage, Father. Thank you for your concern."

Azerick and Raijaun walked the parapet and took positions a few hundred yards apart to cover a wide front. Azerick sent his arcane power into the wall beneath his feet. Stone spears erupted from its surface like the many spines of a hedgehog, piercing the flesh of the ravagers piled up against its surface as they fought to reach the summit. The mounds of creatures toppled as the protrusions stabbed into their bodies. He used his abyssal magic to cause the stone to weep poisonous acid that decayed the flesh of anything touching it.

Alex led the humans in a full retreat from the wall while Azerick and Raijaun tried to buy them time to get clear and reach the rift. It was not going to be an easy feat. Thousands of soldiers and wizards packed the battlements, with thousands more occupying the streets and defenses in the district.

Raijaun scoured the area in front of the wall with gold and silver fire all along its vast length and for a hundred yards or more out from its base. It burned the eyes of anyone chancing a glance in its direction as if they were looking straight into the sun. Even Azerick had to marvel at the power his son was able to draw and wield until a pang of sympathy brought him the sobering reminder of the pain his craft caused him.

Seeing that the humans were fleeing once again, or perhaps they knew their most-hated foes had taken the field, the Scions pushed their minions harder. The dragons began attacking with increased ferocity, and the ravagers ignored the death and destruction Azerick and Raijaun threw against them and charged the wall.

Fire and powerful spells battered at the wards to which the wizards had to devote their full attention. Wards flared like sparks kicked up by logs thrown on a fire as the massive wyrms slammed into them and tried to claw their way through despite the sharp, stunning jolts of electricity coursing through them each time they made the attempt. A huge, dusky-brown dragon landed upon a parapet, shattering the heavy ballista mounted there and snapping up the crew trying to help cover the retreat.

The assault came with so much force it was almost impossible to see the sky through the bursts of magic, gouts of flame, and the dragons' huge bodies. A dragon broke through a ward like an ice bear bashing its way into a seal den and dropped onto a mass of humans. The creature's own ward deflected the stronger spells cast at it while it ignored arrows and lesser magic. Its massive tail cracked like a whip, bashing aside houses as if they were toys and swept away a score of soldiers like dirt from a kitchen floor.

Azerick made to strike at the beast, but Raijaun was faster. A great golden hand came down from the heavens like the fist of Solarian, plucked the dragon up, and bashed it against the castle wall until it and the dragon lay in a broken heap. As impressed as he was with his son's spell, Azerick could not help but worry over the grimace of pain rippling across Raijaun's face.

He was not combining his Guardian magic with his abyssal power, but even the amalgamation with the more closely related Source magic caused him distress. Azerick's distraction cost him when a searing bolt of magic struck him in the side and flung him over the edge of the wall. His only good fortune was toppling off to the inner side instead of it tossing him to the snapping jaws of the horde of ravagers piling up at its base once again.

Azerick rolled just as a huge forefoot came crashing down with enough force to buckle the cobblestone street. The dragon's head snapped down with the speed of a swooping falcon. A hastily cast force strike deflected the huge head and cratered the ground next to Azerick's body.

The dragon rose up and prepared to spew fire as the sorcerer began shaping a ward to shield himself from the impending flames. Powerful rays and lightning struck the dragon in its side before it could release its breath weapon against the prone human. The dragon staggered under the combined onslaught, and Azerick turned to see who had come to his rescue.

Ellyssa, Roger, Allister, Aggie, and Rusty appeared through a windblown wall of black smoke like avenging wraiths. The dragon turned, glared at the wizards who had interrupted it, and spit its fire at the newcomers. Aggie and Allister erected a powerful ward, shielding them all from the inferno, while Ellyssa and Roger struck out at three other dragons circling and strafing.

"You like to play with fire, do you?" Rusty shouted. "Me too."

A horizontal column of fire erupted from his outstretched hands with an intensity equal to that of the dragon's breath weapon. The dragon scratched at the air with an outstretched talon and growled. Rusty's spell splashed against an invisible wall and spread out in a great flaming sheet. Allister turned to his offensive magic and unleashed a twisting ray of azure light. Like an auger, it bored through the magical shield and the dragon's armored scales.

The creature roared in agony as the magic tore and seared the powerful muscles beneath the hard plates and tough skin. Azerick shaped the head of his staff into a spear and hurled it with all his formidable strength. The arcanum blade sank deep into the dragon's neck. Runes carved along its shaft flared and sent a burst of arcane power into the dragon's body, ending its pain and continued existence. A quick thought and the staff reappeared in Azerick's hand.

"This place is going to hell with a quickness," Allister said. "Let's get out of here before your wife comes and drags us out by our ears."

"Where is Miranda?"

"Waiting at the gate, and she won't leave until you're through it. It was all I could do to keep her from coming with us."

Azerick nodded and turned to the wall where Raijaun still fought to impede the ravagers' siege. "Raijaun, time to go!"

Raijaun glanced down, conjured a rolling fog that burned like fire, and glided down to the ground. Azerick witnessed his son's pain and fatigue when he landed a bit hard and took a few stumbling steps. Raijaun waved off Azerick's concerned inquiry before he could speak it. Already, ravagers were beginning to pour over the distant ends of the walls where Raijaun's incendiary cloud did not reach. It was definitely time to make haste.

"Azerick, would you like to make a gate to the rift?" Aggie asked. "It's a bit far for us."

The sorcerer nodded and opened a portal to the plaza. The city's remaining defenders still crowded the area as they continued their orderly retreat through the large rift and the remaining gate. Thanks to Ancalon's portal, the challenge no longer lay with getting people through but trying to clear them away from the exit point in the valley so more could pass. The task was made especially difficult due to the vertigo traveling through the portals caused.

Miranda spotted the group almost immediately from her higher vantage point and pushed through the crowd to reach them. "Azerick! Thank the gods you made it."

"We're fine, but it looks as though we are not yet finished. This is taking too long. Raijaun and I need to buy more time."

"I'm going with you!"

"No, you are not. You have your place in this war, but this is not it," Azerick declared.

"My place is by my husband's side."

"There is nothing you can do to help. That makes it more likely you will be a hindrance. I do not mean to sound callous or belittle your abilities, but your skills are not fit for this duty and could cost people their lives if you insist on applying them to the task."

Miranda knew he was right, but hearing it burned in the pit of her stomach. She swallowed her frustration and pride and nodded. "Fine, but I'm waiting at the gate, and I will not pass through it without you."

"Fair enough."

"We're with you, boy," Allister insisted.

"I need Raijaun for what I have in mind. You all help reinforce the plaza against any ravagers that might still reach us until everyone is through."

The archmage looked dour. "It's been a long time since I was second fiddle in the orchestra. I gotta tell you, I don't like it."

Aggie threaded her arm through his and kissed him on his mushy cheek. "You are a distant third, and in the triangle section."

"Hateful old woman," he grumbled.

Azerick and Raijaun stood at the edge of the plaza. Many buildings already lay in ruins, but much of the district still stood proudly defiant. That was soon to change.

"I want to drop these buildings into the streets to create as great an obstacle as we can. I know it's a poor barrier at best given how they move, but at least they will not have a clear run at us."

"I agree, Father. We should be able to make it a greater challenge by igniting the combustibles as well."

Azerick nodded. "This is going to require the blending in of abyssal magic, and I know how difficult that is for you."

"I will manage as I always do, Father. It is my purpose."

Father and son began weaving the threads of a complex spell. Black fog formed around their hands and began curling through the streets and between buildings like smoke but with the sentience of a living creature. Everywhere it passed, wood rotted, iron rusted, and stone crumbled. Walls cracked and supports failed, causing the homes and businesses to topple and choke the streets. Many fell and crushed the invading army beneath their mass, killing hundreds and trapping thousands under the rubble.

The corruption complete, arcane and Guardian magic tracked along the ebony streamers and set the ruins ablaze. What was once a skyline of twisting black columns of smoke became a curtain of flames and choking darkness, hiding the grotesque stage and actors while stagehands erected new, horrific scenes.

Ravagers pushed heedlessly through the hellish destruction, driven by the silent commands of their creators and the unslakable bloodlust inherent to their existence. The death toll extracted by the defenders and Azerick and Raijaun's most recent destruction was incalculable, but still the enemy came on. Fierce battles erupted in the clogged alleys and atop the smoldering mounds of rubble all around the plaza.

The park was nearly clear of everyone not valiantly trying to stave off the unrelenting incursion. Raijaun studied the scene and knew those actively engaged in combat would not be able to withdraw through the portals without help. Combining the three elements of his magic, he ringed the plaza in fire that consumed wood, stone, and iron as if it were coal feeding the intense fires of a forge.

Seeing Raijaun's spell was creating the opportunity for a mass exodus, Azerick focused his power on the skies to drive away the dragons' constant aerial harassment. Rusty sent tendrils of magic into the cloying smoke, gathered it up like black snow, and created a thick screen to blanket a large section of the city and hide them from the dragons' eyes. Allister, Aggie, and Ellyssa reinforced the ebony cloud with magic, giving it solidity capable of warding off the bombardment if only for a short time.

"Everyone, through the rift!" Azerick shouted with a magically amplified voice.

Scores of defenders, mostly the wizards who were using their powerful magic to hold the ravagers' advance at bay until the soldiers could retreat, used the last of their physical reserves to sprint for the rift. Azerick and Raijaun moved in a more orderly manner, eyes peeled for any enemies managing to break through their hasty defenses.

"Miranda, go!" Azerick shouted upon seeing his wife standing next to the rift.

"I told you, I'm not going through without you!"

"Go, Father," Raijaun urged. "I will close the rift and use the gate to make my escape."

Azerick grimaced and balked, but he looked at Miranda and relented. "Be swift, and do not take any unnecessary risks."

"I will be fine, Father."

Azerick nodded, clapped his son on the shoulder, and led Miranda through the rift. Raijaun stood alone in the eye of a vortex of pure chaos and nightmare. Pushing aside the thoughts of the certain death clawing to reach him, Raijaun turned his focus to the rift and sent his magic deep into its ethereal weave. The power of the rift and the perfection of magic used in its creation filled him with awe.

It was unlike anything he had experienced before yet he felt a deep connection within its form. He began unraveling it with his magic, taking care to avoid leaving a scar in the world for the dragons or Scions to exploit. They would face their enemies again all too soon, and he did not want to hasten that meeting by leaving a door open for them to walk through.

Raijaun did more than close the rift. He sealed it and twisted the weave to make its construction as indecipherable as he could manage in the short time he had. He doubted even his skill could thwart the Scions' power for long, but he hoped to confound them enough to make it not worth their while. Raijaun tied off the last threads of his weave and made to hasten to the gate still standing proud amidst a field of destruction. A powerful explosion sped his retreat as a concussive wave sent him airborne and deposited him just a few yards from where it stood.

The Guardian sprang to his feet and scanned the sky. A huge ship had somehow managed to breach the shell over the plaza and floated a few hundred feet overhead. The vessel bristled with heavy weapons he was certain were far more lethal than their mundane appearance implied.

However, it was not the armament capturing his attention but the figure leaning over the rail with an all-too-familiar, satisfied smirk upon his visage. Raijaun wanted to blast the ship out from beneath him, but he was exhausted, in agony, and several dragons were pouring in through the breach behind the ship. Daebian flicked his brother a two-fingered salute from his brow as Raijaun leapt through the portal.

CHAPTER 24

"Destroy it," Raijaun ordered the moment he stepped through the gate and entered the valley.

Wizards assigned to control the gates promptly obeyed. Special runes lit up along its surface, and the stone columns crumbled into dust.

The gates and the rift opened near the center of the valley several miles from where the massive army camp stood, in the event their enemy managed to break through or the Scions were able to reopen them. Even this far from the main body, ten thousand heavy infantry, a thousand archers, a thousand cavalry, and two hundred of Azerick's constructs stood vigil over the gates in orderly ranks. This was but a fraction of the host occupying the east end of the valley.

The duchess, General Brague, and several of Azerick's people waited in the crowded clearing near the gates, shuffling their feet and wringing their hands in nervous anticipation. They rushed forward, pushing past the last of the people coming through and still trying to get their feet beneath them. Mellina and Miranda embraced, gushing words of relief for each other's safe return. General Brague greeted his officers and counted survivors, and several mages barraged Azerick with questions about where he had been and what was going to happen next.

Azerick brushed the queries aside with short, vague answers and an occasional scowling shake of his head. His only concern at the moment was Raijaun who appeared ready to collapse.

"I will be all right, Father," Raijaun said in a voice heavy with pain and exhaustion.

"I am sure you will be in time, but right now you are anything but. Lie down in one of the wagons for the wounded."

"I can walk."

"Barely. You need to recover as quickly as you can, and you will best achieve that by resting as much as possible and as soon as possible. That means starting now."

A rider wearing the black chain mail of a Blackguard galloped in and reined his mount to a skidding stop. "Lord Giles, His Majesty requests you and your people come to the command hall with all haste."

Azerick looked from the rider to his son.

"I'll be fine, Father. Jarvin needs your counsel more than I need you hovering over me." Azerick nodded and turned, but Raijaun grabbed his wrist. "I saw Daebian."

"Where?"

"Aboard one of the flying ships, their flagship given its size, just before I went through the gate."

Azerick took a steadying breath, but his voice still quavered. "Was he a prisoner?"

Raijaun shook his head. "Knowing him, he was captaining it. He struck at me with one of the ship's weapons."

"You are sure it was him?"

"No one else can project that much arrogance across such an expanse."

"I thought he was wiser than that," Azerick said with a rueful shake of his head. "Smarter at the very least. The Scions will never honor whatever bargain they made him."

"Then perhaps some justice will prevail no matter the outcome," Raijaun said with a bitterness Azerick had never before heard from his son.

"Rest. I will see you in the camp."

Azerick joined the rest of the retinue and mounted the horse he was offered. Despite the phenomenal exertion of his experience and subsequent battle, he was certain he could have opened a couple of portals and reached the camp in seconds. However, once he sat in the saddle and the rush of battle wore off, Azerick was glad he had not tried. His strength seemed to roll away like rain cascading down a window to be drunk up by the parched ground.

Miranda rode close by his side, watching him as if he might suddenly bolt like a fugitive. Perhaps she feared he would simply vanish, possibly of his own accord, or be snatched away by the gods or something worse. Such thoughts would seem like lunacy, but his life made it barely unreasonable. He returned Miranda's attention and forced a smile. Azerick did not have the clairvoyance of a seer, but he was certain there would be no happy ending for them. His fate was the tug of a riptide, invisible but drawing them inexorably apart. She was close enough that he could lean over and touch her, but she may as well have been in Sumara.

They rode in silence, but the grim, terrified faces of the people they rode past spoke volumes. In those thousands of pairs of haunted eyes, the history of Valeria, of their known world, played out from beginning to end. Their story began as one of pain and fear, then bravery and the joy of freedom. Now it was coming full circle again like the never-ending cycle of the seasons. Winter was upon their hearts and minds. Would they ever see another summer? Would history and the joyous victory be repeated, or would they all die beneath the ice and snow of defeat?

Trenches lined with sharpened stakes, abatises, and bulwarks built of stone and timber destroyed the valley's once pristine symmetry. It was no longer an unspoiled stretch of nature but a field built to slaughter. Every square foot of ground was crafted to cause the death and debilitation of their enemy.

Azerick had planned out the camp as well as the battlefield, but nothing could have prepared him for the reality of it. To call it a camp was greatly inaccurate. It was a sprawling city of nearly half a million humans and horses. Tents covered mile after mile of ground that was once blanketed with grass and foliage but was now churned into the mud and waste of human settlement.

Tens of thousands of people shuffled along "roads" between tents arranged into districts similar to those of the cities they had recently evacuated. Soldiers kept the new arrivals moving and directed them to the shelters where they would stay. The noncombatants, mostly the elderly and women with children, would only stay until rested and provisioned.

They would begin the march to the mountains where a series of deep caves stockpiled with grain and fresh water would provide them with a safe place to hide until the war was over. If it went badly for them, they would collapse the cave entrances and seek refuge with the dwarves. Already, caravans were underway as a river of people flowed eastward toward the Great Barrier Mountains.

There were a few solid buildings, mostly built of rough timber or a mix of stone and wood. Some of the soldiers, wizards, and engineers had garrisoned here for the better part of a year as they constructed the battlefield, erected tents and structures, and gained expert knowledge of the land and how to deploy the massive army.

The building designated as the king's residence as well as the command hall was a sturdy affair built of solid logs atop a low hill surrounded by a palisade and abatis. Catapults, ballistae, archers, and a dozen constructs with their wizard controllers occupied the higher ground and kept a constant vigil over the heart of the kingdom's army. Half a dozen Blackguards stood against the walls with an equal number of men wearing the distinctive armor of the Sumaran palace guard.

It took Azerick only a moment to spot his former mentor and who he assumed was his brother, the king. The two Sumarans leaned over a stout table covered with a large military map of the valley. King Jarvin Ollander and commanders from both nations also hovered over the map and its many troop icons. Jarvin's son, Miles, stood just behind them, hanging on their every word while they discussed strategy and troop deployment. All eyes turned to the newcomers as they entered the room.

Jarvin greeted them as they approached. "Lady Miranda, Azerick, everyone, I am glad to see you made it through. Is Raijaun with you?"

"He is making his way here on one of the wagons for the wounded," Azerick answered.

"Has he been hurt?"

"He is well but greatly fatigued. Combining the differing elements of his magic takes its toll on him, and he needs to recuperate."

"I am glad to know he is well, and I wish him a speedy recovery."

"I am sure he appreciates your concern," Azerick said.

King Yusuf Sabaht rounded the table and held out his hand. "Lord Giles, my brother has told me a great deal about you."

Azerick clasped his hand. "It is a pleasure to meet you, Your Eminence, but it is just Azerick. I am afraid I am no longer afforded the privilege of any honorifics."

Yusuf's thick black eyebrows arched in surprise, and he gave Jarvin a questioning look.

Devlin asked with a smile, "Have you been stepping on toes again?"

"It would be more accurate to say that I found one of them to be gangrenous and cut it off. It would seem that I overstepped my authority as the Defender of the Crown."

King Sabaht turned to Jarvin. "Was his offense truly so egregious? Surely someone who has sacrificed and risked so much to protect you and your people should be afforded a great deal of latitude, or at least leniency."

"Azerick struck down a nobleman within my hall in front of my entire council. Granted, the man threatened to jeopardize our defense and alliance, but under my rule, no one is above the law, and everyone deserves a fair trial."

Azerick grinned. "Everyone?"

Jaw muscles twitched beneath Jarvin's skin and his face reddened. "I will not entertain this discussion. We have more immediate concerns."

"As you wish, Your Majesty."

"What is the state of Brelland?"

"Its destruction is nearly total," Azerick answered. "My son and I razed the majority of the structures still standing and set them aflame to hinder the ravagers as much as we could to facilitate the evacuation. Castle Stonemount still stood, but I imagine the Scions will level it simply out of malice."

Jarvin sighed, his body slumped as if deflating, and he leaned heavily onto the battlefield mockup. "You had warned as much, but to know it has actually transpired...It is impossible to prepare for such a blow."

"Do we know of Brightridge's status?"

"Brightridge's people began coming through the southern gates less than an hour after ours fled through the western. Our most recent report was that the last line of defenders were beginning to evacuate. Their details of the damage indicated a similar level of destruction throughout the city. Even if—*when*—we win this war, few of us will have homes to return to."

King Yusuf laid a hand on Jarvin's shoulder. "You will not rebuild alone. Sumara is here to fight at your side, and we will not abandon you when the battle is over. You and I both understand that war is not finished just because the fighting is done."

"Yusuf, I cannot thank you and your people enough. Most people would have stayed to defend their own homes, but you and your people traveled more than a thousand miles to come to our aid. I will do everything in my power to see that no one ever forgets it even if it means I have to return from my grave to remind them."

"Do not be so quick to lavish me with praise. Were it not for my brother and Azerick's convincing arguments, I would have done precisely that."

Jarvin smiled and did his best to make it not appear forced. "Regardless of the why, you are here and I thank you."

Azerick asked, "Do you have any word of the happenings in Sumara?"

Yusuf looked to Devlin who answered the sorcerer's question. "It is much as you warned. Sumara is not free of incursion, but it is on a much smaller scale than what we face here. We have lost several smaller towns, but our garrisons within the cities have thus far been able to repel the invaders and crush them against our cities' walls. Knowing what our kingdom will face if we lose here, our soldiers stand ready to die to a man to ensure Valeria and all of humanity triumphs in this valley."

The hall door opened, and Headmaster Florent and two other senior wizards entered. Their robes were torn, and in the headmaster's case, scorched. Dust, soot, and blood, some of it dried, some of it still bright and sticky, dotted their faces and clothing. All were exhausted and appeared ready to collapse. Only their pride and decorum allowed them to remain standing.

"Someone get the mages some chairs!" Jarvin commanded.

Several guards jumped to obey and grabbed the chairs placed near the wall. Headmaster Florent and her two associates sat, grateful for being spared the possible indignity of crumpling to the floor.

"Are you well, Maureen?" the king asked.

"Thank you, Highness. We are as well as can be expected under the circumstances. Better than that since we are still alive. I may have made a poor decision in conjuring a series of gates to expedite our arrival. There were five of us, but two were unable to continue after exhausting themselves."

"I just thank the gods you made it. I think we could have waited for you to arrive by wagon."

The headmaster took several deep breaths and nodded. "I was unsure of Brelland's status and wanted to deliver my report with all haste. Seeing Sorcerer Giles and the duchess present, I must assume they were able to retreat successfully."

"We were, Headmaster," Azerick answered. "I presume you were able to defend your gates?"

"We were, but only barely. Had Raijaun not warned us of the trap beneath our feet, I fear no one from Brightridge would be here now. Thanks to his warning, we were able to turn the sewers and aqueducts into a crematorium just before they sprang their ambush. Even so, we nearly lost one of the gates when the dragons began releasing the vile creatures from the sky like bird droppings."

Jarvin asked, "What is the state of the city and its young duke?"

"The city is nearly gone, but Thomas is alive. He is with the Chosen, who are tending to his wounds. He's brave but still young enough to think he is immortal. I hope this experience has taught him otherwise and he commands farther from the front lines. We are still counting survivors, but my best estimates in round numbers put the dead at around six thousand with perhaps fifteen hundred wounded."

Azerick added, "Our losses are likely half again as high, but I consider it a victory under the circumstances."

"A victory?" Jarvin shouted. "Likely twenty thousand of my citizens dead by the end of the day, our four greatest cities lying in absolute ruins, and you callously call that a victory?"

Azerick remained stoic in the face of the king's outrage. "I consider anything short of genocide a victory. Every day we are able to fight is a victory for us all. I understand the losses involved, particularly given the rather short duration of the battles, but our losses will be ten times as high here in the valley. We have yet to see the full weight of our enemy, but that is going to change very soon. It is the very reason I had us all join forces here where we could apply our full might against the totality of their numbers. Had we remained divided, as conventional military doctrine dictated, the Scions' legions would have destroyed us piecemeal. Here, we control the field, and the battle lines are limited by the terrain. Our wizards and catapults can decimate the ravagers while most are bottlenecked behind their own kind. Their numbers now work against them as long as our soldiers can hold the front line."

Yusuf cleared his throat and spoke. "I brought a hundred thousand men, more than half mounted, and five hundred of our wizards and sorcerers. Even so, from what I understand of this enemy, our combined forces are still inadequate to hold for long. We are also far more exposed to those accursed dragons."

"We are, but my people have been training very hard to defend against their aerial assaults. I hope yours have been as well."

Devlin smiled. "Yes, many balked at the intensity of your training doctrine at first, so I asked them if they were going to allow the soft northern wizards to outshine the greatest of Sumara. After that, even you would have been impressed with their efforts."

"Having experienced your insistence at being the best firsthand, I have no doubt your people are very formidable. You are correct, Your Eminence; even with all our preparations, we would stand little chance. That is why I contacted representatives of the other races. This was never a human war, but a war for everyone who wishes to be a free people."

"This is a matter in which I am uncomfortably ignorant," Jarvin said. The tension of not knowing where or if they even had allies was evident in his voice. "It is somewhat difficult to employ our forces to their fullest effect when I have no idea what the other half is doing or if they are even going to come."

"I apologize for not keeping you abreast of matters, but the fact is that I do not have a great deal of information to share beyond what I have already told you." Azerick directed his next words to Yusuf. "The dwarves have allowed us access to their deeper caverns should the war go badly, and Duncan Runecarver, a notable person within the dwarven kingdom, has assured me that they are preparing their people to fight the Scions."

"But are they going to actually come and fight with us, or will they hole up beneath the mountains and fight only if their homes are threatened?"

"I am confident the dwarves plan to join us here in the valley."

"When?"

"That I cannot say. Communication with them is challenging, and my most recent...misadventure...has not afforded me the time to get clarity on their preparedness."

"You spoke of the elves as well. What of them?"

"I have had no contact with the elves since I asked their representative to inform his people of the impending invasion and beg their aid to defeat the Scions once again."

The Sumaran king turned his eyes to Jarvin. "You had a representative of the elven people here in your kingdom?"

"Representative is a rather grand title. He was part of an oddly effective adventuring group I employed. I would put little faith in his ability to rally his reclusive people to come to our defense. He has all the focus and sanity of a drunken house cat."

"I would not judge him too harshly," Azerick defended Tarth. "He is far more than he appears and a little more lucid than he might let on."

"He would need to be a great deal more lucid than what I witnessed just to find his way back to bed after using the privy."

"I have faith in him and our nonhuman allies. Speaking of allies, I made another while I was away."

"We can certainly use all the help we can get. Who are they?" Jarvin asked.

"It is not a they but a he. His name is Ancalon, and he is known as the Father of Dragons."

"He is the father of these murderous, tyrannical monsters?"

"He is, in name and in blood. It is he who opened the rift so our people could escape Brelland. Without his help, at least half the populace of the capital would be dead."

"I'll be the first to admit I know less about dragons than I do the moon, but I find it unlikely his kind does anything for free. What is his price?"

"When this war is over, there will be no retaliation against the surviving dragons."

"Impossible! These creatures are murdering my people! They have razed our greatest cities to the ground, and you and he expect us to let them go—just let bygones be bygones? No! I will personally hunt every last one of those creatures down, track them to the highest aerie, and climb down into the deepest hole to exterminate them from the face of this world!"

"No, you will not. I will not allow it."

Azerick's face looked carved from stone. Jarvin's looked like the face of a volcano about to erupt. Blackguards shifted their weight, ready to leap into battle. The king's hand brushed the hilt of his demon-slaying sword but did not grip it.

"You will fight me? After all you have done for my people, your people, you will fight us to protect the things that killed their fathers, sons, and daughters?"

"I gave my word, and I will not break it."

"What of your word to me? What of your word to defend this kingdom?"

"I feel I am still keeping it. The dragons are as much of this kingdom as anyone, even if you are not their king. You said yourself, the kingdom is more than just one man."

"I ask you again, why would you make such a pact? Why would you put them above your own kind?"

Azerick smiled and wagged his head ever so slightly. "What is my kind, Jarvin? Who are my people? You still think of me as human. Even if I was, what have they ever done but bring me pain and misery? I have watched humans step on the necks of those they call lesser men for nothing more than gold and power, and they do this of their own free will. The dragons are controlled by the Scions. They have never sought to oppress or fight us of their own volition. They are the victims of our one true enemy. When we destroy the Scions, the dragons will go and find refuge away from humanity just as they did before to live with the shame of their weakness and actions for which they are not to blame."

"You ask a great deal of me, Azerick Giles. You ask a great deal of all the people who suffer because of those beasts, willing or not."

"Have you heard of the dragon who fights for us? She is one of my dearest friends, and she fights against her own kind and against incredible odds. Will you sentence her to death as well to appease your vengeance?"

"Of course not! I am not a monster."

"Do you mean to say you could tell one dragon from another? Could the men and women you send out to slay them? I toppled a city as powerful as a small kingdom when I was a far lesser man in part because of her. May the gods have mercy on anyone who hurts her, because I will not."

"Jarvin," Yusuf said softly, "we were enemies not so long ago. War makes strange bedfellows. It may be that one day we will need the dragons to fight an even greater enemy just as I am here fighting with you today."

Jarvin's hand squeezed the hilt of his sword until his knuckles turned white. "I will issue an edict that no dragon be pursued upon the cessation of hostilities. But they will depart, and any damage or harm they cause after this war will mean immediate extermination."

"He expects nothing more."

Jarvin dropped his hand from his sword and let out the breath he was holding. "I think we should all see to some much-deserved rest. Yusuf, I am sure you have many things to take from this meeting back to your generals. We should all meet again in two days. Hopefully, that will settle all our nerves and weary bodies."

"You speak the truth of it, Jarvin. I brought my best bottle of wine from my cellar to share with you after our victory, but perhaps I will bring it for when we next meet. I do not wish to beckon bad luck or tempt the fates, but I think it would be a greater crime to chance letting it go undrunk."

"I look forward to it, Yusuf."

Devlin took Azerick by the arm and steered him toward the door. "I know you are likely exhausted, but I would like to hear about this 'misadventure' you went on. I would also dearly like to meet your son. He sounds fascinating."

"Headmaster, would you wait with me for just a few minutes?" Jarvin asked, stopping Magus Florent before she was able to pry herself out of her chair.

The Academy headmaster nodded to her two associates, and they followed behind the others and shuffled from the room. Even the Blackguards departed, leaving the senior mage alone with Jarvin and Miles.

"I know you are exhausted, Headmaster, but I wanted Miles to see why what we must do is so important," Jarvin said.

Miles looked at his father. "I don't understand. What are we doing?"

"Azerick Giles is a threat to this kingdom every bit as great as the Scions are," Jarvin explained to his son.

"But he is helping us fight them. He is practically our savior."

"It is true that the Scions are the more immediate threat, and he is vital to our defense. But you saw how he threatened to turn on us if I did not bend to his will. This is not the first time he has done this, and it will not be the last unless we do something about it."

"He had given his word, Father. Did you not teach me that my word means everything? Should he be held to a different standard?"

"It is so much more complicated than that, Son. He killed a nobleman in my hall in front of everyone without hesitation, remorse, or consideration for our laws because it was expedient. What other values will he set aside for the sake of expedience? Even if I agreed with his action in that situation, what about the next one? What crimes will he commit, what laws will he violate because he feels himself justified? Who can stop him or hold him accountable?"

"You are talking about assassination. You just said yourself we lack the power to hold him to our laws, so you will set aside your morals and sense of justice, just as he did, for the sake of expediency. So, because he is powerful, we will forgo his trial and discard the laws and rights you yourself created and swore to uphold."

"It is more than just his power, Miles. You saw how easily he rallied not just North Haven to his call, but the kingdom of Sumara, the entire nation of dwarves, and possibly even the elves. They came not just because we all face a common foe, but because he asked them to. More than once he has threatened to remove me from my throne if I do not act or lead as he thinks I should. He toppled a powerful city in Sumara and brutally removed the previous duke of Southport in a fit of vengeance. Granted, he was justified in those acts, but were his methods necessary, or were they simply expedient and gratifying? I do not like this, Miles, not in the least. But as king, sometimes I must set aside my values to defend my people. If I am wrong, then the people will rise up and remove me. Can they do that with him?"

Miles cast his gaze down onto the table, looked at the ranks of figures, and imagined the innumerable horde of savage creatures descending on them to tear them apart. "I understand, but I do not like it."

Jarvin embraced his son, resting his bearded chin in the crook of Miles's neck. He wondered when his son had grown so tall. "Nor should you. I am glad you question me, for actions like this must always be questioned. Your dedication to our laws and your sense of right and wrong make me proud. I included you in this awful affair because if I fall, it may be up to you to carry out Azerick Giles's sentence."

"Me? How could I?"

"The sword I wear was blessed by the gods to slay demons. The headmaster and our clerics believe it will work on Azerick as well due to his demonic nature. If I fall in battle, you must pick up my sword and carry out his execution. How you do it is up to you. Remember what I said about your duty to our people. You may have to sacrifice your values and morals to ensure their safety. I hope this task does not fall to you, for such a reprehensible act will surely stain a decent man's soul, it certainly will mine, and I would do anything to spare you from that taint."

"Miles," Maureen interjected, "you spent several years at the Academy, and although your interactions with the Magus Academy were minimal, I hope you know me well enough to know that I would never agree to something like this if it were not of paramount importance. Azerick was one of my brightest students, and I was very fond of him. He was a troubled but decent young man. I fear some of those troubles and a great many new ones have made him unpredictable and very dangerous. He has been possessed by a demon and then possessed that demon in turn. He spent years as the master of the abyss. No one, not even he, could suffer those experiences and walk away unaffected. It is an awful task, but one that must be carried out. It may not need to be done by you at all. There are four blades in four different hands."

"No, my father is right. As king, it is my responsibility, and I will not ask another to do what I am unwilling to do. It is my duty, and I will shoulder the burden of guilt if I am able."

"I have no intention of dying in this war, Miles, but if I do, I needed you to know and take up my sword."

"I will, Father."

CHAPTER 25

A zerick found the rucksack propped against the alchemy set he had bought so many years ago in Southport. He touched the case containing the apparatus and his mind traveled back to those simpler times when all he had to worry about was avoiding slavers, thugs, and starvation on the streets.

The fact Miranda knew how much it meant to him and ensured that it avoided destruction warmed his heart. He turned back toward the entrance flap, his heart urging him to tell his wife how much her simple consideration meant to him, but the weight of the codex cradled in his hand was an anchor chained to a ship called duty, and it held him fast. He sat at the small desk against the tent wall and opened the codex.

The smell of food wafting through the tent eventually pulled him away from his studies. He stepped from the antechamber into the main pavilion. Miranda sat at the table; a half-eaten meal long gone cold scattered about the porcelain plate before her.

"I see dinner is ready," Azerick said as he sat down at the table.

"Over an hour ago."

"You should have called me in."

"I did, three times. I fixed Raijaun a large plate. He is feeling much better already, or at least he's pretending to."

"Thank you. I'm sorry. I must have gotten lost in my research."

Miranda stared down at her plate. "My husband is dead, isn't he?"

Azerick choked down the growing lump in his throat. "I don't know if I would say dead. Gone might be more appropriate."

"Is he ever coming back?"

"I don't know. You must hate me."

"I hate a lot of things these days, but not you. Never you. I think I finally understand. I kept trying to make you *my* Azerick, the one who was kind and compassionate, but you're not him. You are Azerick, savior of our world, and I cannot hate him either for he does what he must for the sake of us all. What hurts me so much is that I did not stop mourning until I thought you had come back. Now that I understand you never did return, I am mourning your death all over again. I do not mean to sound selfish or put the burden of my sorrow on your shoulders. I know you have more than your share to bear already. I just wanted you to know that I understand."

"I want you to do whatever it takes to ease your pain and get past your mourning. I'm sorry I could not come back."

"I know you are, and I know it hurts you too. I know this sounds awful, but it makes me feel a little better knowing that it does. It makes me feel like a little bit of you did make it back, and I am grateful for it. At least I finally get the chance to say goodbye."

He searched for words of comfort, but they were lost to him just like the possibility of returning to the life he once shared with Miranda.

"I must attend to something important."

Azerick stood and walked from the tent without looking back. He had no desire to see the pain he had inflicted upon his wife yet again. Miranda sat in resolute silence. She had no more tears left to shed. That well of anguish was now dry.

"Goodbye," she whispered as the tent flap brushed closed.

Azerick stalked across the massive camp with his eyes cast toward the ground. It was dark, but even with the hood of his cloak pulled over his head several people recognized him and called out a greeting. The sorcerer ignored their salutations and the occasional questions begging to know what was going to happen next. If forced to answer, he would do so honestly and say that most of them were going to die in the days to come. Better to let them cling to the small bit of hope they earned through their relative victories in the cities.

They all thought they understood what they faced, saw the massive preparations made within the valleys and the enormous army waiting for the Scions and their minions. They simply could not comprehend the vastness of the approaching horde. The Scions had so far engaged them with a certain amount of reserve, but that would change here.

They knew the humans had nowhere else to run, knew that the bulk of humanity was gathered here in the valley and in a few key cities in Sumara. Now they could concentrate their full power on a single battlefront, and he had made it possible for them to do so.

Daebian had told him he could not win this war. His son's words had cut him deep. Not just because of the betrayal he felt, but because in his heart, he knew Daebian was right. Daebian mocked his shortsightedness, but Azerick was not as blind as his son thought. Klaraxis's memories had been his to explore for several years, and within those memories were hundreds of battles. He knew how to calculate the rate of attrition by gauging the numbers of the opposing armies and their strengths and weaknesses.

Azerick had years to study the Scions and their army and knew the forces at his disposal. He knew it was not enough, but he also understood fate and knew that nothing was certain in this world or any other. The actions of a being with free will could unravel the strongest of prophesies and alter the course of the future forever. It was why he fought so hard despite knowing they would fail. Omnipotence was an illusion, and the real outcome of this war would be decided on what none of them could foresee.

It took over half an hour of brisk walking to reach the nearest edge of the camp, but still Azerick continued to distance himself from the tent city. Half a mile from the perimeter, he found a massive boulder jutting from the ground like a colossal grey tooth. The shaft of his arcanum door handle sank into the stone as if it were wet clay. A slight twist and pull opened a perfect doorway in the solid rock.

Azerick stepped into the cavernous chamber of his old laboratory. The Source pool cast the room in silver light and created no need for any other source of illumination. The sorcerer knelt beside the pool and luxuriated in the aura of power it radiated. Focusing on the task at hand, Azerick reached into the well with invisible arcane hands and scooped out a measure of pure Source.

The magical element floated over the pool as a perfect liquid sphere until he coaxed it into a flat disc the size of a dinner plate. Azerick then leached the pure element of the Source from the disc until the plate took on the solidity of arcanum. Able to now physically handle the object, Azerick set it aside and created three more identical arcanum platters.

He carried his priceless treasure up the stairs and out of the tower. As usual, Ancalon's gigantic, serpentine body wrapped around the tower but left the doorway unobstructed. The Father of Dragons' head hove into view as Azerick emerged.

"You have crafted the discs, I see. Your retreat was successful then?" the dragon asked in a voice like a thunderstorm.

"Because of you, yes it was."

"You have relayed the requirements of my assistance to your people, and they have agreed to my terms of allegiance?"

"With great reluctance, they have agreed. No one shall be given leave to persecute the dragons once the war is concluded. However, any dragon causing harm or threatening the people will be dealt with under the king's law."

"This is acceptable. Let us see to our task."

Azerick set the arcanum plates on the ground. Ancalon set a single talon over the first one and began to etch its surface. The nearly indestructible metal took the intricate design as easily as a wax tablet. Despite the tiny size of the disc compared to the dragon's colossal body, the design he carved into the face of it was astounding.

Azerick knew from practice how perfect a rune carving had to be in order to hold power, and Ancalon's was far beyond anything he could possibly hope to replicate. Considering the fact that the disc was little more than a small coin to the dragon made it something of a godlike achievement. Ancalon repeated his etchings upon each disc without the slightest variation in their design. Not even a stamp could reproduce the images with such exacting detail.

"It is done. You know what you must do with them."

"I do," Azerick said with a nod.

"Even with my help, the Scions have the power to resist your trap. They must be weakened or the trap sprung during a moment of chaos, or they will certainly break free."

"I understand. Once we force them to come to our world in their full physical embodiment, I hope to have the power to shake them enough for this to succeed. I simply do not see another way for the races to survive otherwise."

"I wish you success, for all our peoples' sake."

Daebian's armada flew over the teeming horde of ravagers loping through the forests and across the open valleys, killing and destroying everything in its path. Behind his ships, large, glowing slashes in the veil between worlds were still evident even this far away as even more creatures poured through the rifts to add to their already impossible numbers. Scores of dragons flew alongside his armada, rising, diving, and circling in their desire to cause destruction, and agitated by their masters' magical domination.

Black smoke from the burning cities and countryside marred the horizon and cast the entire sky into a depressing grey haze. Blacker specks within the miasma hinted at even more dragons arriving to heed their masters' call. The moment Daebian had been dreading finally arrived when his crew went stock-still and the dragons ceased their wild flight and hung in the air like toys dangling from a giant mobile.

"Your father has returned and taken to the field."

"So I saw."

"Your plan to destroy the gates failed. You failed...again."

Daebian felt a giant hand crush him to the deck of the ship. His skin burned as if a red-hot iron had branded his flesh in a dozen different places. He forced himself not to give in to his urge and grab at his sword. If Zyn discovered what he was hiding within the soul blade, he would kill him without hesitation. He wasn't certain the Scion was not going to do that now.

"M-master, the rift allowing them to escape your wrath could not have been my father's construction."

"It was not. It would appear as though an old acquaintance has sought to turn against us. He will be punished in due time. That does not change the fact that both cities managed to evacuate their wretched populations. You said your plan would destroy the gates. They did not."

"My plan did work! The destruction of the two gates at Brelland would have been disastrous for our enemy there had the rift not appeared. Brightridge's people got away because they were warned, and your creatures did not move swiftly enough. I cannot be held responsible for their failure."

"I will hold you responsible for whatever I deem you responsible for! However, I still find you useful, so I will spare your life once again." Daebian felt the pressure bearing down on him vanish, but the agony remained. *"We know where your father and the bulk of the vile races are now. He does us a favor by not forcing us to ferret them out of every dank hole into which they might crawl to find refuge. He has made the purge much easier for us in his pathetic attempt at defense. He will seek to draw us into this world in hopes of taking the battle to us just as the Guardians and the elven wizards did in the past. When he does, you will kill him, and we shall both have what we most desire."*

"Your will be done, master. I exist only to serve you."

"You speak the truest thing you have ever uttered in your life despite whether or not you truly believe it."

The world returned to life and assaulted his senses with the feel, sound, and smells that had vanished with the Scion's presence. A gust of wind slapped at his face and a hand touched him lightly on the shoulder.

"He was here again, wasn't he?" Eva said.

Daebian nodded.

Eva shivered and hugged him from behind. "I can feel it. It's like I jumped into an icy lake. Was he angry again?"

"He was not pleased they had escaped the city. That's what he said, but I think they are enjoying the hunt. A dog finds more joy in chasing a rabbit than it does actually catching it. I doubt they are any better."

"Daebian, are we doing the right thing? Can we really turn against our own kind like this?"

"Would you rather join them? Do you think the outcome would change if we fought with them?"

"I suppose not."

"The only way to win is to survive, and there is nothing but death down there."

Eva nodded and wiped a tear from her eye as the ship carried them to the only true resistance the races could muster. Once they were destroyed, there was nothing to stop them.

Seeing the entire human army deployed on the battlefield was an impressive sight to behold. Two hundred fifty thousand infantrymen nearly stretched across the entire width of the valley in perfectly square formations of five thousand men each. Their cavalry numbered almost one hundred thousand and was divided into north flanking, center, and south flanking units.

Five hundred of Azerick's constructs created the bulwark of their front line to blunt what was sure to be a powerful initial charge. A reserve force numbering half the size of the fielded army stood at the ready to relieve their fellows when they became too fatigued to fight. In most normal battles, armies tended not to fight after darkness, but the Scions and their ravagers would certainly not relent until they crushed their foes. This made the role of the reserve units vital in sustaining the humans' ability to continue the battle.

Even with such a vast army of horses, swords, spears, and heavy siege weapons, the primary purpose of the men and women placing themselves in the path of death was not to kill but to stop the ravager advance. The true task of slaughtering their enemy was left to the corps of wizards whose arcane power could smite the legions of ravagers by the hundreds or even thousands. The soldiers were the shields, the wizards the swords, but all would spill more blood than the waters of a spring snowmelt before the war was over.

All eyes stared intently westward at the dark shapes circling and streaking across the sky. Those with spyglasses could make out the sleek flying ships gliding toward them, heralding the impending arrival of the greatest threat to humanity and the races since the near genocidal conclusion of the Great Revolution. Even the last of the refugees fleeing for the caverns cast fearful glances over their shoulders as they struggled to hasten their pace. These were the infirm and those too injured to evacuate until there was simply no more time to give them to recover.

Jarvin, his key leaders, and his advisors crowded the war room. The king and his military commanders bent over the map tacked down to the large table and moved the brass and tin figures placed upon it as their scouts arrived with updated reports. Azerick was absent, but Raijaun towered over everyone in the room and stood beside Aggie and Headmaster Florent to advise Jarvin on arcane matters.

"Sire, our most recent scouting reports put the main body perhaps seven hours from our forward lines, but it is getting increasingly more difficult for our scouts to reach us. The dragons are flying ahead and often pick them off. We received our latest reports only by sending ten riders through the forest to the south. Only three managed to deliver their missives," one of his generals reported.

Jarvin made a rumbling noise in his throat and nodded. "At this point, it hardly matters. Order our scouts back to within a mile of our forwardmost troops. I'll not throw away their lives for reports we can do little with." He turned to the three magic users. "Is there anything to add in regards to our magical preparedness?"

Raijaun spoke. "Our wizards and Sumara's mages and handful of sorcerers are in place with two groups of reserves ready to lend additional support and defenses. Thanks to the Source pool, our construct operators are able to control them from upwards of a mile away now instead of the few hundred yards of their previous limitations."

"A good thing too," Headmaster Florent chimed in. "I was very concerned with our younger and less talented mages being so close to the front lines, and I am sure Raijaun's people were as well."

Raijaun nodded. "It was indeed a point of significant worry. It would have been far too easy for them to get absorbed into the press of battle if our front lines buckled by even a moderate measure."

"Can these iron men truly stem the tide bearing down upon us?" Jarvin asked.

"No, but such is not their purpose. The ravagers are simply too numerous, but they can break up the horde into many smaller fronts and bleed off much of the inertia before hitting our shield wall. Without them, the ravagers could cut much deeper into our forward ranks and possibly dismantle our army piecemeal if our mages are not able to do enough damage to break them apart."

"I just wish I had ten thousand more of them. Has Azerick been able to contact anyone from the other races?"

"He was able to speak to Duncan Runecarver last night. The dwarves are in place and ready to strike, but because their numbers are significantly less than ours, they are going to lay an ambush and strike at our enemy's northern flank at the optimal time. They fear exposing themselves too soon and risking being overwhelmed."

The king nodded. "It doesn't give us much information to work with, but at least it's something. What of the elves?"

"Father was unable to contact the northern elves. His attempt to speak with the abyssal elf representative was blocked by magic he could not penetrate."

"I don't know much about either kind and will assume they have chosen to hide—"

A soldier in riding leathers burst through the hall door, cutting off Jarvin's words. The scout fought to gain his breath as he tried to overcome the exhaustion of a brutal ride.

Still breathing hard, the scout slapped a fist to his chest in salute. "Sire, I have news of happenings to the southeast."

"Relax, soldier. What is your report?"

"Our scouts spotted a large number of brutes, mostly goblins, lurking a few hours' ride from here."

Several vile oaths from around the room responded to the report.

"How many do we estimate?"

"Our scouts spotted no more than a few score, but tracks and signs of recent activity indicate there could be a substantial number. Hundreds at the least, possibly several thousand given some of the abandoned campsites we found."

"Did any engage you?"

"No, sire. Despite catching our first scouts by surprise and significantly outnumbering them, they hastened into rougher territory before we could receive reinforcements and pursue. The commander of our company chose not to continue the pursuit into the rough terrain fearing ambush by a potentially larger force."

"It could be just a band of scavengers and opportunists," General Brague suggested.

"Likely, but it could be a war band sent by the Scions to strike at our rear. Headmaster, is there a way you or our wizards can spy them out with magic?"

"Aggie has the best scrying ability I know of." Headmaster Florent replied.

The venerable archmage located a small round mirror hanging near the center of the hall. "I can give it a try."

Aggie focused her magical power upon the mirror and willed it to show her what her eyes could not see. Not knowing exactly what and where she needed to see, the magus summoned an image of their own camp as if seen through the eyes of a high-flying eagle. Aggie willed her "magical bird" to fly to the southeast far faster than even the swiftest of raptors could possibly go.

Within minutes, she spotted the human company arrayed behind hastily constructed defenses. Following the soldiers' eyes, she located several scouts hidden in the dense brush a mile farther on. She continued to track south and east into the nearly impassable terrain near the Forsaken Lands, but as her eyes flew over that wilderness, her vision began to blur and lose color as if delving into a dense fog. Just a mile into the hinterland, she could see nothing but a grey miasma.

"I cannot see them. My scrying is being actively blocked. Whoever is hiding in the backcountry does not wish to be seen."

"Who could be strong enough to block your scrying other than the Scions?" Maureen asked.

"The magic had a definite shamanic origin."

"A savage shaman's magic is stronger than yours?" Jarvin asked in disbelief.

"Shamanic magic can be quite formidable, particularly when worked in concert with other shamans. I am guessing several are working together to prevent anyone from discovering them or their numbers."

"Wretched beasts!" Jarvin shouted. "As if I do not have enough to deal with. General Haskins, order two thousand reserves to aid the scouting company. Headmaster, can we afford to detach some of your wizards to support them?"

"Honestly, no, but I see little other choice. I will have six of our war mages accompany the soldiers. They are not far from our camp, and we can send additional reinforcements should it prove necessary."

"Let us pray it does not." The king slammed a fist against the table. "Where in the six circles of the abyss is Azerick?"

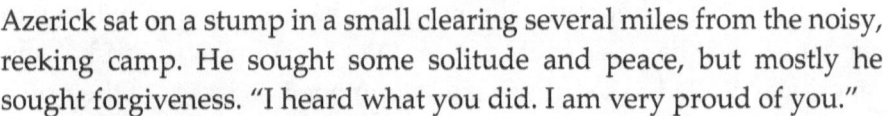

Azerick sat on a stump in a small clearing several miles from the noisy, reeking camp. He sought some solitude and peace, but mostly he sought forgiveness. "I heard what you did. I am very proud of you."

Sandy grunted in response.

"I hope you understand why I did it even if you cannot forgive me for it."

"I met someone after I left. Another dragon."

Azerick raised an eyebrow. "Male?"

Sandy nodded.

"Do you care for him?"

"Very much, but like a grandfather. Even though we only got to spend a few days together, he taught me so much. I think it was because of the link through our blood. I understood what he was teaching me even when he did not speak. I seemed to learn just by being near him. It was different than my egg memories, but also similar."

"I am glad you were able to find someone to help you. I wish I could have done more or something different, but I did not know how, and I was very pressed for time."

"I know. Mordigar helped me understand what you did and told me to look within myself to find my identity and not just the surface."

"He sounds very wise."

"He is, and he wants me to kill him. He was powerful enough to resist their call from within the barrier, but he said he would lose control once they broke free. He told me we would be enemies once the war truly began and we would fight. Even if I could somehow defeat him, how can I hurt someone I love?"

"Because you must," Azerick answered softly, stroking her scales. "Because Mordigar loves you more than himself, just as I do. It is why I have done things I am not proud of. It is why I chose to mar your scales knowing it would pain you and possibly take you from me forever. Like me, he wants you to survive and will pay any price to ensure you do. Sandy, I want you to survive this war. Even if we lose, I am confident you can live on despite not being under the Scions' control if you do not draw attention to yourself. I do not want you to throw away your life by fighting to the death. If all seems lost, I want you to fly as far away as you can."

"What about you?" Sandy asked softly.

"I have been lost for a long time. The races will fight to the last because the Scions will not give us any other choice. We will win, or the Scions will choose how and when the war ends. We have no choice, but you do."

"I choose to fight! You are my family, and I will defend you."

"Of course you will, but when there is no one left to defend, you must fly away."

"You sound as though you expect to lose."

"I do not know if we can win, but I do know I will not."

Sandy narrowed her eyes. "What do you mean?"

"I mean there is no winning scenario for me. Even if we defeat the fallen gods, events in my life and actions I have chosen have ensured that I will not enjoy our victory."

"You are going to leave me just like Mordigar!"

"I will have to suffer the consequences of the things I have done. I wish the people I love did not have to suffer for them, but that is the price of letting love into your heart. For me, it is well worth the cost, and I hope it is for those who care about me as well."

"Is that why you are not with Miranda right now?"

"It has much to do with it, yes."

"You exact a high price for loving you, Azerick Giles, but I would pay ten times as much. Besides, you always said no one can predict the future, not even the fates."

Azerick turned his eyes to the west and picked out a dark splotch just a bit larger than the others flying over the horizon. "No one indeed."

CHAPTER 26

The smell of fear was palpable across the battlefield as the tens of thousands of humans stretching across the valley watched a sea of terror rushing toward them. Hands gripped shields and weapons so tightly they trembled even more than the ground being shaken by a million stomping feet. Just two years ago, most of the men and women standing to defend their kingdom and lives were farmers, merchants, bakers, and other simple laborers.

Today, they were the greatest hope of staving off annihilation. Months and months of intense combat training had turned them from a multitude of professions into the largest, most well-trained army ever assembled, but few if any facing the horde barreling toward them thought they could possibly be enough.

The red-skinned ravagers looked like a tidal wave of blood washing onto the shore to mercilessly sweep everything away with its impossible mass and power. The horde crashed into the iron constructs first, parting like water around boulders jutting through a river's surface. Several of the iron men fell to the overwhelming mass, but most held and began hacking at the creatures as they flowed past.

The forwardmost mages struck in concert with the rows of archers and siege weapons. Fire burst throughout the ravagers' ranks as heavy stones and thousands of arrows fell like rain and hail. The horde did not balk in the slightest and continued to charge through the storm of death. Tens of thousands of ravagers impacted the human shield wall with a deafening crash.

Rank upon rank collapsed under the brutal assault as the defenders fell or were hacked down and trampled. The humans shoved shield and spear into their enemy, and the wall began to hold. The ravagers' momentum broken, the humans fought back with animalistic fury, stabbing, snarling, and spitting into the faces of their foes.

The tide of ravagers began to swell as those in the back surged forward, climbing over the tops of their brethren like a wave reaching the shallow waters of the coastline. The colossal press of bodies began pushing the human lines back once again, and there appeared no way to stop it.

"Dear gods preserve us," Jarvin said as he looked out at the endless sea of attackers through a powerful spyglass mounted on a tripod.

Just as Jarvin and those able to witness the full scale of what they faced became certain of their imminent destruction, sections of the northern hillside exploded outward toward the valley. From out of the dust and rubble of a hundred new caves, twenty thousand dwarves charged down the hillside toward the ravagers' flank with howls of fury every bit as savage as those of their enemy.

The ravagers had no trouble sending an army to deal with the new threat. More defenders meant more for them to slaughter. Without any audible or visual sign of communication, a massive section of the ravager army split off from the rear and center of their advance and charged to meet the new source of resistance.

As the bloodthirsty monsters barreled down upon the newest arrivals, the dwarves' forward rank raised a hobnailed boot high and brought it crashing down with a single, uniform cry. The earth rune carved into the thick leather sole obeyed the dwarves' command and released its pent-up energy. A massive swell of ground undulated away from the dwarves and rolled toward the charging ravagers. Spears of stone and crystal erupted from the ground to stab into their enemy, and deep fissures opened up to swallow them whole.

The ravagers, fearless even in the face of imminent death, charged on, leapt the deep crevices, and bounded across bridges created by the bodies of their fallen. The dwarves took another exaggerated step forward and triggered the rune carved into their other boot. That sigil expended, the foremost attackers stopped and let the second rank step forward. The new front line raised a foot and brought it down with a thundering cry. A third earthen wave rolled out from beneath their boots then a fourth and a fifth until all ten ranks had spent their runic power.

The dwarves tightened their grip upon the hafts of their axes and hammers and screamed into the ravagers' faces as if to blow them away with the power of their combined voices. The stout people looked about to be engulfed by the vast army racing toward them, but the subterranean warriors were not out of tricks just yet. Fierce cavern gnomes backed the dwarven army, and their earth callers raised their gems high. The long slope between them and the onrushing swarm turned liquid and buried the nearest attackers in a mile-long mudslide.

The collapse left the dwarves and gnomes standing upon a fifteen-foot-high bulwark a mile long, creating a highly defendable position. The wall could not stop the ravager attack, but the earth callers were not finished with their foes. Summoning the power of the elements, large globs of mud began rising from the ground even as the ravagers threw themselves against the wall, climbed its face, and leapt high enough to strike at the defenders atop it.

Dozens of huge earth elementals broke through the surface of the mud and used their powerful fists to pummel the attackers or stab them with shards of stone growing from their tireless arms. The ravagers clawed at the elementals, stabbed at them with their short blades, and slowly chipped away at the constructs. The elementals were not indestructible, but the number of ravagers that would fall to them before they were destroyed was incalculable.

Huge war machines rolled out of the caverns, some pushed by teams of dwarves while others moved under the power of the runes etched in their frames. The wildest and most lethal-looking siege engine looked like an onager set on wheels ten feet high. Instead of a single arm and basket, there were five, set like the spokes of a wheel and rotated around a central shaft. Each towed a large cart full of spherically-carved stones behind it.

Runes flared and the arms began to rotate, pausing just long enough for the ammunition to roll down the chute from the cart and settle into the basket, before lobbing the stone in a high arc onto the battlefield. The stones themselves carried a rune to violently explode when the rock struck the ground. The repeating catapult was able to fling twenty stones per minute with a good crew, and all the crews were exceptional.

"The dwarves are here!" Headmaster Florent cried as she used her magic to observe the battle by scrying the chaotic scene in a marble basin.

As glad as Azerick was for their ally's arrival, the dwarves' assault did little to relieve the pressure his people were under from the ravagers' relentless attack. Their numbers were simply too vast. The army besieging the dwarves was largely the countless minions unable to reach the human lines, but it did free much of his reserves from having to guard the northern hillside so they could concentrate on the main battle raging on the valley floor. Jarvin had to amend his first impression when the dwarven war machines began flinging exploding stones deep into the ravagers' ranks. The dwarves may not have mages, but their mixture of rune magic and conventional weaponry was nearly as devastating.

Finally seeing the dwarves and their infernal machines as a true threat, dozens of dragons broke off their relentless assault on the humans to deal with them. The dwarves did not have wizards to shield them from the dragons' aerial attack, but they were not unprepared. Dozens of self-cocking ballistae mounted on chassis to allow them to pivot at high angles launched rune-enhanced bolts at the terrifying beasts as they swooped down to unleash their fiery breath and powerful magic against the short people.

Soldiers hunkered beneath large rectangular shields built to withstand the intense fire and leapt into trenches and foxholes the earth callers dug with their magic. Teams of dwarves stood resilient in front of their precious machines and hoisted shields the size of shed roofs to protect them and their crews. Those close enough to the tunnels rolled back into the caves until the imminent danger passed before lurching back out to fling more stones and spears.

The ferocious battle appeared to be evening out, and Jarvin and his leaders felt a glimmer of hope that they could sustain the fight at least for a time. Although night fell and cast darkness across the kingdom, the two factions did not relent. The battlefield took on a new, nightmarish aspect as the magic being unleashed across the valley threw the world into a chaotic strobe of flashing fire, lightning, and arcane explosions.

An eternity later, the sun began to edge over the colossal mountain peaks behind them, but instead of bringing with it the hope and warmth of a new day, it illuminated a horrifying image. A great swarm of dragons created a black cloud in the western sky. A hundred or more aerial reinforcements swooped in and rained death down upon the humans and dwarves.

Only the mages' quick actions saved them from being routed and destroyed. The wizards shifted their focus to defense and raised powerful wards over much of the army. The dwarves retreated back into their caves and defended the entrances. With much of their offense crushed, the ravager horde began cutting deeper into the human ranks and pushed them farther back into the valley.

Azerick and Raijaun brought their unmatched power to the fore and struck at the dragons with as much of their magical strength as they could spare. Both knew they could not afford to expend themselves against the ravagers or the dragons. That was the duty of the soldiers and mages. Azerick and his son had to be at their peak strength to battle the Scions directly when the time came, but it was becoming apparent that it may not be an option as the defenders continued to fall.

Sandy made a slow, circling pass high above the battlefield. Until now, she had remained at the periphery of the fighting, separating and engaging single targets as they distanced themselves from the skirmish to rest or hunt. It did not appear as though the dragons were able to tell she was not under the Scions' control until she attacked them.

If the fallen gods were aware of her meddling, they showed no interest in her. There were so many dragons now she doubted she could make much difference, but people were dying so fast she had to try. Her friends and family were down there, and if they were not already dead, she needed to try to save them.

She chose a thick knot of dragons assaulting the dwarves who had mostly retreated back into their tunnels, but at least a thousand of the stout, brave creatures were trapped outside, desperately trying to defend the long trench in which they were hiding. The dragons took turns strafing the channel with fire and magic while the dwarves hid beneath their shields and earthen overhangs. Several popped out from their cover to fire powerful crossbows at the attackers as they streaked past but were unable to inflict more than minor injuries on the colossal beasts.

Sandy waited until she was within a few hundred yards of the main group circling and waiting for their turn at the dwarves before striking at them with her rune magic. A powerful fireball erupted near the center of their group, destroying the wing of one dragon and singeing half a dozen others. Even as the crippled dragon made an uncontrolled spiral to the ground into the vengeful arms of the dwarves, she struck out at others with bolts of lightning and bursts of flaming breath.

The young dragon dived through the center of the chaos she created and streaked low over the ground toward the human front line with half a score of furious drakes racing after her. Warding runes tingled across her scaled hide as they instinctively detected an impending attack. Sandy banked hard to her right at the last moment, using the power of her runes to blow her out of the path of the arcane onslaught. Lightning, searing rays, and blinding orbs of destruction streaked past and unleashed their fury upon several ranks of ravagers. Swifter dragons used their higher positions to dive at her and spewed massive jets of liquid fire at her. Sandy juked back to her left but was unable to avoid all the attacks. Her warding runes flared and deflected most of the blast to send it splashing with the others into the enemy army.

The heat of the near miss blistered a large patch of skin beneath her scales, but she ignored the pain and summoned a wind to lift her skyward while conjuring another to blast down upon the backs of the three dragons trying to roast her. The two dragons on the periphery of the gust were able to arrest their dive and bank away to avoid being pushed into the unyielding ground, but the creature at the center of the sudden downdraft was unable to compensate in time and plowed into the swarming ravagers, crushing scores of them beneath its tumbling mass.

Sandy leveled her flight and flew at a narrow but deep canyon with the bulk of her enemies close behind. She sent her magic into the clouds and called for a fierce storm of wind, lightning, and hail. Rain pelted her as she neared the canyon and the unnatural storm brewing above it. Lightning flashed and illuminated the grey walls for an instant before it went dark once more. Small hailstones bounced off her hard scales as she threaded her way into the massive crevasse, but they were growing substantially larger by the second.

By the time the bulk of the hounding dragons entered the canyon, the hail was the size of apples and struck with the force of a mule kick. Many of the dragons were able to ward off the pummeling assault with their magic, but several were taking a brutal beating. Within moments, three dragons lost the ability to control their flight as their wings suffered too much abuse to keep them aloft. Others tried to fly out of the canyon only to be buffeted down and blown into the walls. Those strong enough to withstand the gusting wind and pounding hail fell to lightning strikes as Sandy reached out to them with her senses and guided the bolts to their targets.

By the time Sandy began her steep ascent out of the canyon, only four of the almost two dozen dragons still dogged her. Sharp pain and a massive blow struck her in her left side just as she cleared the edge of the fissure. She instinctively rolled and kicked her attacker away. The dragon tumbled and struggled to right itself as Sandy fell from the sky. With her back toward the rapidly approaching ground, she spotted two more dragons dive at her from where they had been cleverly waiting for her just over the rim of the canyon. She felt the other dragons' magic tear apart her storm, and rays of morning sunlight stabbed through the dissipating clouds.

Sandy tucked in one wing and stretched out the other as she twisted her body in order to right herself. She could see the two shadows just seconds away from intersecting her path and knew she had no time to avoid them. She braced herself and was preparing to pour all her strength into her wards when another shadow eclipsed all three of them. Sandy looked back just as a colossal dragon dropped onto one of her attackers and sank its massive claws into its body and engulfed the second one with a hellish blast of fire.

"Mordigar!"

"Fly away, child!"

"But..."

"Do not mistake my intervention as an alliance. I destroyed those two out of jealousy for stealing my kill and nothing else. The Scions' control will allow me to do little else, and even that bit of resistance is failing. My masters sense my conflict and are even now impressing upon me to destroy you."

"No, you can fight them!"

"No, I cannot, and so you must kill me as you promised."

"Please don't make me!" Sandy cried; the anguish clear in her pleadings.

"It is our enemy who makes you, not I. I am begging you to win our battle and set me free. Do it!"

Mordigar spread his paws and brought them together in a single clap. Thunder rolled out between them and struck Sandy with a concussive wave that sent her tumbling end over end across the sky. It took all her concentration to right herself and she called upon the wind to speed her flight. Mordigar's use of magic was every bit as awesome as his physical form, and he had no trouble keeping up with the smaller, swift sand dragon.

Sandy was certain Mordigar could swat her from the sky with ease if he let himself go, but he was obviously subverting the Scions' will to an extent. She surmised they were able to command him to kill her but not how he was to go about it, not without taking a far more direct role in controlling him. She hoped her theory was correct. It was the only way she could possibly survive.

Sandy heard Mordigar laugh as she dived toward the ravager lines. Her scales tingled and her wards glowed as the elder dragon began drawing in an enormous amount of power. Mordigar released a roar just before unleashing a blazing sphere of magical energy. Sandy was already dipping hard to the right when the orb streaked past her and left a smoldering crater in the heart of the ravager army more than a hundred yards wide. Had it hit her, it would have blown her to bits. The massive dragon swooped after her, spewing long blasts of fire that narrowly missed his target and decimated his "allies."

Both dragons understood the game they were playing as the pair wheeled and dived back and forth across the valley. Mordigar hurled spell after spell at his quarry, always giving her some sort of cue just before he struck so she could dodge away. What Sandy may not have understood was that Mordigar was intentionally exhausting himself so she could defeat him while doing as much damage to the Scions' army as he could. If his death was the only way to be free of enslavement, he was determined to make it worth something.

Either the Scions finally took notice of him, or they no longer found his and Sandy's antics amusing. Whichever the case, Xar's voice filled his head and commanded him to kill Sandy, and then use his awesome power against the human wizards. His gigantic form shuddered beneath the mental assault as he fought to retain what was left of his independence, but the Scion's hold was too powerful.

Several rapid but powerful magical strikes struck Sandy's wards and buffeted her around like a strong wind. Two broke through her defenses to blast away scales and traumatize the skin beneath.

"I am sorry, little one, but my masters have decided our game must end."

Sandy's only response was to coax more wind to push her faster. Mordigar's fatigue was showing as he struggled to keep up. Brilliant flashes of light streaked past as the elder dragon hurled arcane bolts at her in rapid succession. Sandy twisted and contorted as she dived and banked to avoid the lethal magic, grunting in pain whenever she failed. She sped away from the battle toward the mountains once more with Mordigar refusing to give up his pursuit.

Sandy hugged the mountainside and raced upward along its face as Mordigar conjured a powerful squall. Heavy rain pelted her body and greatly reduced her vision. Strong winds buffeted her wings, threatening to shove her into the mountainside even as bolts of lightning reached out and tried to touch her.

Sensing Mordigar close on her tail, Sandy raised a thick wall of stone behind her, but Mordigar was familiar with the tactic and avoided it. Despite Mordigar trying to tire himself out, Sandy was certain she was fatiguing even faster. Just beating her wings was becoming an arduous task. She needed to finish this battle soon before it ended in a way neither of them wanted.

A bolt of lightning seared the tip of her tail but also illuminated a deep cleft cut in the side of a cliff. Sandy aimed for the fissure, using the flashes of lightning to keep her course true. Mordigar's vision was every bit as acute as hers, so she needed to fly into the crevasse without allowing him time to avoid it.

Her heart was torn just like the rent in the air as she conjured a magical gate. Part of her hoped her plan would succeed but she understood the anguish she would suffer if it did. Sandy vanished into the portal and twisted so her long wings would not brush the fissure's walls. She had allowed Mordigar to close the distance between them until he was right on her tail and would have no time to avoid the gate or the crevasse. Sandy heard his sharp bark of surprise a split second before he plunged through the portal. Not even the torrential rain, fierce wind, or booming thunder could mask the sickening sound of the ancient dragon's bones snapping under the impact of his wings striking the narrow canyon walls.

Sandy flew upward out of the fissure and circled back to its entrance. Her keen vision picked out the massive lump of Mordigar's broken body lying almost a hundred yards inside the cleft. She walked hesitantly into the dark crevice as the pounding rain washed away her tears.

"You did well, child," Mordigar said in an agonized rumble. "I am proud of you. Now you must set me free."

"Mordigar, I'm so sorry!"

"Do not be. You have freed me, and we hurt the enslavers in the process. I could not ask for a better death. Now you must end my suffering, please."

Sandy could only nod as her throat clenched too tightly to speak. She laid her front paws on Mordigar's brow and summoned her magic. Mordigar did not resist and sighed as the golden aura warmed him and took away his pain just before it resolved into a razor's edge and cleanly severed his soul from his body.

Sandy lay next to her mentor's body for several minutes before speaking her final farewells and trudging from the cleft. Without Mordigar's guiding magic, the localized storm was dispersing. There was no more lightning arcing across the sky, and the rain had slowed to a drizzle. Turning back to face the fissure, Sandy fought through her exhaustion and called upon her runic power. The canyon walls trembled and collapsed, entombing Mordigar in a cairn worthy of the great dragon.

Thoroughly spent, Sandy lay down near the edge of the rubble and looked into the sky. Her heart sank as scores upon scores of winged shapes appeared over the tops of the distant mountains. For all the damage they had caused, Mordigar had given his life for nothing. The humans and dwarves could not possibly defend against so many dragons. They had all fought valiantly, but it was soon to be over.

CHAPTER 27

"Dear gods," Jarvin exclaimed as he passed his spyglass over the northern range and spotted the flying shapes.

Azerick turned to look at what the king had spotted. "How can there be so many dragons still left in this world?"

"Our wizards are already being pushed back and dying. How can we possibly defeat so many?" Jarvin asked.

"We cannot."

"Father, they do not fly like dragons," Raijaun interjected. "They're birds, enormous birds with men astride them!"

Azerick smiled. "The elves have come."

At least a hundred blood hawks and their riders dived at the backs of the dragons wreaking so much havoc on the mortal defenders. Wizard riders hurled powerful magic, and the silver streaks of elven-enchanted arrows broke the dragons' assault. No longer being pounded by the dragons' relentless magic and fiery breath, the human wizards resumed their offensive, and the dwarves and their destructive machines reemerged from their caves. Within minutes, the tide of the battle turned, and the humans stopped the ravager advance and even began reclaiming some ground.

A handful of aerial riders broke off from the main body and landed their powerful birds near the hilltop from where Jarvin and the others commanded the battle. Ten figures approached and Jarvin waved his Blackguard to stand down. A human warrior, a priest of Solarian, a dwarf, and seven elves, all sheathed in magnificent plate armor save one who wore a rainbow of silken robes and stood a head taller than even most of the humans present, comprised the delegation.

The elf bedecked in golden armor doffed his helm and delivered a short bow to Jarvin and then Azerick. "Your Majesty, I am Duharhuln Oakroot, son of Tuharhuln, chosen king of the elven nation."

Jarvin returned the bow. "I am Jarvin Ollander, son of Harlan Ollander, and king of Valeria. Words cannot express my gratitude for your coming."

"I bring more than my hawk riders, King Jarvin Ollander. Fifteen thousand elven warriors are marching through the northern pass as we speak. I expect them to arrive by midday to bolster our defense and cast these monsters back into the pits whence they came."

"That is welcome news. I pray we can hold out that long."

The rising sun revealed a battlefield every bit as terrifying as when the fighting first began. More so as Jarvin made a tactician's count of their forces. The Scions' army was so vast that their numbers were replenished as quickly as they were struck down no matter how much damage was inflicted upon them. Jarvin began to feel their efforts were as futile as trying to hold back the rising tide.

"Fear not, friend Jarvin. We did not come alone." The elven king turned to Tarth. "Can you contact our cousins, Tarthanalis?"

"Azerick, I rode a bird!" Tarth exclaimed.

Azerick smiled at the distracted elf. "I saw."

"Borik threw up, and I laughed so hard I almost fell off."

"Tarth, our friends?" Duharhuln asked again.

"Oh, right." Tarth produced a polished shell from inside his many layers of silk and spoke into it. "Hello, dear, are you there?" Tarth held the shell to his ear with a look of confusion. "Oh, wrong shell." The elf dipped his finger into the glossy paste filling the inside of the shell and applied a coating to his lips. "Flying is so much fun, but it wreaks havoc on my skin."

"Tarth, please," the elf king urged.

Tarth huffed and retrieved another shell from elsewhere in his robes. "Teraneshala, can you hear me?" Tarth held the shell to his ear and apparently received a reply. "We would love for you to join us now."

A large section of ground near the enemy's front line exploded in a spray of dirt, rock, and ravagers, and left a vast hole in the battlefield. Like a colony of bats, alabaster-skinned abyssal elves poured out of the pit on the backs of wyverns and even a few dragons. Runes painted on their black and stone-grey scales and etched into silver collars glowed with eldritch light. Azerick understood their purpose immediately and wished he had been able to create a less permanent solution for Sandy. Dozens of portals opened near the outskirts of the battle lines and disgorged hundreds and eventually thousands of black-clad warriors and scores of wizards and priests.

"We might actually do this," Jarvin said in a hopeful breath.

"Come on, Borik. Let's get down there and get our blades bloody," Maude commanded.

"I like it up here. I'm more of a command-and-control sort of dwarf," Borik responded.

"You're going to be a foot in your arse kind of dwarf if you don't move it! Today, we become heroes. Now get your knee-high backside to the front lines with me."

"Most heroes die in the end, Maude!" Borik complained as he followed the warrior woman down the hill. "I'll tell you this, I'll never complain about being on a boat after riding on one of those infernal dwarf-eating chickens. Did you see the way it kept eyeing me? Like I was a worm!"

"Malek, Brother Thomas would be grateful for all the help he can get at the hospital tents," Azerick told the cleric.

Malek watched his friends headed toward the battlefield and was torn with indecision. He made his choice and nodded at Azerick. "You're right. The wounded need me most right now."

The battle continued to rage, and by nightfall the combined forces of the races managed to regain much of the ground they had lost. Come morning, the Scion army had resurged, halted their advance, and begun turning the tide yet again. The ravager numbers seemed endless, and the light of a new day revealed a field still choked with their enemy's inexhaustible numbers. Ravagers threw themselves at the races' forward lines, ignoring the iron constructs even as the animated machines hewed at their backs. Wizards and pikemen eventually stopped the feverous drive, but not before cutting a deep swath in their defenses.

Jarvin and his key leaders had been in conference most of the morning, desperately trying to devise a strategy to counter the newest setback. Twice they had been rescued from defeat by the arrival of allies, but now there was no one left to come to their aid.

"There appears to be no end to these creatures," Jarvin said. "If there is, I see us reaching ours far before we find theirs."

"Where are they coming from?" King Yusuf asked. "Surely they did not all travel across the land from Brightridge and Brelland? I read your accounts of those battles, and there did not seem to be nearly so many."

"There were not," Raijaun confirmed. "Father and I think they managed to erect gates near the valley to allow a resupply of forces from their prison world, but the Scions are actively blocking any attempt at scrying them."

"If we do not cut off their resupply, we will never defeat them here. Is there any way we can get some of our people to these gates and destroy them?" Jarvin asked.

Duharhuln answered, "My riders have been trying to get a look at the far end of the valley, but the dragons rally and force us away before we can get near. This indicates they are indeed hiding something from us."

"We must ascertain the existence of those gates and destroy them if that is indeed how they are bringing in reinforcements."

"If we could locate them, it is possible for Raijaun and me to get near enough to open a portal to them," Azerick said. "If we could do that, destroying them should pose little problem. The hard part is going to be getting away afterward. The Scions have already shown a keen interest in protecting their existence, and they are sure to be heavily guarded. Undertaking this sort of action could leave me and Raijaun too fatigued to battle the Scions when they arrive. It is the very reason we have not expended ourselves thus far."

"Well, while you are conserving your power, our people are dying by the thousands! If we do not find these gates and destroy them soon, there won't be anyone left for you to save when these fallen gods do deign to show themselves."

Azerick sighed and nodded. Jarvin was right. He and Raijaun could not continue to let the soldiers and wizards bear the brunt of the fighting. They were dying too fast. What good would it do to fight the Scions if there was no one left to fight for?

A soldier burst into the hall. "Sire, something new occurs on the battlefield!"

"Gods, bad news is like mold. Once it sets into your cheese it just spreads," Jarvin complained as he stormed out of the door followed by his officers and leaders.

A low, thick fog rolled over the northern range and blanketed the valley floor in a blindingly thick miasma. Were it not for the continued sounds of fighting and the aerial battles raging overhead, the region would have appeared clean and serene, like a waste dump hidden beneath a fresh layer of snow.

"This cannot be natural," Jarvin said.

Azerick replied, "It is not."

"This is disastrous! Our wizards are almost useless if they cannot see. Is this more work of the Scions?"

Azerick extended a hand as he sent out his consciousness and felt for the magic involved in the fog's creation. "There is a heavy necromantic aspect to it. It feels almost identical to the fog we encountered at End's Run, which covered much of Valeria."

"Are you saying we are going to have to fight the dead as well? There must be twenty thousand or more of our own dead on that battlefield and at least ten times as many enemy. If they rise to fight us..."

"Then this battle has likely met its conclusion," Azerick finished.

The fog drifted from east to west and cleared away to reveal the mostly human army as it rolled over the enemy ranks. As it passed, the fallen, both ally and foe, stumbled to their feet, shambled toward the front lines, and began hacking and clawing at the enemy.

"They're fighting for us!" Jarvin shouted, then motioned to his fellow kings to peer through his powerful, tripod-mounted spyglass.

"This is truly a miracle of our gods," Yusuf said with a relieved sigh.

"I do not sense the power of the gods in its creation," Azerick said. "Not directly anyway. Only Sharrellan would deign to use such detestable magic, and I have felt firsthand the signature of her power. Someone else has been tasked by the gods to play a part, and their piece has just been put into play."

"As awful a move as it is, I'll take it," Jarvin replied. "Perhaps now we can locate those gates and destroy them."

"Raijaun and I will search for a way, but it may take time."

"Do everything you can, but do it quickly. This black magic has bought us some time, but it does not appear as though it will last."

Already the fog had rolled deep into the ravager lines and left a clear view of the battlefield behind. Although similar to the spell enacted during the night of terror, it soon became apparent that it was far shorter-lived. For the first time in the war, the ravagers faced a foe as fearless and relentless as themselves, and it was taking its toll.

Like any rare good news, it did not last long. A battered and bleeding scout galloped his mount to the very top of the hill and nearly fell out of his saddle at the king's feet. Jarvin reached down and helped the man stand.

"Your Majesty, a massive force has attacked the southern pass! We have them bottlenecked in the pass, but our numbers are too few to hold for long."

"How many?"

The scout shook his head. "I don't know, sire. It was thousands, and more seemed to be coming."

"If they opened a gate to our southeast, we could be facing a battle on two fronts," Yusuf stated. "We do not have the reserves to split our forces if they break through with substantial numbers."

"Yusuf, it is time we led our people into battle. We must gather everyone we have available, plug the gap, and find out if there is another gate. Duharhuln, can you spare us a few of your hawk riders? I think the Scions were relying on this to be a surprise attack. If there is a gate, we need their eyes to find it."

"Of course. I can pull a company of my archers from the battle to go with you."

"There is no time. We must take everyone who is ready to ride right now." Jarvin turned to his son and laid a hand on his shoulder. "Miles, you will lead in my stead. Begin pulling as many of our troops from the rear ranks as we can afford, and get them ready to ride south if we fail to stop them."

"Father, I should go, not you!"

"No, you are a brilliant soldier, but a mission like this must be led by the king. If I fall, I know you are ready to wear the crown. You are the future of Valeria, and the people could ask for no one better to lead them."

"Allister and I will go with you," Aggie said.

"What are you doing volunteering me for a suicide mission, woman?" Allister snapped.

"Are you going to let me go by myself, you old goat?"

Allister chewed on his bushy, white mustache. "No, but I'll darn well make you feel guilty about it."

The two human kings gathered all their available cavalry and rode for the southeastern pass. Five thousand horses thundered across rough terrain and along animal paths for over an hour before reaching the new battlefield. The regiment guarding their southern flank was down to a few hundred men desperately fighting to keep the horde of ravagers bottled up within a narrow pass. Only the handful of wizards sent to augment the contingent had kept them from being overrun, but they were near to collapsing from exhaustion.

The air was thick with the smoke of burning sagebrush and manzanita piled together in a desperate attempt to prevent the ravagers from climbing over the pass and going around them. The sight of several secondary skirmishes showed it was only moderately successful.

Their reinforcements arrived just in time as the defense was near to shattering as more men were forced to abandon the pass to defend their rapidly failing flanks. Jarvin looked to his fellow king, nodded, and drew his sword. Signalmen blew their horns to order a charge. The cavalry split into three groups with the largest one thundering into the mouth of the gorge.

The exhausted footmen cheered and gladly made way for the mounted soldiers to take control of the battle. With the two archmages' and five wizards' arcane help, the humans managed to take back the pass, but their advance was stopped cold upon reaching the enemy's main body. At least ten thousand ravagers surged toward the pass or climbed over the steep butte to brave the fires set all across its height and face.

The elven hawk riders landed near the humans' rear, firing their arrows over an impossible distance yet making incredible shots from atop their winged mounts as they waited for a runner to relay their scouting report to those in charge. Jarvin, Allister, and Aggie broke away from the battle and approached the elves.

"You've found a gate?" Jarvin asked.

"Yes, Your Majesty, perhaps five or six miles farther up the gorge. Hundreds of these fell creatures are pouring through every minute."

"How well is it defended?" Aggie asked.

"Other than the hordes streaming through, they have three dragons circling overhead. They drove us away before we got within a mile of it. Thank the gods they stayed there and did not come to the pass, or it would likely have fallen before we arrived. It is strange. There are several avenues that would allow these creatures to go around this pass and avoid your fighters, but they continue to stream through the gorge like ants."

"Hmm, likely a more adept analogy than you think," Allister answered. "We know they do not operate at a human level of intelligence and use very little in the way of tactics. Yet they are able to respond very quickly to changes in the battlefield. I suspect they are of a hive mentality and communicate with some sort of telepathy. It would explain how the rearmost elements are able to respond so quickly to changes on the front lines."

"We must close that gate quickly before we lose control of the pass. My son is gathering our reserves as we speak, but it will take at least half a day for most of them to get here," Jarvin said.

"Is there any way you can get us near that gate," Aggie asked.

"Our hawks cannot support two riders, but I can teach you some basic commands. The dragons are going to be a problem, but three of us may be able to draw them away to allow you to get close enough to destroy the gate."

Allister cast the enormous predators a doubtful glance. "You want us to ride those things by ourselves?"

"It is not so different than controlling a horse except for a few additional commands to urge them to ascend and descend. They will mostly follow the others and their own instincts. You will need only to hold on until you reach the gates."

"Magus, we must destroy the gate at any cost," Jarvin said.

Allister agreed but not until after a bit more grumbling. Two elves surrendered their mounts, helped strap the two wizards in place, and gave them brief instructions on controlling the stubborn but highly intelligent birds. Securely mounted, the flyers took to the sky and raced south in a desperate attempt to avert disaster—if it was not already too late.

The hawk rider leader pointed at the river of ravagers flooding the long, twisting gorge. "There is already a significant increase in their numbers, and they are still growing," he shouted over the wind buffeting their ears.

The wizards nodded; their eyes fixed near the horizon where they could see the dragons circling above two large obelisks planted in the ground between which spewed more of the ravenous creatures.

The dragons ceased circling and made straight for the intruders. The three elves surged ahead and dived at the dragons to gain their attention and draw them away from the gate long enough for the wizards to complete their mission. Arrows streaked from their powerful bows and bit into the dragons' hard scales, but only two of them chased the bait. The third one banked and dodged the stinging shafts but kept heading for the two mages. Their hawks parted in opposing directions as the dragon blew a long column of fire that passed harmlessly between them.

The dragon took up the chase after Allister when he dived toward the gate. Fire and magic streaked past as the blood hawk twisted and dodged the lethal attacks. Aggie tried to strike at the dragon with her magic, but weaving a spell from the back of a bird was a challenge at best. Her flight was too unsteady to create her more powerful and complex magic, and even the simpler spells were erratic and rarely found their target.

Allister was forced to break off his attempt to reach the gate as he needed to regain altitude. Aggie guided her hawk beside his when the dragon chose not to pursue them and resumed its vigilance over the gate.

"This isn't working," Allister shouted. "I can't weave a strong enough spell to destroy that thing even if I could get close enough."

Aggie nodded her understanding. "Let me see if I can draw the dragon away. He can't chase us both."

Allister gave her a thumbs-up sign, and they both wheeled their flying mounts back around for another attempt. Far in the distance, they could see the elves locked in combat with the other two dragons. Whenever the wyrms tried to break away from the fight, one of the riders would swoop in and launch harassing attacks with claw and arrow until it resumed the chase. The elves had their hands full and could not provide any more help. If they were going to destroy the gate, they would have to devise a way to do it themselves.

The dragon went on the offensive the moment they approached the gate. Aggie struck out with some moderately powerful spells until her mount wheeled away to avoid the dragon's return strikes. Turning in her saddle, she sent arcane orbs streaking out behind her, but they were little more than an irritant to the powerful beast.

Allister guided his hawk toward the gate, but the dragon broke off its chase and dived after him. Aggie looped around and struck at the creature's back, but she could not deter it. Allister was forced to break off his attack, but Aggie stayed true and tried to reach the obelisks as the dragon gave chase. Seeing what was happening, the dragon twisted in midair and attacked Aggie with its magic.

Knowing what the human wizards were trying to do, the dragon sent its arcane power into the sky. Black clouds formed above the gate, and fierce winds swept across the gorge, forcing the blood hawks to dip their wings one way and another to maintain flight. It made for a very bumpy ride and the already difficult task of casting magic from their backs all but impossible.

"We cannot do this from up here!" Aggie shouted.

"Well, we can't go down there! The instant one of them sees us, the whole lot of them will turn around and swarm us."

Aggie looked serious as she nodded. "I know."

"Blast your wrinkly old hide, woman! I told you it was a suicide mission."

"We're not dead yet, you old coot! Do you want to live forever?"

"That was the plan!"

"Well, plans change!"

Allister jerked the reins of his aerial steed with a loud, unintelligible shout at the wind and rain, and the two mages raced for the stone pylons once again. The dragon's defense was simple but strong. It knew the wizards were unaccustomed to flying and could do little to harm it or the gate as long as it did not allow them to land. Even if they did manage to reach the ground, the disgusting ravagers would likely tear them apart within minutes if not seconds.

The blood hawks flew wide as another jet of fire scorched the air between them, but instead of trying to draw the dragon away, they regrouped as the dragon sped past and continued to dive at the gate. The wyrm flipped around with incredible grace for a creature so large and pursued them. Allister and Aggie aimed for the area behind the pillars where it was mostly free of ravagers.

Less than a hundred feet from the ground, the two wizards released the straps securing them to their saddles and threw themselves over the side. A simple spell arrested their uncontrolled fall to the speed of a quick jog. The dragon, finally taken by surprise by the unexpected maneuver, continued to chase after the blood hawks until it realized neither of them held a rider. It tried to loop back around, but the giant birds attacked it mercilessly, tearing out scales and digging into the flesh beneath with their formidable talons.

The archmages took a moment to study the obelisks and found them heavily warded against magic. It would take a powerful spell to bring them down, one which the ravagers were not going to afford them the time to cast. It took only seconds for the first creature to become aware of the intruders and even less time for it to relay the alarm to the rest.

Ravagers stopped in their tracks and spun around by the hundreds to kill the interlopers before they could bring down the gates. For now, the gate gave the wizards two advantages. The ravagers on the other side could not see or reach them from directly in front of it, and the ones pouring out of it hampered those racing back up the gorge to attack them.

"Aggie, you need to shield us until I can bring this infernal thing down."

"How long will it take you?"

"At least a minute, but not much more. This thing has some strong wards carved into it."

"I'll do my best."

Aggie conjured her most powerful ward as scores of ravagers leapt at their exposed position. The creatures howled and slashed at the barrier with fervor when it prevented them from reaching their foes. Sweat began streaming from her brow as she continued to pour power into the shield in order to maintain it. Every pounding fist and slashing blade weakened it, causing invisible cracks in its surface, and these required a continual flow of energy to repair.

"How much longer, you old coot?" Aggie asked.

"About twenty more seconds, thirty if you keep nagging me!"

Aggie shut up and focused her attention on the barrier, shifting her sight between the magic making up the ward and the creatures clawing to get through. She blessed Azerick for his foresight and courage in creating the Source pool. Had he not, she would never have been able to create and maintain such an impassable barrier.

She gasped as several smaller, blue-skinned creatures leapt at the barrier without impediment. She summoned arcane energy to her hand and lashed out, striking down three of the vile creatures but failed to stop a fourth before it leapt onto Allister's back and plunged a bone-bladed knife into his neck. Aggie cried out and struck with her magic, and the creature's head exploded like a lanced boil. Anger and anguish drove her to draw in more power. A ring of flesh-rending magic and nearby stones swirled around the outside of the barrier in a powerful vortex.

Aggie dropped to her knees and pressed a wad of her robes against Allister's neck in an attempt to stop the bleeding even as she maintained her focus on the powerful spells.

"What are you doing, woman?" Allister demanded as he gazed past Aggie at the spell swirling around them. "You're gonna burn yourself up."

"I'm going to get you out of here," Aggie promised as sweat beaded and dropped from her face.

"Don't be stupid. That nasty critter hit an artery. I knew your nagging was gonna be the death of me one day." Allister coughed, flecking his snow-white beard and mustache with blood.

"Shut up, you damn old coot. It's going to be the death of us both."

"You can still get away."

"I can't cast a portal far enough to get past those creatures even if I wanted to. Besides, I can't leave without destroying the gate, and I can't work a strong enough spell to do that without losing control of the ones keeping those creatures away from us."

"Are you saying you can't...take down...the gate?" Allister struggled to ask as he began losing consciousness.

Tears flowed down the old archmage's face and spattered onto Allister's wrinkled forehead like rain. "There's one way, my love. Go stand at Solarian's side. I'll see you very soon."

Aggie gently laid Allister's head onto the ground and stood. She faced the furious horde but looked beyond them to the shimmering well of power residing far away in another dimension. The archmage opened herself completely to the flow of magic, holding nothing back.

"Damn...fool...woman," Allister mumbled, then coughed and breathed a final shuddering breath.

Aggie's tears burned with silver light, blinding her as the Source poured into her body far beyond her ability to control it. She struggled to contain the power as long as she could. Brilliant argent light shot from her eyes and mouth as she released a silent, anguished scream. Aggie was unable to contain the magic any longer, and the pent-up energy exploded with cataclysmic violence. The powerful blast destroyed the gate and scoured the gorge clean for half a mile in every direction.

CHAPTER 28

Jarvin and Yusuf's forces were unable to hold the pass. The relentless ravager assault had pushed their men out of the gulch and into the expanding basin just beyond it. The human front stretched thinner as the ravager lines widened, and every minute the horde pushed them back farther and thinned their lines closer to the breaking point.

A titanic explosion shook the ground beneath them and was so powerful it was visible even over the tall butte. The sky above the horizon lit up with a light bright enough to force anyone looking at it to turn away and shield their eyes despite it being a clear afternoon, and a huge column of dust rose into the sky like a colossal mushroom.

"I think the wizards have done it!" Jarvin exclaimed.

Yusuf gave a grim nod. "Yes, surely good news on the whole but likely too little and too late for us."

Jarvin's excitement evaporated under the heat of reality. There were still tens of thousands of ravagers trying to shove through the pass, and more were climbing over it and descending into the gulch to decimate his people. The soldiers fought valiantly, their morale and courage bolstered by their kings fighting alongside them. Most armies would have broken ranks and retreated under such disparaging odds and brutality, but his and Yusuf's men would fight to the last knowing their leaders would die beside them for a cause greater than the lives of any man, even a king.

The shuddering of the ground ceased, but another source of shaking replaced it, and it was growing stronger. Thunderous battle cries and shrill trilling resonated across the battlefield as a horde of ogres, orcs, and goblins poured over the eastern hills and descended upon the humans' left flank like an avalanche.

"Damn cowardly jackals!" Jarvin raged as he watched doom fall upon his already beleaguered forces.

His mouth fell open and his eyes narrowed in confusion as the first of the brute horde fell upon the ravagers climbing over the butte to their front before slamming into those filling the valley.

"I think you judge too quickly," Yusuf called out with the laugh of a man pardoned just before the headman swung his axe.

Goblins sprinted around and through the legs of ravagers, leaping onto their backs and plunging their blades into them with psychotic fervor. Orcs and massive ogre warriors waded into the fight with more organization and discipline but with equal brutality. What truly held Jarvin's attention were the three figures wearing plate armor of incredible blackness.

"By the gods, they are wearing Dundalor's armor," Jarvin said with reverence and a bit of fear.

"What is this?" Yusuf asked.

"They wear the armor created by the dwarven master smith Dundalor Ironforge and gifted to my ancestor to fight the dragons during the Great Revolution. How could they have such a thing?"

"It appears yours was not the only ancestor gifted, nor the only hero to stand and fight."

Jarvin slowly wagged his head. "How much of our history has been forgotten? How much of it is an outright lie?"

"Let us be more concerned with the truths of today than the lies of yesterday."

"You are a wiser man than I, Yusuf."

"Better-looking as well!" The Sumaran king chortled. "Yet another truth of today."

A ravager's blade spun over the forward ranks of warriors and slipped between the narrow gap of Jarvin's helm and breastplate. Yusuf dropped from his mount and caught Jarvin as he swayed and fell from his saddle. The Sumaran gently lowered the king to the ground and slipped off his helm.

The knife was buried in the hollow of Jarvin's throat, and he was bleeding profusely. His jaw worked up and down but the blade made it impossible to speak. Several of his Blackguards tightened their defensive ring around the king and pulled him and Yusuf away from the press of battle. Jarvin reached for the handle of the knife protruding from his throat but Yusuf held his wrist fast.

"No, my friend, if we remove it, you will surely die."

Jarvin pulled his hand toward the hilt again, and his eyes pleaded with Yusuf. They had no Chosen with them, and they both knew he would never live long enough to return to the valley. Jarvin waved forward the Blackguard who had retrieved his fallen sword. The elite soldier placed the hilt of the saint sword in his king's hand. With another beseeching look to Yusuf, the Sumaran gently extracted the lethal blade.

"For...my...son," Jarvin said in a raspy, gurgling voice. "He knows...what must...be done."

Yusuf gripped Jarvin's fist tightly in his hand. "I will see he gets it, my friend. You have my word."

Jarvin forced a smile onto his face and squeezed Yusuf's hand. Yusuf knelt at Jarvin's side until Solarian's life-giving flames went out in his eyes, and his soul ascended to their god's celestial palace like a cinder borne upon the wind.

The ring of Blackguards tensed and lifted their blades high as an enormous shadow draped itself across the knot of humans. Yusuf did not even have to stand to see the source of their unease. Towering above the group stood a massive figure bedecked in gleaming, black plate armor from head to toe. Yusuf found himself lost in the armor's depthless ebony sheen. The Sumaran forced himself to focus, stood, and motioned Jarvin's elite warriors to stand aside. Yusuf stepped boldly to the outer ring of men and stood before the hulking ogre.

Sefket doffed his gold-trimmed onyx helm and held it in the crook of his arm just above the handle of the massive battle-axe hanging from his thick leather belt. "Are you the human king?"

Ogres were little more than folklore in his kingdom, but the stories regarded the creatures as subhuman brutes, barely more intelligent than animals. But when Yusuf looked into the piercing yellow eyes of the creature standing before him, he did not see an animal or even a savage tribal chief; he saw a being of strength, pride, and nobility every bit the equal to his own.

"I am Yusuf Sabaht, king of the Sumaran people." Yusuf extended an arm toward Jarvin's body. "There lies Jarvin Ollander, king of the Valerian people."

Sefket turned his huge palms toward the sky and growled something unintelligible to the humans' ears. "He died defending his Kin. There can be no more honorable death than that. I am Sefket, king of all the Kin. Your people are too few, and a king has fallen. Take your soldiers and return the king to his people. The Kin shall defend this pass and wipe this scourge from our world."

"Thank you, Sefket. We owe your people a great debt. I hope we can repay it one day."

"There is but one way your kind can show their gratitude."

"How? Name it and it is yours if it is in my power to give."

"Remember today. Remember what the Kin have never forgotten and will never forget."

"I will, Sefket," Yusuf swore. "Your deeds will be written in a hundred books and upon a thousand scrolls. We will carve it into the walls of our greatest cities to remind everyone of what you have done for us."

"We shall see." Sefket donned his helm, took his enormous battle-axe in his hand, and waded back into the fray.

Yusuf commanded the Blackguards to secure their king's body and ordered a retreat. The crack of lightning and the cacophonic booming of thunder punctuated the clarion calls of horns as the human survivors formed ranks and left the fighting to the Kin. The Sumaran looked back toward the battle.

Angry clouds stabbed at the ravagers with lightning. Even blacker clouds of what appeared to Yusuf to be massive swarms of birds or huge insects dived, split apart, and raced over the battlefield. Yusuf looked to the three remaining wizards riding next to him as the air tingled with the presence of magic.

"Not us," one said in answer to the unspoken question. "There is a powerful shamanic and even druidic influence to it."

"Will it be enough for the brutes to hold the pass?"

"We did not get a good estimate of their numbers, but their forces appeared to be quite strong. Shamans may not be able to stand toe to toe with a mage, but once their ritual magic gets ramped up, it can be devastating over a much larger area than any of us can achieve. Assuming those savages don't break and run, they will provide a good bulwark for our southern defenses."

"They are not savages, magus, and it will do us all good to understand that," Yusuf said in rebuke. "The misunderstandings between all our peoples has contributed to the disaster we face today, and we must learn from it, or we are sure to repeat them until we either learn or our ignorance becomes our end."

The wizard had the decency to look chastised. "You are a wise king, Highness."

"Good-looking too," he responded with a grin directed at Jarvin's shrouded body tied onto the saddle of his mount.

It was a long, somber ride back to the valley. The sun was just settling into the horizon when they reached the southern battle line reinforced with every available fighter Prince Miles was able to pull from the reserves and battlefront. The air filled with the droning of hundreds of muttering voices as the contingent passed through the lines with more than half the horses carrying dead soldiers, many of them riding double, but it was the shrouded form borne at the head of the procession which drew everyone's eyes.

Miles pushed his mount toward the riders, leapt from the saddle, and began pulling at the straps securing Jarvin in place. "Father!"

Yusuf dismounted and restrained the anguished prince in a tight embrace. "Be strong, son. Do not let your grief overwhelm you. There will be time for grieving later, but right now, you must be a pillar of strength for your people. You are now their king, and you must be a shining symbol of your father's heroic sacrifice."

"I'm not ready!"

"Yes, you are, my son. Your father knew you were ready when he left you to defend our people. I see in you much of your father's courage and wisdom. His last thoughts and words were of you." Yusuf presented Jarvin's sword and crowned helm to the heir to the Valerian throne. "He knows you are ready for both of these and asked me to give them to you with his final words."

Miles replaced his own sword with his father's and held the helm in his hands. "You say I am wise, but I know I'm not my father. Will you help me?"

Yusuf embraced Miles once more. "You already show wisdom beyond your years. I pray my foolish sons do as well one day. Your father was my friend, as are you. I and my people will always stand with you. You will not fight this war nor suffer its ravages alone. Speaking of the war, how fares the battle?"

"It is bleak. What you see here is the bulk of our reserves, and they were fighting on the front not more than a couple hours ago. We are all exhausted, and I fear none of us will be able to rest for long."

"Has Azerick been able to close the enemy's gates?"

"No. He and Raijaun have devised a plan, but they cannot get near enough to them to enact it. Our defense is as tenuous as ever, and it is failing fast."

"Let us confer with him. It may be time to roll the dice and strike with all our might without regard to what happens next. Otherwise, we may not get a chance to face the fallen gods at all."

Miles and Yusuf galloped up the hill to the heart of the allied command and left a squad of Blackguards to act as a funeral detail. The two kings found Azerick and Raijaun studying the battlefield with worried expressions while the elven king spoke in conference with one of his aerial scouts.

"Azerick, are you able to reach the gates and destroy them yet?" Miles asked, the desperation evident in his voice.

Azerick looked to his son. "Raijaun?"

"Not yet, Father. Sandy is unable to fight past the dragons to reach the gates."

"Yusuf, I am glad to see you returned. Where is the king?" Azerick asked.

"I am saddened to report he fell in battle. Miles is now your king."

"Highness, your loss is shared by us all. Long live the king."

Miles's voice caught as he touched the saint sword's hilt. "Thank you, Azerick. Your condolences are appreciated. We shall mourn as a nation when this is done."

"Where are Allister and Aggie?"

Yusuf cleared his throat and spoke. "There was a great explosion deep within the gorge. It may be they perished while effecting the gate's destruction."

King Duharhuln broke away from his conversation with the rider and approached. "That was one of the riders I sent south. He says the two wizards were near the gate when the explosion occurred. I am sorry, but it is very unlikely they survived."

Azerick felt as though he had been punched. Aggie was beloved by all who knew her, and Allister had become a surrogate father to him. The world felt a much lonelier place now.

"Duharhuln, can your riders help clear a path to the gates?" Miles asked.

"They have been trying, but we have suffered grievous losses and they are overwhelmed by the might of the dragons."

"Azerick, I know you and Raijaun have been reserving your strength to fight the Scions, but I fear it is no longer an option. If we do not destroy those gates now, facing the fallen gods will be all but pointless."

Azerick's face fell and he nodded his agreement. "You are likely right. Headmaster, contact your people and have them gather where we discussed. Yusuf, please ask Devlin to do the same. Miles, you must know that even if we are able to carve a path to the gates, it is unlikely very many of us will return. The ravagers will likely envelop our contingent, and we will have only the elves' wizards to lend their arcane support if we do not all return."

"I understand, Azerick, but I see no other option if we are to cut off their unending supply of reinforcements. If you think there is any other way, I would gladly hear it."

Azerick shook his head, knowing that even if they severed the gangrenous limb, they would likely bleed to death. "I wish there was."

CHAPTER 29

In a world far removed from any war, four gods looked down upon the raging battle, helplessly watching their followers die by the thousands. Sharrellan and Serron's faces remained impassive, Solarian tried his hardest to appear stoic despite his grief and anger, and Ellanee wept openly.

"We cannot stand by and just watch them die," the goddess of nature pleaded.

Solarian stroked her long, flowing hair. "We do not dare move before the Scions, or we will fail."

"My Hand is going to lead the wizards in a charge to destroy the gates," Sharrellan said. "Even if they succeed, the races lack the strength to defeat the Scions' minions with the loss of nearly all their arcane might, and he and Raijaun will be too weak to force the faceless ones to the battlefield of our choosing."

"Either path we choose leads to destruction."

"There is a third option," Serron stated. "We send another army to break through the horde thus sparing our Guardians and wizards so they may still employ their power as needs be."

"We do not have another army!" Solarian shouted in exasperation.

Sharrellan flashed Solarian a coy smile. "I do."

Solarian glared at his dark counterpart. "Your creatures are forbidden from entering the mortal world en masse. You would unleash another scourge upon an already beleaguered people."

"Are you still so petty that you cannot trust me? Do you think I would risk my existence in some childish attempt to become the dominant deity of this world?"

"What about when it is over?" Ellanee asked. "Will you willingly send your demonic army home, in its entirety, without hesitation or duplicity?"

"I make it my most sacred vow. Do not forget, those are my supplicants dying down there as well."

"I second the motion to release the demons upon the Scion minions," Serron declared.

The sun god and the goddess of nature exchanged worried looks but nodded their assent. The four gods placed a hand upon the large, flat-topped crystalline column in the center of the celestial palace's Hall of the Gods. The four-colored crystal—amber, sapphire, emerald, and onyx—flared with light as each god touched its surface.

"Only the lesser demons, Sharrellan," Solarian insisted. "We cannot risk your lords breaking free and pillaging the world."

"You tie my hands, Solarian, but it shall be as you command."

Azerick, Raijaun, Headmaster Florent, and Magus Skinner hastened down the slope toward the wizards' gathering point to act as the tip of the spear they hoped would be strong enough to stab deep into the enemy ranks and cut out its heart. None of them paid much heed to Tarth as he hummed and skipped along behind them.

As they neared the base of the hill, the ground shook and large plumes of dust, ash, and fire erupted into the air as massive fissures reaching all the way to the abyss opened up. Demons swarmed from the pits like ants from a disturbed mound. Grackin and succubi flew into the air and attacked the dragons as balrogs, harunden, powerful tar'raun'atu, and the devilish kamaris threw themselves at the ravagers.

"What in the abyss...?" Azerick exclaimed.

Maureen looked at the sorcerer. "You would know better than the rest of us."

"Father, can you communicate with the demons and get them to clear a path for Sandy?"

"I...don't know."

Azerick closed his eyes and sent his consciousness outward. He found the violent thoughts of a succubus and tried to speak to her mind. It did not appear he was getting through so he "shouted." The demon halted its attack on a dragon and broke away from her sisters who were swarming the furious serpent.

"*You!*" she sent back.

"*Yes, me. I need you to command the demons for me.*"

"*You are no longer our master. We need not obey you.*"

"*I am the Hand of Sharrellan and her chosen one to act in this war. You will obey me or suffer both our wrath.*"

The succubus formed several vile thoughts but acquiesced. "*What would you command us to do?*"

"*I have a dragon friend who carries powerful objects capable of destroying the gates the Scions are using to replace their fallen.*" Azerick sent an image of Sandy to the demon's mind. "*Help her reach the gates. It is crucial in order to win this war and fulfill the wishes of our goddess.*"

"*Our goddess?*" the demon chuckled. "*Send your dragon. We will get her there.*"

"Raijaun, contact Sandy and tell her to make for the gates. The demons will clear a path."

Raijaun nodded and reached out to Sandy much like Azerick had done with the demon. His blood contained only a diluted amount of dragon essence, and mind-linking was a challenge that allowed only a limited form of communication.

"She understands, Father."

Sandy heard Raijaun's muddy sending and circled back toward the ravager lines once more. She had been trying to reach the gates for the better part of the day, and she was exhausted. Demons thronged the battlefield and dotted the skies. Their numbers were not as great as the ravagers, but their fearlessness and ferociousness shifted the press of the attack back onto the Scion legions.

Succubi hurled balls of fire and stabbed at the eyes and softer parts of the dragons' anatomy in concert with the bat-like grackin. Neither demon could match the speed of a dragon, but the sky was thick with them, and the demons latched onto their scales like ticks, drawing blood and wounding them with magic, claws, and blades.

Sandy picked an opening between the dozens of aerial battles and summoned a wind to speed her through. A few dragons spotted her and tried to ignore the parasitical demons stinging them like swarms of bees. She clutched the four arcanum spheres Azerick had brought back from his tower earlier that day tightly in her forepaws. It would not do to drop them where they would be instantly and irretrievably lost in the swarming mass below her.

She urged her runes to ward her body from the pursuing dragons' unwavering attacks, but she was tired and unable to shield herself from the assaults in their entirety. Fire, lightning, and magic ruined several patches of scales and blistered her flesh. Sandy now understood why Azerick had etched so many redundant runes all over her body. Her scales would grow back along with the sigils decorating them, but for now they were all she had.

Sandy conjured fierce winds and choking dust storms in her wake to hamper the dragons' pursuit. The powerful gales collided and created miniature tornados, sucking in and flinging away any dragon failing to avoid them. Through the haze of her black blizzard, Sandy spied the first gate and spotted two others a moment later.

The dragons became more numerous as she approached, but swarms of winged demons dropped from the sky and savagely attacked to distract them long enough for Sandy to deliver her gifts. Sandy considered her speed, altitude, and the weight of the orbs to plot the trajectory. A hundred yards from the nearest gate, she let one of the arcanum spheres slip from her grasp.

The orb fell as a silver streak to anyone watching from the ground and landed in some brush some fifty feet away. Sandy was disappointed in her aim but was not concerned. Azerick had told her the explosion would be powerful enough that it only needed to be close. Still, she thought herself as something of a perfectionist and it bothered her.

Using what she had learned from what she considered a practice shot, the next sphere came to a stop an arm's length from one of the gate pillars and a third butted right up against the other. Sandy increased her altitude and searched the area for another gate. She decided that if there was one, she was not going to be able to find it as the dragons began winning their battle with the demons and directed their attacks toward her. Sandy sprinted for the safety of the human lines, dropping the fourth arcanum bomb in the midst of the ravager legion on her way past.

"*Raijaun, it is done. Do it now!*" Sandy mentally shouted.

Raijaun relayed the news to Azerick. "Now, Father."

In Azerick's open palm lay four coins made of pure arcanum with a single rune perfectly etched upon their face. The sorcerer fed magical power into each of the coins. Identical runes on the spheres Sandy dropped glowed for a brief second before they exploded with the force of a powerful meteor strike. Yet more cataclysmic power scarred their world deep enough to leave a reminder of what happened in this valley for hundreds, possibly thousands, of years.

Azerick turned to King Miles. "It is done. The gates are destroyed."

"Praise be, we may have a chance," the young king said with a heavy sigh of relief. "What happens next?"

"We continue to fight until the Scions are forced to face us themselves. It should not be long now. Our gods have landed the first blow, and the Scions will feel the need to retaliate. Opening the abyss to help destroy the ravager horde may have saved us, but it is an invitation and open declaration that it is time for all the gods to take the field."

Witnessing the teeming throngs of ravagers had filled Miles with the greatest fear he thought imaginable, but the prospect of soon facing angry, vengeful gods raised it to stark terror. Only his discipline and knowing he had to stand strong despite his fear kept him from breaking down and weeping like a babe.

CHAPTER 30

The banished gods watched the destruction of their gates with mild annoyance. It was not an unexpected setback, but the mortals' audacity piqued their ire nonetheless.

"The usurpers have thrown down the gauntlet," said Xar, first amongst the forsaken.

Doaz replied, *"I believe it is time for us to pick it up."*

"Agreed," the remaining three concurred.

The majestic crystalline fortress left the grey space between worlds and shimmered into view above the battlefield like a shining star hovering just a few hundred feet over the land. Hundreds of thousands of eyes could not resist gazing upon the magnificent sight. The distraction cost many of them their lives. The brilliant intensity increased to blinding just before a searing beam lanced out from the crown of its center spire. The beam washed over the foremost ranks of mortals, searing thousands of them to less than ash in seconds.

The fortress dimmed and glided silently forward, its crystal walls shimmering and flickering as it gathered the energy for another devastating strike. The rhythmic strobing reached its crescendo. The instant before it struck another mortal blow, four massive runes carved into the valley floor burst to life, sending their own dazzling rays skyward. The beams did not strike the fortress, but came to a peak high in the sky, surrounding it within a colossal prism. A ray of light lanced through the clouds from the apex of the pyramid to seemingly stab at the heavens. The Scions' bastion began to shake and quiver as it tried to break free of the trap.

Daebian stood on the deck of his flagship and watched the spectacular scene unfold while stroking the soul stone with a grin plastered on his face. He knew what his father was trying to do, just as he knew it was destined to fail.

"Gloom, go find Father."

The crow dropped over the rail of the ship and sped across the battlefield. The moment Daebian had been expecting came as the world around him froze. The deafening sounds of battle ceased and the wind stopped blowing. Even the stench of fire and death vanished when Zyn appeared before him. Much like the Scions and their citadel had resided between worlds, Zyn preferred to speak with his favored pet in the tiny spaces between time as it allowed him to appear within the world of mortals without the chaotic distractions.

"It is time to fulfill your primary purpose. Your father and brother have created something of a nuisance. We could break free of their pathetic trap if we desired but do not wish to expend the energy. Let them think it is working and exhaust themselves as they try to hold us in stasis. It also provides the perfect distraction for you to successfully carry out your assassinations."

"Your wish is my command, master."

"My command is your command. I wish nothing."

"Please forgive my turn of phrase, master. Also, please forgive my presumption, but I would beg another token for going beyond our agreement by killing my brother as well."

Zyn was taken aback. Not by the audacity of his slave asking to be rewarded beyond being allowed to exist, but because he could not ascertain what the unusual creature wanted. The sudden lack of omniscience threw the Scion off balance.

"What is it you desire?"

Daebian caressed the soul stone and turned his eyes toward the gods' fortress. "How strange you don't already know."

Daebian stepped out of the shadow, and his feet touched soil for the first time in weeks. Just a few paces away, his father, Raijaun, Headmaster Florent, and an unusually tall elf stood in a circle pouring arcane power into a silver disc the size of a serving platter set in the center of their ring. With his soul blade already in his hand, Daebian strode toward the ring of magic-wielders as nonchalantly as if he were headed to the market to buy cheese.

Raijaun felt a sharp prick in his back but dared not break his focus on the incredibly powerful spell meant to rip the Scions from their fortress and send them to the lifeless world where Father had secreted away his tower and the Source pool. He turned his head to ascertain the source of pain and stared into his brother's grinning face.

"Hey there, ugly. Having fun?"

"You!" Raijaun exclaimed. "Tell me why I shouldn't tear you apart right now!"

"For one thing, you would lose control of your spell, not that it's going to work anyway. But I suppose you and Father are quite accustomed to failure by now, so it won't come as much of a shock."

Azerick glared at Daebian but still maintained his control over the magic. "Daebian, whatever you are here to do, do not do it, or I will end you."

"Father, is that any way to greet your only son?"

"Raijaun is my son!"

"Is that any way to greet your only attractive son?" Daebian amended.

"You are vile and do not deserve to be called my son."

"You're certainly half right. Still, it's rather rude considering the wonderful present I brought you."

All eyes glanced at the large cloth sack he gripped in his free hand as Daebian upturned the bag and spilled its contents. It was a miracle and a lifetime of training that allowed them to maintain control of the magic when the large grey head rolled onto the ground and glared balefully with its star-filled eyes at those within its purview.

"Meet Zyn. He thought he was my master."

"*Wretched…traitorous vermin, I will take…great pleasure in…dragging out your death…for a thousand years!*" the Scion railed, its voice sounding like a man barely on the edge of consciousness.

"That's about enough out of you. Let's see if your death is traumatic enough to shake your fellows up a bit."

"*Fool…you may have hurt me…but you cannot kill me. I am…a god!*"

"Nothing is impossible if you have the right tool," Daebian said, then plunged his sword through Zyn's eye. "*Klaraxis, shred this creature's soul without hesitation. Do not attempt to feed on it or absorb any of its power, or it will destroy us both."*

"I am not a fool, my prince."

A psionic keening tore through the minds of every living creature for hundreds of miles. Men and women dropped their weapons and clamped their hands over their ears despite the uselessness of the gesture. Ravagers began writhing on the ground in agony, clawing at the dirt, their brethren, and even their own bodies.

"Focus!" Azerick shouted. "The Scions are shaken!"

The fortress seemed to cry out in pain. Light flashed chaotically and cracks appeared across its surface. The beam stabbing into the sky from Azerick's trap doubled in intensity and cast the Scions from their world. The four powerful wielders of magic broke the ring and stepped away. Headmaster Florent fell to the ground but waved away Tarth's helping hands, preferring to just sit and fight for breath.

"Daebian, I cannot begin to understand you," Azerick in a hoarse voice.

"Of course not. You lack vision, just like everyone else."

"Whatever your motivations, you may have saved us all and I thank you."

"Well, that's much nicer. If I had known all it took to earn your respect was the head of a god, I would have done it ages ago."

"Daebian…"

"Not now, Father, you still have things to do, and time is wasting. If you don't mind, I'll go find Mother while you are off fighting gods. I'm sure she's been absolutely intolerable with worry since I left. Gloom, go find Mother!"

"Your mother is in the caves to the east with the other noncombatants."

Daebian laughed and shook his head. "It's true, some things never change. Paramount among those invariable things is your blind ignorance. So long, Brother, Father."

Azerick did not have time to think about Daebian's words. He pushed away the image of Miranda fighting on the front lines, burned a sigil into the ground with his staff, and imbued it with power from the Source. A world away, Ancalon sensed the rune flare to life, reached out to it with his awesome power, and tore a hole between the two realities so his allies could pass over.

A soft voice made Azerick balk as he stepped toward the portal. "Azerick, I believe I shall go with you."

"Tarth, I have great respect for your power, but this may not be the best place for you."

"My grandmother was the last of the Guardians, and she saved me from Klaraxis's tortures. I think it only fitting that I return her gift by upholding her cause. Do not worry about me. I will do my best to stay out of the way."

Azerick nodded and stepped over the threshold to the other world followed by his son and the elf wizard. They did not appear near the tower, but they all clearly felt its proximity. The sounds of a fierce battle echoed not far from where they stood, and the air was electric with spent arcane power. The Scions had been forced from the mortal world once again, and they were not pleased about it.

"We need to hurry," Azerick ordered. "Ancalon will not be able to hold them long by himself."

Tarth smiled at Raijaun as Azerick wove a gate to take them to the battle. "You know, Lissandra was my grandmother and your mother. That makes you my father even though I am hundreds of years older than you. You owe me a lot of birthday presents."

Raijaun gave the strange elf a confused look and followed Azerick through the gate without comment. No one was there to notice Gloom swoop through Ancalon's portal just before it snapped shut and vanish into a long shadow cast by a nearby tree.

Daebian stepped from a man's shadow just as a ravager blade hewed him down like a tree. The moment of his arrival was fortuitous for him and his mother. Had the man died a second sooner, his shadow would not have been where Gloom showed and Daebian would have been forced to make a blind jump through the shadow ways. As it was, he emerged just in time to block the ravager's next strike aimed for his mother. Daebian interposed his blade between the ravager's knife and

Miranda and slew the creature with three swift cuts, all in the blink of an eye.

"Hello, Mother."

"Daebian!"

Miranda grabbed her errant son by the arm and pulled him back through several ranks of soldiers until she found a spot clear of immediate fighting. She ripped off her helm and glared at him with barely suppressed fury.

"I don't know whether I should hug you, stab you, or put you over my knee and beat you until you can't sit!"

"Let's go with the first one and see where it leads us."

Miranda dropped her sword to the ground and wrapped her arms tightly around her son with a gush of tears. She pushed herself away, tore off her gauntlet, and slapped Daebian across the face.

"That is for trying to kill your father!"

Daebian could have easily avoided the strike but chose to let his mother have it. "I did not try to kill Father. If I had tried, I would have succeeded. Father had something I needed, and what he had he didn't need, so I took it, and we're both better for it."

"That does not excuse you for stabbing him. What are you doing here?"

"What are you doing here?" Daebian countered. "Father thinks you are at the caves hiding with the other useless people."

"They are not useless, Daebian. They are women, children, and people who are better kept safe than letting them die needlessly on the field."

"Apples, oranges, they're both fruit. Anyway, I came to help."

"Have you switched sides yet again? I never thought anyone could be so incredibly capricious."

"I have not switched sides, Mother. There has only been and will always be but one side—my own. Trust me, my coming here and doing what I do is completely self-serving."

"You fought against us! You and your ship killed your own people. You sided with the Scions!"

"Sometimes one must take some strange paths to reach one's destination," Daebian replied cryptically, then smiled. "Besides, they made me call them master and hurt me, and when someone hurts me, I hurt them back. Father is certainly proof of that."

Miranda's eyes filled with sadness and she stroked Daebian's cheek. "Azerick never meant to hurt you."

Daebian shrugged. "I never meant to be brilliant and gorgeous, but that's what happened, and we all have to live with it." Daebian looked to the sky. "Watch, Mother, the show is about to start."

Several of the flying ships, including the huge flagship, turned their weapons against the other Scion vessels and any dragons flying near them. Fireballs and lightning bolts flashed across the sky. Although far fewer in number, the four vessels crewed almost exclusively by Daebian's people ravaged the other ships with their surprise opening salvo. Miranda could only shake her head, unable to comprehend who or what her son was.

Azerick, Raijaun, and Tarth emerged from the portal near the edge of a fight between four angry gods and the Father of Dragons. Ancalon writhed in agony as the Scions used their power to punish him for aiding their enemies. Acres of tall grass, trees, and shrubs lay crushed and mulched from his tormented struggles.

"Release us, worm, before we decide your use no longer outweighs the trouble you have caused."

Ancalon's answer was a roar of defiance and pain that shook the already trembling ground. Azerick, Raijaun, and Tarth struck at the fallen gods with all their power. Kaz and Doaz raised a hand and the shimmering, multihued rays struck an invisible barrier without effect.

"More vermin has arrived. We shall deal with you later. You and your children will be punished for your transgressions," Xar promised.

The eyes of four vengeful gods turned toward the interlopers, and it felt like the weight of the universe was weighing down on them. It was a soul-rending feeling that filled them all with enough fear to induce a cold sweat. The gods flicked a casual wrist at the three arrivals as if brushing crumbs from their dining table. Azerick and Raijaun pulled deeply from the Source pool and erected a silver barrier around the three of them.

The disdainful assault struck the shield with incredible power and drove the glimmering orb through the woods, carrying the three passengers with it like beans in a jar. The force of their repulsion shattered trees and plowed a furrow in the ground several feet deep and half a mile long. When their silver cocoon finally came to rest, they stood facing the Scions once again. The Scions did not fly or step through a gate; they were simply there because they willed it to be so. Such was the power of gods.

"You no longer amuse us, and your continued interference ends now," Xar said without inflection or emotion.

The three powerful wielders of magic sensed the gathering of power on a scale none thought possible. It was a hundredfold stronger than the swatting they had just received, and Azerick knew there was nothing he could conjure to stop it. Even with the full power of the Source pool at his command, the Scions could crush any ward he erected as easily as an eggshell.

Azerick felt the titanic concussion hit him for a brief instant before numbing darkness fell over his world. He existed in a state of perfect oblivion, floating in a black void without sight, sound, smell, or touch. His body or soul, whatever his existence was at this point, flew upward. The sound of raging water filled his ears, and his body was tightly wrapped in a swaddling blanket of pain. Azerick opened his eyes and found the three of them lying on a grassy plateau. Sitting up, he saw a smoking crater probably two hundred yards wide half a mile away.

"The fallen ones are right," a deep, powerful voice spoke. "Your fight is over. This is a battle suited only for gods."

Azerick turned his head and winced in pain. Four figures stood nearby appearing not the least bit unusual to the casual eye, with the exception of the tall, muscularly lean figure wearing nothing but his blue-green skin. Despite their mortal appearance, no one could miss the aura of immortal power radiating from them and mistake them for anything but gods.

Solarian stood resplendent in his golden armor and wielded a sword forged from the very essence of the sun. Ellanee wore chain-like mail woven from thin vines sprouting flowers and thorns. Sharrellan had no trouble striking a seductive pose even in the face of potential destruction in a suit of form-hugging black leather crafted from the skin of demons who displeased her.

"Solarian is right, my Hand," the dark goddess said. "You have performed wonderfully, but this is now our fight."

"We must go. The Scions are aware of us, and you do not want to be caught in the middle of our battle," Ellanee said.

The gods took a single, mundane step forward and faced their most hated and feared enemy. The Scions turned their depthless gazes from the smoldering crater to their usurpers.

"So the children seek to kill their parents once again."

"We are older, wiser, and stronger than before," Solarian replied. "This time, you will never return to harm the mortals of our world."

"You are infants, and you lack your precious Guardians. Take comfort that we shall show you mercy and destroy you utterly instead of inflicting upon you the tortures of a banished existence.

CHAPTER 31

Raijaun was just beginning to stir when the gods began trading blows. The ground quaked, and expended power electrified the air. Great swaths of forest were flattened and lesser hills crushed flat just in the first exchange.

Azerick grabbed Tarth's still unconscious form and shouted to his son. "Raijaun, get up! We need to get out of here!"

The sorcerer tore open a gate and leapt through with Raijaun staggering after him. Their first hop took them nearly five miles from the clashing titans, but still the ground shook and the air carried the concussive waves of cataclysmic explosions. Azerick opened a second portal and dashed through with the elf slung over one shoulder. He laid the wizard on the ground high above the valley where gods sought to destroy one another. Raijaun sat on a boulder as he regained his constitution. Azerick looked over at Tarth and saw blood running in tiny rivulets from his ears and nose.

"Tarth, can you hear me? Tarth?"

The elf moaned, began to stir, and his eyelids fluttered open. "Are we dead? I did not expect the afterlife to be quite so noisy."

"We are alive, and the gods have arrived to take over the war."

"Oh, goodie. Help me sit up."

Azerick helped Tarth to a sitting position and propped his back against a boulder. Far below their mountain perch, the battle raged on and wiped forests bare, set shattered timbers aflame, and scoured the earth down to the bedrock and beyond.

"Father, are we not going to help them?" Raijaun asked. "Isn't that why Lissandra created me?"

"I had thought so, and perhaps one day you will find the kind of power the original Guardians wielded, but even as powerful as we are, we are but children compared to them. They would, and almost did, crush us like insects. I think our job was to set the battlefield and draw the Scions out where the gods could engage them."

"Will they be strong enough to defeat them?"

"We must pray that they are. The Scions are only four now. Hopefully, that will be enough to shift the balance."

Using scrying magic to get a closer view, they watched the calamitous struggle rage on from a distance, ready to leap through another gate should it begin spilling over toward them. A fiery meteor streaked from the sky and struck with enough force to shake the mountain upon which the three spectators stood. A colossal earth elemental, towering a hundred feet tall, crawled from the ground, spit magma, and tried to stomp the Scions flat. An intense ray shot down from the bright sun and seared a perfect hole in the ground a hundred feet wide and half a mile deep.

The Scions shattered the elemental with a thought, snapped the top off a mountain like the tip of an icicle, and nearly succeeded in crushing Sharrellan beneath its awesome mass. The dark goddess vanished into the shadows, reappeared more than a mile away, and sent streamers of caustic, shadowy black tentacles to choke the immortal life from the fallen gods.

Serron picked up an entire river and wielded it like a mile-long whip, lashing out at the Scions with the power of millions of gallons of water moving faster than even Azerick and Raijaun's superior eyes could track. The Scions deflected the striking mass of water like a master fencer parrying a flurry of sword thrusts. To the watcher's eyes, the battle appeared to be evenly matched until horror struck.

The Scions seemed to grab hold of Serron's aqueous whip with a giant, invisible hand. The river looped, and an undulating wave raced back toward the god of the seas. The massive streamer of water wrapped and constricted around Serron like a serpent and froze solid.

The Scions pulled every particle of heat from the water until it was so cold Azerick and the others could feel a drop in the ambient temperature from where they stood. The faceless ones then shattered the god-encasing glacier with a sledgehammer of arcane power.

Massive blocks of ice flew through the air and skittered across the land, crushing trees and cutting huge scars into the ground. When the scene cleared, Serron was nowhere to be seen.

Azerick witnessed the death of a god, and his faith in their victory died with him. "We have to do something."

"As you said, we are but children compared to the gods," Raijaun said.

"Yes, but even children can set a trap to catch a bear. I have been studying the Scions, the way they fight and wield their magic. They act as a single being, like a collective mind. That is why the death of the one Daebian slew affected them so much. A blow to one is a blow to the collective. I think that is why Daebian was able to keep secrets and use the soul blade against them. The Scions' mentality is structured on logic and order above all else. It is why they feel the need to enslave all intelligent life so they can control it. It is why they despise freedom and free will. Daebian is a being of chaos. Sharrellan once told me that not even the sisters of fate were able to see Daebian within the strands. We cannot face them as a collective, so we need to devise a way to separate one from the whole. Only then will we have a chance to fight it."

"How can we isolate one from the group? Even if we managed, do you think our power is enough to defeat it?"

Azerick sounded far more hopeful than he felt. "We have to try."

"No, we do not have the strength to slay the god even then." Azerick and Raijaun's eyes went to Tarth. "But I think I may know a way to defeat it."

"What do you mean, Tarth?" Azerick asked the elf.

A distant, haunted look filled his eyes. "I know something about true chaos. This pseudo-world seems to mirror our own, yes?" Azerick nodded. "We must try to send one of them to my home on this world where my connection is strongest."

"Tarth, you cannot face one of them alone," Raijaun said.

"Face it, yes, but none of us can fight it even together. I have a better chance of removing it from the battle alone than if we try brute force together."

"Are you sure, Tarth?" Azerick asked softly.

Tarth smiled. "I have not been sure of anything for hundreds of years."

Azerick laid a gentle hand on the elf's shoulder. He had grown fond of Tarth, had been inside his mind and understood his tortured existence like few could.

"Ancalon!" Azerick called out.

The huge serpent slithered out of a hole in the air not far from where they stood. The Father of Dragons had shrunk his form down to a more manageable and less noticeable size of a petite hundred feet in length.

"The war goes badly for us."

"It does, but I have a plan I hope will change that, but I need your help again. Are you well?"

"I am deeply abused, but that is a shadow of the tortures I will face if the Scions are victorious. What do you require of me?"

"We have to separate one of the Scions from the group. Do you know the place of the elven nation in this world, and can you open a rift strong enough to force one of them there?"

"The task is far easier than forcing the four of them to this world was, but it is still beyond my ability to do it alone."

"What if we all strike at the Scions at the same moment with all our power? Will that be enough to weaken their resistance?"

"It is possible, but far from certain. Only the death of the one shook them enough to allow me to pull them here. But, as I said, this is by far a simpler task. Perhaps it will be sufficient to shift one, but it will be impossible for me to hold it. The creature is a god and will able to return to the fray with little more than a thought."

"It is the only chance we have," Azerick said. The sorcerer focused his thoughts inward and called out. "*Sharrellan.*"

"*I am a bit busy, my Hand. We have lost Serron, and I fear our time draws near.*"

"*I have a plan. We must strike at one of the Scions at the same time. I hope to separate one from the whole and disrupt their collective mind.*"

Sharrellan's deep laughter filled Azerick's mind. "*I knew I chose my Hand well. Call upon us and we will answer.*"

"Our gods understand what we are trying to do. Ancalon, please send us where we need to go. I will call out when the moment comes."

"I will hear you and act," the great dragon promised.

Ancalon slashed two small rifts in the air and directed Tarth to one and Azerick and Raijaun to the other. Father and son stepped onto the open plain where the battle still raged just a few miles away. They had to erect powerful wards to protect themselves from the arcane destruction being unleashed even this far from the fighting. Azerick sent Sharrellan his need for a few seconds of respite, opened a gate between exchanges, and leapt through with Raijaun.

"Now!" Azerick shouted with all his might in both mind and voice.

Azerick and Raijaun lashed out with everything they had the moment they arrived. Energy from the Source pool streamed into them faster than they could unleash it. They opened themselves up to its power and held nothing back. The three gods struck simultaneously with equal effort, focusing their awesome might into a single, concentrated point instead of their previously expansive, devastating blows. Ancalon opened a rift behind the Scion nearest Azerick and Raijaun, similar to the one he had used to send Azerick to the magically dead jungle world only smaller and more concentrated.

The Scions faltered under the intense, focused attack for a brief moment, but that moment was enough. The Scion called Doaz was violently pulled through the rift and vanished only to appear in a beautiful stand of trees the elves called the Grove of Heroes. Before Doaz could take in the copse, a powerful magical strike strong enough to make him take a step back lanced into him. Doaz faced his attacker and nearly laughed at the pathetic elf who sought to challenge him. Tarth flew back and was pinned against the trunk of a large tree with a thought.

"*Pathetic elf, did you think you could defeat me?*" The Scion studied Tarth for an instant. "*The blood of a Guardian runs through your veins. I know its taste, although it is greatly diluted. You spring from the line of the last true Guardian. We were denied justice for her transgressions, so you will bear her sentence.*"

Tarth felt the Scion sliding into his thoughts and tried to push it away.

"*Fool, your blood is too thin to resist me.*"

"Resist you? On the contrary, I invite you to share my madness."

Doaz felt the thin barrier between his consciousness and the elf's shatter beneath his mind's eye like thin ice covering a pond. The Scion plunged deep inside the lake of madness and flailed for the surface. Doaz found himself drowning in every chaotic thought, emotion, and event in Tarth's long life.

Unable to cope with the swirling insanity, the Scion experienced the full effect of Tarth's decade-long torture in the hands of the most brutal demon lord ever to inhabit the abyss. The current of chaos poured in through the blood link with his grandmother, and the faceless one spun out of control in the turbulent memories of all the pain and anguish inflicted upon the races during the Great Revolution. It was more than the false god could bear, and he sank screaming in madness into the darkest depths of Tarth's mind.

Doaz's terror and madness lashed at the minds of the three Scions in a powerful psychic feedback. The world shuddered under their combined psionic shriek. Azerick and Raijaun staggered beneath the combined physical and mental assault. The gods struck swiftly and in unison. Their renewed attack rocked the Scions with a brutal assault. Again and again the true gods attacked, driving the Scions back and inflicting real pain and injury for the first time since their battle began.

Xar and his fellows took the brutal beating and did their best to shield themselves from the assault while they collected their strength and adjusted to the unexpected change. The loss of Doaz to some sort of insanity was a terrible blow, but it was far from critical, and they were nowhere near defeated. The usurpers had the momentum now, but that would change very quickly. It was still the three elder gods against three children. The balance of power had not shifted that dramatically and would soon favor the elder gods again. But first, it was time to remove the one chaotic variable they had mistakenly ignored until now.

The Scions' power resurged, and the gods' assault stopped dead against their wards as they directed their attention to Azerick and Raijaun. *"Your meddling has proven more problematic than we had anticipated. We had wanted you and the pathetic mortals to witness the death of your gods, but your interference ends now."*

The Scions shifted so fast they existed in two places at one time for the smallest fraction of a second. Azerick knew there was nothing he could conjure to block the faceless gods' killing blow, so he tried to rip open a portal to whisk him and Raijaun away. It was an equally futile gesture. Even as Azerick began drawing in the Source to create his gate, the Scions stood before him, radiating power like the heat of the sun.

Ellanee interposed herself between the Scions and the mortals' champions. The world around them vanished in a massive explosion of power. When the dust cleared, Azerick, Raijaun, and Ellanee stood on an island surrounded by calamitous destruction. The Scions glared balefully at the nature goddess for thwarting their will. An invisible hand punched through Ellanee's ward, wrapped around her, and sought to crush her like a dry leaf. Xar poised a blade of pure psychic energy over the goddess's heart and stabbed.

Everything happened in the space between breaths. High overhead, a solitary crow cawed, and Azerick glimpsed a flash of motion. Daebian leapt from the Scion's shadow and plunged his sword deep into Xar's back. The fallen god released a horrific scream as Klaraxis sank his ethereal claws into the Scion's soul.

"Hold or you shall die with her," Daebian warned.

"*Neither you nor the demon I sense within the gem can destroy me before I kill her.*"

"Are you sure? Can you look into my mind and foretell the moment I decide to strike? No, you can't, and you have less tolerance for ignorance than I do. Less than total control and absolute omniscience drives you to the brink of madness."

"*You pretend to comprehend things beyond your understanding. Slay me and she will die. This I know. Once again, we will stand even and continue this war until there is only one still standing.*"

"Which of you will stand in the end? Whose side will emerge triumphant? You were certain of your ability to kill our gods, yet I see only three of you still around and one a thought away from oblivion. Let us end this now. We both know you cannot predict the outcome of my involvement, and it scares you."

A silent war waged within the minds of the Scions. Thousands of scenarios played out in an instant, and in none of them were the Scions certain of total victory.

"We fear nothing, but mutual annihilation does lack logic. We will accept banishment to end this war. Perhaps this was not our time to return, but that day will arrive."

"Can we imprison them?" Raijaun asked. "They were banished once and returned in what is little more than a heartbeat for the gods."

Solarian answered, "We predicted this outcome as one of several possibilities and have spent the past two millennia devising a better prison, one with far fewer resources for them to exploit. It will not last forever. Nothing can contain that kind of evil power for all eternity, but it should keep our people safe for a very long time."

"Very well, send us away. We will not resist."

Ellanee felt the crushing fist holding her vanish. The three gods merged their power into a single spell and transported the Scions to a place of bleak existence. Daebian looked at the naked sword he still held extended in his hand for a moment before sliding it back in its sheath.

"So, is that it?" Raijaun asked. "Is it over?"

"We are done here, but there is much rebuilding to do," Solarian answered. "We will take you home now."

"What about Tarth? Where is he?" Azerick asked.

"He has found some peace here in this world. He has trapped the mind of a god inside him, and it is best if he stays here where there are no distractions. Do not worry about your friend. I will ensure he is well taken care of," Ellanee assured him.

There was no sense of movement or sign of a rift or shimmering gate. Azerick and the others simply found themselves standing atop the hillside in front of the humans' command hall and amongst the bustling people of Valeria. Miranda was the closest and the first to notice their return.

She threw herself into Azerick's arms and wept. "Thank the gods you returned!"

A sharp keening rang out over the battlefield, and the great crystal fortress fell from the sky and shattered onto the diminished ranks of ravagers. With the Scions banished once again, the citadel and few remaining flying ships lost the magic keeping them afloat.

Azerick spotted Ellyssa nearby and called her over. "I am glad to see you made it. How are we doing with the ravagers?"

"Most of the wizards are exhausted, but the demons turned the tide of the battle, and most of those not killed have fled. I thought for sure we would be fighting them until the last, but their spirit seemed to finally break. There are still thousands of them on the field, but the soldiers are dealing with them."

Azerick nodded. "With the Scions gone, there is nothing but their own vile natures guiding them."

"So, you did it? The Scions are truly dead?" Miranda asked.

"Not quite. One is dead and another is suffering a worse fate. The remaining three have been banished once again."

"Banished? We suffered all this and they still live to try again one day?"

"It was the best we could achieve, and it will be a very long time before they get the chance to return, if they ever do," Azerick assured her.

King Miles Ollander trotted his mount up the hill, dropped from the saddle, and knelt before the gods. "Glorious Ones, you grace us all with your presence."

"Arise, young king," Solarian commanded. "It is we who bow to your and your people's courage. We bow to all the peoples of all the races who set aside their petty differences and joined together to fight a terrible foe. If you truly wish to honor us, then remember all who fought to achieve a victory this day."

"We will not forget again." Miles stood and faced Azerick, his hand gripping the hilt of his sword in a seemingly casual manner. "Azerick Giles, we owe you a special thanks. Without you, we would have been horribly unprepared. I truly wish there was some way I could justly reward your service."

"Do not think too much on it, Highness. You have the welfare of the people to think about, and it must take precedence."

No one could shake the feeling that there was far more meaning in their words than what was being said. There was a tension in the air like the silence that often precedes a battle. Magus Skinner, the headmaster's attentive aide, edged closer to the knot of people around Azerick.

"Sharrellan, it is time to return *all* your demons to the abyss," Solarian intoned.

Miranda looked out across the battlefield. "But the demons crawled back into the ground and vanished when you stole the Scions away."

"He means me," Azerick clarified.

Miranda's face fell and went ashen. "What? No, the demon is gone now. Daebian removed it from you with the sword!"

"Klaraxis was only part of what made me what I am. I do not belong here."

"Yes, you do! You belong with me! I know I said goodbye, but I was wrong. I cannot let you go again!" Miranda turned her furious eyes onto the dark goddess. "You cannot take him from me again!"

Sharrellan tossed her head back and laughed. "Child, I am a god. I can damn well do what I please. Besides, he was mine long before he was yours. I did not take him; he gave himself to me."

"You lie! You are the god of lies!"

Sharrellan waved a hand, and a perfect scene appeared as if they were all looking out a window to watch a strange scene happening just a few feet away.

A young boy who could be no one except Azerick sat up on a sleeping pallet in some dark room and shouted at the ceiling. "I will be your Hand, goddess of death. I will be your Hand against everyone who threatens me or those close to me! I will send you so many vile, tainted souls you will have to open another circle of hell to keep them all in!"

The goddess flicked her hand again and the image vanished. "You see, he gave himself to me of his own free will."

"He was just a child!"

"And already a killer."

Azerick stopped Miranda before she threw herself at the goddess and tried to claw her eyes out. "It's okay, Miranda. I would never have been allowed to remain here regardless." He turned his head toward Miles. "Isn't that right, Your Highness?"

Miranda looked at the king and saw his face flush. "What do you mean? What were you going to do, Miles?"

"Do not blame him or whoever else may have laid plans to deal with me after this war."

"Deal with you? They were going to kill you?" his wife demanded. "You ungrateful bastards! If you ever try to hurt anyone in my family,

I will personally strip the crown from your head and shove it so deep up your arse not even the dwarves will be able to dig it out!"

"I did not leave them with any choice, Miranda. I secured my sentence through my actions, culminating in the murder of Lord Atwater. I was too dangerous to exist unchecked. I told you that I feared I was becoming a tyrant, and it was only a matter of time before it came true."

"But you are not an evil man! The demon made you angry and influenced your emotions. You weren't in your right mind."

"Klaraxis was never the source of the danger I represented. The real threat was the bit of humanity I could not let go of. As long as I clung to it, I could not avoid imposing my power if I thought it needed to be done. I already cast aside justice for expediency once, and I would certainly do so again if I felt I must."

"But you did those things to save us and protect us."

"It is not my place to enforce my will upon others because I think I am right. Every dictator and tyrant who ever existed thought their causes and methods were justified. It is why the gods seem aloof even when they could prevent so much pain and hardship, and I lack the wisdom of centuries of life to check my own power. I understood this, and I made Jarvin understand it too so he and others could devise a way to counter the threat I represented, because I did not trust myself to do it for them. I might live forever, but I still have the heart of a fallible, mortal being."

Miranda pressed her face into Azerick's chest. "Then this is goodbye again."

"It is."

"Well, Father, it appears you may not be quite as blind as I thought you were," Daebian quipped.

Azerick broke free of Miranda's embrace and faced his troublesome son. "Daebian, I still cannot begin to understand you, but I want you to know that I love you, and I am proud to be your father."

Daebian's eyes became glossy and his voice caught in his throat. "Father, that is all I ever wanted from you."

Azerick made to embrace Daebian. "Is it truly? I didn't understand…"

Daebian ducked Azerick's grasping hands and pushed him away. "No, you great damn narcissist! Just when I think you start to see, you open your mouth and say something else stupid. This is why you vex me to no end. My actions have nothing to do with you. I act the way I act and do the things I do because I want to, not because of you or the demon or any other damn reason. You just never got it. You can't help but feel like you are the center of everyone's universe. 'My son's a great big pain in the ass because of me.' No, I'm a pain in the ass because I like to be a pain in the ass. You could never just accept me for who I am. You don't get credit for my greatness! It's all me and it's all mine. Now, it's time for me to go, and I need a horse."

Sharrellan stopped the irate young man. "Daebian, you have something that belongs to me."

Daebian faced the goddess and looked as though he was going to defy her. With an annoyed sigh, he pulled the blade from its sheath and held it out. Sharrellan clasped her hand over his and smiled when Daebian was reluctant to release it. He finally loosened his fingers enough for Sharrellan to slip it from his hand. As the hilt slid through his fingers, he felt the soul stone come loose. With the deftness of a master pickpocket, he slipped the stone into his pocket, never taking his eyes from the goddess's smiling face.

"Now I need a horse and a sword!" Daebian spun, stalked over to the young king, and shoved him hard enough to knock him to the ground. "This is a nice one."

Several Blackguards drew blades and charged. Daebian grabbed the wrist of the first one to strike, gave it a twist, took his sword, and shattered his nose with the pommel. "Thank you."

"Let him go!" Miles shouted as he regained his feet.

His elite bodyguards ceased their attack but held their swords at the ready.

Daebian leapt into the saddle and smiled at the king. "This place is a wreck. I hope you get it cleaned up. I might like to conquer it someday." He looked once more to Azerick and held out his hand. "Pirates never work for free, Father."

Azerick shook his head, dug into the pocket of his tattered cloak, and retrieved a single gold coin. Daebian took the token and slipped it into his pocket with a smile.

"I'm starting to get quite a collection of these."

"Daebian, wait!" Ellyssa called out. "Take me with you."

"Ellyssa, please don't," Azerick begged.

Ellyssa looked at Azerick and Miranda and wiped the tears from her face. "I'm sorry, but there's nothing here for me anymore. I need to get as far away from all this as I can."

Daebian reached down and lifted Ellyssa onto the horse's rump. "When you all start erecting statues to my father and brother and all those you want to portray as the saviors of the world, I hope you have the decency to at least remember that it was I, Daebian the pirate king, who was responsible for defeating the fallen gods."

"Your actions were extraordinary, Daebian, and we cannot thank you enough," Azerick said.

"You're right, *you* can't." He looked at the three gods and made a show of taking count. "There appears to be one of you missing. 'Daebian, god of the sea' has a rather nice ring to it. No? Think on it."

Neither he nor Ellyssa looked back as they galloped down the hill toward the wreckage of one of his flying ships. Men were gathered around looking bewildered or picking through the destruction in search of their fellow crewmen.

Tobias!" Daebian called out. His first mate shouted back and waved from atop the pile of timbers. "Oh good, you're still alive. Round up what's left of our crew and find some horses. It's a long damn way to the ocean."

"Aye, sir!"

"Where's Eva?"

"Sorry, sir, she didn't make it."

Daebian turned to Ellyssa. "Well, that avoids a potentially awkward situation."

Miranda watched her son ride away without a backward glance, leaving an aching void of loneliness in her heart for the second time. "Daebian!"

"Let him go," Sharrellan said. "You all have far greater things to worry about."

"Like what?"

"Like what happens when he gets bored playing pirate. Azerick, it is time to go."

"One more moment, please." Azerick took the arcanum door handle from his pocket and gave it to Raijaun. "This will open a door to the old tower. You need someplace safe away from anyone whose fear and lack of understanding might cause them to act foolishly. I think Ancalon will appreciate the company and so will Tarth. They are very much your family as well."

"Thank you, Father. No matter what Daebian says, I know you love us both and did your best."

Azerick hugged his son and wife once more. "Say goodbye to Sandy for me. And someone go find Wolf and make sure he's okay. I doubt he let the ravagers catch him."

"I will, Father."

Sharrellan opened a doorway to the abyss. Azerick looked out across the battlefield at the fighting, death, and ruin stretching to the horizon and beyond. He could only shake his head and sigh before stepping through the portal.

EPILOGUE

A zerick emerged onto the red, rocky surface of the Fifth Circle of the abyss and felt the tension of the past several years drain away into the ground. He attributed it to finally ending the war and knowing his family and the people of his world were safe, but another part, a part he tried hard not to recognize, felt as if he had returned home.

The great onyx fortress stood before him, nearly covering the wide expanse of the horizon. It looked much as he remembered, but there was some damage evident from what must have been a titanic battle. Colossal black stones the size of small houses lay scattered across the ground, some of them hundreds of yards away.

As Azerick approached the tall doors, the two insectoid demon sentries crossed their spears to bar his path. Azerick came to a stop just a few feet from them and stood without speaking. The demons exchanged looks, uncrossed their spears, and the doors opened with a silent command.

The sorcerer strode down the gloomy halls without hesitation, passing numerous demons that immediately ceased their chattering and activities and watched him pass without question. Azerick felt the tension of his presence, but not a single creature sought to challenge him as he navigated the halls and entered the vast throne room.

Morta'sha relaxed upon the throne of bones and ebony soul stone striking a seductive yet amused pose. "Normally, I would have any unwelcome intruder eviscerated on the spot, but your presence and my minions' reaction to you intrigues me. It is lucky for you I am extremely bored. The gods denied me the pleasure of participating in their grand battle, and I would enjoy hearing its accounts. You will entertain me with the details before I slowly strip the flesh from your bones and dine upon your pleas for an end to your tortures for your trespass."

"I see you managed to attain the lofty perch you so desired," Azerick said.

"Yes, thanks in large part to your bastard offspring, hence my warm welcome."

"Morta'sha, we seem to have a small problem."

A wry grin curled the corners of her seductive mouth and revealed rows of fang-like teeth. "What problem would that be?"

"You are in my chair."

Azerick thrust his staff at Morta'sha and struck her with a twisting ray of black and silver power. The beam hurled her from the throne and pinned her to the wall. The demon lord wailed in agony as the amalgamated magic incinerated her flesh until she was nothing but a spot on the wall and a small pile of ash on the floor. Azerick climbed the steps of the dais and took his rightful, if not deserved, place on the throne. The great chair dwarfed his human body and he shifted about uncomfortably. He focused his will and took on Klaraxis's natural form.

Azerick sighed contentedly. "Ah, that's better."

Sefket stood next to Bron and his two high chiefs, the leaders resplendent in their ebony armor. Stretched across the southern ridgeline, the brute army gazed down into the valley at the humans regrouping after their titanic battle with the enslavers' hordes. Elves circled overhead upon the backs of their blood hawks, keeping a vigilant eye on the few dragons that were slow to shake off the effects of their compulsion and flee the battlefield.

The dead replaced the once green grass of the valley floor in coverage if not numbers. Across to the northern side, dwarves marched back into their tunnels, pushing massive siege engines ahead of them in case they ever needed them again. They had all suffered grievous losses, but this time the brutes fared better than the humans did.

Their fight had been brutal, but with their shamans and Bron unleashing nature's fury against the ravagers and the might of the almost untouchable chieftains, they were able to rout them in short order. The human king called Yusuf and a young human wearing the dead king's crown looked up, spotted them, and extended a hand in recognition.

"Do you think they will remember?" Bron asked.

Sefket shrugged his broad shoulders. "Who can say with humans? Even if they do forget our part, they will remember that we still bear the armor. That at least will make them reconsider any foolish actions in the future."

"If not, we can always kick their butts," Trielle said, then yawned and curled up on Bron's shoulder. "But not today. I'm tired."

"You fought well, little one."

Trielle answered with a loud snore. The brute races turned from the valley, disappeared over the crest of the hill, and returned home. They needed no words of praise or recognition, least of all from the humans, dwarves, and elves. Theirs was a quiet, dignified withdrawal…until they got back to their lands. Then the celebrations would last a season.

Sandy watched the last of the dragons disappear into the distance. She had lost so much during this war, but no more than tens of thousands of others but less than probably twice that many. At least she was still alive, but now she was all alone. Azerick had disappeared, back to the abyss Raijaun said. Raijaun was going to take the codex to wherever it was they had moved the old tower and said he would likely stay a while. He wanted to seal off the energy emanating from the Source pool like his mother and the Guardians had done when they possessed one. Mortals were not meant to have access to so much power. She could go and find Wolf and Ghost. She was sure they were okay. Wolf was too sly to let the ravagers catch him, but she knew he was not the company she needed right now.

Maybe Ellyssa was right to run off with Daebian. Well, maybe not with Daebian, but Sandy understood her desire to get away from all this and everyone who reminded her of what she had lost. Her happiest recent memory was of Mordigar, but he was gone too. She stared at the grey horizon. Maybe she could find a connection with another dragon like the one she had with him. Would they accept her after she had fought and killed so many of her own kind? She didn't know, but she had to find out. If she could not find another connection to this world, she would surely become lost within it.

Sandy was exhausted in every conceivable meaning of the word, but she forced her wings to beat, pulled the last vestiges of power from her runes and spirit, and took to the sky. There was no urgency to her flight. She did not know where she was going nor did she care how long it took to get there. The only thing that mattered was leaving all the death and destruction behind her.

Sharrellan glanced at the black stain on the wall. "You seem to have settled in nicely."

Azerick looked up from the bowl of blood he used to view the goings-on of the mortal world. "It is customary to knock before entering one's home."

"Goddesses are granted much leeway when it comes to protocol, especially when you are in my home. You are simply renting a room. However, I am glad to hear you say you are at home. I was worried you would sulk and become intolerable like you did last time."

"I understand my place in the world now. You should not confuse it with enjoyment, nor should you think to consider me just another one of your demonic puppets. I will rule this circle my way. It shall be a place of punishment for those who deserve it, but also one of atonement if they are willing. I will not allow cruelty simply for the sake of being cruel. If that is unacceptable to you, then you may send me somewhere else or do away with me as you please. I am beyond caring."

The dark goddess smiled. "My dear Hand, you would be boring if you did anything less. It is why I value you above all others. I have any number of toadies who would love to occupy your throne. If I wanted one of them, I would never have allowed you to destroy Morta'sha. I want you to make this place yours. Rule it as you see fit. Whatever makes you happy."

"Happiness is fleeting and something I have long been denied. There is only sufferance."

"Perhaps you will learn something better eventually. After all, you have all eternity to find it."

To be continued in:
RISE OF THE ORDER
Book Nine of The Sorcerer's Path

FROM THE AUTHOR

I hope you enjoyed this tale and will try my other works. Feel free to look me up on Facebook! You can also check me out on my website http://brockdeskins.com/ where I write serial fiction, free for your enjoyment, and answer questions!

Author page:
https://www.amazon.com/Brock-Deskins/e/B005M6VQ1O

Facebook:
https://www.facebook.com/brocksbooks/

Twitter:
@brockdeskins

PLEASE REVIEW MY BOOKS (Especially if you liked it). Customer reviews are the primary means of enticing others to purchase them. I am dependent upon the sales of my books to earn a living that will allow me to continue writing stories that I hope bring you some measure of entertainment. Thank you for your support.

OTHER BOOKS BY BROCK E. DESKINS

The Sorcerer's Path is an epic fantasy series.

The Sorcerer's Ascension: Torn from a life of comfort and luxury, his family destroyed by political intrigues and aspirations, a young boy must quickly grow into a man before the deadly streets of Southport devour him. Follow Azerick through a page-turning adventure that pits him against thieves, thugs, murderers, and men of power that will stop at nothing to achieve their goals.

Azerick must fight just to survive, but for him survival is not enough. A hunger to avenge the wrongs committed against him burns deep within. But that is not all that lies within the young man. There is a power waiting to be unleashed that may be the key to achieving the justice and security he seeks--if it does not destroy him first.

The Sorcerer's Torment: Azerick flees The Academy but quickly falls prey to powerful beings that use his skills and power for their own amusement. What these creatures do not understand is the power of the young sorcerer's will and the lengths he will go to for vengeance. Despite becoming a prisoner, Azerick finds his first true love, but can he keep it?

The Sorcerer's Legacy: Azerick has found himself a home and tries to settle down. He takes on an apprentice and tries to put all the death and desire for vengeance behind him. But when the Rook finds him, Azerick is once again pulled back into Ulric's schemes. Knowing that all he has worked toward and everyone close to him is in danger as long as these schemes are ongoing; Azerick decides to put an end to it, once and for all.

The Sorcerer's Vengeance: After narrowly avoiding being killed in his own bed by the land's most feared assassin, Azerick leaves his school behind to find out who sent him and to put an end to the threat once and for all. Azerick's search will take him to the very pits of the abyss and back to unleash hellish fury upon those that threaten him.

The Sorcerer's Scourge: With the siege broken and Ulric dead, Azerick can finally relax, study his magic, and run his school in peace. Unfortunately, Jarvin's reign is far from uncontested and the true usurper decides to make his move. Jarvin escapes with help from an unlikely source—a vampire named Landrin who still clings tenaciously to his own humanity. While Azerick and a large force from North Haven race to save the king in exile, evil forces are preparing to unleash a nightmare upon the kingdom that may well destroy them all.

The Sorcerer's Abyss: Now the master of the Fifth Circle of the abyss, Azerick is challenged by another demon lord for supremacy. Azerick must face this threat as well as his innermost demons, all the while searching for a way to escape his hellish prison.

Ellyssa fears she is going insane as she plagued by nightmares of her capture and enslavement. Deciding the key to saving herself lies in the total destruction of the object of her fears, she embarks on a crusade to find and kill the slaver, Captain Jake, and eradicate the slave trade.

Ellyssa's nightmares and battles spill out onto the streets of North Haven and gains the attention of The Academy. Fearing Azerick's school is turning out rogue wizards, The Academy decides to hunt down and destroy the rogue and place the school within their control.

The Sorcerer's Return: Azerick has come back from the abyss in order to try to unite all the races against the return of the old gods who seek to destroy them and subjugate the few they allow to survive a brutal purging. However, fighting ancient gods may be the least of his troubles as he battles to save a fractured kingdom, a brilliant son traveling a dark path, and the splintered soul of his own humanity.

The Sorcerer's Destiny: Brutally purged of his demonic influence, Azerick continues the struggle of uniting the kingdom to face the coming of the Scions, ancient gods banished by the mortal races during the Great Revolution two thousand years ago. The fallen gods' prison is crumbling, and Azerick is powerless to stop them from breaking free and enacting their cataclysmic vengeance upon the world.

The humans must ally with the other races in a final battle against impossible odds while their entire world crumbles to the ground and is trod beneath the feet of an unstoppable foe. How can they set aside their distrust of each other when they fear the very person trying to save them?

Rise of the Order: Banished to the abyss after helping defeat the Scions and saving the world from eternal darkness, Azerick languishes in perpetual misery as Lord of the Fifth Circle. The denizens of his hellish realm view him as a usurper and outsider. The chaotic creatures form an alliance with one goal in mind: destroy Azerick Giles, but Sharrellan stands in their way.

A powerful spell tears through the demonic planes, and when the dust settles, the dark goddess is nowhere to be found. It is up to Azerick to return her to her seat of power, but he has a price: return him to his mortal form and send him home.

Back home, a vast empire is on a crusade to conquer the world, and it has set its sights on Valeria. Their goal is to unite the world under a single banner, eradicate the spawn infestation unleashed by the Scions, and replace the gods who they feel have forsaken them with their mystical rulers.

Can Azerick save the dark goddess from the clutches of her demonic subjects and become mortal once again? Will he have the power to protect his people from The Order if he does?

Descent Into Chaos: The Order has arrived in force, and the fate of Valeria, and perhaps all the world, is poised to come under their iron-fisted control. Azerick and Daebian are forced to flee Southport and make a contentious alliance when King Miles capitulates to the invaders. Reduced to insurgent warfare, Azerick and his allies attempt to battle The Order's vastly superior forces in a series of hit and run strikes, but the enemy legions may not be his biggest threat.

Princess Sylvian Attar, daughter to The Order's godlike emperor and empress, has taken a personal interest in Azerick. Herself a powerful sorceress, Sylvian hunts Azerick in hopes of removing Valeria's legendary hero from the battlefield thus sapping her enemies' will to fight. Azerick decides there is but one course of action he can take against this unstoppable foe. It was time to inject a little chaos into The Order.

Brooklyn Shadows is a modern-day vampire tale. Full of action and snarky dialogue, Brooklyn Shadows is an enjoyable read for anyone who enjoys the supernatural underworld and butt-kicking vampires.

<u>**Shrouds of Darkness**</u> (Brooklyn Shadows Book 1) Leo Malone has been a vampire for the better part of the twentieth century. Once a prominent Sherriff (vampire cop), he now earns his living as a private eye and occasional bodyguard for anyone that requires some serious protection. Leo is hired by the daughter of a mob accountant who has gone missing.

The fact that her father is also a werewolf has Leo following a trail of grisly murders that will lead him through a web of intrigue and conspiracy involving his fellow vampires and the local werewolves that make New York their home, all the while trying to keep one particularly determined cop off his back and himself out of jail. Leo is not some pretty-boy vampire that all the girls ogle over, but a hard-eyed, remorseless killing machine who does not take crap from anyone.

<u>**Blood Conspiracy**</u> (Brooklyn Shadows Book 2): While dealing with the aftermath of the failed vampire council coup, Leo discovers that the modified Cure has fallen into the hands of a black ops government project designed to create vampiric super soldiers. When the inevitable happens, the off-book Homeland Security operation forcefully enlists Leo to help them resolve the situation. Worse yet, he has to work not only with an antagonistic werewolf named Meat, he is reunited with his hated creator, Lesile.

<u>**Primacy of Darkness**</u> (Brooklyn Shadows Book 3): Jack the Ripper, sadistic madman of old London, once thought long dead, has returned

to New York in an effort to quench his thirst for blood and mayhem. When the city's vampire enclave finds itself insufficient to deal with a madman of Jack's caliber, Vincent, the enclave head, enlists Leo Malone to put the maniac down before he reveals the existence of vampires as he throws the city into the throes of chaos and terror. Leo soon finds that Jack is not the only monster with which he must contend. A ghost from his past has also seemingly crawled from its grave and seeks to put an end to him and the rest of his kind.

The Transcended Chronicles is the story of an outlandish young man as he goes from being a troublesome youth to one of the kingdom's greatest secret agents. Blessed (or cursed) with an amazing ability to both fight and abuse his body with every conceivable vice known to man, Garran Holt is either the kingdom's greatest hero or its biggest embarrassment.

The Miscreant (The Transcended Chronicles Book 1): Garran Holt is a troubled young man. Unable to tolerate his self-destructive ways, his mother sells him into indentured servitude as part of a work crew building King Remiel's new trade road. When mercenaries sent to disrupt the road's construction attack his work camp, Garran discovers an inner power capable of turning him into a warrior of unparalleled ability. When the leader of his work crew recognizes Garran as being one of the transcended (a fighter able to slip into the swifter currents of time), he is trained as an agent, one of the kingdom's elite spies. Crude, abrasive, and deeply committed to destroying himself with drugs, alcohol, and debauchery, Garran might be the kingdom's only hope against falling to The Guild, the powerful trade cartel bent on becoming the true and undisputed power in the land.

The Agent (The Transcended Chronicles Book 2): The Guild rules the kingdom through their puppet monarch, and Garran must race to save the last living heir to the throne before the powerful syndicate's assassins complete their extermination of anyone who could oppose them. Garran and Prince Adam Altena struggle to find allies in hopes of rescuing Adam's sister, who was forced to marry the usurper in order to prevent even the thought of rebellion, and raise an army capable of defeating The Guild. With The Guild now in control of Anatolia's powerful army as well as their legion of mercenaries, their future is grim. How can a disreputable agent and a deposed prince convince their neighboring rulers to oppose The Guild, an organization that has had them cowed for decades?

Empire of Masks is an exciting and explosive new series that takes place in the world of Hedon and takes you across the land of Eidolan where ships sail through the skies and men and women wage war with magic, swords, muskets, and cannons.

<u>**Highlords of Phaer**</u> (**Book one of Empire of Masks**): Born a slave, descended of kings, Jareen Velarius just wants to provide the best life he can for his family, but Eidolan is a realm that challenges even the most stalwart of souls. Caught between his masters and those brave or foolish enough to strike against them, Jareen struggles to reconcile his role as a dutiful slave with that of a man who desires to be free. His goal: to return his people to a life stolen by the highlords more than a millennium ago.

Auberon Victore, sorcerer, alchemist, son of a powerful overlord, and Jareen's master, creates an alchemic compound he is certain will change the world; he just does not know how. Jareen sees it for the weapon that could break the sorcerers' iron grasp wrapped around the necks of every lowborn in the empire. It will change the world, but not in the way his master desires.

Across the Tempest Sea, a mighty storm has raged for a thousand years, keeping a terrible, long-forgotten enemy at bay, an enemy whose cruelty knows no bounds. Only the perpetual storm and their fear of the sorcerer highlords keep the Necrophages from returning to Eidolan and cloaking the empire in death and darkness. But the tempest is waning, and the dissidents' freedom may well come at the cost of their total destruction.

<u>**Nightbird**</u>: The Great Revolution ended the highlords' tyranny two hundred years ago, but the legacy of that epic war, and that of the principal architects' descendants, lives on. With the highlords' death and their taking magic, as it was once known, to their graves, Eidolan

fell into a time of darkness and its cities lived in isolation. However, some people, dubbed arcanists, discovered a new form of magic and the airships returned to the skies, rejoining the cities in trade as well as conspiracy, but a new darkness, more dreadful and deadly than any they faced before, is coming.

Kiera is a fifteen-year-old nightbird, one of many who flit about after dark, stealing whatever they can find in order to survive. She lives on a derelict airship in the poorest part of the city with Wesley, a young man who plies his trade as an escort to wealthy older women, and his little brother Russel, an autistic savant who communicates only through sign but who could secretly be the most powerful techno-arcanist the empire has ever known. Deep in debt to the underlord Nimat, Kiera dives into evermore dangerous schemes that put her at the heart of a secret war that could spell the destruction of not just the city, but the very empire.

Kiera is caught in the center of several factions on the brink of war. When she can no longer tell friend from enemy, there is only one side she can trust—her own.

Mourningbird: A creature of darkness lurks in the shadows of Velaroth, wearing the skin of its victims, and grips the city in terror. Dorian, a Necrophage bent on sowing chaos and paving the way for his people's invasion, has declared war on the humans of Eidolan, and there appears to be no one capable of stopping him.

Kiera's world is shattered by those who hold power, and she is forced to seek an ally. The nightbird is coming into power of her own, but can she stay alive long enough to seize it? Russel's behavior has taken a turn for the worse, and his actions have drawn the attention of those who would use his amazing talents for their own gain...and everyone else's loss.

The battle for Velaroth, and perhaps the world, has begun. Who will win? Who will live to mourn the dead? Will there be anything left for the victor to claim as their prize?

Standalone books

The Portal is a fun and exciting story of some less than popular teenagers that accidentally open a portal to a mystical land during one of their role-playing games. Drew, a dour and anti-establishment teenager, is pulled through and captured by evil creatures lying in wait on the other side. Now it is up to his friends and older brother to rescue him, but who will rescue Drew's captors from him?

Amelia (Battle for Ardentia): Amelia is a precocious, ten-year-old girl with a powerful imagination. In her alter-ego guise of a demi-goddess warrior princess, Amelia fights against a powerful demonic sorcerer named Romut and his horde of monsters in a never ending series of battles to protect the people of her imaginary world. However, the true battle strikes home when Amelia is diagnosed with a brain tumor. Now Amelia must fight not just the evil living in her imagination, but for her very life.

ABOUT THE AUTHOR

Brock Deskins was born in a small town located in rural Oregon. At age twenty, he joined the army and served as an M1A1 tank crewman, dental specialist, and computer analyst. While in the military, he became an accomplished traveler, husband, and father of three wonderful children. His military career completed, attended college to brush up on his skills as a computer analyst and gain new skills as a writer. Brock received his degree in computer networking and is now devoting his full time and limited attention span to writing.

BIBLIOGRAPHY

THE SORCERER'S PATH
The Sorcerer's Ascension
The Sorcerer's Torment
The Sorcerer's Legacy
The Sorcerer's Vengeance
The Sorcerer's Scourge
The Sorcerer's Abyss
The Sorcerer's Return

The Sorcerer's Destiny
Rise of the Order
Descent Into Chaos

BROOKLYN SHADOWS
Shrouds of Darkness
Blood Conspiracy

THE TRANSCENDED CHRONICLES
The Miscreant
The Agent

EMPIRE OF MASKS
Highlords of Phaer
Nightbird
Mourningbird

OTHER BOOKS BY BROCK E. DESKINS
The Portal
Amelia: Battle for Ardentia

Curious about other Crossroad Press books? Stop by our website:
http://crossroadpress.com
We offer quality writing
in digital, audio, and print formats.

Subscribe to our newsletter on the website homepage and receive a
free eBook.